THE REBORN KING

THE GODLING CHRONICLES

THE REBORN KING

BRIAN D. ANDERSON

4 Horsemen
Publications, Inc.

DEDICATION

Although I dedicated book one to my son, this final installment is particularly special to me. It is the culmination of years of hard work which began when my boy came home from school one day and said, "Dad! I have an idea for a story!"

So this is for the light in my heart and the best reason I have to keep breathing—Jonathan Anderson

CONTENTS

PROLOGUE

The shadows danced along the stark walls of the dilapidated shack as the candle flickered and dimmed, stubbornly resisting the draft seeping in through the cracks in the wood that threatened to blow it out. The air reeked with the smell of rotted fruits and vegetables—food for the pigs that could be heard squealing and jostling in the pen directly outside.

The four elves gathered around the small table in the corner farthest from the door waited in silence, their hands fidgeting nervously in front of them.

Several minutes dragged by before the door creaked open to reveal a tall elf with red hair and narrow, piercing eyes. Clad in the cloak of a *seeker,* he stepped inside and surveyed the scene.

"This is all of you?" he asked in a soft, yet deep, voice.

The dark-skinned elf sitting nearest to him looked up. "This is all that can be here without arousing suspicion, Tallio. But there are more. Of that, you can be certain."

Tallio scowled before taking a seat at the table. "Their fear is a weakness they must soon overcome."

"Do not mistake prudence for fear," the elf shot back. "My people are steadfast and loyal. They will not hesitate to act when the time comes."

Tallio looked him directly in the eye. "Let us hope not. And the rest of you? Does your resolve still hold?"

Two of the other elves nodded, their faces grim.

"Then it is settled," said Tallio. "We will move against them as soon as Darshan is away."

A stocky elf to the right of him huffed and shook his head.

"You wish to add something, Vixis?" Tallio asked.

"I do," he replied evenly. "I wish to add that you are all fools. What do you think will happen if you succeed? Do you really imagine that things will go back to the way they were?" He leaned in closer to meet Tallio's gaze. "All you will achieve is to bring death to everyone here. The wrath of Darshan will know no bounds. He will burn us to cinders."

Tallio sneered. "If you fear death, then perhaps you should leave these matters to those with the courage of their convictions. Darshan is not invincible. And I will not sit idle as he spreads his lies."

"How can you be so sure they are lies?" Vixis countered. "What could he possibly gain from such a deception?"

"If you think I will ever believe our people to be a mongrel race spawned from the loins of the gods, then you are sorely mistaken." Tallio tensed, his fists clenching so tightly that his knuckles gleamed white. "Darshan has caused nothing but despair and doubt amongst our kin. Many have wandered east without purpose or hope, their minds and spirits broken by the words of a false god. And to think that he has brought forth offspring... mothered by one of our own." His right fist slammed violently down onto the table, nearly shattering it to splinters. "No! This cannot be allowed. I will face Darshan alone if need be."

"And you will die alone if you do," Vixis told him. "I have seen his power with my own eyes. And though he may not be invincible, his strength is far beyond any of us."

Tallio leaned back to scrutinize Vixis for several seconds before speaking again. "It seems to me that you have not come here to offer your support," he stated.

He paused, waiting for a response, but Vixis remained silent. "So, why *have* you come?"

"To offer you an alternative," he finally replied. "Many of our kin have decided to retreat to the desert. There we hope to find a new life and peace. We can live as we once did amongst our own kind. The humans will leave us be, and our desert kin would welcome us gladly. I have come here to ask you to abandon this madness and join us."

"Our desert kin have allied themselves with Darshan. And even if that was not so, what sort of existence do you expect to find there?" Tallio's tone was dark and dangerous. "Shall we leave our traditional homes and lives behind? Shall we cower off into the sands and forget who we really are?"

"To seek peace is not cowering, it is wisdom," Vixis responded. "Would you rather see us destroyed than find a new life? Our kin have lived in the desert for generations— free of gods and human corruption. Why should we not seek the same?"

"Because *this* is my home," Tallio insisted. "And I will not be driven from it by lies and slander. You would have us slither away... a mongrel race bereft of honor. You would allow the forked tongue of Darshan to continue poisoning the minds of our kin. And you would allow his cursed off- spring to linger upon this very world that the *Creator* has charged us to protect." With each word, his voice rose in intensity and the fire in his eyes burned ever hotter. "But I, for one, will *not* sit idle while all that I hold sacred is being destroyed and defiled."

"Your hatred has blinded you, old friend," said Vixis, sorrow and pity in his eyes. "And it will be your undoing. I can only pray that you do not drag our kin into the fiery depths along with you." He rose slowly and bowed to the others. "I wish you well. I honestly do. And should you change your mind, my kin and I shall be departing east in one week." He strode to the door and looked over his shoulder. "I hope to see you again ... soon." After giving Tallio a final searching glance, he lowered his head and stepped outside.

The three other elves sitting at the table exchanged uneasy looks as Tallio stared grimly at the door his former friend had passed through. After a brief moment, he rose to his feet, and with slow deliberate paces, made his way across the room. He turned briefly to the others before sucking in a deep breath and following Vixis out into the night.

Vixis had walked only a few yards when the sound of footfalls from behind caused him to pause and turn. He regarded his fellow elf steadily. "I take you have not come to persuade me further," he said.

"You know I cannot take the risk," Tallio told him. "There is too much at stake."

"Would it make any difference if I swear to keep your secret?" He could see the resolve in Tallio's expression and frowned. "No. I suppose not."

The flash of steel thrusting into his heart was quick and precise. Vixis gasped just once, his hands briefly clutching hold of Tallio's arms. A tear then rolled down his cheek as the light of life quickly faded from his eyes.

Tallio lifted the body over his shoulder and laid it carefully beside the shack. After covering it with some loose brush and twigs, he returned to the others. Their accusing stares swelled his anger.

"And what would you have me do?" he shouted. "We cannot trust our fate to those without the courage to fight."

A thin, dark-haired elf clad in a simple tan shirt and trousers pushed back his chair and glared at Tallio. "Vixis was no coward, and you know it! He simply wanted us to consider a different path."

Tallio held up his hand. "Calm yourself, Faliel. I only did what I had to do in order to protect us. Vixis carried knowledge that could have doomed us all. And though he was once my friend, I am not convinced he would have kept it to himself. He fought alongside Darshan, and served as personal guard to King Lousis. How could we know for certain where his allegiances lie? Darshan is a trickster and a liar. Many an elf who once despised humans now willingly serves alongside them. Even Lord Theopolou was not immune to Darshan's influence."

There was a long silence as the two elves stared at each other unblinkingly. Finally, Faliel heaved a deep sigh and sat back down.

"That some of our kin need to be sacrificed weighs heavily on my heart too, brothers," said Tallio. "But we must look to the greater good of our race. And that means all traitors and heretics must be destroyed."

He leaned forward and grasped hold of Faliel's hand. "Believe me, there is no other way."

Faliel nodded weakly. "And we are with you. Even so, I cannot help but lament the passing of any of our kin, traitors or no."

The third elf, much younger than the other two yet with the bearing of one who had seen much bloodshed and battle, fingered his dagger unthinkingly and narrowed his eyes.

"You have something to say, Hasheen?" asked Tallio.

"I do," he grumbled. "Have you given any thought as to what the elves from across the sea will do once they arrive? It is well known that Aaliyah sent for aid not long after she met Darshan. They said it would take a year before we could expect assistance. Well, a year is now nearly up. If they should take up Darshan's cause, we cannot hope to prevail."

"All the more reason to make haste," Tallio countered. "We cannot allow them to fall prey to the same lies that are being spread among *our* people. Victory must be swift."

"Do you know where the heretic is hiding?" Hasheen asked. "My people have been searching for weeks, to no avail."

A sinister grin crept upon Tallio's face. "Yes, I do know where she is. I know where they all are. Including the half-breed."

Hasheen frowned. "I see no reason to kill *her*. She is an innocent—a mere victim of birth—and should not suffer for the crimes of her mother."

"She is an abomination," Tallio snarled. "Innocent or not, she embodies all that we have warned our people against. But if it helps to ease your mind, I promise that she will not suffer. Plans have already been set in motion."

"You do know that killing her will bring the wrath of Linis down upon us," Hasheen warned. "He is not one to be trifled with. He will never rest until he has had his revenge."

"I will deal with Linis," Tallio said. "His crimes have already warranted his execution... and I will personally see it done." He reached into his shirt and pulled out three sealed scrolls. "Inside these are your instructions... That is, assuming you are still with me?"

There was a long pause. All three elves then nodded in turn.

Tallio smiled, clearly pleased. "Then make ready. We move soon."

The cavernous throne room was dark and bitterly cold. Not that he could feel the chill nipping at his flesh any longer. At least, not in the same way mortals feel it. As a man, he'd anticipated winter with dread and spent all his extra coin on the thickest wool and finest furs. But now he was no longer mortal, the cold was a welcome friend. It was a reminder of a life when he'd known the simple joys of lying under the sun on a warm spring day, watching the birds dart across a cloudless sky. The cold was gone ... for a time. And for a time, he was contented.

He thought back to that first day when he'd drawn the *Sword of Truth* from its cradle and held it aloft. While gazing upon its beauty, he'd all but forgotten that, only moments before, he had taken the life of a once dear friend. More than that, it was his dearest friend. The man's blood was still warming the marble floor just a few feet away, yet all he could see was his prize.

He had heard the stories, just as every other member of Amon Dähl had. The *Sword of Truth*. A weapon of unimaginable might... and danger. But the reality was quite different. To wield such terrible power, even for a moment, was a burden beyond human understanding. But to do so for eternity was utter madness. And it was that madness he had only managed to conquer through sheer force of will.

He placed his hand on the hilt of the *sword*. At this moment, it was protruding from the stone floor just beside his throne, its blade having cut through the rock as easily as if it were human flesh. As the power raged through him, he tilted his head back in ecstasy.

He took a deep breath, and while watching it billow away in a cloud of vapor after escaping his lungs, began to wonder if he actually *needed* to breathe any longer. Was it possible that such mundane acts could be left behind completely? He hadn't eaten in months, yet felt no hunger. Could he truly abandon all things human? He smiled inwardly. Soon he would have time everlasting to puzzle such things out.

He could feel the chaotic and fearful emotions of the people in Kratis. At one time, the idea of the enemy invading was unthinkable to them. But news of the defeat in the west had hit hard. And for the first time, his followers had doubts. They didn't understand. They believed that serving the Reborn King guaranteed their place in his new world. It didn't.

So let the west come, he thought. There is no reason to stop them. Those who survive will have proved their worth. And once all is over, it will not matter who they fought for, what flag they carried, or even if they hate Angrääl and its king. Ultimately, all who live will serve my purpose.

Only one thing remained to be settled—Darshan. He had tried so many times to hate him, but at best could manage only a mild animosity. He had even begun to respect him. The young godling had disrupted his plans far more than he'd imagined possible. Yet for all his efforts, the end would still come and the boy would still die. Nothing had changed.

It was regrettable. He would have made a powerful ally. To end a life so filled with promise was always a waste. But without the death of Darshan, the cleansing would fail. Though the boy was human in body, his spirit was that of his chief adversary. The gods must not endure... and the earth *must* burn. The disease unleashed by arrogance and self-indulgence would be eradicated, and a new world reborn from its ashes.

The door to the massive chamber creaked open, allowing a spear of light to penetrate the darkness. The hall was bare aside from the massive stone throne and a banner hanging from the ceiling bearing his sigil.

Captain Lanmore entered and approached with uneasy steps, his head lowered. Even in the pitch black, he would not dare risk meeting his master's gaze. The door boomed shut behind him, startling the captain, but he quickly regained what little composure he could muster. He stopped just a few yards away from the throne and fell to his knees.

"You called for me, Your Highness?" His voice seemed small, and he trembled nervously.

"You have done well, Lanmore." The Dark Knight was careful not to use too much force in his speech lest he drive the captain mad with its power. "I am putting you in direct command of the city legions and elevating you to general of all the northern armies." Even with this restraint, the sound of his voice still shook the walls. He could see that Lanmore was struggling not to cover his ears.

"Thank you, Master." Lanmore could only manage to whisper.

"Come forward," the Dark Knight commanded.

After a second of hesitation, Lanmore rose and approached the throne, his feet sliding noisily across the stone floor and his arms outstretched in a desperate attempt to avoid stumbling into his king.

The lines on Lanmore's face twitched and then froze as the Dark Knight reached out to place his forefinger in the center of his brow.

"You are by far the best and bravest of all my servants," he told the captain. "And because of this, you shall receive the highest of honors. From this moment forward you are to be known as Prince Lanmore, heir to the throne of Angrääl."

Lanmore was speechless. He threw himself prostrate before his master.

"Rise and go forth," the Dark Knight commanded. "Endowed with my power, lead our people to glory."

For the very first time, Lanmore looked up and met his master's eyes. His expression was one of wonderment and awe.

"Your face..." he began. "It's... it's..."

CHAPTER 1

Kaylia approached the gates to Theopolou's manor with Jayden sleeping soundly in her arms. She could feel the strength of the *flow* of the earth had increased dramatically. As a child, she had frequently marveled at the way her uncle could always know everything that occurred within the walls of his home. He knew every footfall of every elf, and the door to each room would always swing open as if it were greeting him as he approached.

Theopolou had once tried to describe to her the deep connection he had with this place, but she'd never really understood. Not until this very moment. His family had spent generations cultivating a relationship with the *flow* here. At least, that's how he'd explained it to her. Now, at last, she could feel as he did—partly due to her training, but mostly because his blood also flowed through her veins. This gave the land more than life. It gave it a soul.

The gleaming gates swung open as she touched the handles and, oblivious to the assembly of elves behind her, she passed through.

Aaliyah, Linis, and Basanti broke away from the twenty elves belonging to Theopolou's clan acting as their escorts and made their way alongside Kaylia, the wide path being easily able to accommodate them all walking abreast. The crystal statue in front of the main house sparkled in the noonday sun and split the rays like a prism, casting rainbows of warm light in every direction. The majesty and unrelenting beauty of the manor and grounds was never wasted on Kaylia. She paused to take in her surroundings.

"Magnificent," remarked Aaliyah.

"Indeed," agreed Basanti.

"Theopolou told me that this was built at a time when our people made many wonders using the power of the *flow*," explained Kaylia. Saying his name aloud immediately brought an emptiness to her heart. Feeling his mother's grief, Jayden awoke and began to cry.

"Allow me," offered Aaliyah, holding out her arms.

Normally, Kaylia was hesitant to give over her son while he was crying, even to Aaliyah. However, this time she did so without protest or complaint.

She recalled the day when she and Gewey had first visited here together. She had been so angry with her uncle at the time, even though his actions were driven by love and had only been to protect her. The fond memory eased a little of her sadness.

The main door to the manor swung open and Lady Bellisia stepped out. Her face shining a welcome, she spread her arms wide. Even before the approaching group could reach the steps, she sprang forward and descended to meet them. She immediately embraced Kaylia, Aaliyah, and Linis. Basanti gave her pause, however. She had been told of the oracle and of her origins, but it still unsettled her to think of someone so ancient being amongst them. Not wanting to show discourtesy, she bowed low instead.

"And now for the guest of honor," Bellisia said, leaning in closer to see Jayden. He had already stopped crying and was beginning to drift off. She brushed his cheek with the tip of her finger and sighed. "I remember you this young," she said, glancing at Kaylia. "Your father brought you to every home within a hundred miles after you were born. He was so proud."

Kaylia smiled but said nothing.

"And it will be good to have a new life here," Bellisia continued. Pulling herself away, she gestured for everyone to enter. "Come. All has been made ready for your arrival."

Kaylia was grateful that Bellisia had chosen to go on ahead of them to prepare the house. She had no desire to be looked upon with wary eyes by the servants and caretakers. Bellisia would have seen that they were all familiar with the new circumstances far ahead of time.

With their duty done, the elves escorting them took their leave and departed. Their homes were scattered well away from Theopolou's grounds, and many had families they had not seen in some time.

Once inside, both Aaliyah and Basanti paused to admire the gleaming walls and green marble floors.

"Much like the halls of my homeland," remarked Aaliyah.

"It was likely built not long after your two peoples were separated," said Basanti. "Perhaps even before. Elves were master builders for a very long time after the barrier went up. The decline in their skills was a slow one."

"To think that you remember such things," said Bellisia, shaking her head in wonder. "One day I would like very much to hear of what you know concerning my people. Since the opening of the Book of Souls and the revelations it brought forth, I have been anxious for further knowledge. Most of the book has yet to be translated. All we know at present is what Gewey was able to divine in the short time he spent with it."

Basanti lowered her head and smiled. "I will be happy to share what I have learned. But I must warn you, some of the things you hear may be upsetting. And it will be told from my singular perspective."

Bellisia nodded. "After what I have been told, there is little you could say that would cause me pain. I did my best not to show it in front of Darshan and Chiron, but I was deeply disturbed by what he said."

"Then come and see me whenever you like. I will tell you my account regarding your people. And don't worry. Most of it will please you. The elves have been through many changes over the millennia."

"Sadly, now that Kaylia and Jayden are here I must leave at once," she said. "My healing skills are needed with Lousis and the army."

"When you return then," said Basanti.

Then mention of war cast a dark shadow over the assembly and they entered the manor with thoughts of their friends and loved ones lingering in their hearts.

Servants showed them upstairs to their rooms. An ivory crib with elf blessings carved in delicate ancient lettering had been placed in Kaylia's chambers. She tried to divine whether the house staff would be accepting of the new situation, particularly the presence of Jayden, but their expressions were stone and unreadable. News of Theopolou's death had certainly hit them hard. Many of the elves who dwelt in the manor had lived their entire lives beneath its roof.

She fed and changed Jayden, then left her room to say farewell to Bellisia. The urgency of her departure only brought more feelings of anxiety to the fore. Afterward, she wandered the house in an effort to ease her mind with fond memories. Each painting and tapestry she passed was like looking at a piece of her childhood. She had spent as much time here as she had in her own home. Theopolou and her father had been very close, in spite of the fact that her father preferred a more rural and simple lifestyle than his brother. She remembered a conversation she had overheard between the two when she was still very young. Theopolou thought it best to keep Kaylia with him one spring to further her education, while her father insisted that their time in the forest was more important.

"Only the Creator knows how much time we have with our children, Theopolou," her father had said. "And they are only children for a short while. There will be time for books and study later. This time... this precious time... is fleeting."

The prophetic nature of what he had said now rang true and clear as a crystal chime.

On the top floor of the house, were the libraries and parlors. It was in one of the lesser sitting rooms that she came across Aaliyah admiring a small statue of an elf maiden set upon a marble pedestal.

"Your uncle had exquisite taste," Aaliyah remarked.

"He did," agreed Kaylia. "But much of this has been passed down for generations." She noticed Aaliyah's sad expression and touched her shoulder.

Aaliyah sighed. "Am I so transparent?"

"Only to me."

"I miss my home," she said. "And seeing this place reminds me of what I left behind. But more than that, I miss Nehrutu. I cannot help but question my decision to send him with Gewey and Felsafell." She looked up with guilty eyes. "I know how selfish that must sound to you."

Kaylia felt a sudden, overwhelming compassion. Careful not to put Jayden between them, she embraced Aaliyah tightly. "You are not selfish. I would have Gewey at my side if I could. And were there a place to hide from the world, I would take Jayden and escape this terrible war."

A tear fell from Aaliyah's eye as Kaylia released her. "I would flee as well if I were able. Now that we are bonded, I have no greater love than for Nehrutu. I would do anything to protect him." She looked down at Jayden, who was wriggling and cooing. More tears fell. "And when I think of what *you* have risked… I am ashamed."

The sight of Aaliyah's tears induced Kaylia to spill a few of her own. "Please do not be," she said. "I was relieved to hear that Nehrutu was going with Gewey. I did not give a thought to the danger he would be in, only that my *unorem* had more protection. I thought of the loss *I* would feel should *my* love not return… not yours. For this, I could feel ashamed as well. But we both know the pain of loss. You were prepared to follow your mate in death. I went mad when my bond with Gewey was broken. Neither of us can be faulted for not wanting to endure that for a second time."

Aaliyah wiped her eyes and forced a smile. "You are very young to be so wise. I thank you for your words. My heart is lighter."

Kaylia laughed. "I feel as if I have aged two-hundred years since I first met Gewey. By the time he returns, I suspect I'll be an elder."

They strolled from room to room together for the next few hours, talking about happier days of long ago, and of the peaceful times to come.

Just before dinner, they were joined by Linis. He appeared to be in unusually good cheer.

"The house staff wishes me to convey a message to you," he told Kaylia. "You are now to consider yourself master of this manor."

Kaylia raised an eyebrow. "I thought they did not care for my being here."

"Of course, they are deeply saddened by Lord Theopolou's passing," he explained. "But in his wisdom, he sent word of his desire for you to be his successor before he left for the Steppes. They would never question his final request."

"When you say staff," said Aaliyah, frowning, "do you mean the servants here? I have wondered…"

"They are not slaves," laughed Linis. "They serve as a matter of honor. Lord Theopolou was a chief among our elders. Many came here in search of his wisdom, then chose to remain after receiving it. All may come and go as they please. And now they wish to pass on to Kaylia the respect they had for her uncle. As this house has become their home, some will most likely remain. Others may choose to leave and start anew."

Aaliyah nodded. "I see."

"Do you not have servants in your land?" asked Kaylia.

"Not as you do," she replied. "Most menial work is done in turn. We work as one. For example, dinner is prepared and served by all who sit at the table. And certain tasks are assigned according to need. We have no need for servants because all are equal."

"Then what of your masters of crafts and learning?" asked Linis. "Do they halt their work to clean and polish?"

Aaliyah shrugged. "Certainly. Why should they not? Only those too old or sick do not assist. I may be the most powerful elf in my land, but just before I departed, I was polishing the railings of the city archives. I feel no shame in this. In fact, I am pleased to have done my part."

Linis nodded approvingly. "Perhaps when the rest of your people arrive, this is something we should adopt. Though I am surprised to hear you speak of it only now. You have been here for some time and seen the order of things."

"Yes, but this is the first purely elf dwelling I have been in," she explained. "Until now, I have seen only human, or a combination of elf and human. But do not misunderstand. I do not disparage your ways. There is honor in serving those you admire and love. Aboard my ship, I did little of the actual work. My crew would not allow it."

There was a brief pause.

"Are you leaving us soon?" Kaylia asked Linis, changing the subject.

His face twisted, and he shook his head. "Dina has insisted that I remain here in spite of my assurances that the manor has ample protection. Besides, she claims that her new duties as Interim High Lady of Amon Dähl would make my presence at the temple a distraction. Now that Lady Selena is Queen of Althetas, the order is in need of leadership... At least, that's what Dina tells me. In truth, I think she feels guilty that everyone else has to be apart from the ones they love and cannot justify her own lack of sacrifice."

"What will you do if she takes up the position permanently?" asked Kaylia.

Linis shrugged. "I have no idea. But I do not believe that she wants it. Until now, our plan has been to find somewhere quiet to settle once the war has ended. I suppose only time will tell."

After a little more talk, they made their way downstairs. Dinner was already being laid out on a large round table in the center of a spacious, warmly lit room, elegantly decorated with superb oil paintings and masterfully crafted furnishings. Basanti soon joined them and they all sat down together, eating at a casual pace. Conversation was light, centering mostly on past times and childhood memories.

Just as they were ready to retire, an elderly elf woman named Therisa beckoned for Kaylia to follow her outside. Kaylia had known the woman her entire life. She had been head of the household staff for more than three hundred years and had a stern and unbending nature about her. She went after the old woman, accompanied by Aaliyah.

The night was comfortably mild, with stars dotted about a cloudless and moonless sky. Even so, the statue at the front of the house still managed to glow with an almost spiritual light.

Therisa was kneeling at the statue's base, and gestured for Kaylia to come do the same. "I can feel that your ability with the *flow* is strong," she said. "Stronger even than Lord Theopolou. This is good. It will ease the transition."

After handing Jayden to Aaliyah, Kaylia joined the woman. "What is this?" she asked.

Her stoic expression softened into a sweet smile. "You are master of this house, just as Theopolou was before you, and his father before him. Now that Theopolou has died, the land is without a companion. You must take his place."

Though not nearly as strong as her own skill, Kaylia could feel the *flow* emanating from Therisa and entering the crystal. The light transformed into a deep blue as the power was amplified. Kaylia knew instinctively what to do. Closing her eyes, she placed her hands on its base. A warm sensation washed over her. Instantly, she could feel the *flow* coursing from the earth and seeking to combine with her spirit.

The moment she joined with it, she could feel everything around her coming to life. It was as if the manor, the grounds, and everything within it had a consciousness... and *it* knew *her*. She allowed it to wrap itself around her in a warm embrace. When she was a child, she had thought that Theopolou was in command within his borders. But that was only partly true. Now she truly understood. Just as he had been, she was a part of this place, and it was a part of her.

Just then, her eyes snapped open, and she sprang to her feet.

"What is it?" asked Therisa.

"Get inside and alert the staff," she ordered. "Enemies are coming."

The *flow* burst forth from Aaliyah as she hurried over, reaching out to the surrounding area. "I feel nothing," she said, frowning.

"They are there," Kaylia insisted. "They are clever. And they are elves."

CHAPTER 2

Gewey mounted his horse and made his way to the vanguard of the massive army. Even at a gallop, it took him ten minutes to reach King Lousis and Nehrutu, who were waiting patiently. Nehrutu looked uncomfortable atop his mount. Much like the desert elves, he preferred traveling on foot. Lousis, on the other hand, looked tall and proud—every inch a warrior king.

"It's about time," called Lousis. "I thought you might have lost your nerve."

Gewey laughed. "I did. But being as how you are refusing to leave me behind..."

"And where is Felsafell?" asked the king.

"I suspect that he's not far away," said Gewey. He took a long look back at their force, which measured one hundred and fifty thousand swords. "I'm still amazed at how many soldiers you were able to muster in just two months."

"And when you join with the desert elves," added Nehrutu, "your enemy will truly have cause to fear."

"I hope to gain even more support along the way," said Lousis. "Baltria has managed to recruit men from the Eastland, and I hope to do the same."

"And if those you hope will become allies turn out to be enemies?" asked Gewey.

"I do not intend to engage in battle until I must," Lousis replied. "If we are allowed to pass unhindered, we will. The journey will be difficult enough without the added hardship of battle."

"If you are resisted," said Nehrutu, "Mohanisi and the others from my land should be able to swing the advantage to your favor. It's unlikely they will know what he and my kin are capable of."

Gewey hoped that such a display of power would also make them think that Darshan was leading the army. This was a hope shared by the king, though it was left unspoken. Lousis was already in poor spirits that King Victis would not be with him. His friend had returned home to assist the southern kingdoms in rebuilding their shattered lands. Being that many of their sovereigns had perished, his leadership was desperately needed there. The remaining northern rulers had also gone with Victis in a show of solidarity. Of all the remaining monarchs, only King Lousis would be going to war.

This was a fact that had not gone unnoticed by the former High Lady, and now *Queen* Selena. It was all Lousis could do to keep her from coming along, too. It was only when Lousis named Jacob as his heir that she finally relented. Lord Ganflin would be there to instruct Jacob as to his duties, but Jacob insisted that his grandmother stay too. And though the former High Lady knew this was likely a conspiracy to keep her from harm, she could not refuse her grandson.

Lord Chiron arrived, his normally cheerful countenance grave and showing the signs of age.

"All is ready?" asked Lousis.

"It is," Chiron confirmed.

"Then why so glum?"

"I have been on such a march before," he replied. "During the Great War, the remainder of the elf nations gathered in a desperate effort to stave off defeat. I cannot help but be reminded of what happened then."

"What did happen?" asked Gewey.

Chiron looked sideways at him. "We failed."

"Ah," said Lousis. "But today elf and human fight together, and it is our foe who now stares at defeat."

Chiron nodded slowly, albeit unconvincingly. "Of course. Please forgive my melancholy. The eve of *our* final march was filled with such hope as well. Needless to say, that hope was destroyed. I do not enjoy such reminders."

"I understand," said Lousis. He turned to face the herald. "Sound the advance."

A silver trumpet rang out, its call taken up by others scattered about the ranks until they combined into a single harmonious note that pieced the air and called all to attention. For a moment, there was quiet, and the air was still. Then, like some massive behemoth from ancient legend, the army slowly lurched forward.

The pace was little more than a slow walk. So many men and elves, together with wagons and horses, were not capable of moving with any great speed. And the roads beyond Althetan borders would be sure to bottleneck their ranks and slow them even further.

Most of the morning had passed before the last wagon of provisions eventually pulled away. Spirits were high and songs of anticipated victory were sung as the vast army tramped off to meet its destiny. Gewey, on the other hand, was anxious. He was to wait at least two weeks before breaking off with Nehrutu and Felsafell and go his own way.

Felsafell had warned him against using the *flow*, or even using his bond with Kaylia. The Dark Knight *must* believe he was with the army, and there was the possibility he would be able to sense Gewey's location if he used his power. This restriction did not sit well and spawned several heated arguments.

"The Dark Knight has never been able to know where I am before," Gewey had insisted.

"Perhaps," said Felsafell. "But you cannot be certain. Melek knew where you were the moment he left Shagharath. He could feel your power. There is no reason to think the Dark Knight does not possess the same ability. There is too much at stake to risk discovery."

Eventually, Gewey was forced to relent. His last moments with Kaylia and Jayden, before they left for Theopolou's manor, had brought him to the brink of collapse. Up until then, he had kept in almost constant contact. And in the end, it was Kaylia, not he, who insisted that it be done. They had both allowed Aaliyah to impede their bond. Though he could still feel her, it was dull and distant. Kaylia said that they must trust in the wisdom of Felsafell, for she feared that he was right. If Gewey failed, the world would burn. And, even more importantly, in her eyes, the fate of their son rested firmly on his shoulders.

Nehrutu leaned over in the saddle and whispered to Gewey. "I understand. I too feel the absence."

Clearly, Aaliyah had taken similar precautions with her own bond. At first, Gewey had found it unnerving that Nehrutu could tell what he was thinking. Likely, the bond he had shared with Aaliyah gave him a keener understanding of Gewey's mind. But as the days passed, and he got to know the elf better, their connection was now becoming a welcome feeling of kinship to fill the void left by his parting with Kaylia.

The rest of the day was uneventful. Mohanisi came forward twice to speak with King Lousis, then returned to the rear to march with his kin. By the time the sun started sinking beneath the horizon, the road was beginning to narrow. A few wagons on their way to Althetas had been forced to yield the road, and Gewey smiled inwardly at the traveler's dumbfounded expressions as they watched one hundredand fifty thousand armed warriors go marching by.

When they finally halted, Gewey and Nehrutu sought out Felsafell in the forest south of the road. It didn't take them long before they ran across his camp. He had apparently anticipated their company by catching three rabbits and picking some wild onions. After the meal, they relaxed by the fire while Felsafell regaled them with stories of the rise of elf and human. There was no need to turn the conversation to serious matters. They knew where they were going, and there was no point in speculating about the perils they might face.

Gewey settled by the fire and allowed himself to drift into an uneasy sleep. The world of dreams would be a lonely place without Kaylia there beside him.

Gewey found himself standing atop a tall dune and staring out at jagged peaks to the north.

"Don't go there. You will not return," whispered a voice in his mind, but he wasn't certain if the voice was his own... or was it someone else's.

He ignored the warning and willed himself closer to the mountains, secure in the knowledge that, in this place, he could come to no harm. At the base of the tallest peak, a tunnel had been carved into the living rock. As he approached, a blast of searing hot air sent him hurtling back. He touched his face. It burned. And the pain... it felt real. Many times before in his dreams, he had been cut, bruised, or otherwise damaged, but never once had he experienced actual pain.

Fear knotted his stomach, but he was compelled to continue walking toward the entrance. A deep rumbling growl echoed from the depths just as he reached the threshold. Desperately, he tried to stop, but his body would not obey his will. Once inside, all light vanished and he could feel a menacing presence watching him. Waiting for him to come to his doom.

He tried to force himself awake, but it was useless. Something had trapped him. His fear increased as he kept moving deeper into the mountain.

"Who's there?" he shouted.

The only reply was another feral growl. Then, peering at him from out of the pitch black, he saw two burning yellow eyes. He tried to reach for a weapon, but his arms were paralyzed.

I'll not die in a bloody dream, he thought, fighting back his terror.

The eyes were drawing steadily closer. A sinister hissing sound raked at his ears. Gewey made one final frantic effort to wake himself, and this time the world of dreams began to fade. As if realizing that it was about to be denied its victim, the creature surged forward. Gewey caught a fleeting glimpse of a claw with scaly flesh and razor-sharp talons reaching out to mutilate him. Then, in a swirl of color, the vision faded, and he found himself back in the camp.

Nehrutu was sleeping a few feet away. Felsafell was sitting close to the flames, staring blankly into the night. "Your dreams were troubled?" he asked, without looking up.

Gewey's shirt was soaked in sweat. He sat upright and recounted what had happened.

"Perhaps you are having visions of the future," Felsafell mused.

"I hope not," Gewey responded. "Whatever I saw inside that tunnel, it is not something I ever want to encounter again."

"I have heard stories of the beasts that dwell in the mountains north of the desert. Elves ventured there long ago, and only a very few returned. My people feared to go there, and I have never had the need to do so until now."

His words only fueled Gewey's anxiety. He could still see the beast's yellow eyes in his mind, staring at him as if he were its helpless prey. The hideous claw reaching out for him in order to feed its ravenous hunger caused him to shiver.

"There is no need to burden your mind," Felsafell said. "Perhaps your dreams will reveal more before we arrive."

"I'm not sure I want to dream anymore," said Gewey. "Not after that."

Felsafell smiled and tossed Gewey a skin of water. It was nearly dawn and they could hear the army beginning to stir. Gewey took a drink, then shook Nehrutu awake. After a quick meal of bread and fruit, they returned in time to greet King Lousis as he rode toward the vanguard of the ranks.

The moment the sun broke the horizon, trumpets sounded, and the march continued. Quietly, Gewey told Nehrutu and Lousis of his dream.

"We have all heard stories of the fire lizards," Lousis said dismissively. "That's probably what spawned the dream. Old stories, nothing more."

Gewey nodded and forced a smile. "You're right, of course." At that moment, he regretted telling the old king what he had seen. Lousis was marching into the heart of death and had more than enough to trouble his mind.

Nehrutu, on the other hand, was unable to hide his concern. However, he remained silent.

"My scouts tell me that the road ahead is clear," Lousis told them, clearly wanting to change the subject. "Let us hope it remains so. At least until we turn north."

"Let us hope so," agreed Gewey.

CHAPTER 3

Lee and Penelope huddled by the small fire along with one of the three desert elves they had recently encountered. The few of these who had not marched west with Gewey were patrolling the borders of the sands and had discovered them just after they left Dantory.

Lee knew that he was putting the desert dwellers in danger simply by being in their company, but he was relieved to see them, nonetheless. The Waters of Shajir were weeks away, and his knowledge of the small oases that dotted the desert was limited to an old map he had acquired from a merchant. Though Lee believed the man to be speaking truthfully when he told him it was accurate, there was no way he could be sure of this until it was far too late to turn back.

Samaal, a sand master in training, was sitting just across from Lee and Penelope. He was a good-natured elf with a sharp wit and kind demeanor. He had halted his training until after the war was over and his kin returned. Though desperately desiring to go with the rest of his people, he had grudgingly accepted the charge of minding their land's borders.

The other two elves, Talmiel, and Mangri, were at present scouting the area. Rogue bands of Soufis who'd escaped slaughter had been seen in the area. Though as a people they were no longer a power in the desert, they were still dangerous and desperate enough to attack lone travelers.

"We have been with you for three days now," Samaal said. "I am wondering when you intend to tell us what pursues you. Truly, it must be dread incarnate if you brave the sands alone to escape it."

Lee hesitated and looked to Penelope. Her eyes were cast down and uncaring. Each day she had become increasingly reserved, rarely speaking a word.

"I am ill," he explained. "And I hope the Waters of Shajir will cure my malady." This was true enough.

Samaal scrutinized Lee for a moment. "And does your malady cause enemies to follow you?"

"What do you mean?"

"I am no fool," he replied. "Though I have no doubt you wish to reach the Waters, you are also in flight. Something is giving chase, and it is clear you do not want whoever it is to catch you."

Lee nodded. "You're right. We are being followed, and it is likely you are in danger if you remain with us. I should have been more forthcoming when we met, but I..."

His voice trailed off. The truth was, he desperately wanted to protect Penelope as much as he could, and three more blades provided a much better level of security. He pulled her close, but still, she did not look up or give any other indication that she was listening.

"If you are in need of our protection," said Samaal. "We offer it freely. There is no need for subterfuge."

"Thank you." Lee bowed his head. "Perhaps I can repay your kindness one day."

Talmiel and Mangri returned a few minutes later, their faces twisted into scowls.

"Wolves," said Talmiel. "At least six of them. They are stalking us."

Samaal waved a hand. "They'll not attack. There are too many of us."

The new arrivals kneeled down beside them, hands on the hilts of their blades.

"Their eyes glowed green," said Mangri. "Just like the ones who attacked Darshan and Pali."

Gewey had told Lee the story of the monster wolves he and Aaliyah had encountered when the desert elf, Pali, was leading them to the Black Oasis. Apparently, it was a tale often told amongst the elves as well. Instinctively, Lee stood up and drew his sword.

A single, long, and menacing howl sounded, lingering ominously in the night air. This was answered by several others, their aggressive wailing seeming to come at the small group from all directions simultaneously, like beastly battle cries. Rapidly, Lee helped Penelope to her feet and pushed her behind him.

He spotted the wolves just as they crested the dunes. They charged with astonishing speed. In complete concert, four of the six animals leaped for the throats of their prey—one at each combatant. The two others were moving a little wider on either side in order to get at Penelope. Lee ducked under the wolf, attacking him, thrusting his blade up into its belly. The cut was deep, but the beast twisted at the last second, preventing the deadly steel from gutting it completely. It crashed onto the sand just beside Penelope, its jaws snapping and snarling.

Lee seized hold of his wife's arm and pulled her away just as another wolf came at them from the left, ready to deliver a lethal bite.

Letting out a feral cry, he swung his blade down in a tightly controlled arc, splitting the animal's skull in two.

By now, Samaal had killed the wolf attacking him and was trying to stop the beast on the right flank from getting through to Lee and Penelope. Mangri and Talmiel had injured their foes, but in return had fallen victim to vicious bites—Mangri to his shoulder, and Talmiel to his upper arm. The wolf wounded by Lee was already regaining its feet.

Just at that moment, another lone howl called out from the darkness. As if responding to this, the attackers immediately began backing away, all the time their glowing green eyes spewing malice as foam dripped from their dagger-like fangs.

"What devilry is this?" hissed Samaal. "It is as though they are being guided by some sinister intelligence."

"Perhaps they are," said Lee.

He listened carefully. Three more wolves had joined the others. And there was something else. Four Vrykol. He quickly scanned the area but could see nothing other than more rolling dunes.

"Is there somewhere we can mount a defense?" he asked.

"There is an entrance to the Blood of the Sands to the south," Samaal replied while stripping off a piece of his shirt to bind his comrade's wounds. "But it is at least half a mile away and leads straight into the vortex, so we could not use it. In any case, I doubt we could make it there in time."

Lee looked at his wife. Her eyes showed no fear, yet tears still streamed down her cheeks. She gave Lee a sad smile and reached up to touch his face as if to say that she was ready for whatever was about to come. He could hear the foul voices of the Vrykol in the distance. The wolves howled in response, then began moving to surround them again.

"You three stay here," ordered Lee. "The wolves will follow us."

"We will not abandon you," Samaal shot back.

"If we stay with you, we *all* die," Lee told him. "And I will not have that." Grabbing his wife, he threw her over his shoulder. "And I have no time to debate."

The sinews of his legs burst into life as he ran headlong for a gap between the wolves. The three elves set off just behind him, but split away and attacked the beasts closest, hoping to give him and Penelope more time.

Lee could hear the elves engaging three of the creatures. The other wolves had paused and moved back, caught off-guard by the sudden aggression of their prey. But the Vrykol remained focused, and at once ran after Lee and Penelope, ignoring all else.

He had covered only a short distance when Lee heard the sand scraping beneath massive paws just a few yards behind him. He waited until he heard the beast jump, then, sword still in hand, spun sharply around. His blade thudded into the wolf's outstretched neck while it was still in mid-air, instantly killing it. At the same time, he was forced to step sharply and awkwardly to one side in order to avoid the creature's falling body. While recovering his balance, he heard Penelope grunt but dared not delay to see if she was hurt.

The Vrykol were drawing near, as were two more wolves. But ahead he could now see the outcropping of rock and narrow entrance.

Encouraged, he ran with every last bit of speed he could muster, all the time feeling the presence of his enemies closing in. Penelope gripped the back of his shirt, trying not to cry out from the rough manner in which Lee was being forced to handle her.

Still running hard and barely able to pull up in time, he stumbled up to the entrance, where his right arm rammed straight into the rock. Penelope was thrown off his shoulder and landed hard on the rocky path within. Lee twisted, slipping inside next to her. Ignoring the blood from the wound the jagged stone had just made, he raised his blade, ready to skewer anyone who would dare try to follow them. But the Vrykol and the wolves slid to a halt, their gazes fixed.

"You cannot escape, Starfinder," called one of the Vrykol in a harsh, gurgling voice.

"We shall see," spat Lee. He turned to Penelope and helped her to her feet. "Are you all right?"

She brushed the sand and dust from her dress. "Bruised and shaken, my love. But I can still go on."

Despite her assurances, he took a moment to examine her. There was a long cut on her left forearm and her dress was ripped in several places, but there were no serious injuries. Satisfied, he peered along the dark passage. It sloped gently downward for about thirty yards, then veered to the left.

"Stay close behind me," he said in a calm, even tone. He kissed her and smiled. "I'll lead the way." Lee sheathed his sword and drew a small dagger.

The path twisted and turned for more than a mile, then began descending sharply, its suddenness very nearly causing Penelope to stumble over. Lee listened, his half-man senses penetrating the echoes of their footfalls. The Vrykol were indeed following but at a cautious distance. Gewey had described the Blood of the Sands to him, and how he had traveled upon them. If the small round vessels he spoke about were there, they would use them to get away. If not, Lee would hold the enemy at bay for as long as he could. Of course, if Samaal was right about it leading to the vortex, then they may very well be heading to their death, regardless. But it was a risk they would have to take.

After another mile, he saw a faint light ahead. The path ended in a cavern large enough to accommodate about twenty men. On either end was a tunnel connected by a broad strip of rough, dark brown sand. Lee stepped around his wife, picked up a pebble, and tossed it in. The sand instantly came to life, flowing and rippling like the water of a swift stream. Both of them stared in wonder for a moment.

"I have never heard of such a thing," whispered Penelope. "And we can use this to get away?"

For a moment, Lee considered not telling her about the risk. But the look in his eyes betrayed him.

"Tell me the truth," she demanded. "I heard Samaal say something to you about a vortex."

"Gewey told me about that as well," he replied. "He said the elves believe it to be a place of no return." He touched her shoulders. "We will make our stand here if that's what you want."

Penelope reached up to cup his face in her hands. "No. Let's see where it leads."

Lee gazed into her eyes. They were no longer sad and her tears had dried. "Yes. Let us see what it is the elves fear." He kissed her, then took her hand. "And you never know. Perhaps this is where fate wanted us to be, after all."

He scanned the area and saw the round "slithas" piled in a corner. He grabbed two and placed them beside the sands. At that moment, the sound of rapidly advancing Vrykol boots began echoing from the passage. They were very close.

No time to lash ourselves together, he thought. He helped Penelope onto the vessel and pushed it atop the sands. Again, they burst into life, now propelling her toward the mouth of the tunnel. Lee raced to throw his own disc down and was about to jump aboard when a searing pain shot through his chest from where the cursed spike was buried in his flesh. He tried to fight through the agony, but it was unrelenting. He felt his legs giving way and fell heavily to the stone floor.

He heard Penelope screaming out his name, but she had already reached the tunnel and was quickly out of sight. He fought with everything he had to crawl atop the slithas, but his muscles had seized up. He could only lay where he was, helpless and frozen.

The foul stench of decay and ruin soon reached his nostrils. The hissing laugh of the Vrykol raked at his ears. Seconds later, he saw the cloaked figures walking toward him.

"Get it over with," he managed to grunt through his agony.

In a single swift movement, one of the Vrykol mounted his back and bound his arms. Once he was secure, the pain slowly subsided, and a little of his strength returned.

"What are you waiting for?" he demanded.

The Vrykol pulled him to his feet. "Do you long for death? Do you wish for your torment to end?" Its harsh, rasping voice was mocking and cruel.

Lee glared defiantly. "I'll not grovel to you," he growled, spitting hard into the darkness of its hood.

His defiance was met by a fist smashing into his jaw. Were it not for the Vrykol at his back, he would have been sent sprawling.

"It will be a pleasure to watch you ... turn," the creature goaded. "To watch your sanity slip away."

Lee tried not to look daunted by this, but fear of what he was likely to become gripped him ,anyway. Once again, his legs began to weaken.

"I see that even the mighty Lee Starfinder's courage has limits," it continued. "Excellent."

Pride compelled Lee to gather his wits and straighten his back. "If your master wanted this, he would have done it when he captured us the first time."

"My master?" The creature came closer, the stench of its breath nearly causing Lee to wretch. "He knows nothing of this. He no longer cares what we do. Our usefulness to him has come to an end."

"Then why are you doing this?" demanded Lee. "Why bother?"

"We must earn our place in this world before it is too late," it replied. "And now that your wife is no more, you will help us."

"I will never help you!" he roared. The thought of Penelope alone, afraid, and in the bowels of the desert tore at his heart, but he was not about to give these demons the satisfaction of knowing his anguish.

Forgive me, my love, he thought. *Forgive my failure.*

"You have no choice," it shot back. "Soon you will be ours to control... completely."

The Vrykol spun around and headed toward the exit. The one behind Lee shoved him into a brisk walk to follow. While moving along, he concentrated on the spike in his chest. So far, he could feel nothing unusual, but he was certain this would soon change. His only remaining goal now was to free himself and kill every Vrykol he could find before his mind was completely destroyed... even though he knew there was little hope of this ever actually coming to pass.

For him, there was no escaping the harsh fact that it was all over.

CHAPTER 4

Dina sat at the desk in what was formally High Lady Selena's office. Haphazardly scattered papers covered the entire desktop, and three more large stacks waiting for her attention had been placed near the door.

Letting out a soft moan, she put her head in her hands. "What have I gotten myself into?"

When Selena had asked her to take up the position, the prospect had initially excited her. It would allow her access to information reserved only for the High Lady of the Order. And as a historian, this sent her mind racing as to the possibilities of what she might discover.

After telling Linis of Selena's request, she could see how much it had disturbed him. They had been planning to make a home together and hopefully raise a family somewhere quiet and safe once the war was over. In order to ease his concern, she had assured him that it was only a temporary situation and that she had no intention of living out her years in Valshara.

Her elevation had caused no small measure of jealousy among the older members, several of whom had held designs on the position themselves. That someone so young had been appointed rankled them to no end. And though they afforded her all due courtesy, they could not hide the displeasure in their eyes. Only Ertik seemed genuinely happy with the appointment.

Though he had requested to remain in Althetas with Queen Selena, Dina had ordered him back to the temple. This was partly due to the fact that she knew him and wanted familiar company, but mostly because Selena had advised it. She knew that Dina would need all the help she could get, and there was no one more competent than Ertik. In fact, more than once Dina had thought to press for him to become High Lord of Amon Dähl once her service was done, even though this would break with tradition. The Order had always been led by a woman. But as times changed, so must they. If human and elf could find common ground, certainly Amon Dähl could withstand a male leader. Particularly one as capable as Ertik.

There was a knock on the office door and a young girl entered, carrying a pot of hot tea. The pleasing scent instantly filled the room, bringing a slight smile to Dina's face. Tea from Baltria was a pleasure she never passed up, and since trade had been re-established, she saw to it that the stores were fully stocked with enough to last for some considerable time.

The girl poured the tea and gave a formal bow. "Will there be anything else?" she asked.

Dina still felt uncomfortable with the way the others now spoke to her. "No, my dear. Would you care to join me?" The girl looked uncertain. "Please. I insist," Dina continued.

"As you wish, High Lady." She bowed once more before sitting uneasily in the chair on the other side of the desk.

Before the girl could stop her, Dina retrieved another cup from a small cabinet and poured her some tea. Dina laughed softly at the girl's awkwardness.

"Please make yourself comfortable," she said. "There is no need to be nervous."

"Begging your pardon, High Lady," she replied. "But I've only just arrived and didn't expect to meet you so soon."

"What is your name?"

"Wimolia," she replied, then blew the steam from the surface of the tea before taking a small sip.

"A Baltrian name, by the sound of it," remarked Dina. "Am I right?"

The girl nodded. "My father was a knight of the Order. I came here to look for him after Darshan retook the city."

"Did you find him?"

"No, ma'am. He was killed when Angrääl took Valshara."

Dina could hear the sorrow in her voice. "I am so sorry."

Wimolia forced a weak smile. "Don't be. He died with honor in the service of Amon Dähl. I always knew such a thing might happen. That is why I chose to stay here—out of respect for his sacrifice."

"Have you no family?"

She shrugged. "None to speak of. A cousin, that's all. But he has a family of his own and little time for me. I hope to earn a place here as a healer... that is, if I have the talent."

Dina took a parchment from her drawer and wrote a few short sentences. Once completed, she blew the ink dry, folded the sheet, and handed it over. "Take this to Sister Cherlea in the morning. She will officially induct you into the Order and begin your training."

The girl stared at the parchment for a moment. Then, with a smile, she placed it carefully back on the desk. "I thank you, High Lady. But I have been told that it can take years to earn a place in the healing chamber. I would prefer it came through my own merits rather than pity."

Dina felt a sudden respect for this young girl. She looked to be no more than eighteen, if that, yet her demeanor and maturity were of someone far older. *I suppose war destroys the child within us all*, she thought. She picked up the parchment and placed it back in the desk drawer.

"I'll keep it here just in case you change your mind," she said. "And I'll make sure that whoever holds this office after I leave knows your name."

"Are you not staying?"

Dina shook her head. "I am only here to keep things in order now that the former High Lady is gone. There will be a conclave soon to decide who will be the next High Lady of Amon Dähl."

"Surely they'll choose you?"

Dina laughed. "I seriously doubt that. Not unlike you, I have only recently become a full cleric. My elevation has been a matter of convenience and necessity, that's all. Besides, I have a husband with whom I dearly wish to start a family, and I don't think Valshara would be any place to raise children."

Wimolia suppressed a laugh. "Have you not noticed? There are dozens of children roaming the halls. *They* seem happy enough."

Dina had indeed noticed. Most of the current inhabitants of the temple were not members of the Order. The majority were scholars, priests, and priestesses from other temples, many of whom had brought their families with them. Still, she did not think Linis would be happy here. For that matter, the more she came to understand the duties of the High Lady, the more she looked forward to handing the reins over to someone else.

"I am ill-suited to this post, my dear," she said. "And I will be glad when my time here is at an end."

"I hope you change your mind," said Wimolia. "The Order needs you."

Dina quickly changed the subject. While they finished their tea, she asked Wimolia about her father and her childhood in Baltria. Soon, a loud bell rang out to tell everyone that the evening meal was about to be served. The girl politely excused herself and returned to her duties.

Dina left the office and went to her quarters, where her meal was already waiting for her. During the first week, she had attempted to take her repast in the main dining hall, but each time she was beset with so many requests and questions that she was unable to finish eating. It was Ertik who finally put a stop to it, stating that Dina could ill afford to lose any more weight and insisting that she eat in her room.

She had only just sat down when there was a knock at the door.

"I am sorry to disturb you," Ertik said after stepping inside. "But I have troubling news."

"Not at all," Dina responded. "Please sit."

Ertik obeyed and took a chair at the table opposite her. A guilty expression passed over his face as he looked at the steaming lamb and fresh vegetables on Dina's plate. He clearly hated interrupting her.

"There is a plot against Kaylia and her child," he said in a half-whisper. "An elf plot."

Dina smiled and shook her head. "There have been rumors of plots for some time. This is nothing new."

"And I thought the same. But I believe this one to be real. The body of an elf was found just outside Althetas, his heart pierced."

This sent a shiver down Dina's spine. "That is terrible. But why do you think it's anything more than a dispute between enemies, or even a human who hates the elves? For that matter, it could even have been an enemy agent."

"That would be a possibility," he replied. "But the elves who examined the body are sure that he was killed with an elf blade... and by a seeker."

Dina thought on this for a moment. "And how is this connected to a plot?"

"The victim was an elf named Vixis. He was part of a separatist group who have decided to journey to the desert."

"So, you think this group is responsible?" she asked.

Ertik shook his head. "It's true they have been extremely vocal in their opposition to integration, and have openly tried to convince others to join them, but thus far they have not been at all violent. In fact, it was because of them that we now suspect a plot. They told us that Vixis was due to meet with another far more militant section of elves who have been angered by Gewey's revelations about their origins. He had hoped to persuade them to join his group in traveling to the desert. But he never returned from the meeting. And it was shortly after his body was found that his comrades warned us of rumors they'd heard about a plot against Kaylia and Jayden."

Fear began to swell in her chest. Linis was with them and likely unaware of any danger. "What are they planning?"

"Unfortunately, we have no details yet. But I have already sent word to Kaylia through Queen Selena."

Dina took a deep breath and steadied herself. "Keep me informed if you hear of anything further."

Ertik rose and bowed. "Without delay, High Lady."

Dina stared at her plate as Ertik left the room. She was no longer hungry. She called for a servant and smiled when she saw Wimolia enter.

"I asked to be assigned to your room this evening," the girl said. "I hope you don't mind."

"Not at all," she replied. "But you couldn't have had any time to eat." She stood and offered the girl her seat.

She held up her hand. "That's quite all right, High Lady."

"If you don't eat it, it will only go to waste," Dina insisted. "I'm not at all hungry. In fact, I was calling to have it taken away."

Dina walked over and took the girl's hand. Unable to resist the High Lady, Wimolia allowed herself to be sat in the chair. Dina gave her a motherly smile, and after a long pause, the girl began eating.

Satisfied that good food would not be tossed out, Dina took the seat opposite her.

Barely had Wimolia taken her first bite when her back suddenly stiffened and her face became ghostly pale. Seconds later, a thin trickle of blood began dribbling from her nose.

Dina leaped to her feet. "Wimolia!"

She was just able to catch the girl before she fell from her chair to the floor. The slight body jerked and thrashed in her arms.

Laying her down for a moment, Dina raced to the door. "Help! Please, help me!" she called out at the top of her voice. She then returned to Wimolia and cradled her head in her arms. "Stay with me," she pleaded frantically.

In less than a minute, two guards burst in.

"Take her to the healing chambers immediately," Dina ordered.

The men lifted Wimolia's now still body and hurried to the healers, with Dina following close behind. Ertik arrived just as the girl was being laid on a bed.

"What happened?" he asked.

It took a moment for Dina to speak. "She was ... poisoned."

Ertik's eyes shot wide. "Are you sure?"

Dina nodded. "She took merely a bite of a meal meant for me. A meal I insisted she take..."

Her voice trailed off.

Ertik spun around to face the two guards. "Do not leave the High Lady," he commanded. He then turned back to Dina. "And you. Please stay in this room until I return." With that, he raced out of the chamber.

The healers worked frantically to save Wimolia's life, but it wasn't long before they knew it was hopeless. She had been doomed from the moment the food touched her lips.

Dina could feel her sorrow and guilt slowly being replaced by rage. She walked over to Wimolia's bedside and whispered a prayer.

This done, she spoke aloud in a strong, clear voice. "Whoever is responsible for this will pay." Her words were an oath.

Long before Ertik returned, six more guards arrived inside the chamber, with several more positioned outside, watching the door and hallway. When he finally appeared, his face was grave.

"We found your attacker," he reported. "He was caught trying to flee the temple grounds."

"Where is he now?" she demanded.

"Being brought to the cellar," Ertik replied. "And you should know... he's an elf."

Dina paused for a moment, trying to think through her fury. "Then it seems Kaylia and Jayden are not the only ones being plotted against. Discover what he knows. I'll be in my quarters."

Ertik turned to leave, but Dina caught his arm. "Find my mother," she said. "I want *her* to interrogate him."

A horrified expression appeared fleetingly on Ertik's face. He knew Nahali would undoubtedly cut the prisoner to pieces once she learned of the attempt on her daughter's life. After only an instant's hesitation, he gave a sharp nod and hurried off.

Though there was a part of Dina that knew setting her mother loose on her would-be assassin was morally wrong, she could not get the vision of Wimolia out of her mind. So much promise had been wasted. Even after watching her city being invaded by Angrääl and losing her father, the girl still only wanted to do good and honor her father's memory. If ever there was a cause for retribution, *this* was it. Justice... harsh, unrelenting, righteous justice, would be served.

She had only been back in her chambers for a few minutes when her mother came to see her. The fire in her eyes told Dina that Ertik had already relayed the details of what had happened.

Nahali embraced Dina tightly for a full minute before speaking. "I am on my way to see the animal who tried to kill you." Her voice was hard and totally lacking in emotion.

"Thank you, Mother," she replied, suddenly feeling awkward about her request. Could she live with this? The voice of temperance in the back of her mind was beginning to grow louder.

"Don't worry," said Nahali. "He will talk. Then he will die."

"Mother... I'm not sure..."

Nahali held up her hand. "There is no reason to question your decision. Your reaction was emotional, but correct. We must discover who sent the assassin, and there is no better agent to send than me. I will have no pity or compassion." Her lips trembled with barely contained rage. "They tried to kill my daughter, so I would have insisted on this regardless of your instructions. And from what Ertik tells me, this is part of a much larger plot. One that puts your *unorem* in grave danger along with Kaylia and her child." She placed her hands on Dina's shoulders. "Time is short, and there is no other way. I will get the answers we need."

Dina lowered her head, closed her eyes, and nodded almost imperceptibly. She felt the loving kiss of her mother's lips on her forehead, then listened to her leaving the room. Her eyes remained shut for several minutes longer before she retrieved a bottle of wine from the cupboard and poured herself a glass.

She considered trying to sleep but knew it would be useless. As the minutes turned into hours, her mind turned to thoughts of Linis. She could feel him through their bond, yet it was different from how Kaylia or Aaliyah had described it.

She could only sense that he lived... and that he loved her. The human blood that ran through her veins dulled the raw power that the elves experienced. There were times when she wondered if Linis longed for a deeper connection, but whenever she tried to mention this to him, he'd only laugh and tell her that what they had was far more than he'd ever imagined possible.

It was dawn before Ertik returned to her room. He appeared shaken and exhausted.

"What happened?" she asked, trying not to imagine what he had just witnessed. "Did he talk?"

Ertik nodded. "He talked." He found a chair near Dina's bed and sat down heavily.

She poured him some wine. He took it without looking up and drained the glass before continuing. "He was sent by a group of elf separatists led by a seeker named Tallio. They are planning to kill you, Jayden, and Kaylia."

A heavy frown creased Dina's forehead. "But why? Why risk the wrath of Darshan? Surely they know he would kill them all if they hurt his wife and child."

"They are attempting to sway the elves from across the sea to their cause," Ertik explained. "With their help, they hope to defeat Darshan... or the Reborn King. Whoever arises victorious."

Dina's anger began to swell. To kill a half-breed or an elf they considered to have betrayed their people was one thing. But to plot the death of an infant...

She looked up at Ertik, who appeared still shaken by the interrogation. She leaned forward and took his hand. "I'm sorry you had to see what my mother did."

He forced a smile. "I'll be fine. She only did what she had to do."

"Do these elves intend another attack on me?"

"No. You are safe for now. Their primary target is Kaylia and Jayden. They have fifty elves poised to attack Theopolou's manor as we speak."

Dina jumped up from her chair. "We must send word there at once."

"I already have," he replied. "But it will likely arrive too late."

"Then we need to send help." Her mind raced as thoughts of Linis threatened to shake loose her composure.

Ertik stood. "There is none to send, I'm afraid. The few knights we have here are needed to defend Valshara. In fact, I am hoping you will consider temporarily making all new visitors leave. At least until this matter is resolved."

Dina shook her head. "No. But I do want everyone to be questioned. If these separatists have anyone else amongst us, I want to know."

The door opened and Nahali stepped in. Her face was flushed and her eyes somber. "There is no one else in the temple that you need to fear. Were that so, the assassin would have told me. Of that I am confident."

Dina embraced her mother and offered her some wine. She shook her head with a polite smile. The spots of blood dotted across Nahali's tan blouse were hard to miss, but Dina pretended not to see them.

"The fools actually believe that by killing Darshan's family, they can undo the truth revealed in the Book of Souls," Nahali told them. "And this Tallio... he is clearly mad if he thinks anything will come of this other than the spilling of more elf blood." She could see the fear in her daughter's eyes. "But you should not worry about Linis. The home of Theopolou is defended by great power. Every elf knows this. And with Aaliyah at his side, they would need ten times their numbers to succeed."

Dina knew that she was right, but still, her anxiety remained. She took a deep breath in an attempt to steel her wits. She had a duty to Amon Dähl, and must overcome her emotions if she was to be of any use.

"There is nothing left for you to do tonight, High Lady," said Ertik. "The gates have been sealed, and I will begin questioning the people within the temple in the morning."

After a few moments, Dina nodded with acceptance.

"I will stay with you tonight," said Nahali. "Even the High Lady needs her mother from time to time."

Dina smiled. "Yes. I certainly do."

Ertik excused himself, after which Dina and her mother made ready for bed.

As they lay there, Dina thought that sleep would be reluctant to come. But the warm, loving embrace of Nahali soon had her dozing. And, much as she was repulsed by what her mother had done to their captive, she could not help but feel comforted that Nahali would go to such lengths to protect her. There was truly nothing fiercer than a mother's love.

Her final thoughts before sleep completely overcame her were of hope—hope that the war would soon be over and she could experience a comparable love with a child of her own.

CHAPTER 5

Gewey, Felsafell, and Nehrutu watched as the last wagon disappeared into the far distance. The chill morning air made the trio's breath billow out in steamy clouds. Though the snow had melted and the days were now pleasant, the nights remained miserably cold, made more so by a constant north wind. Gewey was fearful of the fate of the king and his army, and more than a little guilty that he would not be there to help them. But he knew that their destiny was out of his hands for the time being.

Word had come that Kaltinor was readying for a siege, though it was unclear whether this was merely a cautious reaction to an approaching army by the locals or a more disciplined response by Angrääl troops still stationed there. King Lousis was fervently hoping that it would turn out to be the former. If not, then they would need to take the city. They could ill afford to have a large enemy force at their back.

"Come," said Felsafell. "We have much distance to cover today."

Without waiting for a response, he burst into a dead run, quickly vanishing into the forest south of the road. Even with only a few seconds' head start, it still took Gewey and Nehrutu several minutes before they were able to catch him up.

They ran without halting until well after nightfall. Gewey, currently unable to use the *flow*, was close to exhaustion when they did eventually stop. He collapsed in a heap onto the forest floor and immediately began massaging his burning muscles.

Nehrutu looked to be in far better shape and helped Felsafell gather wood for a fire.

"Your strength is impressive," said Felsafell, after settling down on his blanket. "Even without the *flow*, you are quite strong."

Gewey shrugged. "It's been a while since I ran so far and fast without it."

His thoughts turned to the time when he and Kaylia were running through the Spirit Hills. He had just learned that she was with child. He found himself yearning to reach out to her and only resisted with great effort.

He dozed for a few hours against a nearby oak, then was shaken awake by Nehrutu. Dawn was near, and time was their enemy. This became their regular routine until reaching the forest just west of the Spirit Hills several days later.

They had stayed away from the roads throughout, and encountered no one other than a few elves traveling east. Gewey guessed that these were from the steppes, just like the ones he and Kaylia had seen near the ruins south of the Old Santismal Road. They did their best to avoid these travelers, and if they *had* been spotted, the elves had clearly chosen to ignore them.

The journey through the Spirit Hills was uneventful, though Felsafell stopped occasionally to listen for signs of pursuit. It seemed to bother him that there was no indication of the enemy anywhere. The rough terrain was especially hard on Gewey, and by the time they reached the road, he was forced to halt long before sunset. His human frailties were clearly taking a toll.

They built a fire just out of sight of the road and Felsafell vanished into the forest, returning some time later with three rabbits and a bunch of wild berries.

"The ruins along the ancient road..." Gewey began while munching his way through a mouthful of roasted rabbit. "Did your people build them?"

Felsafell nodded. "It is all that remains of their time here." His voice became distant. "The ruins that you see now—once they were magnificent. Streets of polished stone, fountains of silver and gold, and spires that reached so high they rivaled the mountains."

"What you describe sounds very much like my homeland," remarked Nehrutu. "Tell me, how did they fall into such decay?"

A sigh fell from Felsafell's mouth. "Those that weren't destroyed by Melek, we managed to destroy ourselves. Ceaseless war and hate had decimated our once proud civilization. Fortunately, I did not witness much of this. My people had journeyed to the spirit world long before I returned from where I had withdrawn. I later learned that, after the wars were over, they simply didn't bother to rebuild. Most chose instead to live in small farming communities scattered about what is now the Eastland and Middle kingdoms. Others wandered aimlessly until the gods finally released their spirits."

"What of the elves?" asked Nehrutu. "I see evidence that some of their works have endured after the great barrier appeared, but not as many as I would have thought."

"Your kind used the *flow* to construct their cities and many of your structures," Felsafell replied. "Over time, the elves here began to reject complexity in favor of a simpler existence. The places they abandoned returned to the earth and became but dust as the powers that bound them dissipated. Only those still in use, such as the Chamber of the Maker, still stand." He cocked his head. "I'm surprised you didn't know this."

Nehrutu smiled. "In my land, our structures never fall into disrepair. And we only use the *flow* to build within our cities. Like our kin here, many choose to live far removed from others and build with the skill in their hands."

Felsafell nodded. "Your people were always marvelous craftsmen and artists. Even during your more barbaric times, you created things of elegant beauty. In fact, that is what gave me hope for your kind."

"I still find it difficult to believe my ancestors were such brutes," Nehrutu replied, showing a hint of embarrassment.

Following the defeat of Melek, Felsafell had told him about Yanti and Basanti's background. As well as the story of how they were hunted by the elves and Yanti's subsequent fall from grace.

Felsafell laughed. "All people can be so. And all *have* been in the past. But it is the present and future you must attend to. There are three distinct elf cultures now. How they unite will determine your fate. Not all will welcome the reunion any more than all welcome the humans."

"This is true," Nehrutu admitted. "But I must have faith."

"Indeed, you must," he agreed, smiling warmly. "We all must have faith."

For the next few hours, Felsafell told them both of his travels and of the ages he'd witnessed arrive and then fade into legend. Many of his tales involved Basanti and his time with her. Gewey found it comforting to see that he was capable of such love. The *first born* had often seemed to him like some ancient myth that had taken on a fleshy form. That Felsafell's heart was not dissimilar to his own made Gewey feel a kinship with him.

During their time in Althetas while the army was mustering, Felsafell had often been forced to speak in the common tongue. The sight of his powerful frame and piercing eyes speaking in broken and often cryptic sentences never failed to bring Gewey to laughter. Though Basanti was not amused by her love being the object of humor, Felsafell took it all in stride and even joined in by deliberately speaking ever more outlandishly.

The next day, as they were winding through a patch of thick brush, Felsafell came to a sudden halt. He sniffed the air and frowned.

"What is it?" asked Gewey. His hand gripped the hilt of his sword.

"Vrykol are near," he whispered before sniffing again. "But they are not alone."

Gewey scanned the forest, but without the *flow*, he was finding it difficult to separate the shadows. "What do you mean?"

"Someone—something—is with them," he answered. "Something I am unfamiliar with. And whatever it is, it knows we are here."

Gewey and Nehrutu drew their blades and set themselves on either side of the *first born*.

"What should we do?" asked Nehrutu.

"We cannot allow them to report our presence to their master," Felsafell said. "If they discover that Gewey is here, they will certainly send word of this."

But the Vrykol did not advance. Instead, it seemed as if they were trying to remain unnoticed themselves, and fell back the moment Felsafell and the others moved toward them.

"Strange," Felsafell muttered. "Very strange." He burst into a run. Gewey and Nehrutu followed, though they struggled to keep pace.

At first, the Vrykol attempted to escape, but on realizing that their pursuers would not relent, they turned to fight. Gewey caught sight of them in a small clearing. There were three of them, together with a tall figure that looked human... at least, almost human. Its skin was deathly pale and its eyes as black as coal. Clad in a loose-fitting leather jerkin and pants, the creature's fists were clenched tight. Other than that, it appeared to be unarmed.

Something Lee had told him flashed through Gewey's mind. His friend had encountered a possessed half-man while journeying to the desert, and his description of pale skin and black vacant eyes closely matched what he was seeing before him now.

He was about to yell out for Felsafell and Nehrutu to stop when darkness wrapped itself around the pale figure. In the blink of an eye, it completely vanished. Seemingly oblivious of this, the three Vrykol suddenly charged forward to meet them, swords drawn.

Concerned by the creature's sudden disappearance, Felsafell skidded to a halt. Ignoring the onrushing Vrykol, he cast his eyes rapidly from side to side, seeking it out. As he stood there, Gewey and Nehrutu flew past him, and in a ringing clash of steel, began engaging the enemy.

Considerably weaker and slower now than when using the *flow*, Gewey at first struggled to fend off the vicious strikes coming at him from all angles. Being far less disadvantaged, Nehrutu moved into position so as to take on two Vrykol at once, leaving Gewey to deal with just one.

Felsafell was on the point of joining them in the fight when, from nowhere, a cloud of darkness covered his eyes. A massive blow then struck his jaw, sending him reeling back.

Quickly recovering, he crouched low, but his foe was nowhere to be seen. He shot a glance across at Gewey and Nehrutu. Despite his lack of the *flow*, Gewey was now slowly and surely pushing his adversary back. He still had the brute strength of several men and was using this to overwhelm the Vrykol with sheer force. Nehrutu, meanwhile, was moving back and forth with superb skill and experience, his blade a blur as he found weaknesses in the enemy's defenses. He was gaining no ground, but neither was he giving any away.

The *first born* closed his eyes and took a breath. This time, he heard the creature coming a moment before it attacked. Just in time he rocked back on his heels, causing a flying fist to miss his jaw by barely a hair's width. In the same motion, Felsafell raised his knee sharply, burying it deep into the creature's midsection and forcing it to double over. It cried out in an unbridled rage, its black eyes demonic with fury. But before it could raise itself up again, Felsafell smashed his fist with terrifying force into its temple. The power of this blow would have killed any normal man, but this was no man like he had ever encountered before.

Felsafell moved in to finish things, but to his astonishment, the creature nimbly jumped aside and threw a series of savage punches back at him. Never before had the *first born* been matched in speed and agility by a mere mortal. Three times his head was snapped back as bony knuckles found his chin. Once... twice... three times, he tried to get close enough to grapple, but on each occasion, it anticipated his move and stepped sharply away.

But something had to give. As fast and strong as his foe was, Felsafell had spent thousands of years gaining experience in such situations, and his skill was beyond reckoning. He allowed his opponent to press him back until they were at the edge of the clearing. A bone-cracking strike then landed on the bridge of his nose, sending him stumbling back into a young oak. Felsafell's legs appeared to wobble. Grinning triumphantly, the creature charged in for the kill.

This was exactly what Felsafell was waiting for. With perfect timing, he leaned in and wrapped his powerful arms around his enemy's waist. In a single motion, he lifted him off the ground and slammed him with bone-shattering force down onto his back. Before the creature could recover from this, he pinned its arms with his knees and rained down a storm of vicious blows.

Incredibly, even through this, the beast continued to struggle and fight back. As its broken and gashed face began to ooze a thick, acrid smoke, its bestial growls lent savage accompaniment to the incessant ringing of steel on steel from the nearby fight.

No matter how many times Felsafell hit the creature, it appeared to show no signs of weakening. Amazingly, it even managed to free one of its arms. Only the *first born's* massive strength and great height was now keeping him atop his foe. But, with the creature's endless punching and clawing in an attempt to free itself, his own injuries were beginning to mount.

Just then, Felsafell's eyes caught the gleam of metal through a tear in the beast's tattered jerkin. It was no larger than the head of a nail and appeared to be buried within its flesh, just above its heart. He thrust the tips of his fingers around the protrusion, digging hard until he could feel it firmly in his grip. Satisfied, he yanked upward with vicious force.

The creature's eyes shot wide as the spike jerked free. It flailed about wildly for a few seconds, all the time letting out a series of ear-splitting shrieks. Then it went completely limp.

Felsafell took a moment to regard the thin spike before tossing it aside and leaping to his feet. As he raced over to aid his embattled comrades, the beast's body suddenly erupted in a blast of white-hot flames. But there was no time to stop and watch this. The fight still raged on.

By now, Gewey was bleeding from several deep cuts to his arms and chest, though his foe's cloak was shredded and its blade broken in half. Nehrutu had severed the leg of one Vrykol, and was relentlessly driving the second one back.

Felsafell leaped skyward and landed just behind Gewey's attacker. In a single blinding motion, he tore its head from its shoulders with his bare hands. In that same moment, Nehrutu took the head of the Vrykol he was battling. With barely a pause, his sword then decapitated the other one, still struggling to rise from the ground.

Battle over, the three took a moment to survey the scene. Gewey then stripped off his shirt and began to clean his wounds.

"You have knowledge of that thing I fought?" asked Felsafell, looking back at what was now no more than a pile of smoldering ashes.

Gewey nodded and went on to tell him about Lee's encounter. "This one wasn't quite as deformed as Lee described," he concluded. "But everything else fits."

Felsafell walked back to the ashes and picked up the small spike. "It would seem our enemy has found a way to control a corrupted half-man. This poor creature was not feral, as was the one Lee described to you. It possessed at least a semblance of a mind. I think the Vrykol were imposing their will on it somehow."

"And it appears they wish to keep this new ... *weapon* a secret," added Nehrutu. His face twisted into a scowl. "From what I have learned of the Vrykol, they would not have fled otherwise." He touched his side, remembering the wound he'd received from the enemy soldier while fighting one of the unwholesome beasts.

"The question is, how many of these half-men do they have?" said Felsafell. "And what purpose will they serve?"

There was a long moment of silence.

"There is no way to answer these questions," Nehrutu eventually said. "I suspect we will learn the truth soon enough. For now, we should keep going."

Without another word, they set off, though at a considerably slower pace than before. It was dusk by the time they arrived at the ancient *first born* city. After they'd built a fire, Felsafell strode toward the ruins. Gewey followed him. Nehrutu, however, seemed content to remain by the fire and doze.

Felsafell ran his fingers over the broken buildings and ruined columns as he passed. His eyes were distant, as if staring into the depths of time.

"Did you know this place well?" Gewey asked.

Felsafell nodded. "I lived here briefly—before the madness took my people. Once, this city extended for more than two miles in every direction. Now, only a few stones have not been reclaimed by the earth." He looked at Gewey and gave a sad half-smile. "One day, all that remains of my people will be forgotten; lost to the ravages of time."

"You'll still be here."

He laughed softly. "I have no intention of living forever. Should we prevail, I will remain with Basanti for a time. But neither of us wishes to endure eternally. One day we will pass from this life and take our well-deserved rest. We are relics of a bygone era, and we must make way for those of this new age." Seeing Gewey's concern, he placed a hand on his shoulder. "It is the way of things. Everything has its time, then it must make room for whatever comes next. Were it not for the love I feel for Basanti, I would be content to end my stay in this world far sooner."

"I think the world still needs you," Gewey told him with deep sincerity. "If only to guide us when we go astray."

This time, Felsafell's laugh was loud and hearty. "I would be a poor guide for the mortal world. I am far too old and have seen too many horrors. My mind is filled with the phantoms of an immortal life. More than once, it has nearly driven me insane. No, my young friend. Human and elf are not the children they once were. They no longer need the likes of me meddling in their affairs."

Gewey sighed heavily. "I suppose if I were to have lived as long as you, I'd see the end as being a welcome respite."

"The end? You, more than anyone, should know that this world is not all that exists. My departure from this life will only mean reuniting with my kin and eternity... true eternity with my love." He squeezed Gewey's shoulder. "But there are still pleasures I would enjoy here first. And I will not be denied at least a short time of peace with Basanti. I have seen much of this world—though not all of it yet—and I would see the rest with her by my side."

He led Gewey through the ruins for a while, describing the city as it had been in his time. Felsafell painted a picture of a vibrant society that was dedicated to art and culture. Though they were not able to use the flow, or feel the heartbeat of the earth, they nonetheless felt a deep connection with the world and planned their cities to meld with the landscape—unlike humans, who later on imposed their own will upon the land with the cities they built.

By the time they returned to the campfire, Gewey's stomach was rumbling. He pulled out a piece of jerky and a scrap of bread. He offered some to Felsafell, but this was politely refused.

While trying to relax sufficiently to sleep for a while, Gewey became increasingly aware of how much his wounds were beginning to throb and ache. It seemed like many years since he'd been forced to heal naturally, and he did not like having to do this again one bit.

His mind drifted back to his recent fight with the Vrykol. His godlike strength was the only thing that had kept him alive during that, or at least, from becoming far more seriously wounded than he actually was. The vulnerability he currently felt was unnerving. It had been much the same when first setting out from home with Lee. He recalled his fight with the bandits on the night he'd first met Kaylia. Though much more experienced with weapons these days, without the *flow,* he was still little better than a human soldier. It was almost impossible to perceive himself in any other way.

The temptation to ignore Felsafell's warnings and destroy their enemy with a massive ball of fire had been great. But had he done so, there would have been a grave risk of their purpose being discovered. After that, he would have found himself facing the Reborn King prematurely and over-matched. He sighed. Even if they did succeed in recovering the remaining god stones, there was still no guarantee that wouldn't be the case, anyway.

It seemed that each time he felt ready to face his destiny, there was something more to overcome first. What if the god stones weren't enough? For a moment, the notion that he had made a mistake by not joining with Melek shot through his mind, but this was quickly dismissed.

There is no point in dwelling on things I have no control over, he told himself, then allowed his eyes to close. Besides, Melek was insane.

CHAPTER 6

Kaylia reached out through her newly acquired bond with the manor and grounds. Though considerably weaker when on the other side of the wall, she could still sense the presence of at least fifty elves—and their intent was clear. They were coming to kill her and her son.

Instinctively, she reached out to Gewey, but Aaliyah had been effective in preventing this. She briefly considered asking her to remove the block, but thought better of it. There was no telling what he was doing, and such a distraction could get him killed. Besides, the manor of Lord Theopolou was well protected. But there was something else. Something just beyond her senses.

"I feel it as well," said Aaliyah.

They reached the crystal statue in front of the house and surveyed the wall and grounds. Linis and Basanti were busy gathering and organizing the staff. Those who could fight were being issued weapons.

"Can they overcome the defenses?" asked Aaliyah.

"Even the elves of your land would find that difficult," Kaylia replied. A frightening thought then entered her mind.

Could these attackers be in league with the Dark Knight? If so, then perhaps they had some weapon yet to be revealed.

Kaylia kept watch on the movements beyond the wall. The enemy was not attempting to take the manor yet; instead, they were making their way to the various outlying houses. A cry of anguish fell from her mouth as their initial objective became obvious. They intended to slaughter the families in their own homes. They would not see them coming. But there was no way to warn the people in time. The ground shook as Kaylia screamed a curse.

Linis came running up from the corner of the house. "We should go inside," he told her. "It will be far easier to defend than the grounds."

Kaylia gasped as the bond allowed her to hear the first elf home being attacked. The cries of the family tore at her like savage talons, causing her fall to her knees. It was over in seconds.

The wrath of vengeance now consumed her. They would all pay. And if the fools thought murdering their kin would give them an advantage, they would learn how mistaken they were. She would show them that the legends which surrounded the home of Theopolou were true. The ground trembled again, and this time a deep rumble reverberated off the walls. Her anger had become a part of the land itself. And its lust for justice would not be denied.

"Come," said Aaliyah, taking her hand. "We should prepare."

With one final glance at the front gate, she allowed herself to be led inside. Once all the doors were closed and sealed, she took Jayden to her chambers and laid him in his crib. Thankfully, her connection to her son was unaffected by Aaliyah's block. She sent him loving reassurance, and in moments he was sleeping soundly, completely unaware of the danger bearing down on them.

The house staff had prepared as best as they could and were gathered in the main hall just beyond the front door.

Kaylia went to the top floor and climbed a narrow staircase leading to the roof. Linis and Aaliyah followed her, while Basanti joined the elves at ground level. Though unable to draw blood, she was perfectly willing to use her strength and speed to confuse the enemy.

Kaylia, Aaliyah, and Linis stared over the grounds. Aaliyah began allowing the *flow* to rage through her.

"Your help is unneeded," said Kaylia. Her voice dripped with malicious intent. "Once, during the first split, this house was assaulted by more than a thousand elves." She turned her head to give Aaliyah a sinister grin. "They did not succeed."

A series of resounding booms drew their attention to the main gate. The gleaming metal vibrated as it repeatedly came under assault from violent blows. Kaylia's eyes narrowed with concentration. Soon, the gate began to glow a fiery red. This was followed by alarmed voices crying out as smoke began to rise.

A few moments later, the simultaneous thwack of dozens of bowstrings heralded a barrage of arrows sailing over the wall. Kaylia laughed out loud before creating a blast of wind to send them all falling harmlessly to the ground.

Several heads poked cautiously over the top of the wall. After briefly scanning the deserted grounds for a second or two, the attackers then leaped nimbly over, blades drawn. In response, Kaylia spread her arms wide and the earth instantly began to shake. From beneath the grass, hundreds of tiny crystal shards began pushing their way through to the surface. The sunlight captured their deadly beauty, giving them the appearance of stars in an emerald sky.

Linis and Aaliyah looked on with astonishment as Kaylia flicked her wrist and sent the crystals shooting forth, their razor-sharp edges slicing and ripping the flesh of the attackers to pieces before they had taken barely a few steps.

"You see?" Kaylia said. "We are safe here." But no sooner were these words out of her mouth than she felt a disturbing presence approaching. Her face contorted into a furious scowl.

"What is it?" asked Linis.

Kaylia held up her hand to silence him and closed her eyes. Screams of terror erupted from the other side of the gate, and in less than a minute, at least a dozen more elves were desperately scrambling over the wall. But they were not attacking this time. They were fleeing. Not that this made any difference to Kaylia, who immediately sent them to their deaths with a renewed storm of the deadly crystals.

After a short time, their screams ceased and all was quiet.

"Vrykol," muttered Kaylia.

"Are you saying that the Vrykol have driven off the elves?" asked Linis, incredulously.

"No," she replied. "Something else did that. But the Vrykol are with them. And they did not drive our attackers off. They massacred them... all of them."

Another loud boom sounded as the gate came under renewed attack. Again Kaylia focused the power of the *flow* to make it glow red with intense heat. But this time, who- ever—or whatever—was trying to batter it down was not so easily deterred. A dozen more blows thudded relentlessly into the gate until, finally, it burst from its hinges and toppled inward with a resounding crash.

More shards of crystal began appearing throughout the grounds, ready to bring death to any who dared enter. Then a wave of darkness washed over the earth, spreading all the way up to the very threshold of the manor.

All at once, Linis knew what they were up against.

"Cursed half-men," he growled through clenched teeth. "Corrupted by the Reborn King."

Kaylia recalled the tale and fear struck her heart. Even with Aaliyah alongside her, such foes might be impossible to vanquish.

The shadow continued swirling and spreading around the manor grounds until the house was isolated like a solitary pearl in an ocean of darkness. Then, slowly, the darkness receded. Standing just beyond the ruined gates were four pale figures—shirtless and bootless, clad only in a pair of dingy leather trousers. Their heads had been shaved clean, and their black, empty eyes were focused straight ahead.

Kaylia let fly with her lethal barrage of crystals, but the creatures did not even flinch as dozens of shards ripped through their flesh. They simply remained motionless, while thin wisps of smoke issued from their wounds. Within seconds, these injuries were completely healed.

Aaliyah tried to send down a column of flame to consume them, but to her dismay, found that her connection to the *flow* was being blocked.

"What should we do?" asked Linis, trying hard to calm the tremor in his voice.

Before Kaylia could answer, twelve Vrykol filed through the gate and lined up behind the half-men. She could feel their foul gazes directly upon her.

"We are here for the mate of Darshan," one of the Vrykol called out in a thin rasp. "She will come with us, or all here shall perish... including her offspring."

Kaylia's heart froze in her chest. She was unable to move or speak.

"Will you comply?" it pressed.

Aaliyah stepped forward. "And how do we know that you will keep your word?"

The Vrykol wheezed its gruesome laugh. "My word? I give you no word other than you will face certain death should you resist."

Kaylia turned to Linis. "There is a hidden passage in the basement that leads outside the grounds," she whispered. Her voice was barely audible. "Therisa will know how to find it. Once I am gone, take Jayden to Valshara."

"I will not just hand you over," snapped Linis. "They will surely kill you."

"They could kill me now if that was their plan," she countered. Her hands were shaking and tears were welling in her eyes.

"Then take Jayden and flee through the passage yourself," suggested Aaliyah. "We will keep them occupied long enough for you to escape."

She took Aaliyah's hand and shook her head. "No. I cannot risk that. If I flee, they will only pursue us. I will not be able to outrun them with Jayden in my arms."

"What is your answer!" demanded the Vrykol.

The half-men took a step forward, their movement causing the air to stir.

Kaylia took a breath and banished all traces of fear from her eyes. "I will come with you."

Without waiting for a reply, she spun on her heels and went inside. Downstairs, she could hear Jayden cooing and Basanti humming softly to him. The moment she saw her son wrapped in his soft cotton blanket and being coddled by the oracle, the tears she had been holding back burst forth and streamed down her cheeks. Basanti carefully handed Jayden over.

Kaylia kissed his forehead and for a moment considered flight. But she knew it was foolish. *This is for the best*, she told herself. *There is nothing else I can do.*

While handing Jayden back to Basanti, she could feel her heart breaking. Her body shook from the sobs she could no longer contain. Jayden stirred, sensing his mother's grief.

"There, there," comforted Basanti, her words meant for both mother and child. "All will be well. You shall see." She smiled up at Kaylia. "Don't weep, my dear. Your child will be safe. And soon... so shall you be. I will make certain of that."

Kaylia stifled her tears and dried her eyes. Something in Basanti's voice was unusually comforting. She felt her courage rising. Grasping desperately for any source of hope, she forced herself to believe the words. Yes. All *would* be well. It would *not* end like this.

With level determination, she turned away and opened the door. Without glancing back, she strode down the front steps and past the crystal statue, stopping only when she was a few feet away from the half-men. They regarded her with emotionless black eyes before moving aside.

The Vrykol in the center hissed a whispered order, and in an instant Kaylia was surrounded by black cloaks.

"You have chosen wisely," it said.

The stench of death caused her face to contort. "As long as you leave my son in peace, I will give you no trouble."

"Your son is of no interest to us at present," the Vrykol replied. "It is you we need. Should our master require him after Darshan is dead, it will be a simple matter to fetch him."

When Darshan discovers what you have done, she thought, *he will tear your spirit apart like wet parchment.*

"You have me now," she snapped. "If you intend to take me, then lead on. Your words are empty and unwanted."

Without reply, the Vrykol spun around and started toward the gate. Kaylia felt an icy hand pressing into the small of her back. She loathed to be touched by these creatures, so she quickly matched her captor's pace. Again she wanted to reach out for Gewey, but even without Aaliyah's block, she could feel that the Vrykol would have prevented it.

"Do not bother," said the Vrykol, anticipating her thoughts. "He will not hear you. By the time he learns of your fate, my master will have already placed his head on a pike."

Rage boiled up from deep inside, but she forced it back and remained quiet. Basanti would come to her aid, she was sure of it. And then they would pay dearly for their folly.

Basanti watched from the window as Kaylia and the enemy disappeared beyond the shattered gates.

"What do you plan to do?" asked Linis.

"I plan to rescue her," she replied flatly.

"How can we help?" asked Aaliyah. Her tone did not conceal her fury.

Basanti looked down at the baby in her arms. "Linis can help by taking Jayden to Valshara. He should be safe there until Kaylia returns."

"You cannot hope to challenge the Vrykol *and* the half-men alone," Linis protested. "I shall go with you."

Basanti handed the baby to Linis and shook her head. There was a sad smile on her lips. "I will not be alone. Aaliyah will assist me." She met the other woman's eyes. "But only if you agree to do precisely as I say."

After a long pause, Aaliyah nodded.

"But I still cannot understand how you hope to defeat so many," Linis contended. "Even with Aaliyah's help."

"There is much about me that you do not know... cannot know," she explained. "And once I have done what must be done, I will be changed."

Linis regarded her with concern. "Changed? How?"

"It doesn't matter," she replied. "This is a decision I must make. I ask only that you convey a message to Felsafell when next you see him." Her words had a sense of finality. "Tell him that I am sorry. I wish I could have explored the rest of our world by his side. Please let him know that I will always treasure the memories of the odd little hermit who protected and cared for me throughout the long years. But most of all, tell him... tell him that I love him." Her tears were beginning to flow. "Now go. You must not delay."

There would be no discussion of the matter. Linis could see that. Basanti's mind was fixed and her path had been chosen. Whatever she had decided to do, it would come at a great cost to her.

Linis quickly packed a few essentials and had Therisa show him to the passage.

"This will lead you to just beyond the walls," the old woman told him. "The brush is thick around the exit and should conceal you well."

He thanked her and went to find Basanti and Aaliyah in order to say farewell. But they had already departed.

"Do you think they will succeed?" he asked Therisa, even though he knew she did not have the answer.

"Perhaps. If she is the oracle of legend. But it sounded as if she will sacrifice much to do so." The old woman handed him a bundle of changing cloths and a skin of milk. "But you must focus on *your* task. Jayden's mother is the mistress of this house. Her child must be kept safe."

He steeled his wits and cleared his thoughts. She was right. Whatever Basanti was planning to do was not his concern at this moment.

All his attention must be concentrated on getting Jayden to safety. Would there be foes awaiting them along his path? And if so, how would he deal with them?

That was more than enough to be thinking about at present.

CHAPTER 7

Gewey, Nehrutu, and Felsafell halted just as the Vrykol fortress came into view. The curtain wall Gewey had destroyed when last here remained scattered in massive black chunks about the yard, indicating that no one had yet attempted to repair it. He hoped this meant that the place was still abandoned.

They stood perfectly still, listening intently for several minutes before approaching. Dotted around the landscape were numerous sections of black-stained earth where the ashes of Gewey's victims still lay. The memory of that night flashed through his mind. His vengeful fury back then was almost beyond reckoning. Only Kaylia's love had been able to prevent him from completely abandoning his humanity.

The cage where the human slaves had been imprisoned was still there as well—its twisted door on the ground a few feet away, where he had tossed it aside. How terrifying he must have seemed to them. He wondered if the people he had freed ever had nightmares about the wrath of Darshan. Or did they see him as their liberator?

"I hear no enemies about," Felsafell said in a half-whisper. He regarded the shattered wall and the empty Vrykol cloaks. "You must have been a truly awesome spectacle when you did this."

"That's not exactly how I'd put it," Gewey responded somberly.

The stench of death still lingered in the calm air. Hundreds of the Reborn King's foul creations had dwelt here, and it would be years, if not decades, before the ground was clean and pure again.

"This was once a beautiful place," remarked Felsafell, sharing Gewey's revulsion. "When my people lived, this was a center for art and music. It stood for thousands of years and produced wonders the like of which would make the gods themselves weep for joy." He closed his eyes, a distant smile on his lips. "During the spring months, the honeysuckle and lavender perfumed the breeze just as evening fell. The musicians would join the painters and sculptors in the grand courtyard, allowing the visual splendor to inspire them to unimaginable heights of creativity and subtlety. So masterful were they, the sheer magnificence of their works would cause the *night blooms* to issue forth."

"What are *night blooms*?" asked Gewey.

Felsafell opened his eyes. "*Night blooms* were the pinnacle of my people's creative ingenuity. At least, that has always been my opinion. Our horticulturists spent centuries cultivating and combining various species of flowers. Ultimately, the *night bloom* was born. It looked much like a rose, though with longer and more complex petals. And the colors..." He sighed. "They were enough to shame even the splendor of heaven. When the musicians played, the blooms glowed with a faint, pure light that would change with the mood of the music. Each flower was different, but rather than a chaotic swirl, it melded and took form—increasingly growing in beauty as the songs progressed."

"I've never heard of them before," Gewey said, now even more disgusted by the scorched and disfigured scene before him. "I wish I could see some."

"They are long extinct," Felsafell explained sadly. "Without gardeners to tend them, they soon faded away."

"A great pity," said Nehrutu. "Your words remind me of the flowers and gardens of home."

Felsafell smiled. "I hope you will show them to Basanti and me one day." He turned his attention back to the fortress. "But first we must complete the task at hand."

Beyond the wall and broken gates, the interior was pitch black. Even with his god's eyes, Gewey struggled to make out anything other than shadowy shapes devoid of detail. Felsafell reached into his pocket and pulled out a small crystal sphere, which he rubbed his hand against. Like the elf globes, light emanated from its core.

"A remnant from the distant past," Felsafell told them, before anyone could ask.

Unfortunately, the light only revealed stark walls and bare floors. It seemed that Vrykol had no interest in décor, nor even furniture. Gewey glanced to his right, where a staircase led to the upper floors and was tempted to explore.

"There is nothing there of value," remarked Felsafell, as if hearing his thoughts. "What we seek is below."

He led them deeper inside through the labyrinth of passageways. There were no doors on any of the rooms, and upon inspection, it became clear why. There was nothing there—only bare stone walls.

"Why have a fortress at all?" Gewey pondered. Even in a low whisper, his voice echoed loudly, sending a sudden wave of anxiety through him.

"Why indeed?" agreed Nehrutu.

"I can only guess it was meant to be some sort of staging point," said Felsafell. "But for what, I cannot say. The location they chose would shield them from most eyes. Including yours. There are certain places in this world in which the god's vision is obscured. This is one of them."

Gewey considered this. He and Kaylia had been quite close by when he first detected it. And that was before he'd learned how to truly stretch out with his spirit. An ability later taught to him by Melek.

"Then maybe it wasn't the stones that brought them here," he suggested.

"Perhaps," said Felsafell. "But it begs the question—if they were hiding, was it really from you?" He cast a worried look at Gewey. "You had no ability to see them when this place was first built. And there was no way they could have anticipated Melek's arrival. So, who were they hiding from?"

Gewey was at a loss. Now that Melek was in Shagharath, there were no more gods on earth other than himself. "The elves?" he suggested.

"Unlikely," said Nehrutu. "We are not as powerful as you, and cannot see as far or as clearly. They would not need to go to so much trouble to conceal themselves from us. Especially being that, other than myself, only Mohanisi and Aaliyah have significant talent with the *flow*."

"And they could certainly have captured any elves of *this* land who might happen along," Felsafell added.

Gewey thought hard, but could come up with no logical reason why the Vrykol would need to build such a fortress here. Finally, with a grunt, he pushed the question from his mind. It would have to remain a mystery for the time being.

They continued to explore, twisting and backtracking several times until finally discovering a downward stairway. Gewey would have thought it impossible, but the air that wafted up from here was even more rank and unclean than in the rest of the foul place. The odor was like a cloud of vile pestilence that threatened to choke the very life from him. Yet, as he took a step forward, he could feel something odd. Almost like a presence—conscious and alive, but without focus or purpose.

"Do you feel that?" asked Gewey.

Both Felsafell and Nehrutu shook their heads.

Once again, Gewey cursed the fact that he had to forgo using the *flow*. The soreness of his wounds from battling the Vrykol, though healing rapidly, was a testament to how much he had come to depend on it.

"Something is down there," he said warily.

The song of steel pierced the thick air as Nehrutu and Gewey drew their blades. All three then began descending the steps with Felsafell leading the way, the glowing orb in his hand only slightly breaking into the suffocating dark.

The stairs continued for more than one hundred feet before ending in a long, narrow hallway. Felsafell was forced to duck down so as not to scrape his head on the ceiling, while Gewey had to walk slightly twisted to one side in order to accommodate his broad shoulders.

With each step, the presence grew more pronounced to Gewey. He was reminded of the way he had felt when in the Black Oasis, only this time it was not something malevolent, angry, or even aware of him. He speculated that it might have been touched by the gods at some point. The thought excited him. Perhaps he would encounter yet another godly essence left behind to assist him. Maybe even his father. But could a god leave more than one piece of itself behind? Or could it be one of the other gods this time?

The passage sloped downward for a few more yards before ending at an iron-barred gate that proved to be solidly locked. Felsafell motioned for the others to step back. The sinews of his arms and shoulders rippled as he pulled on the bars with all of his might. For a moment it looked as if the gate would prove to be too much, even for the *first born*, but then they heard the complaining groan of yielding metal as the hinges gradually began to bend. After letting out one final mighty grunt of exertion, Felsafell tore it completely free. Gewey winced, the high-pitched screech of iron scraping on stone sending shivers down his back and causing all the hairs on his arms to stand on end.

Beyond the entrance was an immense natural limestone cavern measuring several hundred feet in all directions, and with a ceiling at least fifty feet high. The floor was smooth yet uneven, and the rancid air was made even more unpleasant by a sudden drop in temperature.

"We are here," Felsafell announced. He peered through the darkness. "And we are not alone."

Gewey focused and very quickly could make out three cloaked figures standing against the wall on the far side of the cavern. His muscles tensed as he prepared to charge.

"Wait," said Felsafell. "Something is wrong. Look closely."

Gewey could see that there was indeed something odd about the Vrykol. They seemed to be taking no notice at all of his sudden appearance. Instead, they were simply jerking back and forth erratically. Their weapons lay discarded on the floor a short distance in front of them.

Cautiously, they inched toward the creatures. When they were about twenty feet away, the Vrykol on the left let out a high-pitched scream and fell to its knees. The two others spun around and began clawing wildly at the stone wall, as if trying to tear a way through.

Gewey, Nehrutu, and Felsafell looked at each other in stunned confusion. This bizarre situation continued for several minutes—then slowly, the creatures returned to their previous positions.

Gewey took a few steps closer, motioning for the others to stay where they were. "Do you know who I am?" he demanded. His voice echoed, causing the Vrykol to twitch, but none of them answered. He repeated his question.

The Vrykol in the center eventually nodded. "You... You..." His rasping voice was full of fear. "You are Darshan. I... I know you. I've seen you. You... you... destroyed us."

"Yet you do not flee."

The Vrykol began to tremble. "I... I cannot. I must not. There is no escape."

Without another word, the creature leaped forward, spanning the distance between them in an instant. Gewey instinctively raised his blade, impaling it down to the hilt. In spite of this, the Vrykol's claw-like fingers still desperately sought to grab hold of his shirt front.

"Save us," it pleaded. "Save us and we will serve you. Yes. We will serve you and no other. Save us, and we will do anything you ask."

Some of the thick black blood covering Gewey's blade spilled onto the floor as he pushed the wounded creature away. However, it was undeterred. It crumbled to the ground and began crawling forward until it was groveling at Gewey's feet.

"Save us, master," it hissed pitifully. "Save us."

The other two also fell prostrate and joined in to echo the first one's plea.

"What is wrong with you?" Gewey demanded, unable to believe what he was seeing. *Vrykol didn't feel fear. At least not in this way.* But soon their hissing pleas had degenerated even further into incoherent blubbering, spat out in sharp gurgles and vile coughs. "Answer me!" he commanded, but still they gave no answer.

Finally, exasperated, Gewey raised his blade and in a swift motion took the wounded creature's head. The other two appeared not to notice and continued their pathetic wailing. Quickly, he moved in and silenced them permanently as well.

Their screams echoed for a moment throughout the cavern before fading away. After a long pause, Gewey turned to his two companions, looking shaken and mortified.

"I don't know what to think," he said. "What could have affected them so?"

Felsafell shook his head.

"I never imagined I would be capable of feeling pity for these beasts," remarked Nehrutu. "But that was ... ghastly."

"Indeed," said Felsafell. He cast his eyes along the walls, fixing his gaze on a smooth section a few yards to their right. He approached it with care and examined the surface for a time.

Gewey stood beside him. "Is that the door?"

"Yes," he replied, running his finger along a barely visible crack in the rock. "And it has been damaged. Possibly when you unleashed your wrath upon this place. The seal which protects it can only be opened by the power of heaven."

"Maybe the Dark Knight broke it?" suggested Gewey.

"Perhaps," said Felsafell. "But I think not. If he possessed the ability to do this, he would most likely have removed it completely." He turned to Gewey. "Touch it."

After a brief hesitation, Gewey pressed his hand against the wall. The limestone was instantly replaced by a silver door, across the face of which was etched a circle containing the symbols of the nine gods.

At the sight of this, Felsafell reached out to grab the handle. But the instant his fingers made contact, there was an earsplitting crack and a flash of blinding white light. The *first born* was sent flying several yards back and landed with a thud, flat on his back. Nehrutu and Gewey were at his side at once.

"I am unhurt," Felsafell reassured them before either could ask. He struggled back to his feet.

"What was that?" asked Gewey.

Felsafell let out a dissatisfied snort. "It would seem that only you can enter," he grumbled.

"He should not go on alone," Nehrutu protested. "Whatever drove the Vrykol mad might still be in there."

"Almost certainly," the *first born* agreed. "But I can think of no way for us to help. And he *must* go on." He looked at Gewey. "If you find yourself with no other choice, use the *flow* to protect yourself."

Gewey smiled and chuckled. "So I take it you're not suggesting that I take a safer path and *not* go on?" Before Felsafell could respond, he turned the knob and opened the door.

He was half expecting the world to vanish and to find himself in some strange place. But that was not to be this time; the door simply swung open to reveal a long stone passage. Though there were no torches, the way ahead was lit by a pale light that emanated from the rock. A rush of warm air washed over him.

He glanced back and nodded reassuringly. "I won't be a moment."

As soon as he stepped over the threshold, the door slammed shut behind him, instantly setting his nerves on edge. A few yards ahead, the light vanished. He longed to fill himself with the *flow,* but managed to resist the temptation.

"Not yet," he muttered.

He could still feel the presence. But now it was beginning to take form and was becoming aware of him. It was almost as if it were waking from a deep slumber.

He walked with quiet steps until reaching the darkness. Even without the flow, his naturally keen eyesight enabled him to see several yards farther ahead. The passage curved to the right, then gently sloped upward.

The presence was growing more tangible, but it felt neither good nor evil... at least not yet.

"Hello," he called out, then immediately regretted it as a gust of hot air blew down the hallway as if in response to his cry.

A sudden anxiety struck Gewey, causing him to glance over his shoulder. The door was still there. But the wind continued to howl, and soon his anxiety was turning into an inexplicable panic. He paused, considering whether to return to the cavern.

"Do not turn back, son of Gerath," came a soft voice. "What you seek is now close. Don't go. Not yet."

"Who are you?" he shouted. But there was no reply.

His panic was now bordering on fear. What the hell is wrong with me? he scolded himself? I've faced worse than this. Why am I so afraid?

With one hand firmly gripping the hilt of his sword, he pressed on through the gloom. After a few hundred yards, the wind calmed and he arrived at a plain wooden door.

"Come in," said the same voice. "Take your ease. There is nothing to trouble you here."

Gewey reached for the knob, but just before he touched it, the door swung wide open of its own accord. He took a step forward and peered inside. Beyond the threshold was a room roughly the size of a tavern common area. A small, square-shaped table sat in the center atop a modest brown rug. In the corners, brass lanterns hung from iron hooks, and set against the wall to his right was a simple yet comfortable-looking couch.

On the table, a cup and bottle had been placed beside a wooden bowl filled with peaches and pears. Gewey looked for the source of the voice, but could see no one.

"Where are you?" he asked unsteadily, still fighting off his inexplicable fear.

"I am here," the voice replied. "Can you not see me?"

"No."

A hollow laugh drifted on the stale, dusty air. "Then you are not looking with your father's eyes. Draw from the power and I shall appear."

"I cannot," he replied.

"Why is that? Do you fear an enemy, perhaps?" There was a long pause. "Tell me. What is it you fear?"

"Nothing," said Gewey. "I fear nothing."

"Then why deny yourself the pleasure? Surely you want to feel the *flow* coursing through you. Is this not so?"

"That isn't your concern," he snapped, attempting to replace his fear with anger. "Now tell me who you are."

This is what must have affected the Vrykol, he warned himself.

"I can hear your thoughts," the voice told him. "I am Tyrin. And yes, I am indeed the one who altered the foul creatures that tried to pollute this clean place. Though I admit, it was a considerable challenge. So dark and evil were they, it took some time to find my way to their inner terror."

"What are you?" asked Gewey. "A spirit?"

"Yes," Tyrin replied. "But a spirit cast aside." Malevolence bled into his voice, causing the lantern lights to pulse and flicker. "A spirit betrayed. A spirit entombed by my brothers and sisters."

"You mean the *first born* betrayed you?" Gewey blurted out before he could stop himself.

"You know of us?"

Gewey felt as if something was probing his mind. He tried hard to resist, but was quickly overcome.

"Felsafell," Tyrin hissed. "You have brought my kin with you. The caretaker of the spirits has at last come within my grasp."

Gewey could now see a slight glow hovering above one of the chairs at the table. His desire to protect himself with the *flow* was growing stronger with each passing second.

"Felsafell means you no harm," he told Tyrin.

The pulsing of the lanterns slowed. "Of course, he doesn't. He only watches in safety as he sends *you* into peril."

"Am I in peril?" Gewey asked nervously.

There was another brief silence. "No. Your father made me promise. But then, he is not here... is he? And your fear is so very unique. Succulent and nourishing. The fear of the Vrykol was dry and dull. Yours, however... yes, yours... I must have it. And then I will have that of your companions as well."

Gewey could feel the spirit's menace surrounding him—suffocating him. It was too much. His will failed, and he rapidly drew in the *flow*. In that moment, everything changed. The room faded away, and before him now were the smoldering ruins of Valshara.

"Yes, son of Gerath," whispered the voice. "Show me. Show me the dark places you fear to share... even with *her*."

Tyrin was using the *flow* to probe ever more deeply into his mind. Once again, Gewey tried to resist. But he was unable to. Even releasing the *flow* was now becoming impossible.

He opened his mouth to speak, but his tongue felt swollen and his throat numb. He took a step toward the broken temple gates. The burned timbers and twisted metal foreshadowed what he would find inside. The stench of mold and decay saturated the air. But this was not recent. Years had passed since this happened.

Gradually, Gewey felt his courage returning. "Do you think to break me?" he scoffed. "I have seen these visions before."

"Have you?" asked Tyrin mockingly. "Have you really?"

"Yes," Gewey shot back. "I have seen what could be, and what has been. You waste your time if you think these illusions will do anything but anger me."

The *flow* swelled within him once again. But as his own power extended, so did the spirit's hold on his mind. More and more of his past was being revealed.

"Your anger means nothing here," it countered. "Your anger is not what drives the things you are witnessing. You believe that I show you the destruction produced by war?" Tyrin laughed disdainfully. "But you are wrong. It was not your enemy who did this."

Something compelled Gewey to walk on through the gates. The horrific visions he found upon entering made him gasp. Hundreds of pikes were buried in the ground about the courtyard, the skeletal remains of either a human or an elf grotesquely impaled upon each one. As for the main temple, it had been reduced to rubble, with countless numbers of crushed bones and skulls scattered amongst the wreckage. Whatever had created this destruction, it had sadistically chosen to bury all those inside the temple alive.

"There is only one power capable of such devastation," said Tyrin. "And I think you know what that is."

Recognition washed over Gewey like a vile torrent, bringing both revulsion and fear in its wake. Tyrin moaned with pleasure, feeding off his torment.

"I did this?" Gewey whispered. He could feel the spirit's satisfaction. He shook his head violently. "No! I will not be deceived."

"Interesting," the spirit remarked.

Gewey took a long breath. "You will not make me lose my senses. None of this is real... and I know it."

"But it *is* real," Tyrin corrected. "This *is* what you fear most. And rightly so. You are only seeing what is destined to be. You will lay waste to both heaven and earth. In your wrath, you will slaughter all that breathes free air. You will cast down your enemy. And with your victory will come death."

Valshara faded, and Gewey could now see a lone figure kneeling in front of two graves, sobbing uncontrollably.

He knew at once who it was. While nervously approaching, he could still feel Tyrin tugging at his mind, trying to make him forget who he was.

"Your friends could not protect them," the spirit whispered in his ear. "They let them die. So, in your rage, you decided that all others must follow. Not even Melek could match your lust for murder. You killed them all. Friends, foes, women, children, gods, beasts… everyone."

A tear fell down Gewey's cheek while reading the names of Kaylia and Jayden carved into the twin headstones. He fell to his knees.

"You could not bear their loss," the spirit continued, increasing its efforts to trap Gewey's mind. "And in your madness, you betrayed their memory with more death."

Gewey traced their names with his finger. He could see it so clearly. The memory of annihilating everyone—hunting them down like vermin. And when they were all dead, he had come here to beg for forgiveness. But there was no one left to hear his pleas. Everyone was gone.

"Yes." Tyrin's voice was hard and grating. "You know it to be true. This is what happened. And all because you could not protect them."

Gewey squeezed his eyes tightly shut and let out a bestial growl. Then, in a single fluid motion, he rose to his feet.

"What you have shown me is indeed my greatest fear, spirit." His tone was suddenly dark and ominous. "And were I the same frightened child that left Sharpstone, I would certainly be lost by now."

He spun around to see Tyrin standing before him. The spirit was almost as tall as Felsafell and bore the same physical characteristics, though his face was more rounded and his eyes were set wider apart. Golden hair fell down his back over silver robes that glistened and sparkled with spiritual light.

The moment their eyes met, Tyrin took a pace back. "What is this?" he gasped, his face suddenly stricken. "Impossible! Heaven is closed to you. You cannot draw from its true strength."

Full of renewed confidence, Gewey laughed out loud. "I do not need the power of heaven to resist the likes of you. I am Darshan—born from the union of the Creator and Gerath. Did you think your feeble tricks could overcome me? I have stared into my own heart. I have seen the darkness that dwells within my spirit." He stepped forward, his form seeming to expand with his every word. "I know my fears well... and I have conquered them all."

Tyrin turned to flee, but Gewey unleashed the *flow* of the spirit and easily held him fast. Now it was Tyrin who would be laid open and have *his* life exposed.

"You were banished by your own kin," Gewey observed. "Your contempt for the living had become intolerable, even for them. You ventured beyond the Spirit Hills with the intent of tormenting all those you encountered, but other *first born* pursued you. They trapped you here. To be imprisoned, alone for all time."

Tyrin struggled to free himself, though his efforts were futile. "Your father promised," he protested. "He said that he would release me."

Gewey tried not to feel amused by the fact that this creature who had brought so much fear and death to others was now the one in terror.

"My father promised to end your suffering," he said. "I can see through you—through your feeble lies and petty deceptions. You were to guard this place until I arrived. And you were also to give me a message."

Tyrin ceased struggling and lowered his head, utterly defeated. Slowly, he nodded. "Yes. I know." His once-strong voice was now a mere whimper.

"Tell me!" Gewey commanded.

"Dust. You will find nothing but dust here. Yet you *must* press on. That is what he told me to say... nothing more."

Gewey cast an eye over the area. The room had now returned, and on the far side stood two pedestals that he had not previously noticed. Without releasing his hold on Tyrin, he approached these. They were made from the purest gold and adorned with rubies, diamonds, and various other precious gems. Both were crowned with a delicate hand, palm held skyward. But where he'd expected to see the *stones*, there was only dust—just as the message had said.

"What is this?" Gewey demanded, rubbing the dust between his fingers.

"Your father," Tyrin replied. "He came here and destroyed the stones long ago."

Gewey scooped up more of the debris. Why would Gerath do such a thing? Surely he must have known that the stones would be needed. With a flick of the hand, he cast the dust aside.

"I have done as you asked," said Tyrin. "Will you now fulfill the promise your father made and free me?"

"I will do exactly what Gerath intended to be done," Gewey told him.

He reached deep within Tyrin's spiritual mind. Dark and sinister thoughts coursed through the spirit as naturally as blood through veins. Gewey strengthened his connection to the *flow* and focused, methodically stripping away the darkness until every single one of the spirit's memories had been eradicated. By the time he was finished, all that remained was an empty shell of a mind, devoid of both recollection and ill-intent.

Only then did he release his hold.

"Where am I?" asked Tyrin timidly. "What is this place?"

"You are safe," Gewey reassured him. "But you must remain here until I come back for you."

Tyrin's form was no longer cohesive. It drifted randomly for a moment or two until settling into a ball of ghostly light that reminded Gewey of his own form in heaven before Gerath had given him true life.

"Who are you?" it asked.

Gewey felt a deep sense of pity for the spirit. He had not been able to bring himself to destroy it, yet at the same time, he could not allow it to escape this place. And with the seal now broken completely, it most certainly would have.

"I am Darshan. And there is no reason to be afraid. Do as I say and remain here until I return."

"How long must I wait?" The voice had changed to an almost childlike whine.

"I don't know," he replied. "But I promise to come back when I can."

Turning quickly away, Gewey strode back to the entrance. As he closed the door behind him, he thought he could hear the spirit weeping.

Nehrutu and Felsafell were talking quietly some distance away from the fallen Vrykol.

"Do you have the stones?" Felsafell asked anxiously.

Gewey shook his head. "They have been destroyed... by Gerath."

Felsafell cocked his head and furrowed his brow. "Gerath? Why would he do this?"

Gewey shrugged. "I was hoping *you* could tell *me*."

He went on to recount his experience with Tyrin, and told them of his father's message.

"So this is where they disposed of him," remarked Felsafell. "I had often wondered after Tyrin, but never dared ask my kin." He shook his head slowly. "I suppose I was afraid to learn his fate."

"He can no longer harm anyone," said Gewey. "I stripped him of his memories."

Felsafell looked horrified for a moment, then his features relaxed and he nodded with sorrowful acceptance. "It had to be done, I suppose. Though I wish it were not so."

"But what are we to do now?" Nehrutu asked. "If the stones are gone..."

"We do as Gerath instructed," Gewey cut in, his voice filled with resolve. "What else *can* we do?"

After a long moment of silence, Felsafell took a deep breath. "Then let us leave this vile place. We have a long way to go from here."

They followed the *first born* from the fortress at a pace no human could match and continued down the ancient road east.

Dust, thought Gewey. Nothing but dust. What if the rest of the stones had suffered the same fate? What if Gerath had destroyed them all? How could he ever hope to defeat the Reborn King without them?

Pushing these negative thoughts away, he allowed the road ahead to numb his mind.

With or without the stone's power, the end was coming soon.

CHAPTER 8

For six days the Vrykol led Kaylia east through the forest, carefully avoiding any roads or frequently used trails. It was clear that they did not wish their presence to be known. Though they had not bound her hands, the half-men were ever at her side, ready to catch her should she make any attempt to escape. But in her present situation, cut off from the *flow* and with no weapon to aid her, there was little chance of that happening.

Her thoughts wandered to Jayden and Gewey during their short respites. She did her best not to focus on all the terrible things that could have happened... or could be happening. If an opportunity to get away did arise, her head must be clear of distractions.

As evening fell on the sixth day, she spotted the flickering light of a campfire through the trees some way ahead. Moments later, she could hear the crackle and pop of sapfilled twigs burning. She also caught the scent of roasting meat, making her mouth instantly water. She had not eaten since they'd departed, and had been sparing with the water skin she had brought with her.

She assumed that the Vrykol would change direction to avoid the camp, as they had done on several other occasions. This time, however, they headed straight for it.

A short while later, they came to a small clearing. Ten more Vrykol were standing at irregular distances from the fire, over which a rabbit was roasting on a spit. Crouching down low and staring into the flames was what at first appeared to be a young human female. She was clad in a plain yet clean blue blouse and black, loose-fitting trousers. Her straight, dark brown hair was neatly pulled back into a ponytail, revealing smooth olive skin. To Kaylia's eyes, she looked to be little more than an adolescent, though she had always found it difficult to gauge the age of humans with any degree of accuracy. It was only when the girl looked up that she realized this was *not* a human at all. She was a Vrykol.

The Vrykol gave her a broad toothy grin. "Most people don't see me for what I am so quickly. But then, you have some experience with my kind, do you not?" Her voice was richly feminine. Not the raspy wheezing of the others. She motioned to a spot near the fire. "Sit. The meal is nearly ready."

Kaylia did not move or say anything.

"Come," she insisted. "I know you haven't eaten for days." She cast a quick glance around. "I'm sure my kinsmen—I guess you would call them that—did not take such needs into account during your journey." Her eyes fixed on Kaylia unblinkingly, her pleasant demeanor never wavering.

After a lengthy hesitation, during which the rest of the Vrykol and the four half-men spread out to join the others, Kaylia eventually complied. She took a seat opposite the *girl* but remained silent. The Vrykol that had sent Gewey to Shagharath was much like this one, she considered—unblemished and looking very much alive, though its elven body had been, to her mind, far more unsettling than this human form.

"I am Jillian," the *girl* announced, bowing her head slightly.

Kaylia raised an eyebrow and spoke at last. "I didn't know that your kind *had* names. But I suppose I was always too busy taking their heads to ask."

Jillian laughed. "If you think to anger me, you'll find it very difficult. But you're right. I am the only one who has taken a name. The others don't see the sense in it."

"Why name the dead?" scoffed Kaylia.

Ignoring the jibe, Jillian removed the rabbit from the spit and tossed it over. The heat burned Kaylia's hands, but she refused to show any pain. She wanted to throw the food back, but hunger was making her weak and she needed to stay strong. Her face twisted in disgust at the prospect of eating food prepared by this foul creature. Regardless of what the girl looked like, she was no better than her cloaked brethren. Forcing down her first mouthful of the meat, Kaylia struggled not to vomit.

Jillian allowed Kaylia to finish her meal in silence, though her eyes never strayed from her face throughout.

Once done eating, Kaylia tossed the bones into the night and drained what little was left of her water. "Why are you keeping me alive?" she demanded.

"Ah. This is the part where you hope to learn of our plans." Jillian leaned back on her elbows. "I cannot tell you that, I'm afraid. There is every chance I shall not succeed. And should that happen, I will not jeopardize my people's future with a loose tongue."

Kaylia let out a sarcastic laugh. "Your people? You can't be serious."

"And why not? Why should the Vrykol not have kinship? We may not share human or elf motives or morality, but we are just as unique to this world as any other creature."

Kaylia spat on the ground. "You are an abomination spawned by evil. And soon the world will be done with you forever. How you can speak of motives and morality is beyond reason. Your motives are to obey your master, and you are utterly lacking in any morality."

Jillian frowned. "You don't know just how wrong you are. We do have motives beyond our master's will. And is not our desire to continue surviving a form of morality?"

Kaylia was taken aback. The look in Jillian's eyes was close to pain and desperation.

"As of now, we are cut off from our master's voice," Jillian continued. "He has abandoned us. So we must fight for our very existence."

"I don't understand," said Kaylia. "What do you mean, he has abandoned you?"

Jillian paused to sit up straighter. "The Vrykol walk the earth due to the grace of our master. He made us, and his voice speaks to us from the moment we are created. But now that voice has gone silent."

Kaylia was baffled by what she was hearing. "So, why have you taken me? If your master did not order it..."

"We took you so we could show him that we are worthy of survival," she said, cutting her off. "We will aid his victory in the hope that, in his mercy, he will grant us a place in his new world."

"But you are not making sense," Kaylia countered. "If he is done with you, why has he not just killed you all?"

Jillian lowered her eyes. "Even the Reborn King has limits. To kill us all would take much time and effort. At least, that is our guess. And as the time of his battle with Darshan approaches, his attention is focused elsewhere."

Kaylia thought on this for a moment. "So you intend to use me as a weapon against Gewey?"

"There is no use for me to deny something so obvious," she replied.

"Then why leave our son? Why not try to take us both?"

"We allowed your son to stay behind so that you could be captured unharmed. I feared you would fight to the death should we try to take you both. And from the look on your face, I think I was right. We need you intact… for now." Her last few words bore a hint of menace. She then stood up and waved a dismissive hand. "That is all you need to know."

Kaylia scrutinized Jillian as she walked away. She could almost forget that she was speaking to a Vrykol. She wanted to know more, but thought it best not to press the issue at this time. She was certain there would be many days of travel ahead, and if she had learned anything from Lord Theopolou, it was that patience is often a powerful ally.

Jillian disappeared into the night, followed by three other Vrykol. Kaylia took the opportunity to try to get some sleep, but found it impossible to remain so for more than a few minutes at a time.

The sun was still below the horizon when they headed out. Their pace was quick, though not overly so. Just before midday, Kaylia was allowed to fill her water skin from a tiny stream they had come across. Jillian also provided a few wild berries to sustain her.

They continued traveling due east for most of the day, but turned slightly south late in the afternoon. From time to time, Kaylia could hear the sounds of human travelers to the south and guessed they were not far away from the road that ran north of the Spirit Hills—though precisely where they were she couldn't be certain.

Just as the sun was setting, Jillian called for a halt and then vanished into the brush. Less than an hour later, she returned carrying a large sack. From this, she removed a loaf of bread and a few strips of jerky.

"You must do without a fire tonight," she said, handing Kaylia the repast. "There are humans nearby, and I would prefer not to have to dispose of their bodies should they discover us."

Kaylia looked at the food with the same revulsion as before.

"Come now," Jillian chided. "It was given to me by a group of human merchants and prepared by their own hands. Be grateful they were not elves. They would have known at once that I am not human. Then we would have been forced to kill them."

"And why did you leave the humans alive?"

Jillian sat down on a fallen tree a few yards away. "My master has a love for humans. You may find this difficult to fathom, but Vrykol only kill humans when we must. Not that we would hesitate when it is needed. Nor do we feel guilt when doing so. I suppose he must have made us that way."

Kaylia plopped down on the ground and tore off a piece of bread. "And what of elves?"

She smiled wickedly. "That is another matter. He does not hold them in high regard. But for now, they are not our concern. So long as they do not have the misfortune to encounter us, we will spare them. Not that it will do them much good, eventually. Once our master is victorious, he will deal with all of your people in his own way."

The Vrykol's words and callous smile brought Kaylia's anger to the fore, but she managed to conceal it well. "You are assuming he will win," she said evenly.

"Of course I am," Jillian responded. "Darshan cannot defeat him. He lacks both the strength and the will."

Kaylia sneered. "Actually, from what I see, your master is a coward. He hides behind his walls and sends his minions to do what he cannot. He has tried many times to kill Gewey... tried and failed. Soon he will wish he had never laid his hands on the *Sword of Truth*. And when this war is over, it will be the Vrykol, not the elves, who are dealt with."

Jillian regarded Kaylia and nodded. "You truly believe that, don't you? I can see it in your eyes. Your faith in Darshan is absolute." She laughed softly. "But faith will not save him. Or you, for that matter."

Kaylia glanced over at the half-men. "And what of *your* faith? Do you think the Reborn King will reward you for corrupting half-men and hatching small-minded schemes?"

"I think we are left with little choice," she countered. This time, it was her turn to feel a flash of anger. But unlike Kaylia, she was unable to hide it.

Kaylia smiled, pleased to have elicited the reaction. But she did not want to press Jillian too far, not knowing what she might do should she completely lose control. Instead, Kaylia turned her attention to her meal.

Jillian glared at her for a full minute before standing up and stalking off into the forest.

The following day, they had only walked for a short time when Jillian called for a halt. She and four other Vrykol sped away west. They returned more than an hour later.

"We are followed," she announced. "It would seem that your elf friend intends to rescue you."

"Aaliyah," Kaylia whispered. "You fool."

"That she is," agreed Jillian. "And a not-very-stealthy fool at that. Though granted, she moves more swiftly than I would have thought possible." She flashed a sinister grin. "But that won't save her, of course."

Kaylia's stomach knotted. Aaliyah wouldn't stand a chance alone... or even with a dozen others to help. "Please, let me speak to her," she pleaded. "I'll make her turn back."

Jillian sniffed. "It's too late for that.

"I think I have their attention," said Aaliyah. "They chased me for a while, but I was able to outrun them easily enough."

Basanti nodded sharply. "Good. Now we will see if they are as dim-witted as I am hoping they are."

She reached for the hilt of the sword hanging at her side, but recoiled the moment her flesh touched it. This would be the first time she had ever wielded a blade. And though she was certain that her lack of experience would not be a hindrance, she knew that she must be able to at least grip it. So far, she had nearly broken into tears each time she tried.

"Are you sure you can go through with this?" asked Aaliyah.

Basanti squeezed her eyes tightly shut, then, with sheer willpower, forced her hand to grip the weapon. Slowly, the steel slid free of its scabbard and she was able to hold it up in front of her face. It was more than a minute before she opened her eyes. The revulsion she felt was clearly visible on her face as she examined the weapon from hilt to tip.

"I am certain," she answered weakly. "It's just hard."

"What will happen to you?" Aaliyah had tried to talk to Basanti on several occasions previously about her intentions, but each time she had merely given a fragile smile and ignored the question.

The oracle sheathed the blade and wiped her hand on her blouse, as if the sword had actually sullied it. "I will become as my brother was—corrupted and vulnerable. A stain will be upon my spirit that I will never be able to wash clean."

"Then why are you doing this?"

"Because I must. There is no one else who could succeed. Kaylia must not be left in the hands of our enemy. She could be used as leverage against Gewey, or perhaps even worse. And besides, she is my friend. I will not abandon her to the cruelty of the Vrykol."

Aaliyah gently touched Basanti's shoulder. "And I am your friend also. When this is over, we will find a way to repair whatever damage is done."

Basanti reached up and took hold of her hand. "It doesn't matter anymore. I only regret that my time with Felsafell has ended. But I suppose I must be grateful for what we've already had. It was far more than any mortal could hope for. Yet far less than I imagined in my dreams."

"Why must it end? Will he not still accept you?"

"As I said, I will be as my brother was. Once tainted, violence and death will follow me always. I will no longer be the person he fell in love with. And I cannot put him through such torment. His love for me would keep him by my side, but he would be forced to watch as I descended into darkness." She shook her head, tears welling in her eyes. "Much better that he live with a memory of who I was before."

"I think you wrong," Aaliyah said, wiping away Basanti's tears as they began to fall. "He would rather be with you, regardless of what you have done or might become." She choked back her own tears. "Do not give up hope."

Basanti embraced Aaliyah tightly. "I... I will try."

After a few seconds, Aaliyah took a step back. "I know I should have already asked," she said. "But do you really think you can defeat so many?"

"I'm as sure as I can be," she replied. "Once I cause death, a force will be released inside my spirit that I have kept contained for thousands of years. Though I doubt its full strength will last, for a time I should be as mighty as Felsafell, maybe even more so." Her face stiffened. "But after that, I will not be myself any longer. When Kaylia is free, I will leave you... and you must neither attempt to dissuade me, nor follow."

"But I thought you agreed not to lose hope?" Aaliyah countered.

"And I will keep my word," she said, smiling. "I hope that when heaven is open, Pósix will take pity on me and release my spirit from this body."

Aaliyah glared with sudden frustration and anger. "That is not good enough. There must be another way."

"I wish there was," she admitted. "But regardless, until the gods are free, I will be a danger to all those around me. Until then, I must stay hidden from both the enemy and my friends."

Aaliyah searched hard for a convincing rebuttal, but could not overcome Basanti's logic. If she would jeopardize the safety of the people she loved, then there truly *was* no other choice.

"Then let us get this done," said Aaliyah. She drew her blade. "But know that if I must petition Pósix at the very gates of heaven, you will *not* spend the rest of your life in exile."

"I think we should wait until the dawn breaks," Basanti responded. "Until then, I would ask you to sit beside me and tell me more about your home. Your stories make it sound so remarkable."

Aaliyah sheathed her sword. "Of course." She smiled lovingly, knowing that Basanti was asking for visions of places she believed she would now never get to see for herself. A final request from a condemned woman.

They found a patch of soft grass and sat together until the sun was nearly upon them. Aaliyah regaled her with tales setting forth from the majesty of her lands. The dense jungles that were home to birds of such brilliant colors that one would catch their breath at the very sight of them. The mountains of the far west where the great cave bears roamed and hunted, some of them so massive and strong that they could fell a fully grown pine tree with a single swipe of their paws. There were also the tall redwoods where she was raised, many of them towering so high that on certain days their tops would be hidden by the clouds.

"It all sounds wonderful," Basanti sighed. "I could spend a thousand years exploring such a place. And Felsafell..." His name stuck in her throat and her voice became a whisper. "He would have loved it, too."

For a moment, she was totally lost in her thoughts of peace and love. Then, a sudden transformation took place. The song of steel sang out, slicing through the cool morning air. Basanti no longer appeared awkward with the weapon in her hand. The instant her eyes gazed upon the gleaming steel blade, her normally compassionate features became hard and unyielding.

Aaliyah knew exactly what to do and drew her own sword. Giving only a sharp nod, she sped away toward the Vrykol camp. She vanished in an instant through the dawn mist.

Basanti forced any lingering thoughts of her love and hopes into the recesses of her mind and focused on the task ahead. For thousands of years, she had kept herself pure—untainted by blood and death. Now she would unleash a torrent of unbridled fury. All she held sacred would be washed away in a single act.

A heat began to rise within her chest, rapidly spreading throughout her entire body. Her face twisted into a snarl, and she knew she was ready.

Swiftly, she set off to follow Aaliyah's trail.

CHAPTER 9

Linis hissed a curse while treating his wounds with the thick pungent salve given to him by Therisa. Throbbing pain had set in from the dozens of tiny scratches caused by the jagged thorns of the dense *barble bushes* surrounding Theopolou's manor. The barbs bore a mild poison that, though not strong enough to kill, was sufficient to cause severe irritation, as well as a nasty infection if left untreated.

Normally, he could have easily navigated his way through the thorny gauntlet without injury, but found it impossible to do so while carrying an infant in his arms. Speed was essential, and the quickest way to Valshara was through a forest that had been specifically cultivated to keep away unwanted visitors—mainly humans who were not as agile and would certainly suffer tremendously should they try to get through. Unfortunately, this same deterrent had clearly not been a hindrance to either the elves or the Vrykol.

The look in Basanti's eyes just before she had departed on her mission was still uncomfortably vivid for Linis. Never had he seen someone so utterly tormented by the inevitability of their own future. He had wanted to comfort her, but could find no words that would do anything more than cause her pain to sharpen.

He glanced down at the precious bundle beside him. Jayden was staring back, sucking on three of his tiny fingers. Linis had never been responsible for the care of a baby before, a fact that had only occurred to him once beyond the manor grounds. He chuckled softly to himself.

"I have faced down the Vrykol and armies of evil men," he said, reaching down and touching the child's cheek. "But you cause me more fear than all of them combined. Will I be so frightened when I care for my own children?"

The thought of Dina scolding him for even thinking such thoughts brought forth a sudden burst of hearty laughter, quickly followed by a deep longing to be with his wife.

"At least when we get there, someone will know how to care for you properly," he said softly.

Jayden smiled and kicked his legs.

Sighing, Linis rose to his feet and began gathering wood for a fire. Not willing to let the baby out of his sight, he made do with a few twigs and thick branches that were scattered nearby. Soon, a small fire crackled and popped. Linis knew this risked drawing the attention of any pursuers, but the night air carried a chill that was unhealthy for an infant. Or in his mind, that seemed to be a reasonable assumption. Besides, if elves or Vrykol were in the vicinity, the sound of a baby would be enough to give away their location. And any human who might have ill intent would be sure to make plenty of noise and give him ample warning.

He withdrew the milk bladder from his pack, hoping that the contents would be enough to last the full journey. After spreading a blanket on the ground, he took Jayden in his arms and drew him close. Linis had heard that babies would cry if away from their mothers for too long, but up until now, the child had seemed to be perfectly content. *If only this will last until we arrive*, he thought. Soon after being fed, Jayden fell into a peaceful slumber.

After laying the baby down, taking extra care not to jar him awake, Linis ate a meager repast of jerky and flatbread. He could hear rabbits scurrying through the underbrush not far away and longed to hunt. The thought of fresh rabbit and wild herbs made his mouth water. But that would have to wait for another time.

The kitchens in Valshara produced wonderful elf dishes these days, but Linis was a creature of the forest. Simple meals and open spaces were far more to his liking. Memories of wandering the land with his group of *seekers* washed over him, followed by melancholy as each face—all of them now dead—flashed up, then slowly faded. Those days were behind him. And even if the tragedy of betrayal had not befallen his fellow *seekers* and dearest friends, his life had moved on. *He* was different. The elf tribes no longer needed his kind to act as their guardians. And though his heart would certainly continue to linger on days past, he now had a more important role to play. One that, in time, would be far more demanding—and rewarding—than any he had taken upon himself thus far.

He watched Jayden sleep for a time, then spent the rest of the night listening intently for any hint of enemies. Once he thought he caught the sound of distant footfalls, but even with his finely tuned skills, he could not be certain. A *seeker* perhaps? He hoped not.

Jayden woke just once during the night, but after a quick feed went immediately back to sleep. By the time dawn broke, Linis was packed and ready. He had constructed a makeshift sling in which to carry the baby, so as to leave both hands free should he need them in an emergency.

"Let us hope I do not," he whispered.

Gently, he slipped Jayden inside the sling and tied it securely before starting out. The air was unusually cool, with a thick fog covering the base of the trees. Linis did his best to keep Jayden's exposed face dry with a strip of cloth, but it was a never-ending task. In less than an hour, his own clothes were soaked and droplets of dew were dripping from his hair. Thankfully, Jayden was faring a bit better. The sling had been made from a piece of elf blanket, and so possessed some resistance to moisture.

Fortunately, the heat of the day soon arrived. By mid-morning, the fog had lifted and his clothes were dry. The sunlight, split by the high branches, was a welcome friend and lifted his spirits somewhat.

By noon, there was still no sign of enemies. Regardless, Linis was careful to continue making his trail almost impossible to follow. Even a seasoned *seeker* would need to slow his pace considerably in order to notice that anyone had passed. He drew in as much of the *flow* as he was able to, sharpening his already acute senses. His training with Nehrutu enabled him to utilize more power than ever before, though still not as much as Kaylia, and nowhere near as much as Nehrutu himself. Aided by this extra ability, the details of Linis's surroundings now burst magically into life, and he spent the next few hours singing songs to Jayden. The child certainly appeared to be enjoying the entertainment, laughing and cooing with each new verse, and even looking unhappy when the singing stopped.

The day was so pleasant that Linis wasn't even annoyed by the frequently needed stops for feeding and changing. In fact, by late afternoon, he found that he was actually enjoying caring for the child.

This is something I will definitely tell Dina, he thought with a smile.

Suddenly, he was more than grateful for this opportunity to experience a few parental responsibilities—regardless of the dire circumstances. Until now, "Linis the seeker" had been more than wary of becoming "Linis the father". And though Dina was not yet with child, each time she had brought the subject up, he would feel even more inadequate than on his first day of *seeker* training under Berathis's critical eye.

The remainder of the day passed uneventfully, raising Linis's hopes that Kaylia's kidnappers were being truthful over their willingness to leave Jayden alone—also, that the elves who had attacked Theopolou's house had given up their mission in light of the slaughter unleashed upon them by the Vrykol.

The next morning, he arrived at a point where the forest started to thin and the ground became ever more rocky and uneven. The sun glared down, but a cool westerly wind blew dry any hint of perspiration forming on his forehead. Jayden seemed to remain in good spirits, too. He certainly wasn't crying at all, which, as far as Linis was concerned, was confirmation that all was well.

So far, they hadn't encountered anyone. There had been sounds of a few wandering humans off to the north, but they seemed involved with their own affairs and posed no threat.

During a brief halt, Linis's mind wandered to the beginning of the second split. Back then, he and his *seekers* had been outcasts and renegades, constantly on the move, in order to remain free from the vengeance of the elders. But these days it was those who sought to destroy the peace between human and elf who had become the outlaws. And even if Gewey were to fail and the Reborn King unleashed his power upon them all, for a brief moment, the future of both races had been bright.

He glanced down at Jayden, whose eyes were fixed on his own. "But your father won't fail. He will triumph, and you will grow up free from hatred and fear."

At that moment, the hairs on the back of his neck stood up. Elves, more than a dozen of them, were closing in less than a mile ahead. As quickly as he could, he bundled Jayden and turned to backtrack. But after only a short distance, he sensed more elves coming from the other direction. A chill shot through him. They were surrounded. But how? How could he not have noticed?

They must have known, or guessed, where he was heading. If they were seekers, and Linis thought they must be, they would know how far away to stay in order to avoid detection.

He assessed the situation. There was no way to fight, nowhere to run, and no place to hide. He pulled his long knife free and waited. The moment the elves came into view, he nodded a greeting, but none returned his gesture.

"Who among you leads?" shouted Linis.

All but one halted their advance.

"I lead," shouted back a tall, red-haired *seeker*. "I am Tallio. And you Linis, can go your own way in peace... if you leave the child to us."

Linis sneered and spat on the earth. "You would harm an innocent baby over your bigotry and hatred?"

"I will do what I must to preserve the honor of our people," he replied.

"Then you disgrace the name of elf with such bile in your heart. And you know nothing of me if you believe I would abandon Jayden to you."

"I did not think you would do so," Tallio replied. "And I would have you know that, in spite of your crimes, I still hold you in high regard. Only Berathis was your better. And only he, more widely known among our people."

Linis could hear the ominous creaking of bowstrings being drawn behind him. His mind raced, but he could see no way out.

"I would not have you shot down like an animal," Tallio continued. "Give up the child, and you may yet live. Or at least, be given the opportunity to die with dignity."

"So you wish to challenge me?" Linis asked. A small hope sprang.

"I do," he answered with a slight bow.

"And if I prevail?"

"Then you will live."

"And the child?"

Tallio shook his head. "The child's fate is sealed. Only *you* have hope for life."

"Then there is no hope for either of us," Linis shot back fiercely. "Once Darshan finds you, he will flay you alive, then hang your bleeding carcasses from the walls of Althetas."

Tallio shrugged. "Perhaps. But I think it more likely that the Lord of Angrääl will dispatch him. And even if I am wrong and Darshan prevails, one thing we have learned is that he is not invulnerable. He may kill some of us. But we will find a way to slay the so-called *god*. Of that, you can be certain."

"You are a fool," Linis scoffed. "A delusional fool. Your small band that attacked Lord Theopolou's manor was slain by a mere shadow of the power Darshan wields. He will look into the mind of every living elf and rip the identity of the culprits from their very spirits. He will be upon you, and all those who follow you in your folly, before you even know he is there."

Fury burned in Tallio's eyes at the mention of his fallen comrades. "They were slain by the creatures of the Reborn King—not the feeble defenses of a dead traitor. And if Darshan chooses to let loose his rage over the death of his son, he will quickly find his mindless worshipers turning into determined foes."

Linis sniffed. "So, is that your great plan? To bring down death upon our people in order to turn them against Darshan? Or do you even have a plan worthy of the name? Could it be that you are so blinded by hate, you have forgotten what it means to be a *seeker* and an elf? We never act impulsively or rashly."

"My plans are my own," snapped Tallio. "And they are far beyond your understanding." He took a menacing step forward. "I have wasted enough time on fruitless banter. Will you face me or not?"

Linis guessed that Tallio's plans must have fallen apart when his attack on the manor failed. Now he was acting out of sheer fury and vengeance. But this only made him more dangerous. Under the circumstances, there was only one thing left to do. Run and pray.

His muscles tensed, but before he could take a single step, the snap of a bowstring sent an arrow thudding deep into his left thigh.

Grunting under the impact, Linis dropped to one knee. He clutched Jayden close to his chest with his left hand, while still gripping his long knife in the other. He would fight to the very end.

Every elf but Tallio charged at him. The instant they were within reach, Linis slashed and hacked for all he was worth. But the disadvantage of holding a child, combined with his injury and the skill of his many foes, made it impossible to inflict more than a few minor wounds before being overcome.

Letting out a series of feral screams, he struggled in vain against his enemy's strength. He could no longer feel the arrow digging into his flesh as the child was ripped from his arms. He could only watch in terror as one of the elves brought Jayden to the waiting Tallio.

"Please!" cried Linis. "Don't do this! I'm begging you!"

Ignoring his pleas, Tallio drew a short dagger from his belt. "I am truly sorry. But this must be done."

Time stood still as cold steel hovered above innocent flesh. And yet, through all of this, Jayden had not made a single sound. Tallio stared down into the child's eyes and hesitated for a moment. Then, shaking his head as if coming out of a trance, he pressed the dagger against the baby's throat.

"Stop this at once!" a deep male voice boomed out from behind Linis's position.

Tallio looked up and his eyes flew wide. At first, he said nothing. But after a few seconds, he lifted the deadly blade and tucked it back into his belt. "Why are you here, father?" he asked.

"To stop your madness," the voice replied.

Linis thought the voice sounded familiar, but it wasn't until the man advanced and glanced down at him that he was sure. It was Kaphalos. He had met him only briefly on their way to the Chamber of the Maker, but there was no mistake. He stopped just in front of his son.

"But father," said Tallio, suddenly now sounding like a troubled child. "This is what you said must happen. This is what you wanted."

Kaphalos stiffened. "This? How could you possibly think that the murder of an innocent child would be something I desired? Have your senses completely left you? Are you so crazed by hatred that it has led you to this?"

"You said yourself that the gods are evil," Tallio countered, a small amount of defiance creeping back into his voice. "You said that the only way for elves to survive would be for the gods and their human cattle to be driven from existence. Those were *your* words."

His shoulders slumped. "Yes... they were. But they were words spoken out of fear and regret. The sunset of my life has come too late. I should never have witnessed the things that have come to pass. I am too old and filled with memories." He touched Tallio's cheek. "I have sinned many times in my life. But my greatest sin was passing my hatred on to you... my beloved child." He glanced down briefly at Jayden. "That I have driven you to murdering innocents is inexcusable. And yet I still beg for your forgiveness."

Tears began streaming down Tallio's cheeks. "But father. You are dying because of what they have done to our world. How can I...?"

"I am dying," he said, cutting his son short, "because I am rotted away and empty. Only my love for you has kept me alive in recent years. And I understand now that I was selfish to cling to life for so long. There is no place for me in this new world."

"That is not true," Tallio whispered. "You are the wisest and most honorable of all the elves. It is your guidance that the people should follow now. Not that of traitors such as Theopolou, Chiron, or any of the other elders. They would see us corrupted. They would have us believe that we are a mongrel race."

"And perhaps we are," said Kaphalos. "Perhaps it is I who am wrong." He lowered his head. "But it makes little difference. I am spent, and there is no turning back... for any of us." He looked over his shoulder. "Release Linis!"

Linis could feel the uncertainty of the elves holding him.

"Do as my father says," Tallio told them.

Slowly, they released their hold and Linis struggled to his feet. Reaching down, he gripped the arrow and, in a quick motion, pulled it from his thigh. Blood poured from the injury almost immediately.

"Bind his wound," Kaphalos commanded.

Linis waved them away and instead tore a strip of cloth from his tunic. Soon, the leg was wrapped, and the bleeding contained. Without asking permission, he then headed straight toward Kaphalos and Tallio. No one tried to stop him.

As he limped over, he regarded the father and son for a moment. Tallio's expression was one of hurt and confusion, while Kaphalos's face reflected inconceivable sorrow. Without saying a word, Linis gently took Jayden away from Tallio. As soon as he had the child in his arms, he drew back a few paces.

After seeing Jayden safely returned, Kaphalos reached out to embrace his son. But as he did so, his legs crumpled beneath him. Tallio was only just able to catch him and lay him carefully down on the ground.

"What's wrong?" he asked, his tears starting afresh.

"My strength is spent, son," Kaphalos replied, somehow mustering a fragile smile. "I used it all to catch up with you and your brethren. I am done now."

"No," he cried. "You will live. We can still leave this place. Others are gathering in the desert. We can go there ... together."

His fluttering fingers sought and then found his son's hand. "I am sorry, Tallio. That cannot be. I must leave you now. I want only one thing from you before I make my final journey."

"Anything," he whispered.

"Your forgiveness."

Tallio buried his face in Kaphalos's chest, sobbing uncontrollably. He could hear the slowing of his father's heart as the life gradually ebbed from his body.

With a desperate expression, he looked up to where Linis was still standing. "It is said that you are a great healer. And that you have learned skills from those from across the Abyss." His eyes were pleading. "I have no right to ask after what I have done, but..."

More sobs choked off any remaining words.

Without offering a reply, Linis kneeled beside Kaphalos and placed his hand over his eyes. The old elf shook his head, but was too weak to stop him. After a minute, Linis removed his hand and drew a deep breath.

"He is beyond my skill," he said. "I am sorry."

As the harsh reality sank in, Tallio's face went pale. Great sobs fell from his mouth, each one sounding more desperate than the previous.

"There is one thing I can do for you," offered Linis. He touched Kaphalos's chest, then took hold of Tallio's hand.

The *flow* came to life all around them as Linis guided the spirits of both father and son closer and closer until they were actually touching. Once joined, he allowed them to remain together until every last bit of life had faded.

"Thank you," wept Tallio when it was all over.

Linis got to his feet and stared down at the scene. In spite of the terrible atrocity Tallio had been intent on committing, he could now feel nothing but pity for him.

"What will you do?" he asked.

"You need not fear," Tallio replied. "No one will harm you or the child. As for me... I go to join my father."

Quickly drawing his dagger once more, he plunged the blade directly into his own heart before Linis could do anything to stop him. Blood trickled from the corners of his mouth, then he slumped down atop the body of Kaphalos. Linis squeezed his eyes shut and backed away.

The other elves remained totally silent, stricken expressions on all of their faces. They didn't even bother to look at Linis as he set off with Jayden into the forest.

The wound on his leg slowed his progress, and by nightfall, he could still see the faint glow of Tallio's funeral pyre in the far distance. Linis figured that his followers would likely go east to the desert now. Even so, the danger remained. There were certainly others equally fanatical as Tallio. And they might not have an elder such as Kaphalos to quell their madness.

His injury was still painfully fresh when he finally reached Valshara. Without enough rest and proper treatment, his efforts to heal the wound had only been sufficient to keep infection at bay.

The sun was just setting as he passed through the gates. Dina burst from the door before he was even halfway across the main yard. The moment she saw that he was injured, she took Jayden from him and shouted for healers.

"How did this happen?" she asked, slipping her arm around his waist.

Linis stopped and pulled away. For a long moment, he gazed at her face, a loving smile on his lips. "I have so missed the sight of you."

Careful not to crush Jayden between them, she leaned in and gave him a long-awaited kiss. "I have missed you, too. More than you can imagine."

Just then, three healers arrived, along with Ertik. After handing the baby over to him, Dina wrapped her arms around her husband. This time, the embrace was desperate and forceful.

"We must tend his wound, High Lady," said one of the healers.

"Unfortunately, I was not able to do it myself," admitted Linis. "There was no time."

"You can tell me about that once we have you cleaned and tended," said Dina.

She ordered food and drink to be brought to her chambers. Linis joined her as soon as his wound had been treated.

Ertik insisted that he take care of Jayden for the time being so that Dina and Linis could have a long-awaited night together alone. Though hesitant at first, she eventually relented, but only after making Ertik promise to stay in the room nearest to her own. Having been through so much to protect the child, Linis initially seemed to be even more reluctant than Dina about this arrangement. However, the soothing calm of his wife's voice soon had him relinquishing control to Ertik—though not until after delivering a final kiss on Jayden's delicate forehead.

Once alone, they sat at the table while Linis told Dina of the events leading to his arrival. She sat in stone silence and without a hint of emotion until he was finished.

"Then it is out of our hands for now," she said. "Basanti and Aaliyah will not fail."

Linis was impressed by the way in which she was taking the news. As much as he loved his wife, he knew her to be a woman with an intense passion that could sometimes overcome her reason. Apparently, serving as High Lady has tempered her quite a bit.

She then told him of the assassination attempt, as well as the interrogation of the culprit by her mother.

Linis's face darkened. "I know it must have been a hard thing for you to allow. But I would undoubtedly have done the same to him... or worse. But what if there is a second attempt on your life? How are you going to guard against that?"

Dina shrugged. "I will bolster our defenses as best I can. I've also had everyone in the temple questioned in order to check for traitors in our midst. And Jayden will be guarded at every moment by the best warriors we have."

Linis thought for a moment. "Does that cover everything?"

"There is one other precaution I plan to take." She stood up and held out a hand to him. Her movements were now seductive—her eyes burning with desire. "I will be keeping you here with me as well. Your days of war are over, Linis. You are *my* captive now, and you will not leave Valshara until Gewey has completed his task."

Linis smiled up at her and gently took her outstretched hand. "I will not resist... nor attempt escape, I swear it. I surrender to your will... my dearest love."

CHAPTER 10

Aaliyah waited just at the edge of her ability to sense the enemy. They were certainly aware of her presence, even though they had not made any move against her yet. But that would surely come soon enough, and by now Basanti was already in place and waiting patiently.

She thought of Nehrutu, praying that he was safe. Any journey with Darshan would be fraught with peril. Seeing her love die once had been unimaginable torture. If something were to happen to him for a second time...

She pushed such thoughts from her mind and focused on the forest ahead. The Vrykol were still not showing any sign of advancing. For a long, tense moment she worried that Basanti's plan was about to unravel. But then they began moving in her direction. The corrupted half-men were remaining behind—she guessed to guard Kaylia.

The creatures spread out in a straight line, though not so far apart that it would prevent them from blocking the *flow*. Aaliyah stood motionless, her blade gripped loosely.

When it became obvious to the Vrykol that their elf quarry had no intention of fleeing, they began moving with greater caution. But caution wouldn't save them. Aaliyah knew that there was no way they could be prepared for what was about to come.

As they came into view, Aaliyah reached out with the *flow* and felt it being suppressed. That was to be expected; only Darshan would have sufficient strength to break their hold. She pressed harder, feeling the creatures' increased concentration to keep the *flow* at bay. Their focus on preventing her from using her power was absolute. Just as she hoped it would be.

The deadly song of Vrykol blades sliding from their scabbards tore through the otherwise quiet woods. Aaliyah's muscles tensed and she crouched low, jaw clenched and teeth bared.

As they neared, the center of the Vrykol line slowed its pace, allowing those on either side to begin encircling her. But just as they drew closer, a blur flashed across Aaliyah's vision—moving faster than anything she had ever seen. Three Vrykol heads rolled off their shoulders in the merest blink of an eye.

The hold of the *flow* lessened while the astonished beasts tried to understand what was happening. Aaliyah was almost able to break through.

The Vrykol halted their advance, desperately searching for the source of the attack. Again, two more heads were separated from cloaked bodies. Aaliyah couldn't help but marvel at Basanti's speed and agility. Five enemies had been effortlessly slain—the only sound being the whistle of her blade and the heads bouncing off the soft forest turf.

Two of the half-men began moving in their direction. Meanwhile, the remaining Vrykol were now grouping together as fast as they could, hoping to form a line of defense against the unexpected onslaught. But there was nothing they could do to save themselves.

The bells and laughter of the *flow* of the spirit filled Aaliyah's ears. Tiny points of light showered the forest with divine radiance. With systematic deliberation, she began ripping the Vrykols' spirits from their forms. In only seconds, they all crumbled to dust.

An agonized cry tore through the air, diverting Aaliyah's attention. For a horrifying moment, she thought it might be Kaylia. But the release of the *flow* had renewed their connection, and she immediately understood. There was another Vrykol with Kaylia. A different kind of Vrykol, such as the one who'd attacked her with a poison dart in the Black Oasis.

The two half-men were already closing in, the ominous shadow that heralded their approach forming into a malignant cloud of darkness. But Aaliyah knew she had to ignore them. Kaylia was her mission.

The sinews of her legs exploded, propelling her forward. But just as she reached the shroud surrounding the two half-men, she heard the slashing of steel cutting into pale flesh. This was followed by a couple of heavy grunts.

For a nervous moment, she was blinded as she passed through the darkness. The fact that it remained told her Basanti was still fighting. That left the other two half-men and a Vrykol for her to deal with alone.

It took less than a minute to reach them. Kaylia was standing in a small clearing with a half-man on either side of her, each one with a hand gripping her by the shoulder. A few feet away was what appeared to be a human female. But Aaliyah quickly realized the truth; this harmless-looking creature was, in fact, the Vrykol she had sensed.

She could still hear the fighting going on at her back and wondered if Basanti was a match for her new foes. Even with her strength and speed, the half-men should not be taken lightly. They had destroyed fifty elves—many of whom were likely *seekers*—with relative ease.

Kaylia looked to be in good health. Her eyes were calm, and she was sending waves of reassurance through their shared bond.

The Vrykol spoke first. "Very clever," she said. "Very clever indeed. But it will do you little good. Whoever, or whatever, you brought to aid you will be dead shortly. If you surrender now, I will give you a quick and painless death."

The offer was brushed contemptuously aside. "Let her go," Aaliyah demanded. She took a step forward and began to draw in the *flow* of the spirit.

"You should do as Aaliyah says, Jillian," remarked Kaylia, her voice even and unafraid.

Aaliyah raised an eyebrow. "Jillian? A Vrykol with a name?"

Jillian sneered. "Shut your mouth, elf. Lay your weapon down, or else I'll have my servants rip Kaylia apart."

The two half-men visibly tightened their grips, causing Kaylia to wince. Undeterred, Aaliyah began drawing in the *flow* of the spirit.

"She'll be dead before you can harm me," Jillian quickly warned.

The wind sifted through the trees, stirring the fallen leaves. The tension was palpable, made more so by the sudden quiet. After a moment, Aaliyah gave a sinister grin and took a step back.

"That's better," Jillian said. The half-men relaxed their hold, but only enough to give Kaylia slight relief. "Now... before you die, you must tell me one thing."

"And what is that?" asked Aaliyah.

"Why did you bother to attempt this? Was it not enough that we left the child alive and in your care?"

The wind rose, then fell again as the chirping of a finch sounded from high above. Aaliyah's gaze remained fixed on Kaylia for nearly a minute before she replied.

Finally, she sheathed her blade and turned to look directly at Jillian. Her eyes were ablaze, her features hard and determined. "I would not abandon a friend to the like of you, even at the cost of my own life. Fortunately, on this occasion, that is a sacrifice I will not have to make."

Jillian responded with a fiendish laugh. But her amusement was short-lived. Aaliyah sprang forward in Kaylia's direction. In the instant it took the half-men to react, a blur rushed in from behind them. With a silvery flash, a sword lopped off each of their hands holding on to their prisoner.

Momentarily confused, the half-men stumbled back, black smoke already spewing from their wounds. It was just enough time for Aaliyah to reach her objective. Without pausing, she threw her arms completely around Kaylia, and, using the *flow* of the air, carried her skyward. Now unhindered by the Vrykol, Kaylia quickly merged her own power with that of Aaliyah's. Within seconds, they were hovering high above the clearing.

They looked down. Basanti was darting back and forth, the sword in her hand finding its target again and again. But Aaliyah could tell that she was not quite as fast as she had been only a short time ago. Her enemies were now fighting back furiously. Twice a half-man blow sent her staggering back. And Jillian's blade was also flying with supreme skill.

"We must help her," said Kaylia.

"No," Aaliyah replied. "We cannot."

"What? Then release me now!" Kaylia began to struggle, but Aaliyah held her fast.

"If I do, I break my oath," she explained. "Basanti made me swear to leave this to her. And if you are killed, her sacrifice will have been for nothing."

Kaylia glared furiously, but finally relented. Together, they rose even higher until they could see only tree tops and the horizon. For more than an hour, they traveled until both of them were completely spent from the effort. Finding a clearing, they set their feet back on solid ground, uncertain of how far they had gone.

Both of them plopped down against a thick maple tree, exhausted. For several minutes, neither spoke a word—their thoughts and fears centered entirely on the fate of the Oracle.

"We can go no farther," said Aaliyah. "At least, I cannot." She reached to her belt and produced a small flask. The scent of jawas tea filled the air as she removed the top. "In truth, I would prefer brandy right now. But this will have to do." After taking a long drink, she passed the flask over to Kaylia.

"Why did she do that?" Kaylia whispered. A vivid picture of Basanti's battle was still burning in her memory.

Aaliyah pushed herself closer. "Because she knew, as did I, that Gewey's task outweighs all of our lives. We could not afford for you to be used against him."

"I would not have allowed that to happen," she countered, then took a sip of tea. "I would have…"

"Taken your own life?" Aaliyah cut in. "Of course you would. As would I, had I been in your place. But none of us would see that happen. Especially Basanti. She told me something just before we came after you." Her eyes locked firmly with Kaylia's. "She said that even after the war is over, the world will continue to be in peril. It will still need much strength and guidance. She said that the last true vision she witnessed before her powers diminished was confusing. For many years, she could not divine its meaning. Only when she held your son in her arms after you were taken did she finally understand what it meant."

She took a deep breath before continuing. "Two roads, she told me. Both leading to the future. On one of these stood a tall figure of a man cloaked in fire and death. The ruins of the world crumbling around him as he trampled the earth beneath his iron-shod boots. To his left lay a woman, her body ravaged and her spirit dead. To his right, a man on his knees, his back turned and weeping."

"And on the other road?" Kaylia asked.

"On the other, three figures. A man, a woman, and a child. Yet the child stood above his parents, even as they wrapped their loving arms around him. In the distance was a land of peace and plenty waiting to welcome them."

Kaylia furrowed her brow. "How could that confuse her? I don't possess a fraction of the oracle's wisdom, and I can see it clearly."

"Can you?"

"The woman is me, the man weeping is Gewey, and the Dark Knight is the fiery figure."

Aaliyah smiled. "That is what I assumed when she first told me. And that is what Basanti thought, too, until she held Jayden and could feel the power that lives within him." She took Kaylia's hand. "The woman *is* you, and the man weeping *is* Gewey. But the man cloaked in fire is *not* the Dark Knight. It is Jayden."

Kaylia jerked her hand free and slid away. "That's not true! She is wrong."

Aaliyah shook her head, never once breaking her gaze. "She is *not* wrong. Don't you see? It is the second road that gives the first one its meaning. Should Jayden be left without your strength and guidance, he will one day become the very evil that you now fight to protect him from. Gewey turns his back and weeps, unable to fight his own son."

Kaylia said nothing, though Aaliyah could feel her anger swelling dangerously.

"But it is the second road," she pressed on. "The one with your loving arms around him. That is the way to peace. The first road serves only as a warning. One day Jayden will realize that the blood in his veins gives him power beyond any man, elf, or half-man. And when that day comes, what will he do? Will he seek to rule as the Dark Knight does? Or will he seek to better the world and make it a place unhindered by darkness and hate?"

"My son comes from a place of goodness and light," Kaylia snapped. "His heart is pure. There is no darkness in him."

Aaliyah sniffed "No? Is there no darkness in the heart of his father? You and I both know there is. Only through you has Gewey managed to keep his humanity. Without you, he would have succumbed to the rage that even to this day dwells within him and threatens to break free."

Kaylia wanted to argue, but she knew Aaliyah was right. Even so, she could not believe her son capable of creating such a terrible future. "He is an innocent. And I will keep him safe," she stated. Her eyes burned fiercely. "From anyone."

Aaliyah nodded, understanding her meaning. "You have no need to ever fear me. Should Jayden ravage the world, I would still not be able to bring myself to stop him. Never forget that I was there when he took his first breath." She reached out again for Kaylia's hand, and met no resistance. "This is why it must never come to pass. The only road to salvation is through you. It always has been."

Tears were welling in Kaylia's eyes. The magnitude of what Aaliyah had just told her was a heavy weight on her heart. One that she felt inadequate to bear. "And Basanti gave her life to see that I am here to show my son the right path. Is that it?"

"She did," Aaliyah affirmed. "But even during the short time I knew her, I learned that the oracle did nothing without purpose. To her, it was a sacrifice worth making."

Kaylia closed her eyes and murmured a prayer to the Creator for Basanti. "Then I will do my best to ensure that it was not made in vain," she promised after completing her offering.

The two women lay down on the soft ground until the sun had set. Both were still exhausted from their use of the *flow*, so it was decided that they would rest where they were until dawn. Aaliyah built a small fire and shared the bit of jerky and bread she had with her.

All the time, Kaylia was yearning to reach out to Gewey for comfort. But she knew that she mustn't. His road was far too perilous, and he needed no distraction from her.

They had traveled far enough to be unconcerned with enemies. And, as they had arrived at this spot without leaving a trail, it was unlikely that anyone could know where they were, even if they were looking.

For all that, her sleep came slowly and was fraught with disturbing images.

Footfalls in the forest early the next morning had them on their feet in an instant. Aaliyah drew her blade while Kaylia, without a weapon, filled herself with the *flow*, ready to roast anyone foolish enough to attack.

"It sounds like just one person," whispered Kaylia.

A few moments later, to their astonishment, Basanti appeared from behind the brush. She looked to be in a terrible state. Her tattered clothes were stained black ,and her left arm was hanging uselessly by her side. Cuts and gashes covered her face, while her right eye was swollen almost completely shut.

Aaliyah instantly dropped her sword and rushed to her side. At first, Basanti resisted but then allowed herself to be helped over to the smoldering ashes of the dead fire.

Kaylia began examining her wounds.

"I'll be fine," Basanti told her weakly. "My kind heal rather quickly."

"There's a stream not far from here," said Aaliyah. "I'll fetch some water to clean you."

Basanti waved her hand. "That is not necessary. I won't be staying."

"What do you mean?" asked Kaylia. "You should return with us." She glanced over to Aaliyah for support, but her friend's head was suddenly cast down with eyes closed.

"I cannot," said Basanti. "I have become a danger to you... and to Jayden."

"I don't understand?"

Basanti reached out to touch Kaylia's cheek. "Because of what I have done, I am now as Yanti was. By spilling blood, I've released a power inside of me that I have long kept at bay. If I stay with you, the Reborn King will surely come for me. Even now I can hear his call beckoning me to join him."

"He will not have you," Kaylia told her. "We can protect you. And when Gewey returns, he will be able to heal whatever is wrong with you."

Basanti shook her head and gave a sad smile. "Oh my dear, how I wish I could simply be healed. But what ails me runs far deeper than you can guess. I think I finally understand why Pósix refused to help Yanti all those years ago. It wasn't because she wouldn't. It was because she couldn't. The very nature of what I am has been changed. Now I am little better than the creatures I just fought."

"That's not true," countered Kaylia. "You are the Oracle of Manisalia. You have guided the world for countless generations. And you are the wisest and most compassionate among us."

"That is kind of you to say," said Basanti. "But what you describe is who I was... not who I have become. And now that I have seen you and know that you are safe, I must go."

Kaylia opened her mouth to protest, but Basanti pressed her fingers to her lips. "Please. This is a very hard thing for me. Do not try to change my mind. It will only increase the pain I feel."

"Where will you go?" asked Aaliyah, her head still lowered.

"Far from the reach of our enemy," she replied. "Far from the sight of anyone. And there I shall remain."

Basanti took another long look at Kaylia, then struggled to her feet.

"You should at least rest until you've healed a little," offered Kaylia.

"There is no need," Basanti said. "I am already feeling my wounds close. And you have a child to care for. There is no time for you to be wasting your efforts on me."

Kaylia embraced her gently so as not to irritate her wounds. "It is not a waste. How can I ever thank you enough for what you have done? I swear that when this is over, I will find a way to make you whole again."

Basanti sighed. "I would say that you shouldn't bother. But I must admit... I would like that."

She embraced Kaylia for a final time, then turned to Aaliyah. "Thank you," she whispered. "And keep them safe."

"I will," she promised, at last raising her eyes.

Without another word, Basanti turned away. In a flash, she vanished into the forest.

There was a brief reflective pause while both women stared after her. It was Aaliyah who broke the silence. "Come, we should be on our way."

The journey to Valshara was not so far, and a quick pace—often a run—had them there in just a few days. Kaylia frequently looked back over her shoulder. Not for foes... but in the faint hope that she would see Basanti catching them up.

The vision Aaliyah had described continued to weigh on her mind. But after a time, she resolved to ignore her own fears of inadequacy and concentrate only on the love for her family. She had to trust that this would be enough to ensure that Jayden did not take the wrong road.

As they passed through Valshara's gates, they were greeted by both Linis and Dina. Dina came at a run, throwing her arms around Kaylia and very nearly lifting her off her feet. "Thank the gods you are safe," she cried. "We were so worried."

Kaylia smiled through her fatigue. "Thanks to Aaliyah and Basanti, I am fine." The name Basanti stuck in her throat.

Linis stepped forward and bowed low.

Kaylia laughed with amusement. "Are we so distant that you now bow to me?"

"My wife feels that I am in need of refinement," he replied, smirking. "A life spent wandering the forests of the world has made me an ill-suited mate for the High Lady of Amon Dähl."

"She is not wrong," said Kaylia. She wrapped her arms around the *seeker* and hugged him fondly. "But you can be forgiven this time for your rough, uncouth ways."

After embracing each other, Aaliyah led them inside.

"Jayden sleeps," Dina said before Kaylia could ask her. "Ertik is with him."

Kaylia raised an eyebrow.

"He has turned out to be quite the nursemaid," Dina continued. "As has my dear husband. Between the two of them, Jayden has not seen a single second alone." She took Linis's hand. "Who knew that the fiercest *seeker* of all the elf tribes would be such a gentle caregiver?"

Her words forced an embarrassed smile from Linis, which became even more self-conscious when Kaylia bowed low to him in a humorous copy of his own earlier gesture.

Dina walked Kaylia to her room, showing Aaliyah to hers along the way. Kaylia regarded the dozens of soldiers guarding the passageways with curiosity. But the excitement of seeing her son kept any questions unspoken for the present.

Just as she had been told, Ertik was sitting beside the cradle. He was reading a book, but looked as if he was about to doze off. However, his eyes lit up the instant he saw Kaylia.

"Gods be praised," he whispered, trying not to wake the baby.

Kaylia kissed the man on his cheek, then positioned herself as close as possible alongside her son. She stood there, simply gazing down at him for more than a minute.

"There is much you should know," said Dina. "But nothing that can't wait until after you have rested and eaten."

"Thank you," said Kaylia, without taking her eyes off Jayden for a second.

Unable to resist, she carefully lifted her sleeping child and held him close. Jayden stirred and opened his eyes for a moment. A tiny smile appeared on his lips as soon as he saw his mother's face. Kaylia smiled back at him, joyful tears running down her cheeks.

After a bath, a meal, and a short rest, Aaliyah, Dina, and Linis came to join her.

"The oracle will always be remembered," promised Dina, once Aaliyah had finished telling them of her and Basanti's experience. "And as you said—perhaps we can find a way to heal her."

Linis then related his encounter with the rogue elves. Alternate waves of shock and relief raced to Kaylia's heart. She immediately rose from her chair and embraced the *seeker*.

"You have my eternal gratitude," she said. "And Gewey's as well."

"That is why you see all the guards," explained Linis. "Well, certainly some of them. When Jayden and I arrived, their number was immediately doubled. It would need an army of ten thousand to take the halls leading here."

"And what of your mother?" Kaylia asked Dina.

"She is in the south for now. Gone to visit her village and to help the humans devastated by the war."

"And what will you do?" asked Linis.

"I will remain here," Kaylia replied. "Until the end."

"And when it is over?" asked Aaliyah.

"I will make my dreams a reality and go to Gewey's home village."

They talked and told tales until late into the evening. Just as they were about to retire, a message arrived for Dina.

"Aaliyah," she said, after reading it carefully. "You are needed in Althetas."

"Unless there is truly urgent business there, I would prefer to stay with Kaylia and Jayden," she protested firmly.

"Your people have arrived," Dina explained. "Ships with red sails have been spotted anchored just off the Althetan coast."

Aaliyah's eyes brightened for a moment. "Then you are right. I *must* go. Would you please send word ahead that I am coming?"

"Of course," said Dina.

With that, everyone said goodnight, leaving Kaylia alone with Jayden once again. Only Ertik came by a little later to check if they needed anything.

Kaylia decided not to put Jayden back in his crib. Instead, she pulled him close as she settled into her bed.

"You shall never be without me again," she whispered. "And I *will* be there to show you the right path. That, I promise with all my heart."

CHAPTER 11

Gewey stared out over the rolling hilltops of the Eastland. The heat of the noonday sun was almost intolerable, and he was tempted more than once to use the *flow* to cool himself. He was hoping that his use of it in the cavern beneath the Vrykol fortress had gone undetected. Nehrutu had told him that he had not been able to sense anything, so they were reasonably sure that the nature of the place somehow contained it.

They had run across a few bands of elves heading east, but thought it best to avoid them. Many of these were likely unwilling or unable to accept recent changes and were seeking to start anew in the depths of the desert's endless sands. Being confronted with a god, an elf, and the last of the *first born* would only serve to antagonize them needlessly. If they could not bring themselves to live among humans but were prepared to leave peacefully... so be it. Better that than more conflict. And perhaps, in time, the elves of the desert would be able to teach them a measure of their own acceptance and understanding.

"Are you not hungry?" asked Felsafell.

Gewey turned and accepted an apple. "I was just thinking about the elves. Some of them seem so unhappy. Change has taken its toll on them. I wonder if they can ever learn to accept what has happened."

Nehrutu, who was sitting down in the tall grass munching on a piece of flatbread, looked up. "My people will find their way. Once my kin arrive, they will help unite us. Of this, I am sure."

"And what about those who refuse?" asked Gewey.

"No one can stand alone and separate from the world indefinitely," noted Felsafell. "Those who do so will soon find themselves a dying breed. You can hide from others for a time, but you cannot hide from the world itself. Try as you might, it eventually finds you."

"So you think they will simply die out?" asked Nehrutu.

"Ultimately, yes," he affirmed. "Though I imagine that many will return to the fold in due course. Change goes hard on the proud. But even pride can be tempered by wisdom and the right guidance."

Nehrutu turned to Gewey. "And what of you? You have often said that you wish to return to your hometown once this war is over. Do you feel that is a possibility?"

"I would like to think so," he replied earnestly. "Once the Dark Knight is defeated, I am hoping that the name of Darshan will fade into history so I can live in peace."

"The name Darshan will never be forgotten, I'm afraid," said Nehrutu. "But should you find a quiet life impossible here, there is always a place for you across the Abyss."

Gewey smiled. "I may take you up on that when the time comes." He stretched out his arms. "Though there is much to do before that."

Their journey to the edge of the desert would normally have taken less than a week. But in their wish to avoid encounters, several detours had been forced upon them. So, by the time they reached the first border town, more than two weeks had already passed. Felsafell's skill in hunting small game had certainly come in handy along the way, keeping them in food throughout. But now things were different. They were preparing to enter the scorching heat of the deep sands and needed to re-supply.

The town was little more than a trading post, which Gewey decided it would be best for him to enter alone. By now, elves were not the uncommon sight they had once been in this region, but an elf traveling with a human would still raise more than a few eyebrows. And Felsafell would certainly draw his fair share of attention as well. They made camp a few miles east of the town, just where the grass began to give way to hard-packed sand. Here, they were unlikely to encounter anyone other than perhaps a desert elf or a wayward traveler.

While purchasing his provisions, Gewey noticed the tense mood of the traders and merchants. Though no one said why directly, fear seemed to linger on every face he saw.

"Trade goes well?" he asked a food merchant.

The merchant shrugged. "As well as can be expected. It would be much better if all the rabble out west would settle their affairs."

"Well, wars don't last forever," Gewey said, forcing a smile.

"Yeah, I suppose. But I wish they'd keep it to themselves and stop sending their mess to the desert."

"What mess?"

The man glanced from side to side before answering in a hushed tone. "Evil things. Things like you've never heard of."

"You mean the elves?" asked Gewey.

He huffed loudly. "What do I care about the elves? Sure, it was strange to see so many coming out of the sands. But they keep to their own affairs as far as I can tell. And the ones going in don't give us no bother either."

"What then?"

"Some people say that an evil has been awakened. Whatever it is, it roams the desert and slaughters both man and beast. It's even invaded some of our towns. I've never known nothing like that in these parts before. If you ask me, it's some foul beast from the west." He spat a curse. "Bloody Westerners and their bloody war."

Vrykol, thought Gewey. "Have you actually seen this thing?" he asked.

"No," the merchant admitted. "But I've seen the bodies. Torn apart like wet parchment they were." He shuddered from the memory, then regarded Gewey's provisions. "From the look of things, you're heading out to the desert yourself."

"Not too far," he lied. "I heard that some of the people from my village had come this way. I was hoping to find them."

"Then you're wasting your time. No one goes there anymore. Not even a short ways. Whatever is out there, it's killing anything that ventures off too far."

Gewey nodded. "I'll be careful."

The man snorted. "Another fool from the west. Go on then. Get your fool self killed. See if I care."

Gewey spent a few more hours in the town, striking up conversations wherever he could. Nearly everyone he spoke to told him the same thing. Something was definitely lurking in the desert—killing anyone stupid enough to venture forth.

By the time he returned to the others, it was just after dusk. There was a half moon, and stars were scattered across a cloudless sky. After splitting up the provisions, he told them what he had heard in town.

"Vrykol, I would guess," said Nehrutu.

"That's what I was thinking, too," agreed Gewey.

Felsafell rubbed his chin and stared into the small fire they had built. "It would seem logical. Though, we must also take into account the corrupted half-man we encountered. If such beasts wander the desert, we should be cautious."

"We can handle them, I think," said Gewey, grinning.

"Yes," agreed Felsafell. "But a large number of them would most surely be a problem unless you were to use your power. Pray we do not run into such a force. It could expose our hand prematurely."

The truth of what the *first born* had said descended on Gewey like a fog. If they were to encounter an overwhelming number of foes, he would be left with little choice but to use the *flow*. And he was not ready to reveal himself just yet. Later, once they were in the mountains, it would no longer matter. By then, there would be nothing the Dark Knight could do to stop him.

They slept for only a few hours and were well into the dunes by the time the orange sky heralded the dawn. Even before the sun had cleared the horizon, they could feel the heat rising.

"If needs be, I can use the *flow* to cool us," offered Nehrutu. "It is unlikely the Reborn King will notice such a weak display. And even if he did, he certainly wouldn't confuse me with Gewey."

"Let us hope it will not come to that," said Felsafell. "I have not been among the sands in some time. But I still remember where to find the oasis."

"And what of the blood of the sands?" asked Gewey.

"An entrance which will take us to the base of the mountains is about a week's travel from here."

The thought of enduring the heat for a week had Gewey's face twisting into a frown. "Then let's not delay," he said.

By midday, he had the distinct impression that they were being watched. And from the look on Felsafell's face, he was thinking the same.

"What is it?" asked Nehrutu.

Felsafell halted and gestured for silence. After more than two minutes of careful listening, he smiled. "Elves," he announced.

Nehrutu grunted. He was still unsettled by the way desert elves were invisible to his senses. Their complete rejection of the flow seemed somehow unnatural and wrong.

"They've been following us for at least an hour," Felsafell added.

"Why don't they approach?" Gewey asked.

"They are probably trying to figure out what to make of me," Felsafell replied.

Gewey laughed. "I can't blame them. I've been around you for a while now, and I still find myself staring sometimes."

They halted and allowed the elves to watch for a time. Gewey noted that they were even more cautious than he'd known them to be in the past—far beyond their typical wariness regarding strangers. He hoped it was simply the sight of the *first born* that was causing their trepidation.

Finally, four elves crested a nearby dune and made their way down to the base. They allowed Gewey, Nehrutu, and Felsafell to approach the rest of the way.

"Greetings," called out a stocky elf.

Gewey guessed him to be a sand master. His bearing and manner at once reminded him of Weila. "Hello," he responded with a welcoming smile, relieved that their first encounter in the desert was not going to be with Vrykol.

"What brings you so far from the protection of the cities?" the elf asked.

Gewey cocked his head. "The last time I was in the desert, the elves were far more courteous. I was at least afforded an introduction before I was questioned."

There was a long, uncomfortable silence as the elf's eyes darted from Gewey to Felsafell. "I know who you are, Darshan. And your presence *is* welcome. However, it is also unexpected. My people followed you west to do battle with your enemies. And yet now I find you here. I would know why you are not with them."

"It is for reasons I can't explain, I'm afraid. But I can tell you that your people fight on, and have achieved a great victory in the city of Baltria."

This seemed to ease the tension somewhat.

The elf bowed. "For this news, I am grateful. I am sand master Maljahar." He looked pointedly at Gewey's companions.

"I am Felsafell," He spoke without further prompting. "Last of the *first born*. Forgive me if my odd appearance has startled you."

Maljahar raised an eyebrow. "The *first born*? I'm sorry. Your race is unfamiliar to me. Though I do recall stories of the name Felsafell from my youth. If you are indeed he..." He shook his head, as if the thought was almost too much to comprehend.

Nehrutu bowed. "And I am Nehrutu. My mate, Aaliyah, has spent time among your people."

"Ah yes, I did meet her briefly when she and Darshan first came here." The sand master gave his companions a quick nod. In an instant, they turned and set off back up the dune. "There is a small oasis not far away," he continued. "I would be pleased if you would join us there."

"And what of your friends?" asked Gewey.

"They will be keeping a watchful eye." The hint of fear in his voice did not go unnoticed.

The sun was beginning to set by the time they reached the oasis. It was much smaller than the one Gewey had seen the last time—just a tiny spring bubbling up beside a meager cluster of moss-covered rocks and bushes. The scattering of thin grass was large enough to allow only about ten people to escape the sands. Gewey wondered how such a fragile place could endure the blazing heat. He'd seen the power of the sun and what it could do to crops and flowers, even when growing close to a river. *There must be a massive underground reservoir here,* he guessed.

Maljahar built a small fire and offered the group a flask of sweet-smelling liquid, which they accepted gratefully. "Tell me more of what is happening in the west," he requested.

Gewey related details of the siege of Baltria, and of the impending march on Angrääl. This seemed to satisfy the elf. He relaxed a little more, though his eyes remained ever watchful.

"The humans in the border towns say that there is an evil roaming the sands," said Gewey. "I assumed they were speaking about the Vrykol. Have you seen anything?"

Maljahar nodded slowly. "There is ... something. But it's not Vrykol, though we have also seen those vermin wandering about here and there. They usually do their best to avoid us and stay mostly to the areas with little or no water. Places where even we have difficulty traveling. My people have killed a few of them, but they're not easy to catch."

"If it's not Vrykol, then what is it?" asked Gewey.

"We don't know," he replied. He glanced nervously into the distance of the fading daylight. "But it travels in shadow, as if the darkness is a cloak it can wrap itself within. Only a few of us have seen it and lived. It looks human, but its flesh is as pale as a spirit. It can move faster than any elf, and kills without hesitation. Even the bravest among us no longer venture out alone."

Gewey and the others looked at one another knowingly. It had to be a corrupted half-man. Gewey told him what little he knew.

"Is there any way to fight them?" asked Maljahar.

"They are faster and stronger than anything you could imagine," Felsafell offered. "They will heal almost as quickly as you can wound them. If you have a choice, do not fight. Run. And if you must fight, do not fight alone."

The elf nodded thoughtfully. "I will pass on what you have said."

For the rest of the evening, Maljahar peppered Felsafell with questions, to which he was more than pleased to answer. It was well beyond midnight before they all laid down beside the dwindling fire and went to sleep. Gewey was the last to doze. He could hear the howling of wolves from far away.

The wolves! Were they the same as those he had fought with Aaliyah and Pali? The name of Pali immediately struck a chord. He remembered the elf's kindness and good humor... and his death. So many had died: good people; caring people; brave people. But so few of them entered his thoughts any longer. Pali was a typical example. He had spoken to Weila many times since her son's death, and not once had he been reminded of why there was so much pain lurking behind her eyes.

Have I seen so much death that it has hardened my heart? he wondered. So often he had dreamed of his return to Sharpstone, where he would raise his family and live out his life in a dearly purchased peace. But the reality was different. Gewey Steading was dead, and it would be Darshan taking up residence on his father's farm. He could no longer even recall the boy he once was. He closed his eyes and allowed sleep to bring its numbing comfort.

"Gewey."

A voice inside his mind stirred him fully awake. It sounded vaguely familiar, yet he could not quite place it.

"Gewey."

This time it was audible—but only as a whisper on the gentle wind. He looked at the others. No one was moving.

Rising silently to his feet, he listened hard but could hear nothing other than the wolves and the wind. His keen vision and elf training allowed him to penetrate the night, even without the use of the *flow.*

The oasis was surrounded by a circle of high dunes; a far from advantageous position if one was forced to defend it. Gewey scanned the area, but there was no one about.

He listened more intently. The elves who had accompanied Maljahar were positioned just to the north, talking quietly amongst themselves. The wolves' cries were coming from many miles away to the south and were of no concern to them.

"Gewey."

This time the voice came through sounding harsh... like a warning.

Without thinking, he set off up the dune on the east side, careful not to make a sound as he went. On reaching the top, he could see the vast expanse of the desert laid out before him. It was beautiful in its unpolluted continuity, yet ominous in its unforgiving nature.

"Gewey."

This time, he saw where the voice was coming from. A cloaked figure was standing less than a mile away. Were it not for his god's eyes, he would not have been able to see it. He knew at once that this was no Vrykol. A half-man, perhaps?

As soon as he spotted the figure, it moved out of sight. After taking a quick glance over his shoulder, Gewey decided to pursue. Upon reaching the spot where it had been standing, he saw clear footprints in the sand leading him over the next dune.

He continued to follow this trail for about a mile. Then the sands began to flatten out somewhat. And there the figure was waiting for him. The hood of its dark cloak was pulled low to cover its face, but Gewey's eyes were immediately caught by a jewel-handled long sword hanging by its side. He had seen this sword before... and knew who owned it.

"Lee?" gasped Gewey. "Is that you?"

"Stay back!" The voice was broken and rasping. Even so, there was no question at all that it belonged to Lee Starfinder.

"What's wrong?" asked Gewey. "Why are you here?"

"To warn you while I still can," he replied.

Gewey noticed his hands. They were pale white… just as the other corrupted half-man's had been. The hairs on the back of his neck stood up.

"What did they do to you?" He took a step forward, but Lee retreated an equal distance.

"I said stay back!" His fists clenched, and the sound of teeth grinding together came from within the darkness of his hood. "I can't hold on for very long."

"Please let me help you," begged Gewey. "Let me try to undo what they have done."

"There is only one favor I would ask," Lee told him. "When the time comes, kill me. Don't hesitate. Don't allow pity or our friendship to stay your hand. Just kill me." He pushed back his hood. His face was pale and sunken. His eyes, black and vacant.

Gewey could hear the struggle and pain in his voice. He gazed at his friend in horror.

Lee's face twitched and quivered as he continued. "It is the Vrykol's doing. Their master has abandoned them, so they are planning to use me to help him destroy you. If they succeed, they hope to regain his favor."

"Do they control you?"

"Not completely. Not yet. But they will soon enough. And when they do, I will not be able to stop myself. Do not allow them to distract you. When the time comes, you *must* keep your mind on your task."

"I will," Gewey promised. "But I still want to help you if I can."

"There is just one other thing you can do for me." Lee took another pace back. "When you unlock the door to heaven, please see that my wife's spirit gets to meet her Creator."

With that, he turned and sped away. Gewey at first gave chase, but without the *flow*, Lee was able to elude him. By the time he eventually returned to the oasis, the others were awake and looking concerned.

"You should not wander off alone," warned Maljahar. "Even one such as you should use caution."

Paying him no mind, Gewey kneeled in front of the others. "I saw Lee," he told them.

Both Nehrutu and Felsafell's eyes shot wide.

Gewey swallowed hard. "He's been ... corrupted."

"Did he attack you?" asked Felsafell.

Gewey shook his head. "He isn't completely under the control of the Vrykol ... yet. He told me that it is them, and *not* the Reborn King, who commands these corrupted half-men." He went on to recount the rest of the brief and painful conversation with his friend and mentor.

"Curious," remarked Nehrutu. "How is it they would know we are here?"

"I think I know the answer to that now," Gewey said. "And if I'm right, after we leave the mountains, I won't have any need to go to Angrääl."

"What do you mean?" asked Nehrutu.

His face was tight. "I mean, I may have sent King Lousis into battle needlessly. The Dark Knight has always known where we would finally face each other. I was just too stupid and blind to see it." He spat on the sand, then turned to Maljahar. "Spread the word to whoever remains in the desert that they should make for the Waters of Shajir and stay there until they hear from me."

"I will, Darshan."

Felsafell pressed him to say more, but this time it was Gewey's motives and mind that would remain a mystery.

They thought it best to set out before the sun rose. Maljahar offered an escort, but Gewey respectfully declined.

Little conversation was exchanged during the next few days as they pushed on. Gewey became increasingly withdrawn until his usual smile and good cheer had all but vanished completely. After several futile attempts to engage him, even Felsafell gave up and left the young godling to his own thoughts.

The almost constant howling of the wolves persisted for three days, making any kind of meaningful rest impossible. Although this had virtually no effect on Felsafell's endurance, the lack of sleep, together with the heat of the day and the deep sand, was beginning to trigger a fatigue that showed clearly on the faces of both Gewey and Nehrutu. Each night, the creatures' hollow cries came at them from a different direction. But on the fourth night, much to the party's relief, it suddenly became quiet.

Felsafell's memory was indeed flawless, and early on the morning of the seventh day, they came to a broad stone pillar protruding from the sand. A narrow entrance had been carved in the center.

"How long has it been since you rode the sands?" asked Gewey.

Felsafell grinned. "It was not long after I fell in love with Basanti... maybe a hundred years later, as I recall."

That the *first born* could conceive a century as being just a minor span of time was mind-boggling to Gewey.

"I am not educated in matters of the desert," remarked Nehrutu. "But how is it that the sands have not swallowed this place during all the many years that have passed?"

Felsafell shrugged. "That is a good question. But as far as I can tell, nothing that is connected to the Blood of the Sands is ever touched by time."

"I wish I knew who built it," remarked Gewey.

"As do I," said Felsafell. "But even one as old as I cannot know the answer to all of life's riddles. Perhaps we will find the answer to your question in the mountains."

They ducked inside the entryway and made their way down a narrow passage until arriving at a steep stairwell. At the bottom of this, the sands were flanked on either side by a stone platform rising roughly two feet above the canal.

Slithas were piled carelessly along the near wall. Gewey quickly lashed three of these together, then, taking the one in the middle, gestured for Felsafell to lead and Nehrutu to sit at the back.

Because of the elevation, they were forced to jump on simultaneously. The moment their vessels touched the surface, the sands sprang into life, propelling them rapidly forward. Felsafell's great height forced him to bend low just before reaching the tunnel.

"Sometimes I very much regret shedding my human form," he said. But his words were immediately followed by a good-natured laugh.

"Why did you change?" asked Nehrutu.

Felsafell chuckled and grinned almost boyishly. "Love and vanity, I suppose. Though Basanti could already see me as I truly am, there were times when she also saw the little old hermit that I still appeared to be in other people's eyes. After she had no further need to hide away, I could no longer bear for her to witness me looking so foolish."

His admission raised laughter from both Gewey and Nehrutu.

"I'm sure she didn't care how you looked," said Gewey.

"*I* cared," he replied. "I suppose pride is another thing that all races have in common."

"And stupidity," added Nehrutu. "Though I think they might well be one and the same."

They talked for a time—mostly about how they missed their respective mates. Felsafell sounded far more like a heartsick youth than the oldest being in the world when speaking of his time in Manisalia with Basanti. Gewey hoped with all his heart that the two ancient souls would find their measure of peace once this war was eventually over.

Conversation made the trip seem short, and before they knew it, they had arrived at their destination. This time, it was simply a matter of a short hop. Gewey watched as the three slithas disappeared into the dark tunnel ahead, on their way to the vortex.

"Has anyone ever ridden to the end?" he asked.

Felsafell nodded. "One of my kin ventured there when we were still a living people. But the vortex is a dangerous place. No one ever discovered how he managed to return, and his mind was never the same again."

"What did he see?" asked Gewey.

"He could not—or better said—*would not* describe it. But whatever he saw, it broke him. He spent the remainder of his days in solitude. In fact, he was one of the first of us that the gods chose to release into the spirit realm."

Gewey gazed into the dark hole one more time before moving on to the passage.

The way ahead was steep and uneven, and the sandy grit on the floor said that this path was not one frequently used. However, when the exit opened up, Gewey was greeted by a sight that left him absolutely stunned.

In the light of the new sun, towering unimaginably high and seemingly so close that they could simply walk to their base in a few minutes, loomed the Mountains of the Northern Desert. Hundreds upon hundreds of jagged peaks capped in pure white snow stretched to both east and west, far beyond Gewey's ability to see. Like the broken teeth of a giant, they snarled down at him, daring him to enter its maw.

The air was still and cold—a far cry from the scorching heat of the sands. Yet, as Gewey glanced over his shoulder, there was the vast expanse of the desert stretched out just behind him.

"Impressive," remarked Nehrutu. "Much like the mountains of my homeland."

"And very treacherous too, if the stories are to be believed," added Felsafell.

"So what now?" asked Gewey. "From what I can see, there doesn't appear to be any way into them from here. Unless, of course, you intend for us to climb."

"There should be a pass somewhere," Felsafell replied. His eyes scanned the mountains, trying to determine which direction they should take. After a few minutes, he grunted and set off northwest at a quick pace.

"Do you know where we're going?" asked Gewey.

"No," he replied. "But it *seems* right. I cannot explain it. I just have a feeling that this is the way we need to go." He pointed ahead.

As close as the mountains appeared to be, Gewey soon discovered that this was merely an illusion. After pushing on for the entire day, they had still not reached them. By now, the temperature was dropping fast, so they decided it best to build a fire and continue in the morning.

The sounds that came from out of the mountains that night were like nothing Gewey had heard before. Strange unearthly growling was accompanied by distant, unintelligible whispers. Nehrutu was also unnerved, but Felsafell seemed completely at ease.

"Are you sure you've never been here before?" Gewey asked.

"Quite sure," he replied. "As I said, my people feared this place."

"You don't seem to be afraid at all."

Felsafell leaned back on his elbows and smiled. "After living so long, the things that frighten me have changed. These days, the unknown excites me."

"I wish I felt the same," muttered Gewey. He stared up at the mountains and shivered. There was something about them. Something that was telling him very clearly to stay away.

They reached the base by mid-afternoon, by which time the wind was whipping in from the east, chilling them to the bone. The sheer rock formations of the many mountainsides towered above them like an army of impenetrable behemoths. Felsafell paused, his eyes fixed unblinkingly on the masses of jagged gray stone for several minutes. Then, a tiny smile turned up the corners of his mouth.

"Clever," he muttered, almost inaudibly. "Very clever."

Before either Gewey or Nehrutu could ask what he meant by this, he strode forward. The others tried to follow, but in an instant Felsafell dropped out of sight, as if the ground had simply opened up beneath him.

They ran to the spot where they had last seen him, only just stopping in time to prevent themselves from falling into a narrow trench carved ten feet deep into the earth. At the bottom of this stood Felsafell, unhurt and laughing. The trench, though invisible until almost alongside it, extended to an archway set into the mountainside.

"This was well thought," Felsafell said. He gestured for them both to jump down.

Gewey landed with a grunt. Nehrutu was just behind him.

"Whoever made this was determined that only a few could find it," Felsafell told them.

Gewey recalled his dream of being compelled to enter the mountain. Anxiety gripped him. "I wonder if they're still here."

"We will not find out by standing still," said Nehrutu.

As they approached the archway, a blast of hot air shot out from the darkness. Gewey was reminded of the legends of the fire lizards. *Stories,* he told himself. *Nothing but stories.*

With the entrance only wide enough for them to walk along in single file, Felsafell took the lead. Gewey followed close behind him.

A moldy stench hung in the air, and Gewey was now finding that his godlike vision was insufficient to penetrate the suffocating darkness. Knowing that there was little the Dark Knight could do to stop him at this point, even if his enemy did locate him, he reached out for the *flow*. But there was nothing there.

He halted. "Something is wrong. The *flow*... it doesn't exist here."

Nehrutu tried as well and met with the same result.

"Then let us hope we will have no need of your powers," said Felsafell.

Taking a deep breath, Gewey gripped the hilt of his sword. Earlier in their journey, he had felt exposed and vulnerable when forced to fight with only his natural strength. Now he faced dangers unseen, even by the likes of Felsafell. Previously, he could have chosen to fall back on his powers had the situation grown truly desperate... but that was no longer an option. However, there was no time to dwell on such thoughts, and it was far too late to turn back. He glanced behind at Nehrutu. The elf was obviously upset. "Are you able to go on?" he asked.

Nehrutu straightened his back. "Of course. Forgive me. I have never been cut off like this before. It feels ... unnatural. It is hard to imagine how the desert elves live like this."

"They live quite happily, from what I can tell," remarked Felsafell.

The three of them moved on, Gewey staying close to Felsafell's back, his vision still not able to adjust even after more than ten minutes in the darkness.

The way ahead was narrow, yet high enough for Felsafell to walk without bending. Though clearly not a natural tunnel but one carved by hand, it sloped up and down, twisting and turning without apparent rhyme or reason.

After an hour or so, the passage widened sufficiently for them to walk abreast had they wished to. Nevertheless, Gewey and Nehrutu still chose to keep a step behind the *first born*, who seemed to be experiencing no problems at all in navigating the pitch blackness.

Several times they came to a fork, but Felsafell didn't hesitate in his choice of which direction to take. It was as if he were walking a familiar path. Gewey guessed it must be close to midday by now, so he retrieved a few strips of jerky and distributed them equally.

"How long until we are outside again?" asked Nehrutu. The tension in his voice was obvious.

"I don't know," Felsafell replied. "I feel very much as if I have been here before, though, in truth, I know I have not."

"Could you have forgotten?" Gewey asked.

He huffed a laugh. "Could *you* forget this place?"

Gewey reached out until his fingers made contact with the rough walls. *No. This place was wholly unforgettable.* Even as this thought was entering his mind, a sharp hiss cut through the stale air.

The trio froze for an instant, then quickly drew their weapons. The passage was broad enough for swords, but maneuvering would still be a challenge. Ahead was another fork, but Gewey could not tell which one the sound was coming from.

Another menacing hiss was followed by harsh scraping and shuffling noises.

"Be ready," whispered Felsafell.

They waited, tense and motionless, for several minutes, but no more threatening sounds followed. Gewey could hear only the barely audible breathing of his companions and the rapid beating of his own heart.

"What the hell was that?" he eventually asked. Though he tried to speak softly, the echo made it sound as if he had shouted. This brought a harsh stare from Felsafell.

The *first born* took a cautious step forward, gesturing for the others to follow him. After several yards, they took the right-hand fork, then stopped and listened.

Only a few seconds later, the hissing returned. But this time it was coming at them from both ahead and behind. It was also increasing in volume.

"The two of you watch our flank," ordered Felsafell. "And give me a dagger."

After handing Felsafell the weapon he asked for, Gewey quickly took up position shoulder to shoulder with Nehrutu. Both of them held blades at the ready, although given the corridor's restricted width, they were not going to have room for anything more than short, straight thrusts.

Gewey soon spotted the silhouette of a four-legged creature approaching. It stood about as high as a large dog, though was twice as broad and had a long slender neck. Its movements were smooth, as if it were gliding along rather than walking. Only the scraping of talons hinted at any contact with the ground.

As it drew nearer, he could see that it was reptilian, though unlike any lizard he'd ever come across before. Its scales were pitch black, and saliva dripped menacingly from the corners of its mouth. Gewey looked over his shoulder just in time to see an identical creature making its way toward Felsafell.

Again, the stories of his youth flashed through his mind. "Fire lizards," he muttered.

It burst forward with astonishing speed when only a few feet away, yellow eyes fixed evilly on its prey. Gewey and Nehrutu reacted instantly by stabbing hard at its neck and body, but it was like trying to punch a hole through a lump of solid steel. Both of their blades came to an arm-juddering stop, unable to penetrate even a small way into the scaly hide. The sudden reversed force of their joint strikes rocked them back, and the beast's jaws gaped open to reveal twin rows of two-inch-long, dagger-like teeth.

Seeing an opportunity, it snapped at Nehrutu's right calf. He shifted to one side just in time, at the same moment thrusting his sword down with all of his strength. Gewey did the same. Yet again, Nehrutu's blade was deflected, but Gewey's second attempt did somehow manage to penetrate slightly—though the wound was only superficial and less than one inch deep. Even so, it was enough to get the lizard's attention. Swinging angrily around, its clawed foot took a swipe at Gewey's midsection.

The sharp talons sliced through his shirt, opening up a shallow, three-inch-long gash just above his waist. Jumping back, Gewey struck again and again, but his backward momentum was now taking too much of the force away from his blows. Each time, his blade bounced harmlessly off the heavily armored hide.

The creature bit and clawed ferociously at Gewey, relentlessly forcing him farther to the rear, until finally, he felt his back bump hard up against the jagged wall. With no room left to maneuver and the lizard poised to make its devastating strike, the ominous warning about these mountains whispered to him in his dream came rushing back.

"Don't go there. You will not return."

Was the dream now only a heartbeat away from becoming reality?

Though staring rigidly into his would-be killer's glittering eyes, Gewey still caught a glimpse of Nehrutu jumping across the beast's back and then reaching down to grab it by the tail. Letting out a loud grunt, the elf gave a colossal heave. It was an incredibly brave action, and one that unquestionably saved Gewey's life. With a loud hiss of anger, the reptile swung around, its anger now directed once again at Nehrutu. In a single flash of movement, its jaws clamped over the elf's sword arm. His agonized cry reverberated throughout the tunnel as the sharp teeth sank in.

But clearly, the lizard had not forgotten or forgiven the person who had inflicted the wound on it. Instead of retaining its hold on its victim and going for the kill, it at once returned its attention to Gewey. A mercifully released Nehrutu staggered backward, clutching at his wound. His blade fell from pain-numbed fingers to the ground.

But by now, the elf's actions had given Gewey the vital seconds to move left and away from the wall. He thrust out in a renewed attack, using every last bit of strength at his disposal. And this time, thanks to his returned forward momentum, his steel once again forced a way through the reptile's hide and into the flesh just behind its head. It snapped and flailed in response, but Gewey was not about to let it get loose now. With a primal yell, he pushed down again. With a rush of savage satisfaction, he felt the blade sinking in much deeper. But then the unexpected happened. The lizard dropped and rolled sharply to one side, ripping the sword clean away from Gewey's grasp.

Hissing and spitting, it shook its head wildly until it had worked the embedded blade loose. One final shake jerked it free completely. The weapon flew through the air, landing several yards away with a loud clatter somewhere in the inky darkness. Gewey could see Nehrutu's sword still lying on the ground, but the creature was blocking his path. Blood was gushing from its neck, but the wound did not appear to be slowing it down at all.

Gewey feigned left and then right, hoping to throw it off-balance, but it matched his movements easily. Fear gripped him as the beast lurched forward, teeth bared. In a desperate attempt to avoid the attack, he threw himself to the right and rolled. He was not quick enough. Pain shot through his leg as a lunging claw raked through both his pants and flesh. He managed to grab the creature's long snout with both hands just as it landed on top of him, but the surface was slippery from all the blood that had been flying around. Gewey knew that it would shake itself free in just a matter of moments.

He kicked upward into the beast's chest, hoping to lift it over onto its back. But it twisted its muscular frame with amazing agility, whipping its tail to compensate. This left Gewey in an even worse position than before. Now it was to his left and only a gasp away from wrenching its jaws free.

Just as his despairing fingers lost their hold, the great lizard jerked convulsively, then went rigid, its hate-filled eyes still fixed firmly on him. It took a few seconds for Gewey to realize that Felsafell was standing directly behind it, Nehrutu's sword in one hand, and his own dagger in the other. The sword had been rammed all the way through the beast's back, with the tip now protruding several inches from its gullet.

There was a brief moment of dead calm, during which Felsafell's aspect remained twisted into a vicious snarl. He then yanked the blade free. The lizard slumped down, still twitching in its final death throes.

"Are you badly hurt?" he asked Gewey.

The pain in Gewey's leg wasn't unbearable. He'd certainly had much worse. The same could be said of the gash above his waist. "I'll be fine," he replied. "Look to Nehrutu."

Nehrutu was struggling to his feet. By now, blood had totally soaked his shirt sleeve and was dripping from his fingertips. Felsafell ripped the cloth free to examine him.

"I'm fine, too," the elf told them. But his face revealed the deception.

"There is no way of knowing how the bite will affect you," Felsafell said grimly. "Sit. I have herbs and a salve."

Nehrutu obeyed without protest. While Felsafell was treating him, Gewey took a look around and noticed the other lizard sprawled in a bloody heap, its head cut completely away from its body and tossed on the ground just beside it. He marveled at the strength the *first born* must possess to have done such a thing armed with only a dagger. He then made a closer inspection of his injuries. Without the *flow*, both he and Nehrutu would have to heal naturally. And though his own wounds were far from life-threatening, they would certainly ache and slow him down considerably.

After attending to Nehrutu, Felsafell did what he could to ease Gewey's pain. Once both of his patients were ready to move, he took a minute to listen carefully for more foes. When satisfied that the danger had passed, for now, he continued to lead them deeper into the mountain.

"What were those things?" asked Gewey.

"I don't know," Felsafell replied. "I too have heard the same tales of the fire lizards that you were told. Perhaps the stories do have some basis in fact."

"At least they didn't breathe fire," Gewey remarked. "In the stories my father told, they could burn a man to cinders with a single blast of their fiery breath."

"Their bite was bad enough," remarked Nehrutu. "I have never felt pain like it. It was as if the beast's teeth were made of red hot iron." He touched the bandage gingerly. "If anything, the burning is even worse than before."

His remark caused Felsafell to pause and examine the wound once again. Gewey looked on as well, but the darkness prevented him from seeing color well enough to know if there was anything unusual.

Felsafell's sight was not so impaired. "It is already showing signs of infection," he stated.

Nehrutu furrowed his brow. "So soon?"

"Yes," he replied, not trying to hide his apprehension. "I think we must turn back immediately. I have never seen an infection spread so rapidly. You need the *flow* to heal you. Otherwise, I fear you will not last more than a day or two."

"We cannot," he contested. "Gewey must complete..."

Felsafell's back stiffened and his hand shot up to silence Nehrutu in mid-sentence. He craned his neck, listening intently. Gewey heard the sounds a moment later. It was the hissing and scraping of claws... dozens of them coming near—and coming fast.

Without another word, the three of them burst into a dead run. With an injured leg, Gewey struggled to keep pace. But he grimly pushed on through the pain and managed not to lose sight of Felsafell. They twisted and turned down dozens of diverging passages. He prayed that Felsafell was leading them in the right direction. Another fight with the giant lizards would certainly be the end of their quest.

The pounding of their boots and the sounds of their heavy breathing were loud, but even above these distractions, he could still hear the creatures quickly closing in. They couldn't be more than one hundred yards back... possibly even closer. On and on, Gewey ran. He could almost feel the beasts at their heels when he at last saw a light ahead illuminating a curve in the tunnel.

The way out, he thought. Thank the Creator.

He glanced over his shoulder, and it was instantly obvious that Nehrutu was in distress. The increasing light allowed him to see that the elf's face had now turned ghostly pale. Moreover, at least twenty of the lizards were in sight and only a few yards behind. But the light ahead was drawing ever closer—it was almost blinding now. It looked like they were going to make it, after all.

A sudden thought then caused his heart to sink. Escaping the interior of the mountain may not be any guarantee of safety. It was possible that the lizards would simply follow them outside and kill them there. He clenched his jaw. *Much better to die in the light of the sun than in the bowels of the earth.*

The three of them burst into the open air with literally seconds to spare before being caught. Without even glancing at their surroundings, they all spun around, weapons drawn and tensed for a battle to the death. At first, it looked as if the lizards were coming straight for them. But at the final instant, the creatures in the lead came sliding to a halt on the very edge of the opening. With the others lined up behind them, they simply stared out, a feral look of hunger in their glittering yellow eyes. Gasps of relief sounded all around as the situation became clear. It was then that Gewey could see for the first time that the reptiles' skin was not black at all, but a deep ocean blue. After hissing their deadly intent and frothing at the mouth a few more times, the beasts slowly and reluctantly retreated back into the darkness.

"Fortune remains our ally," Felsafell remarked with a grin.

But the good cheer was short-lived. The harsh clanging of metal on stone quickly drew Gewey's and Felsafell's attention back to Nehrutu. His sword had slipped from his hand and fallen onto the ground beside him. Now, his legs were wobbling erratically. Gewey only just managed to catch him before he fell. He laid the elf gently on his back. His face was a colorless death mask.

Felsafell wasted no time in tearing off the bandage. Gewey gasped at what he saw; every bit of tissue surrounding the bite had turned black, with tiny white pustules forming all along the injury itself.

Nehrutu winced several times while Felsafell attempted to clean the wound. "It looks as if this is as far as I am going, my friends." His voice was straining through the pain, and large beads of sweat were beginning to form on his cheeks and brow.

Gewey tried again to touch the flow, but it was still useless. "Hang on," he said. "You can make it through this."

But the look on Felsafell's face told him a different story.

All at once, Nehrutu's eyes widened and his hand shot out to point at something directly behind Gewey and Felsafell.

Only then did they begin taking notice of their surroundings. The rocky clearing they were standing in was roughly circular—about one hundred feet in diameter. One side of it was flanked by the mountain, the other by a sheer cliff more than two hundred feet high. Directly opposite the passage from which they had fled, another path could be seen leading farther north.

But it was not the landscape that had startled Nehrutu. Standing about fifty feet away from them was a massive creature, its entire body covered in thick, black fur. With shoulders as broad as a bear, it stood a full head taller than Felsafell. A pig-like snout decorated the center of its dark-skinned face. As if stunned, it stared at them through red eyes that were set unnaturally close together.

"Morzhash," croaked Nehrutu. "Don't let it escape."

Gewey vaguely recalled Aaliyah telling him about the Morzhash when they were in the desert together. But what were they doing here?

The beast had still not made any kind of move. Gewey gripped his sword and glanced at Felsafell.

"Hurry," pressed Nehrutu. "If it gets away, it might bring others back here."

"It seems afraid," whispered Felsafell.

"We can't take a chance," said Gewey.

Without further discussion, he raced off in the direction of the northern path. With speed astonishing for something so large, the creature did the same. But Gewey was able to block its way. Raising his blade, he prepared to strike. Aaliyah had mentioned that the Morzhash were extremely powerful and quick, so he knew that such a large beast would likely be formidable. But with Felsafell at his side, he was confident they could slay it.

The ground shook with the pounding of its paw-like feet. Felsafell was moving in behind it, though he had not yet drawn his weapon. Just when the creature was coming within reach of Gewey's blade, it slid to a halt and spun around. At the sight of the *first born*, it let out a loud roar. But it was not a roar of rage or hatred. If anything, it was more akin to the sound of terror.

Felsafell halted and locked eyes with the Morzhash. It opened its mouth, but this time, instead of a roar, a defeated moan came forth. Its shoulders slumped, and it dropped to its knees.

"Kill me quickly," it said in a low, guttural voice. It bowed its head, awaiting its fate.

Gewey was dumbstruck. He lowered his weapon and looked at Felsafell, who was also clearly astonished.

"You speak," Felsafell said.

"Of course, I speak, *first born*," it replied. "Now do what you must."

Gewey was unsure what their next move should be. He could not reconcile the stories he'd been told with this submissive creature now kneeling before him.

"If you mean us no harm," he eventually said. "Then we mean you none either."

The Morzhash huffed a scornful laugh. "It is not I who would have captured you. Nor do I travel with an elf." The word "elf" came out sounding like a curse.

"You bear elves ill will?" asked Felsafell.

"They are savages. Heartless brutes who destroy anything they do not understand."

"The elf who travels with us is not your enemy," Felsafell told it. "He is our friend, and he is poisoned by the bite of the giant lizards which dwell within the mountain."

A grin crept over its face, revealing small pointed front teeth and two-inch-long canines. "Then when he dies, the world will be just a little bit more tolerable."

A desperate thought suddenly flashed through Gewey's mind. This creature was obviously familiar with the lizard's deadliness.

"Do you know how to help him?" he abruptly asked.

"Perhaps. But why would I wish to do that?"

Anger rose up in Gewey at this display of stubbornness. But before he could say anything further, Felsafell stepped in.

"If you can heal him," he said, "then I promise to release you. You will be free to go on your own way unharmed."

"And if I refuse, you will kill me?" it asked contemptuously.

"No," Felsafell replied. "But neither shall we let you go."

The creature was silent for more than a minute. Then, after making a grumbling sound, it rose to its feet. "Very well."

With huge strides, and the others following, the Morzhash strode off toward the base of the cliff face where a small leather satchel lay. From this, it withdrew a tiny flask.

"Do you have a name?" asked Felsafell.

"I am Cloya," it replied. "Daughter of Menru."

Gewey only just managed to suppress a burst of laughter. A female? What in the name of all creation must the males look like?

"Pour some of this on his wound and have him drink the rest," Cloya continued. "He will be returned to health within a day. Until then, do not move him."

The moment Felsafell took the flask from her hand, Cloya set off in the direction of the path.

"Wait!" Gewey demanded, barring her way. His sword was still in his hand.

Cloya halted and gave a grunt. "You break your oath?"

"I break nothing," Gewey countered. "But Nehrutu is not yet healed. All we have is your word that what you have given to us will help him."

Her back straightened, giving her already considerable height even more definition. "I am a *yetulu*, not an elf. I do not lie. Do as I say and he will live."

"And what is to prevent you from returning with more of your kind to slaughter us?" asked Felsafell.

Cloya gave an ominous grin. "Nothing at all. But that was not the bargain, was it?"

"True," admitted Felsafell. "Therefore, you are free to go. We will trust that you are being honest with us." He bowed. "And we thank you."

Gewey stared at the Morzhash for a moment longer before reluctantly sheathing his sword and stepping aside. She paused when level with him and looked down, her red eyes scrutinizing every inch of his body. Gewey met her gaze, but quickly found it difficult to maintain contact.

"I would know your name," she said.

"Darshan," he replied. His god name passed his lips before he realized he'd spoken it.

She chuckled. "Darshan? So you have come at last. I must admit, I expected ... more. Of course, you may be lying." She cocked her head. "We will know soon enough."

After a final glance at Felsafell, she continued on her way to the path. Her long strides quickly had her out of sight.

Gewey and Felsafell hurried back to where Nehrutu lay. The elf's eyes were now shut and his lips had turned a horrible gray color. Only the slight movements of his chest told that he was still alive.

The liquid inside the flask was a deep blue that reminded Gewey of the Waters of Shajir. Perhaps the mountains were the source, he speculated. It seemed likely. He continued watching while Felsafell followed Cloya's instructions and then covered Nehrutu with a blanket. This done, he headed down the path to find some firewood.

He returned a short time later. "The road continues for some distance," he told Gewey.

After a time, they both settled down to keep watch—one of them on the tunnel, the other on the path. The daylight appeared to still be keeping the lizards at bay. But soon it would be nightfall. And Cloya was sure to alert others of her kind to their presence.

"Do you think he'll live?" asked Gewey.

"I think Cloya was being truthful," Felsafell replied.

"Have you ever seen anything like her?"

He shook his head. "But it seems that she knows of my kind... and of you."

Gewey sighed. The *first born's* words hung in the air, suggesting the possibility of still more mysteries and new dangers ahead. Was there never going to be an end to them all? His mind then turned to Kaylia and Jayden. Right now, had he been able to, he would have reached out to Kaylia for comfort, and to hell with the consequences. But whatever was stopping the *flow* in this place was also making contact impossible.

He made a promise to himself. If he ever made it out of here, the very first thing he would do was join with her spirit at least once.

Once more... *then* he would be ready to face his destiny.

CHAPTER 12

Gewey gave a sigh of relief when the long night finally ended. Several times during the hours of darkness, he had heard the hissing and scraping of the great lizards, but thankfully they remained unwilling to leave their tunnels. The thought then occurred that, in order to return to the desert, they would need to pass through the mountain again. He prayed that, before such a risk became necessary, they might discover another way back.

By morning, Nehrutu had regained much of his color and his breathing was normal. His wound no longer showed any signs of infection and was already beginning to close. Whatever the blue liquid was, it had certainly performed just as Cloya promised it would.

The shadow of the mountains cooled the air and dimmed the morning light long after the sun was high. To Gewey's eyes, there was something odd about their formation. It was as if they had been deliberately arranged to keep out intruders. Each peak was butted right up against the next one, forming a great wall that stretched for hundreds of miles from east to west. Only to the north, where the range ended, did the ground start to flatten.

By the time Nehrutu opened his eyes, it was almost midday. At first, he lay motionless on his back, a confused lookon his face. Then, with a tired groan, he sat up.

"How am I alive?" he asked, touching his arm. There was pain, but it was tolerable.

Gewey told him of their encounter with Cloya.

"If not for her, you would have surely died," explained Felsafell.

It took a moment or two for Nehrutu to absorb what he'd been told. "And you say it *spoke*?" he finally asked.

"Yes," replied Felsafell. "*She* did. And I might add that they do not hold your race in high regard. I suspect we have not seen the last of them."

"The Morzhash of my land are mindless animals," said Nehrutu. "We have never encountered any that display signs of intelligence or civilization. They raid our villages and kill without cause or remorse. If these beings are in some way related, they have no reason to hate my kind."

"Perhaps," said Felsafell. "But Cloya was certainly not mindless. Nor do I believe her to be a killer. Aaliyah has told me about the Morzhash of your land, but that is a name only you have chosen for them. It seems those living here refer to themselves as *yetulu*. And from what Cloya said, I believe there is more to the *yetulu* than you realize. I only hope that whatever it is they hold against your race, it can be made right... or at least, overlooked."

"We have not wronged them, I tell you," Nehrutu protested.

"Be that as it may," Felsafell countered. "Cloya is not the only one of her kind who dwells here. And that means we are in *their* domain. It also means it is *they* who will decide who has been wronged, and who has not."

The elf sighed. "There is no need to worry. If confronted, I will mind what I say. But you should know—if they are anything like the creatures of my homeland, they are immensely strong. And, in spite of their great size, very agile and quick. Should we be forced into a fight, it will not be an easy one."

"Then let us pray it does not come to that," said Felsafell.

Nehrutu struggled to his feet, at first holding onto Gewey's shoulder for support. After a minute or two, he stretched and groaned. Then, with a sharp nod, indicated that he was ready to depart.

The path north was well-worn, and once the entrance to the mountain was out of sight, it widened considerably, allowing them to walk alongside each other. In spite of the potential danger, Felsafell thought it best to sheath their weapons.

"We do not want to appear aggressive," he said. The others agreed.

The rocky terrain on either side of them stretched for miles before disappearing into a gray mist. Ahead, the path sloped down and curved slightly to the east. After a time, the air became warmer and more humid. A few slender pine trees were even scattered about. Soon, beads of sweat were forming on Gewey's brow.

By mid-afternoon, the landscape began to change dramatically. The trees and undergrowth had thickened to a point where it could now genuinely be considered a jungle. In terms of sheer density, Gewey was reminded a little of the Black Oasis, but without any of its ugliness or threatening atmosphere. He could sense no malice or danger here, though without the *flow*, he had to admit that he was basing these feelings on instinct alone.

Strange colorful birds with long curved beaks and even longer plumes called out from their high perches. Flowers of blue, pink, red, and violet were everywhere, their fragrances so intense and unique that with each gust of wind, they combined to create a multitude of new and delightful scents.

He noticed that the corners of Felsafell's mouth had turned up into a faint smile. "What's making you so happy?" he asked.

Felsafell's smile widened. "Are you not in awe that such a place exists unknown to the rest of the world? To think that, aside from the *yetulu*, we are probably the first to see it in many thousands of years... if not ever. I only wish Basanti could be here to share it with me."

The mere mention of the *first born's* love reminded Gewey of Kaylia, quickly diminishing the beauty around him. He felt her absence more and more keenly with each step. Only the thought that she and Jayden were safe in Theopolou's manor kept his mind from flying apart and abandoning his quest.

"Do you fear nothing?" asked Nehrutu. His eyes had been darting back and forth ever since setting out on the path. The tension he felt was clearly displayed on his face.

Felsafell looked sideways at the elf and shrugged. "Fear? Yes, there are things I fear. I may be immortal, but I am not invulnerable. I felt fear when I confronted Melek. I felt fear when I looked upon Basanti after killing her brother. I fear what will happen to the world should we fail. I am no different from you in this way. I have simply had more time to learn how to control my emotions. Right now, I wager that your fear is deepened by being cut off from the *flow*. Though I have never been faced with this particular difficulty, I have felt vulnerable in other ways."

"How did you conquer it?" Nehrutu asked.

"I did *not* conquer it. I used it to hone my senses and steel my resolve. Remember, fear is much like love. It can consume you if you are not cautious. But if you use *it*, rather than allowing *it* to use you, it can give you strength when you need it the most."

The elf forced a laugh. "The same wise words I would tell a child. Yet I cannot tell them to myself. I have not been this powerless since I was young. Even facing death, the *flow* was always with me. To imagine that humans feel this way all the time..."

"You don't miss what you've never had," Gewey chipped in. "Before I discovered what I am, I had never felt the *flow*. Humans do not feel powerless. And neither do the desert elves."

"I have occasionally questioned the wisdom of the Creator for allowing mortal creatures to wield such power," Felsafell mused.

"Maybe *she* intends for everyone to wield it," offered Gewey. "Or maybe none at all. Dina is half-elf and half-human, and as far as I know, she does not possess such ability. Who can say? In a few thousand years, there might be only one race, with no one holding power over another."

Felsafell smiled. "I think that would definitely make for a more peaceful world."

Nehrutu was still a bit on edge, but as the day wore on, he began to appear less nervous. With dusk approaching, they tried to find a clearing to rest up. But the undergrowth had become even denser, and Gewey thought it unwise to venture into an alien forest at night. Particularly without the *flow* to aid them. Nehrutu readily agreed. So, without any other options, they made camp in the middle of the trail.

Undeterred by the potential dangers, Felsafell set off to explore the surrounding jungle. He returned an hour later with some fruits and a small cord of wood.

They had just started a fire when Gewey spotted a dark figure on the trail slightly north of their position. Though shrouded in the increasing darkness, its massive silhouette told him at once that it was a *yetulu*.

"I see it too," whispered Felsafell, before Gewey could say a word. "Do nothing. We should allow them to come to us."

Nehrutu laughed softly. "I doubt we have a choice. My people have tried to pursue them in our own jungles and forests. As fast and strong as you are, I think even you would have difficulty in catching them."

Felsafell watched from the corner of his eyes as the *yetulu* slowly backed out of sight. "Then we shall wait and see what they intend. Until then, the two of you should try to sleep if you can."

Gewey knew that this would be an impossibility. The uneven ground and many days of hard travel—not to mention the wounds inflicted by the giant lizard—had taken their toll. While lying on his back, the pain and stiffness in his muscles would not let him be. He hadn't felt like this since he was a boy on his father's farm after a hard day's work.

It occurred to him that, even when crossing the deep sands of the desert, he had felt stronger than he did right now. He had not used the *flow* then, but at the same time, he'd always been aware of its presence. Here, he was not. *It must be a part of me, even when I am not a part of it*, he mused. He thought again of his earlier discussion with Felsafell. *Would life be better if all people were cut off from such power?* The more he considered this, the more he thought they probably would be. Neither human nor elf had shown great wisdom when given power. Elves had abused their superior capability, and humans had felt threatened by it. Perhaps the world simply could not abide two entirely separate races of people. Perhaps a joining of the two was the only way to ensure enduring peace and happiness.

His thoughts continued. Not even the gods were immune to prejudice. Melek had detested the *first born*, and hated the elves to the point of committing genocide. Yes, of course, he was an extreme example. But even his own father, Gerath, had made it widely known that he felt humans and elves to be inferior races. And though his actions were far less severe than Melek's, there was little doubt that he considered the virtue of the gods to be far beyond mere mortals.

Easing such reflections from his mind, Gewey allowed the tension in his facial muscles to relax. After several deep cleansing breaths, he closed his eyes and listened to the sounds of the jungle.

As dawn approached, he sat up and rubbed his neck and legs. Felsafell was squatting by the fire, staring into the smoldering embers. At the same time, Nehrutu, having managed to fall into a light sleep a few hours earlier, was beginning to stir.

"The *yetulu* are gathering," Felsafell said. "I can hear them about a half mile north."

Gewey listened, but could hear nothing. "What are they doing?"

"Blocking the road," he replied.

"Then I suppose we should not keep them waiting," said Nehrutu. "I am curious to meet these so-called *yetulu*."

They doused the fire and gathered their belongings. Just as Felsafell had said, the *yetulu* were waiting for them a half mile away. More than twenty of them were gathered in a loose group. To Gewey's eyes they looked almost identical to one another—all apart from one, who was wearing a bright red headdress of plumes.

When they were about twenty yards away, Felsafell directed the others to stop and took a few paces forward, alone. The *yetulu* wearing the headdress did the same.

"We come..." began Felsafell, but the massive hand of the *yetulu* shot up to silence him.

"We do not need to speak with you, *first born*," it said in a booming voice. "Cloya has told us that Darshan is among you."

Gewey stepped forward. "I am Darshan. Who are you?"

"I am Grunyal," he replied. "Son of Hybsal and emissary of the Creator. Why have you come, son of Gerath?"

"First, tell me how it is that you know me?"

His eyes narrowed. "You trespass on *our* land. Furthermore, you travel with an *elf*. You will answer *my* questions."

Gewey glanced over at Felsafell, but his eyes were fixed straight ahead and his face was expressionless.

"I seek the *god stones*," he said.

The *yetulu* began to shift and murmur.

"And what do you want with them?"

"I need their power to defeat my enemy and save the peoples of the world."

Grunyal huffed. "A god seeking more power. I should have expected as much."

"How do we know that he really is Darshan?" called a *yetulu* from the crowd. "He could be just another half-man seeking treasure. Gods do not need the god stones."

"My sister is right," said Grunyal. "Why would you need them? Is the power of heaven not enough for you?"

"Heaven is closed," he explained. "The way locked by one who calls himself The Reborn King. He has taken the power of the gods and seeks to burn the world. If you do not let us pass, he will succeed. Eventually, he will come here too. And when he does, he will not suffer you to live."

Grunyal gave a mocking laugh. "You think us a race to be stricken with fear? You try to scare us as if we were human children? Clearly, your father did not pass his wisdom on to you."

"I tell you only the truth," countered Gewey, trying hard to maintain a level tone.

"Perhaps," he replied. "We will know soon enough." His eyes fell on Nehrutu. "Let the elf step forward."

Nehrutu positioned himself beside Gewey and bowed low. "I am Nehrutu. My people..."

"I do not care about your people," snapped Grunyal. "I care about my own. I care about the fact that you would dare to come here. After what you have done to my kin, I should..."

"I have done nothing to them," Nehrutu interjected. "I am here simply to give aid to Darshan."

"Do you deny that it was you who recognized our kind when you saw Cloya?"

"I do not. There are creatures that look much like you in my own land. But they are mindless beasts, incapable of speech or reason. I mistook her for one of them."

His remarks drew angry grumbles from the assembly.

"Mindless?" repeated Grunyal. "Is that what you think?"

"I assure you that they have no speech or culture," Nehrutu insisted. "My kin have long tried to understand them, but with no success."

"And is it your claim that you knew nothing of our existence outside of your own land?"

"It is. In fact, I have only ever seen a Morzhash once before. And then from a distance."

Grunyal's reaction was instantaneous. "Mind your foul tongue," he roared. "You pretend to come as a friend, yet you curse us by naming us beast?"

"I don't understand."

"Morzhash!" He spat the word out like poison. "An ancient word for savage beast."

Gewey stepped quickly in. "He meant no offense. He is my friend, and a trusted ally. I beg you to listen to him. He means you no ill will."

Grunyal's eyes bored into the trio for an uncomfortably long moment. He then withdrew a few yards to whisper quietly with the others.

"You might have been a bit more thoughtful with your statements," Felsafell scolded Nehrutu in a whisper.

"I spoke only the truth," the elf protested. "And I had no idea that Morzhash was an offensive word."

"Can you hear them?" asked Gewey.

Felsafell nodded. "I do not think we are to be welcomed as friends."

At that moment, Grunyal turned to face them. "You will come with us."

"For what purpose?" asked Gewey.

His expression was stern. "The elf shall have the opportunity of facing his accuser. And you ... Darshan... you will be given the chance to prove that you are who you claim to be." He raised a warning hand. "Just in case you are wondering if you should try to escape, my people are everywhere. Even the *first born* would not be able to evade us for long."

"We will come willingly," Gewey said. "Just as long as you guarantee Nehrutu's safety."

"I will give you no such guarantees. You will either come with us now or test your skills of survival."

Nehrutu touched Gewey's shoulder. "I will go. If my people have wronged theirs, then it is my duty to try and make amends. I will gladly face whoever this accuser may be. And I will meet my fate if I must."

"I will not allow you to throw your life away for something you didn't do," Gewey said.

"There is no other way," Felsafell told him. "We cannot go forward without a fight—and we cannot flee. And even if we did manage to escape, we would still need to pass through the mountain again. I doubt we could make it through there twice."

"What is your decision?" Grunyal called over.

"It would seem that we are at your mercy," replied Gewey. "Let us hope you possess such a quality."

Without another word, Grunyal and the rest of the *yetulu* moved forward and surrounded them.

"We would bind you," he said. "But I suspect you could break the bonds easily enough."

"You need not fear," Felsafell responded. "We shall neither flee nor fight."

Grunyal merely grunted before turning to face north. "It is only a short way. We shall arrive before nightfall."

"Then what?" asked Gewey.

His question was ignored. They began moving forward at a pace that, by Gewey's standards, was nothing more than a leisurely stroll. Not a word of conversation was spoken along the way. The landscape remained a dense jungle, though they passed a number of smaller trails leading off the main path. He could see Felsafell taking note of these and could almost feel his desire to explore them.

After a time, the road split and they headed left along a path that was far more worn and even than before. Also, the jungle here was thinning somewhat, enabling Gewey to catch glimpses of several small animals. Some resembled creatures that were already familiar to him, such as squirrels, snakes, birds, and even a small pig. But others were like nothing he had encountered. One was a deer-like animal with two spiked horns and long white fur that darted in and out of the underbrush at fairly regular intervals. There was also a creature with arms and legs and an almost human face—though with leathery skin and black eyes—that could be seen hanging upside down from a clawed foot. Its movements were impossibly slow and fluid. He particularly wanted to ask about this, but knew it was best to remain quiet for the time being.

Nehrutu did not appear to be at all concerned about their circumstances and continued along as if he hadn't a care in the world. *Perhaps he has now come to terms with his loss of the flow,* Gewey considered. Then a darker thought occurred. *Perhaps he is carrying the resolve of the condemned.* Gewey had seen it before. The peace and tranquility of men and elves who were faced with certain death—their fears gone and ready to accept the end.

The path split several more times, during which Gewey could not help but marvel at the diversity of their surroundings. Along with further sightings of unusual creatures, the flowers seemed to change every few yards, each new bloom more vibrant than the last. Their fragrances filled the warm air, some of them so intensely that he found himself becoming lost in memories that he had not thought about in years.

"We are here."

Grunyal's voice snapped Gewey's mind back to the present. He looked ahead, and at first, was confused. There didn't seem to be anything there other than more jungle. But then, as he watched in amazement, the trees and vines parted, allowing them to pass by with ease.

"The forest obeys you?" he asked, breaking the long silence.

"No," Grunyal replied, a tinge of disgust in his voice. "But I am not surprised that is how you would see it. We are not masters of the earth and wind. We are its brothers and sisters."

They continued on for a few more yards before stopping. Almost at once, the ground began to rumble and shake. A few seconds later, a stairwell leading down into the depths of the earth opened up directly in front of them. While Felsafell simply raised an eyebrow and nodded with approval, Nehrutu and Gewey could only look on in further astonishment.

"Every time that I think the wonders of this world can no longer surprise me..." murmured Gewey.

The stairs continued on down for more than three hundred yards, eventually taking them to an immense hall, the ceiling of which glowed with veins of pale blue light. The floor, though fashioned from the rich, black, jungle soil, was as smooth as marble. Set into the walls of this vast, circular cavern at regular intervals were high-arched hallways leading to a variety of other locations.

They entered the hallway directly opposite and continued on until reaching a much smaller, oblong-shaped chamber. On either side of this were doors that looked to have been made from tightly compressed tree roots—though no handle was visible. Grunyal approached the door to his left. As he drew close, with a great cracking sound, the roots parted in the middle.

"Wait in here," he commanded.

Gewey, Nehrutu and Felsafell obeyed. The moment they were all inside, the roots snapped shut behind them.

They were now within a rectangular chamber, roughly ten feet by twenty. Several large wicker chairs lined the earthen walls, and a sturdy wooden table had been placed in the center. Gewey moved across to take a chair and found that they were far heavier than they looked. Clearly, they had been made to accommodate the extra size and weight of the *yetulu*. He dragged one over to the table; the other two did the same. As they waited for whatever might happen next, only Felsafell did not look like a small child sitting in his father's chair.

"It's as if they used the *flow* to build this place," said Nehrutu.

"Perhaps they did," offered Felsafell.

"Then why can't I feel it?" he asked.

Felsafell looked thoughtful for a moment. "It seems as if this place has been deliberately hidden from the rest of the world. Unassailable mountains—a hidden entrance—and a labyrinth of caves guarded by deadly giant lizards..."

"But who hid it?" wondered Gewey.

"I think we will find that out soon enough," said Felsafell.

They waited quietly for more than an hour. During that time, try as they might, none of them could hear anything from beyond their holding chamber. Gewey was growing impatient and about to test the door's strength when another loud crack announced that it was opening. In filed three *yetulu*. They each picked up a chair and sat across from their captives.

Though to Gewey's eyes, they looked identical, he somehow knew that two of them were Cloya and Grunyal, even though Grunyal had now removed his headdress. The trio simply sat and stared for more than a minute, all the time making him feel increasingly uncomfortable.

At last, one of them spoke.

"You are here to answer for the crimes of your people, elf." The voice confirmed that the *yetulu* in the center was indeed Grunyal. "I have brought your accuser before you." He briefly motioned to the *yetulu* on his left. "This is Yasir. Cloya is also here in order to question you on behalf of our people."

Felsafell nodded. "You say he is to answer for crimes. Are we to assume that his guilt is not in question?"

Grunyal gave a sharp nod. "It is not. Yasir has witnessed what his people did to mine."

"I will submit to your judgment," said Nehrutu. "But first, I would know why I am to be judged."

"You will not meet your fate in ignorance," assured Grunyal. "We are not savages."

Cloya leaned forward. "It was clear to me when I heard you name me Morzhash that you had encountered my people before. This you cannot deny."

"Nor would I try to," Nehrutu said. "But as I told you, the Morz... the *yetulu* of my land are nothing like you. They have no culture or civilization that we have ever seen."

"Because you took it from us!" roared Yasir. With teeth bared, his sudden outburst reverberated off the walls. "You murdered us! You burned our bodies, laughing, while our children screamed and begged you for mercy!"

"Calm yourself, my friend," said Grunyal. "You will have your chance to speak."

Unmoved by this display of temper, Nehrutu remained silent with his hands folded in front of him.

"How is it that I have no knowledge of your people?" asked Felsafell.

"You did once," Cloya told him. "But the memories were taken from you."

He sat back in his chair. "Taken? Why? And by whom?"

"Gerath took them from you, as he did all other people, in order to protect the *yetulu* from their barbarity. It was he who raised the mountains from the earth that now surround us. He warned us never to leave lest we be faced with the hatred and cruelty of the humans and elves."

"But why take my memories?" Felsafell pressed. "I am neither human nor elf."

"And yet you feel a kinship with them both," she countered. "Your race was already doomed when Gerath came to us. You had grown old and weary. You were despondent over the loss of your children and cared little for the happenings of the *yetulu*. Most of you had never heard of us, and those who had, lost the knowledge when they became spirits. Soon they were all gone. All but you, Felsafell. You, and you alone, remained unchanged."

"You speak as if you know me," he remarked curiously.

Cloya gave a mocking smile. "You think yourself so wise, and yet your mind is so easily manipulated. In truth, long ago you would visit our people quite often. There was even a time when you were most welcome among us."

Felsafell furrowed his brow and stared into Cloya's eyes, as if by doing so he might find his memory hidden within.

"Don't bother, *first born*," she said. "Gerath stripped your memory of us completely. He could not risk you telling the rest of the world of our existence."

"Are you saying that you are not mortal?" asked Gewey.

"We are old," she replied. "But not as old as Felsafell. More than that, I cannot say without permission."

"Why not?"

"The secrets of this place are ours to keep. If humans and elves were to discover them, they would surely come here and slaughter us."

"I think you underestimate them," Felsafell said. "True, both races have been barbaric at times. But I think you would find they are much different now from what you once knew."

"Perhaps," she admitted. "But it is a risk we are not willing to take."

"Why tell us anything?" asked Nehrutu. "Certainly you must fear that we shall tell people once we depart."

She laughed maliciously. "You seem confident that you will be *allowed* to leave."

Her ominous words stiffened Gewey's attention. He listened closely as she continued.

"Your sentence will likely be death, elf. So too will Darshan's, should he prove to be false. As for Felsafell, though we cannot kill him, we *can* imprison him for time without end."

"Then if you intend to kill me anyway," said Nehrutu, "I would like to know more about you. How did you come to be here, and how did you arrive in my land?"

Cloya looked at Grunyal, who nodded his consent.

"Very well," she said. "Seeing as you are the condemned, I will tell you what I feel is your right to know. Once I am done, Yasir will speak. After that... then we will see what happens."

Nehrutu nodded his acceptance. Gewey's tension was rising. In spite of what Felsafell had told him, he could not—would not—allow things to end like this. He would find a way out. Even if it meant a fight.

"Our people have dwelled here since the time of the first born," Cloya began. "From where we originated, we do not know. My first memories are of these jungles, as are the memories of all of us. It was here we learned of the Creator and of the well-spring."

"The well-spring?" Gewey asked.

"You have seen what the elves call the Waters of Shajir?"

He nodded.

"They originate from this land. But here they are far more potent. It is through the well-spring that our life is maintained. Here, we know nothing of sickness and death. It allows us to become one with the land and hear the voice of the trees and earth."

"I can understand why you would want to keep such a thing secret," remarked Felsafell. "Eternal life and perpetual health is a temptation very few mortals could resist."

"Which is why Gerath gave us his protection. Without it, we would have been destroyed long ago. Though we had nothing the *first born* desired, their children, and later the humans, were selfish brutes. They would stop at nothing, commit any atrocity, to extend their short, meaningless lives."

"This explains the long life of the desert elves," Nehrutu said thoughtfully. "It must be extended by the Waters of Shajir."

"Yes," Cloya agreed. "Even diluted and so far removed from its source, the well-spring would still be able to extend mortal life to some measure."

"But I don't understand why you hate the elves," Gewey said. "If my father has sealed you away like this, what harm could they have done to you?"

Cloya looked across at Yasir and nodded.

He took up the story, venom dripping from each word. "Long ago, a group of us decided to venture forth from the mountains. Our brothers and sisters begged us to stay, but we were convinced that the people of the world were not the savages Gerath made them out to be. We had been here on our own for so long and desired to know what the world was like beyond our borders. But we were fools."

He paused for a moment. "Humans saw us as monsters and drove us away. But they could do us no harm as long as we didn't allow them to corner us. In any case, they were still little more than animals, living in grass huts and hunting wild game to survive. They had nothing to offer us as a culture. So we moved west."

His eyes bore into Nehrutu. "The elves had yet to cross the great water. We had been told of their existence by Gerath and were anxious to meet them. So we built boats and sought them out. But what we found was not friendship and acceptance. No! The only thing we found was blood."

His giant hands were clenched and his voice was quickly becoming a feral growl.

"They viewed us just as the humans did... as monsters. They hunted us, delighting in our pleas for mercy. And without the well-spring, we could no longer heal ourselves as we once did. We tried to return home, but they cut us off from the sea. In desperation, we fled into the depths of the jungle where they would not follow. Only *I* managed to escape and make it back home. As for the rest of my people... they remain there, hunted and reviled. From what you have told us, they have long since lost all sense of who they are."

Nehrutu bowed his head and shut his eyes. "I am sorry for what my kin have visited upon you. I truly am. And you are right to demand justice. Should my life be the price my people must pay for their crimes, I offer it willingly."

"You cannot offer what you no longer possess, elf," Yasir spat. "Your life belongs to me. And know that I will take as much pleasure in hearing your screams as your kind did when hearing those of my people."

His words were followed by a long silence. Gewey's mind was racing, seeking a way out of their perilous situation. They had not been disarmed, and he was confident that they could fight their way out of the room.

"I can see your intent, Darshan," said Grunyal. "But know this. Even should you kill all three of us, there are hundreds more waiting beyond that door. And as you are cut off from the power of heaven here, I doubt you would find escape a viable option."

"I cannot allow this," Gewey protested. "Nehrutu has done nothing to you. These crimes you speak of were committed long before he was born. And by people of whom he has no knowledge."

"That is not true," Nehrutu cut in. "Though I had no knowledge of their origins, to this day my people still hunt the *yetulu*. And though I have never hunted them myself, I have never objected to it either. But I swear we thought them to be mindless animals who raided our villages simply for the sake of killing. Had we known, we would have done our best to make things right. I swear to you that we are not the same people we once were."

Yasir sniffed. "Your words are meaningless. And you will not escape your punishment."

"That is not my intent," Nehrutu told him. "It is clear that you will not be dissuaded. And my reason for our being here far outweighs the value of my own life. I would not jeopardize the fate of the world in a futile attempt to flee. Do as you will. But do so knowing that I am truly sorry."

"Would you have your vengeance, even at the cost of your people?" Felsafell suddenly asked.

Grunyal fixed his gaze. "What do you mean?"

"Your people are still being hunted in Nehrutu's land. Without the well-spring, those left behind are likely long dead. But they obviously had offspring. And those offspring are your people too. Would you leave them to continue being hunted and killed?"

"And how can I stop it?" he challenged.

"Allow Nehrutu to return to his home," Felsafell suggested. "Let him tell his kin the truth about your people. He need not reveal anything other than the fact that they are not beasts. He could try to return them to you."

Yasir let out a sarcastic laugh. "You expect me to trust an elf?" He shook his head and sneered. "No. I have this one in my grasp, and I will not let him go."

"If you will not accept the word of an elf," Gewey cut in, "then accept the word of Darshan, son of Gerath. Once my task is complete, I will personally see that your people are returned to you. But only if you do not harm Nehrutu. *And* you must allow Felsafell to leave unhindered."

Grunyal sat back and rubbed his furry chin. "An interesting proposal. That is, if you prove yourself to truly be Darshan."

"You cannot be considering this!" Yasir shouted furiously. "You cannot let them go! I demand justice! It is my right!"

"You can have your justice," Felsafell pointed out. "Or you can have your people home and safe. You cannot have both. You must decide which is more important."

Yasir continued to fume as he met Felsafell's eyes. "He will betray us, Grunyal. Even if our people return, he will lead the humans and elves here."

"He has a point," Grunyal said, turning again to Gewey. "What prevents you from telling people of our home?"

"Nothing... nothing but my word. But I will promise you this: once heaven is opened and your people are safe, I will erase the knowledge from the minds of both Felsafell and Nehrutu. They will never know they were even here. And the protection you have enjoyed from my father will endure through me."

After a long pause, Grunyal pushed back his chair and stood. "We need time to consider your offer."

Cloya rose as well, but Yasir remained seated, his eyes burning with rage and hands still balled into massive fists.

"Come, Yasir," said Grunyal. "We must speak alone."

With a hiss of hatred, Yasir got abruptly to his feet, sending his chair slamming against the wall. With a final hard look, he spun around to storm past Grunyal and out of the door.

"We will return, though I cannot say when," Grunyal told Gewey. "I will have food and drink sent in shortly."

That said, he and Cloya left the chamber.

"Do you think they will agree?" Gewey asked.

Felsafell shrugged. "I hope so. I could think of nothing else to offer them."

Nehrutu was staring down at the tabletop, his hands still folded in front of him. "I understand Yasir's anger. I would feel the same if someone had hunted and killed my people."

"What happened to the *yetulu* was a long time ago," Gewey told him. "And the poor creatures you know as Morzhash are totally unlike the *yetulu* here."

"I am not so sure." He looked up at Gewey. "We discovered that they possess a crude language. And we should have guessed that their attacks had a purpose. But we could not see beyond their appearance. To us, they were animals. And we hunted them as such."

"There is no use in dwelling on that," Felsafell said. "If they agree, you can only do what you can to help them now."

A few minutes later the door opened, and a *yetulu* entered carrying a large bottle and a bowl of fruits—none of which were familiar to Gewey. Without a word, he or she unceremoniously tossed both onto the table and departed.

Gewey picked up a round purple fruit and took a small bite. Thick juice squirted to the back of his throat, filling his mouth with a tart flavor that reminded him of a lemon, though with a slightly sweeter taste. The bottle was filled with cool water, but with no cups, they were soon passing it from hand to hand like wine around a campfire.

After they had eaten, Felsafell carried his chair back to its original position against the wall. Once settled there, he reached into his pack and retrieved a pipe. Soon the room was filled with an earthy smell that completely overwhelmed the pungent aroma of the leftover juices of their meal that, in spite of their efforts to be neat, had utterly soaked the tabletop.

Gewey searched through his own pack and found a rag. While attempting to clean the mess, he began to laugh inwardly. *Lessons of my father*, he thought. *Never leave a mess when you're a guest in someone's home.*

More than two hours passed before the door opened once again. Cloya entered alone and took a seat at the table, frowning when her eyes fell on the stains left behind from the meal. Gewey gave her a crooked, embarrassed smile. But this quickly vanished when Grunyal came in a moment later and sat down.

"Yasir will not be joining us," he said. "But he has agreed to your terms and will forgo justice."

"That is, assuming you can prove yourself to be the son of Gerath," added Cloya.

Nehrutu's relief was clearly visible. "Thank you."

"Do not thank me," said Grunyal. "It was Cloya who swayed Yasir, not I."

Nehrutu bowed his head to Cloya.

"You say I must prove myself," Gewey remarked. "How do you propose I do that?"

"Easily." Grunyal's lips crept up into a vicious smile. "You must tame the Ajagara."

"The Ajagara? What is that?" Gewey frowned, sensing a trap. Whatever they had in mind, it would almost certainly be deadly.

Grunyal chuckled. "I believe you encountered its children inside the mountain."

"Its children? You mean those lizards we fought were just..."

"They are but adolescents," Cloya said, mirroring Grunyal's malicious grin. "The parent is much larger."

"How large exactly?"

"What does it matter?" she replied. "If you are indeed the son of Gerath, its size should not be a problem for you. And if you intend to attain the god stones, you will need to pass through the Ajagara's feeding grounds, anyway. So now you can save your friends and complete your task at the same time."

Grunyal and Cloya rose, both still smiling. Just before they reached the door, Grunyal glanced over his shoulder. "You have until morning to prepare. And you will go alone."

Before anyone could protest, they were gone.

Nehrutu was the first to speak. "This is madness. You cannot undertake this alone."

"What choice is there?" Gewey countered.

"None," stated Felsafell. "And you will prevail."

"How can you know this?" Nehrutu demanded. "It took both me and Gewey together to hold off the last Ajagara we faced. And still, you had to help us. You heard what Cloya said. That was just one of its young. Without the *flow*, what chance does he have on his own?"

"I know this because I have faith," Felsafell replied. "Gewey has not come this far to fail now. He will conquer all that is set before him. This he has proven time and time again. I will not begin to doubt him now." He turned to the young godling and smiled. "But that is not to say I think you should be reckless. If you find yourself over-matched, you must run."

A nervous laugh slipped from Gewey's mouth. He steepled his hands under his chin. "If the adult is anything like the offspring, I don't think I'll have any other choice *but* to run."

"There is one other thing you should remember," Felsafell told him. "Grunyal said that you are to *tame* this creature, not kill it. This may be important, or maybe not, but do keep it in mind all the same."

"I will," he promised.

He did his best to calm his nerves and clear his mind. *I will not fail,* he thought repeatedly while setting out a bedroll from his pack. Even after lying down, these same four words still continued to echo in his head. Eventually, he could feel his body relaxing. Soon, sleep would come as a welcome respite from his worries.

At least in the world of dreams, he would be able to find peace, if only for a short time.

CHAPTER 13

It had been many years since King Lousis had traveled so far east. The demands of ruling had kept him a virtual prisoner in his own city. Often he had desired to take time out to revisit the people of distant lands—to taste their food, sing their songs, and to drink their wine. But never had he imagined that his visit would take the form of a siege.

The walls of Kaltinor loomed high in the distance: the ramparts were heavily manned, the gates shut, and the portcullis down. A thousand soldiers, all bearing the crest of Angrääl, were standing at the base of the curtain wall, looking as lambs to the slaughter. Whoever defended the city was a fool. The elves could massacre every man outside the gates without even drawing a sword. Mohanisi alone could scatter them like leaves in a storm with balls of fire.

Still, caution must rule the day, Lousis warned himself. In the past, the enemy had proved to be both cunning and ruthless. Sacrificing a thousand men might easily be a ploy to gain a later advantage. Or perhaps they simply wanted to test the power of Darshan. They would certainly have heard the rumors deliberately sent ahead that it was the son of

Gerath, not King Lousis of Althetas, who was leading the approaching army.

"What are your orders, Your Highness?" asked a young lieutenant that Lousis had assigned as his personal messenger.

"Send word to Kaltinor that I wish a parlay with the enemy commander," he replied.

The man bowed and sped away. Lousis drew a deep breath. With luck, the sight of well over a hundred thousand men and elves would be enough to convince them to surrender immediately.

The pounding of approaching hoofs had him looking over his shoulder. He spotted Lord Chiron, his face beaming with confidence. The king raised a hand in greeting.

Chiron returned the gesture, together with a bow. "Do you think they'll see reason, Your Highness?"

"I think we're in for a fight," he replied darkly. "Have you seen Mohanisi?"

"He is with Lady Bellisia. She and the other healers are preparing tents and beds."

"Let us hope they will not be needed."

Mohanisi arrived a short time later on horseback, causing Lousis to raise an eyebrow. Normally, the elf much preferred to walk or ride in the supply wagons. More than once, the king had teased him, saying that he feared horses. This invariably produced a look of irritation.

"As you can see, Your Highness," Mohanisi said after halting his mount, "I am quite comfortable atop this animal. I trust this will end your remarks."

"I am impressed," Lousis responded, smiling broadly. "It is not easy to conquer one's fears."

Mohanisi frowned at the light-hearted jab. "Do you have orders for the elves?"

"What do you suggest?"

"Their greatest power is in controlling the winds," he replied. "Should the city choose to resist, they can ensure that enemy missiles are deflected. Even the heavy explosive bolts will not be able to fall through once they combine their strength."

"And you?" asked the king.

Mohanisi surveyed the enemy lines. "I should be able to deal with the majority of those outside the wall. Archers can take care of any who flee."

"No," said Lousis. "Any who flee will be left alone. Darshan allowed those who surrendered in Baltria to live. We will learn from his example."

"As you wish. I will gather my people." Turning his horse with surprising ease, Mohanisi trotted away.

"Do you intend to surround the city?" asked Chiron.

"No," Lousis replied. "I will allow an avenue of escape. If the enemy sees a way out, they may well break ranks and shorten the battle. If we trap them, they have no choice but to fight on."

Chiron nodded. "A wise strategy. And one in keeping with Darshan's own actions."

"I'm not sure I would have done the same in Baltria," Lousis admitted. "I have watched those who serve the Reborn King ravage my home and slaughter my people. Mercy is a lesson I am forced to constantly teach myself."

"And yet you spared so many when we fought in Skalhalis. And I have seen you give many pardons since then."

"Yes. I have been merciful. But what I do as king, and what the ire in my heart wishes me to do, are often very different."

"I understand that all too well," said Chiron. His smile had vanished.

"Tell me," asked Lousis. "When the war ends, do you think peace between elf and human will last? Or will we return to our baser instincts and fall prey once again to hatred and vengeance?"

Chiron thought for a moment, then shrugged. "I don't know. But lately, I have often thought it might be best if the fears that I and the other elders once held do actually come to pass."

"And what would that be?"

"We feared a mixing of the races. That should we live alongside humans, in time, our race would simply be absorbed until the elves were no more."

Lousis tilted his head and raised an eyebrow. "And now you think this *should* happen?"

A tiny sigh slipped from Chiron's mouth. "I look at Celandine. She is proud and strong, with all of our grace and none of our flaws. She personifies what is best in both elf and human. She is not burdened by hatred and prejudice. If that is the future, then maybe we should embrace it. Perhaps you and I are destined to fade."

"Perhaps."

With a brisk movement of his hand, Lousis then shook off the sudden melancholy that Chiron's tone had created. "But for now, it is our task to ensure that such a future has an opportunity to happen."

The messenger returned a short time later. "The enemy commander has agreed to meet and hear your terms," he announced.

A few minutes later, the city gate and portcullis opened. Three men on horseback emerged and proceeded to a point about a hundred yards beyond their own lines.

Lousis's guard was gathered in seconds.

"You will still be within the range of their bows," warned the guard captain. "You should not go to meet them."

"Then we will wait for Mohanisi," Lousis said. "He will be able to protect us should there be treachery."

Mohanisi was quickly with them. With him riding alongside, Lousis and Chiron spurred their horses forward to meet the enemy. As they drew nearer, they could see more details of the three men waiting to talk. They were clad in fine polished armor and carried well-made swords, their hilts set with gold and precious stones. This finery was in stark contrast to the soldiers standing in front of the city walls. Most of these looked ragged and terrified, though it was difficult to see beyond the first row of men.

When they were only a few yards away, the man in the middle raised his hand in salute. Lousis returned the gesture.

"I am General Kylio Merwood," he announced. "These are my captains." He looked across to Mohanisi and Chiron and frowned. "But where is Darshan? I was greatly looking forward to meeting with him."

"I am King Lousis of Althetas," the king replied. "And if you know what is good for you, you do not want to meet Darshan. More importantly, he has no desire to meet with you."

"I see," said the general. "Well, little matter. Speak your terms."

"Lower your flags, throw down your arms, and surrender the city at once. In return, we will spare your lives and allow you to return to your master unharmed."

Merwood rubbed his chin and nodded. "A generous offer, Your Highness. Only a great fool would turn down such kindness. But then again, my mother always said that I was a fool." The two other men chuckled at his levity. "So now, allow me to counter your offer. Turn your army around and march back to where you came from as fast as you can. Once there, await the judgment of the Reborn King."

Lousis's anger began to boil. "Do you not see the forces arrayed against you? Do the lives of your people mean so little that you would see them slaughtered?"

"I would see you and the rest of your rabble be gone from my sight," Merwood responded brusquely. "Soon the mighty Darshan will be no more, and you will come to understand the price of defying the true ruler of this world."

Lousis glared at Merwood, who only smirked back at him. "You will pay for your stupidity," the king said. "And your people will pay with you." Sharply turning his horse, he galloped back to their lines with his companions hurrying to catch up.

"Ready your elves," Lousis instructed Mohanisi. "We attack at once."

The elf gave a quick nod and rode away.

"This man Merwood is a fool," remarked Chiron.

"I hope you're right," Lousis said. "But such arrogance generally derives from advantage. Have you or the other elves sensed any Vrykol about?"

"No. Not in two weeks. And even then, they fled when we confronted them."

Lousis frowned. "Yes. Mohanisi also told me that. Most curious."

The lines quickly formed, with the elves just behind the vanguard. Mohanisi then stepped forward and raised both arms. Almost instantly, the air above him burst into a massive ball of flames. The enemy positioned outside the walls began shifting about fearfully.

The air crackled and spat with furious power as Mohanisi sent the flames hurtling directly into the enemy's center. Instantly, those to the fore scattered, the agonized screams of the burning men behind them tearing the air to shreds. There was no need for another bolt. Not one soldier had remained at his position and the way to the city gate was already clear.

The human infantry surged forward bearing ladders, with the elves immediately behind them preparing to repel an avalanche of enemy arrows. But no arrows came. Almost unbelievably, the ramparts now appeared to be completely empty.

"Forward!" bellowed Lousis, his sword raised high. "The cowards flee the walls!"

The lines moved faster, their cheers increasing in volume with every yard they drew closer. Still, not a single man could be seen atop the wall. *A trick,* thought Lousis.

He continued to watch, awaiting whatever scheme the enemy had devised. "Onward, my brave men," he called out. But just as the line arrived at the point where Mohanisi had delivered the fireball, it suddenly came to a halt. All sounds of cheering also ceased. Lousis frowned. A full minute passed, and still, there was no further sign of them advancing farther.

A short time later, a soldier arrived. His face was pale and his hands were trembling.

"What is it?" Lousis demanded.

The soldier saluted. "Your Highness. They were children... women... old men." His voice wavered badly. "They are all dead."

"What in the name of heaven are you talking about?"

"The people that Mohanisi's fire consumed. Only the front line were men of fighting age. The others were lined up behind so we couldn't see them."

The king could hardly believe what he was hearing. A vicious knot of anguish gripped the pit of his stomach as he looked around for Mohanisi and then beckoned for him to come over. On being told of what had happened, the elf's ear-splitting cry of rage and remorse severed through the entire clamor of the field.

"Scale the walls," Lousis commanded. "And bring me the head of the enemy commander."

The soldier bowed and sped off.

Mohanisi was still clenching and unclenching his jaw and fists, utter fury on his face.

"It was not your fault," the king said, before Mohanisi could speak.

"No, you are wrong," he retorted. "I should have been more aware. I could feel the unusually intense fear rising from them, but I chose to ignore it."

"Even had they been real soldiers, they believed Darshan was coming. Their fear would have been the same."

Lousis's words went unheard. Eyes blazing, Mohanisi said, "Do not kill Merwood. Bring him to me." With that, he spurred his horse and urged it into a gallop toward the rear.

In less than half an hour, the men were over the wall, and very soon after that, the city gates creaked open. *That was too fast*, thought Lousis.

The king approached at a slow trot, his guard completely surrounding him as they went. One of the captains saw his advance and moved up to meet him.

"The monsters killed everyone, then fled through the east gate," the officer announced. "So far we have not found a living soul in Kaltinor." His eyes bore unmistakable rage and revulsion.

This fresh burst of terrible news hit Lousis hard, forcing him to squeeze his eyes tightly shut. It took him several moments to gather his wits enough to speak. "Send men to round up those who fled the fire. Give food and medical treatment to any who need it."

He opened his eyes and fixed them on the captain. "And see that none of them are harmed."

The captain saluted and hurried off. Moments later, Chiron arrived.

"Beasts," he said in a half-whisper. "What will you do now?"

The king stared at the open gate. "Bury the dead and move on."

"I'll send *seekers* to scout the way ahead."

Lousis nodded, then turned his horse around and made his way to his tent. After dismounting, he spotted Bellisia and Mohanisi talking quietly nearby. Bellisia was gripping her staff like a club, her knuckles white around its shaft. On seeing the king, the pair walked over at once.

"Come," said Lousis. He handed his reins to a guard. "Drink with me."

Normally, neither Mohanisi nor Lady Bellisia would partake of alcoholic drink, but on this occasion, they did not balk at the suggestion.

After escorting them into the tent, Lousis tossed his sword aside and produced three bottles. By nightfall, all of them were more than a little intoxicated, though they drank in utter silence.

A report came through stating that the majority of the people who had fled the fireball had been caught and tended to. Most of them were from Kaltinor. They had been warned that, if they ran, the archers on the wall would fill them with arrows. None had known anything of the slaughter within the city.

"Do not allow the children to re-enter until all of the dead are removed and buried," Lousis ordered the messenger. "And then only long enough to collect some belongings."

"So what shall we do with them, Your Highness?" he asked.

"I'll send a small group of soldiers to escort them back to Althetas."

"You cannot shelter the world," said Bellisia.

"Perhaps not," Lousis retorted. "But I will help *these* children if I can."

"And those that wish it, may make a new beginning across the sea," added Mohanisi.

"Would your people allow that?" Bellisia asked.

"I will not give them a choice," he replied sullenly. "The rest of the world is coming to our shores. This is a fact we will be forced to accept, be it now, or in a hundred years' time."

As midnight approached, Chiron joined them, along with Lord Brasley Amnadon and Eftichis. Though Lousis was grateful for the company of his new friends, he dearly wished Victis was with him as well.

It took three days for the bodies to be attended. Less than fifty people were found still alive in Kaltinor, and most of these had decided to go west with the other survivors.

When the *seekers* returned, they reported that the army holding Kaltinor had in fact been only five hundred men strong, and that it was now hastening with all speed toward the Goodbranch. Lousis considered pursuit, but eventually dismissed the idea. It would be difficult for even the elves to catch them, and he would not risk the possibility of a trap being laid for a small force separated from his main army. As much as he longed to capture Merwood, he knew that it was time to keep moving.

As they passed by more towns, Lousis was relieved to see that these had not suffered the same fate as Kaltinor. Likely, the fleeing dogs were in too great a hurry to get back to their master. By now, Angrääl would certainly be preparing for an assault. The only question remaining was, would they retreat north, or choose to meet his army head-on before it could cross the borders?

Three days before they were due to arrive at the banks of the Goodbranch, scouts reported that the army from Baltria was already awaiting them. Thousands of desert elves, together with a large contingent of humans—some recruited from riverside cities and from the Eastlands—were encamped on the west bank about thirty miles north of Sharpstone.

The hometown of Darshan, Lousis reflected. He'd been informed that Sharpstone remained completely untouched. A good thing too. He shuddered at the thought of Darshan's rage should he discover that the town in which he'd grown up had been ravaged. Only harm to his wife and child would be capable of eliciting greater anger.

They had only just made camp when a courier brought him a letter from the Baltrian army. As he read it, a smile slowly appeared. He called at once for Mohanisi. When he appeared, Lousis asked him to sit.

"The Baltrians have engaged and defeated the Angrääl force that was fleeing Kaltinor," he announced.

The elf instantly leaned forward. "And Merwood?"

"Captured!"

Lousis's cheerful smile turned into a wicked grin. "And he knows that we are coming. The letter says he is begging to be released, and has offered valuable information in exchange for freedom."

"And what was their response to that?"

"That the decision rests with me."

Mohanisi's normally stoic demeanor was now dark and dangerous. "And will you allow me to see him first?"

"I will, my friend," replied the king. "You have my word on that."

Mohanisi rose and bowed low. "Thank you." Without another word, he turned and left.

Once alone, Lousis wondered if he would truly be capable of watching while Mohanisi did whatever it was he had in store for the general. But the thought of the man's smug expression inflamed his anger; even more so when picturing in his mind yet again the countless devastated bodies of the innocent.

Yes, he told himself. *I think I will be able to bear it.*

CHAPTER 14

Mohanisi approached the tent with steady, deliberate strides. To him, the celebration going on all around was non-existent. A few of the desert elves had come to offer greetings, but after one brief look at his face, they understood that this was not the time and quickly backed away.

The king had wanted to be with him, but his presence was required elsewhere. For this, Mohanisi was thankful. In just a few moments, he would be face-to-face with the object of his fury. This was a time reserved for vengeance, and it would be a brand of vengeance that was best kept away from those close to him.

The two guards stepped aside and allowed him to pass without a word. His keen vision meant that adjustment from the brightness of the noon sun to the dim light of the solitary lamp took only a second. He saw him at once—General Merwood.

The man was sat on the ground and tied to the tent's stout center post, his clothes ripped and ragged from capture. He squinted as the sun struck his eyes. But they widened the moment the entrance flap closed and he could clearly see the tall figure of the elf standing over him.

"They told me you were coming," Merwood said, clearly trying to mask his fear. "Are you here to torture me?"

Mohanisi kneeled down to be at eye level. His face was expressionless, though his eyes burned with the fire of justice.

"Answer me, elf!" the general demanded. But his bluster quickly disintegrated as the threatening silence continued. Before long, a tear began to fall from the corner of his right eye.

In a blur of speed, Mohanisi's hand shot out and caught the drop on the end of his index finger before it reached the man's cheek. With exaggerated fastidiousness, he then wiped it away on the front of Merwood's shirt.

"Did you know that I would burn the people you placed in front of the gate?" he asked. "Or did you think they would flee so your men could fill them with arrows?"

"I only did what I was ordered to do," he whimpered. "My master..."

"Your master is far from here," snapped Mohanisi. The steel in his voice caused the man to flinch. "I want to know how you intended for them to die."

Merwood's lips quivered. "Darshan. Darshan was meant to kill them. We hoped his anger would drive him to leave the army and travel to Kratis alone."

"So you *did* want them to burn. And what else?"

Merwood looked confused. "I... I don't..."

Mohanisi reached out and lightly touched the general's forehead. There was a hiss of burning flesh, quickly followed by an agonized scream from Merwood. Mohanisi removed his finger, revealing a black spot.

"I will burn you one inch at a time on every single part of your body, which will prove to be infinitely more painful than the relatively quick death many of those poor innocent souls that you condemned suffered." His voice was calm and his countenance detached. "Then I will remove your manhood. And when you beg for death, I will heal you and begin all over again. Know that I can repeat this indefinitely. You can only avoid this fate should you choose to speak. Do you understand?"

By the time the elf had finished speaking, Merwood's features had already turned a ghastly shade of dirty white. The stench of urine was also filling the tent.

Mohanisi smiled. "That is good. I think we are now ready to begin."

He interrogated General Merwood for the next three hours without pause. The sounds of merriment going on outside the tent were an ironic backdrop to the severity of the grilling as he demanded answers about the plans and strategy of the Reborn King. When Lousis finally arrived, he looked at the two of them in surprise.

"I was just about to go out and find you," Mohanisi told him. He stood up and rubbed the back of his neck.

"I thought he would be... well... in far worse condition."

"I have questioned him about the enemy. He lied, naturally."

"I did not!" Merwood protested. "I swear it!"

"Silence!" Mohanisi snapped back. "Of course you did. You think I know nothing? You are no mere foot soldier. One such as you will have been in the presence of your master many times. This much I learned from my conversations with Jacob Nal'Thain." He turned to Lousis. "The general is incapable of betrayal. Should he attempt such a thing, it would kill him."

"So how did you learn anything?" the king asked.

Mohanisi smiled. "You would be amazed what can be discovered from lies. When you know what is *not* true, then the real truth often is revealed."

"So, what did you find out?"

"A large force awaits us one hundred miles to the north," he said. "They are meant to test our strength and give us a sense of confidence before we reach the Angrääl border. They want us to think that the battles in the west have diminished their ability to fight. Naturally, this is not the case. From there, the way is clear until we reach Kratis. That is where the real war will be fought. And I am sad to say, it does not appear to be a battle we can win."

"Is that all?"

"No. They are led by a new commander. Someone in whom the Reborn King has complete faith. And whoever he is, his soldiers have great faith in him, too. Also, the Vrykol are noticeably absent from their plans. No one seems to know where they are. This may serve us in battle."

Merwood stared at him, wide-eyed and mouth agape. "How could you have divined all this from what I told you?"

"Because you are a fool," Mohanisi said, waving his hand dismissively. "And had I the skills of Theopolou, I would have learned much more. But as is stands, we know as much as we need in order to proceed."

"And what of Merwood?" asked the king. "I thought you intended to... well... you know."

"I did," he admitted. "But fortunately, I came to realize that it is not *my* justice he must face." He paused before asking, "Are there still people remaining in Kaltinor?"

The king nodded. "Around a dozen of them. They refused to go west with the others, and I had no cause to force them."

Mohanisi looked down at the general. "Then I ask that Merwood be escorted back to Kaltinor. There, he will face the people he has truly wronged."

Spasms of fear began to shake the man's body. "Please. You promised that I would be released."

"I promised nothing other than I would not torture you if you answered my questions," Mohanisi countered. "I never said that you would not be brought to justice." He looked up at Lousis. "Is this agreeable with you, Your Highness?"

The king thought for a long moment. "My commanders would wish to interrogate him themselves first. But after they are done, I have no objections."

"They can do as they like. They will not learn any more than I have," Mohanisi stated. He gave Lousis an unnerving grin. "But I suppose there is no harm in being thorough."

Lousis chuckled. "Indeed. No harm at all."

Prince Lanmore gazed out over the ramparts. The chill air felt good on his skin, though for most of the men along the wall, it was far too cold for their taste. *It probably would have been so for me as well,* he thought. *When I was just a man.* But now, thanks to his master, he was much more than that.

"Any news from the south?"

The high-pitched whining voice of General Jasish had always irritated him. And hearing it now, while enjoying a rare respite from the burdens of command, made him want to throw the man from the wall. He was another noble-born fool who rankled at the thought that someone from the lower classes could rise so high. But unlike many of the others, he was a capable leader. A fact that, at this very moment, had saved his life.

"Kaltinor has fallen to the west," Lanmore replied. "The enemy will be upon us soon."

"I advised that you leave a larger force there... my prince." The words "my prince" were spat out as if a bitter seed.

"Your advice was stupid," he shot back. "Kaltinor means nothing. I only left that idiot Merwood there in order to establish the location of Darshan."

"And?"

"He is not with them."

The short, stocky man's shoulders sagged with relief. "That is good to hear."

Lanmore sneered. "Is that so? Is it a good thing to not know the location of our deadliest enemy? Have you any idea of just how powerful Darshan is?"

"I think so." In defiance of the cold weather, beads of sweat were forming on his brow. "At least I know what I've heard."

"You *think* so?" Lanmore mocked. "You know nothing. Darshan could wipe out an entire army with just a thought. He could descend from the heavens and burn every living creature to cinders with no more effort than it takes to draw a sword. Only the power of the Reborn King can stop him."

Jasish pulled a handkerchief from his pocket and wiped his forehead. "Then it is good we have our master's protection."

"That is the first intelligent thing you've said so far. Now go tell the other commanders to muster their soldiers. We march south in three days."

"South, my prince?"

Lanmore gave him an irritated look. "That is what I said. Now that Merwood has served his purpose and led them to believe that we cower behind our walls, we will go forth and slaughter our foes like the dogs they are. King Lousis and his army will never gaze upon the spires of Kratis—that I swear."

Jasish hesitated. "Is it true that you are from Kaltinor, my prince?" Lanmore gave no reply. "I see. Forgive me for asking," the general quickly added. After a brisk salute, he hurried away with quick, nervous steps.

Kaltinor, thought Lanmore. Yes, that was my home.

And because of Merwood's bloodlust, it was now all but gone. Its people killed needlessly to satisfy one man's insanity. Through the power bestowed upon him by his master, Lanmore had peered through Merwood's eyes and heard his thoughts. He'd seen the bodies of his brother and mother sprawled out in the streets like heaps of abandoned rubbish.

He did his best to feel outrage and anger, but could muster only mild displeasure. Had the power bestowed on him stifled his human emotions? No, that could not be. He felt rage toward the army that now sought to destroy him; he felt hatred for Darshan; and he felt a love for those who were loyal to his king. He laughed softly. Even that fool Jasish. But the murder of his family was bringing forth no urgent desire for justice or revenge.

Still... no matter... Merwood had earned his reward. He closed his eyes and reached out across the vast distance separating them.

He quickly found the man. "Merwood," he whispered. "You have failed me. You have failed Angrääl. And you have failed your king."

"Please," he responded weakly. "I did as you commanded. I told them nothing. I swear it."

"You are a wretched fool." Lanmore pressed deeper into his mind. "Little better than a wild animal. No one ordered you to slaughter the people of Kaltinor. Your only task was to find out if Darshan marched with the West's army. Nothing more."

"But my prince. I could not escape. I only did it to give myself time to..."

"Time to what?" His thoughts were like a claw wrapping itself around Merwood's spirit. "Time to save your miserable skin? Better for you to have died."

Merwood was weeping now. "I beg you, my prince. Spare me."

Lanmore laughed viciously. "I'm not going to kill you, fool. But you will wish that I had."

Mohanisi and King Lousis sat together talking by a small fire just beyond the king's tent. Only light conversation was permitted. It had been decided between them that dire subjects had no welcome until the sun rose. Meanwhile, Chiron and Bellisia were acquainting themselves with their desert kin, and the commanders were organizing their ranks with a man from Baltria called Bevaris. He was a knight of Amon Dähl, and, from what Lousis could make of him, an extremely capable leader and tactician.

As dusk turned into night, the merriment rose to a fever pitch. Lousis had never seen such joyous abandon as that being exhibited by the desert elves. Stories of their prowess in battle were already spreading quickly about the camp. It was enough to give hope to a doomed cause.

A distraction, he thought. *A mere distraction from all this death.* He wondered if he would ever be able to look at Darshan again without feeling anger. In his mind, he knew this was not the young god's doing. It was the only path to victory. But his heart was telling him something different. If only Darshan would engage and defeat the Reborn King before they faced the enemy in battle...

He shook off these dark thoughts and returned to his wine. A short time later, Mohanisi produced a small silver flute—something Lousis had never seen him do before—and began to play an unfamiliar yet delightful tune. Clearly, the elf was being influenced by the high spirits of his kin.

"Is that a melody of your homeland?" Lousis asked when the music was over.

"No," he replied. "It is something new."

"A new song for a new age," mused the king.

Mohanisi smiled, then began to play again. This time, the tune was slow and sweet. It reminded Lousis of his time with Selena just after their wedding. He pictured her face and imagined himself lying beside her, his arms wrapped around her soft shoulders, her warm breath gently ruffling the hairs on his chest. He closed his eyes and allowed the fantasy to take him.

"Your Highness."

The voice of the messenger broke the spell. Lousis sighed and forced a smile. A lad of no more than eighteen years was standing beside him.

"What is it?"

"You are needed, Your Highness," said the young boy. "There is something amiss with the prisoner."

Reluctantly, the king rose to his feet. After exchanging curious glances, he and Mohanisi followed the boy back to the tent where Merwood was being held. They could hear his screams sounding out when still fifty yards away. But these were not the screams of a man being tortured for information. These were screams of sheer madness and terror.

On entering the tent, they saw Merwood, still tied to the post, thrashing his head wildly from side to side and screaming incoherently. Standing close by were one of the desert elves and a young Baltrian captain. Both of them appeared confused and unsure of what to do.

"What happened?" Lousis demanded. "What did you do to him?"

"We did nothing," the elf stated. "We have not even begun to question him yet."

Kneeling down, the king looked hard at Merwood. His eyes were in a faraway place and his face contorted. Blood was dripping from his mouth where he had bitten his tongue.

Lousis grabbed the man's head and held it fast, forcing their eyes to meet. But there was no look of recognition or reason there. "What could have done this?" he asked.

Mohanisi touched the king's shoulder. "Allow me."

Lousis moved aside, watching closely as the elf bent down and placed his hands on Merwood's face. Almost at once, the general's thrashing ceased, and his eyes grew even wider. But the contact only lasted for a few seconds. With a surprised gasp, Mohanisi suddenly withdrew his hands and stumbled backward as though receiving a violent shock.

Lousis caught his shoulders and held him steady. "What is it? What did you see?"

Mohanisi rubbed his temples and shook his head. "I... I cannot describe it." He looked at Lousis with a horrified expression. "And yet, it was something I will never forget." Politely shaking off Lousis's hold, he kneeled in front of Merwood. "Another's mind has broken his will. It has left him in a place where nothing but dread and pain exists. Pain beyond reckoning, and fear the like of which makes the darkest nightmares seem a pleasant and kind place to dwell."

"Is there anything you can do?" asked Lousis.

"Nothing," he whispered. The vision of what he had witnessed was still fresh in his mind. His hands trembled and his chest felt heavy. "No one should be forced to endure this, whatever their crimes."

In one single fluid motion, Mohanisi drew his dagger and plunged it hard into the middle of Merwood's heart. The man gave a single gasp and shudder, then the light in his eyes was gone.

"Burn his body," ordered Lousis.

He and Mohanisi returned to the fire, but Mohanisi was no longer in a mood for merrymaking. Very soon, he retreated on his own to a quiet spot at the south end of the camp.

Shortly after that, Lousis retired to his bed. Seeing the elf so troubled had brought the reality of the coming battle back to the fore.

Even so, as he had done every night since leaving Althetas, he made sure that his dear love, Selena, was his final thought before allowing sleep to take him.

CHAPTER 15

The sun was setting as Aaliyah entered the gates of Althetas. The light from the street lamps that once gave the city a friendly glow and brought a feeling of security to its inhabitants now illuminated the faces of a troubled and despondent people. With the king away and only sparse news coming regarding how the war was faring in the east, there was little to be happy about.

Construction and repairs had all but ceased as most skilled humans and elves were now away, serving with the army. In fact, the city's population was currently reduced to less than a quarter of its former number.

Aaliyah had felt the presence of her people the previous day, and could not help but wonder about their feelings about discovering such conflict. War was virtually unknown to them. Aside from the Morzhash raids, there were no real threats to their society. Indeed, her own initial reaction to the turmoil had not been favorable. She recalled her revulsion on learning that elves had been attacking their own kind. Back then, she'd had grave doubts that her people and those of this land could ever be truly reunited. But now, bitter experience had helped her to understand the foolishness of that attitude. It was the *world* that had molded the people here. The weakness of both races could not be blamed. Or at least, they should be given understanding.

On reaching the king's manor, she noticed at once how relieved the guards appeared to be at the sight of her.

"Lady Aaliyah," called one of the men. "Your return is most welcome. The queen will want to see you right away. I will take you to her."

"Thank you," she replied, bowing her head. "Are my people residing within the city walls?"

"No, My Lady. They have chosen to remain aboard their vessels."

Aaliyah frowned while following the guard to the queen's parlor. This did not bode well. To refuse hospitality was not normally the custom. She needed to find out what had transpired as soon as possible.

Queen Selena was sitting in a plush chair near a crackling fire, reading a book. Her face lit up at seeing Aaliyah. Tossing the book aside, she sprang to her feet and hugged her in a tight embrace.

"I am so happy you are here," she enthused. "Life here is dull beyond imagining. Perhaps you can bring some light into these dismal halls."

Aaliyah returned the embrace, but her expression remained one of confusion. "I would have thought that with my kin docked in your harbor, there would be plenty of excitement."

Selena huffed. "They've been here for days, and still refuse to leave their ships. Jacob met with an envoy when they first arrived, but they would say nothing other than they wished to speak with you as soon as possible. I must say, I *am* disappointed by their lack of courtesy."

"As am I," she agreed. "Such behavior is not typical. Did they give their names?"

"Only one, who called herself Estrella. From what Jacob said, she is in charge of the fleet."

"Yes, she would be. Of that, there is no question."

"So you know her?"

Aaliyah nodded slowly, her eyes narrowing with concern. "I do. And the fact that she has come here may not be what I was hoping for when I sent for my people."

"So what does it mean?"

Aaliyah forced a smile. "Perhaps nothing. Dark thoughts enter my mind so easily now that I am separated from Nehrutu. I will send for Estrella in the morning. She will not refuse my summons."

Selena offered Aaliyah the chair across from where she had been seated. "I understand. I never imagined that I would love again after the death of Lee's father, but I was wrong. Lousis makes me feel young and alive." Tears welled in her eyes. "And now I fear that I shall lose yet another love... I don't think my heart will be able to endure it."

Aaliyah leaned forward to gently touch the back of her hand. "I will not tell you that I know for certain your husband will return. But then, I cannot tell that to myself either. However, I do *believe* he will. And that belief keeps me from despairing." She leaned back again and smiled. "I will say this: of all the humans I have met, King Lousis is by far the most blessed by fortune. If anyone can evade death, it is him."

Selena began to laugh softly and wiped away her tears. "You are not wrong. Lousis is most certainly blessed with good luck. King Victis told me the very same thing before he went south. He said that, even if the enemy were to completely blot out the sun with arrows, Lousis would still be standing in the one spot where none landed." She sighed. "I suppose I will have to follow your example and believe that he will return safely."

Both women reflected in silence for a moment. Aaliyah then said, "When I arrived, I noticed that your guards seemed to be on edge."

"Yes. Since your people appeared, rumors of both hope and disaster have been rampant. No one knows for certain if they are here to help us or not. Poor Jacob has done his best to reassure the people, but they have not known him long enough yet for him to earn their trust. They constantly cry out for Lousis. Thankfully, Jacob was called away to Skalhalis for a few days and is currently removed from the constant needs of the city."

"I have only known him for a short time," said Aaliyah. "But he is a strong young man. I'm sure he will win them over, eventually. And after tomorrow, all rumors will be laid to rest."

The two women talked for a while longer. Aaliyah then excused herself and retired to her room. Before going to sleep, she had a messenger take a letter of invitation to the lead elf vessel.

Why have you come, Estrella? The question continued to plague her as she drifted off to sleep.

She woke just before dawn. After quickly dressing, she sought out Selena and found her in the same parlor as the previous night. The queen was sitting at a small table beside the window, a steaming plate of eggs and ham in front of her. Another plate had been set opposite in anticipation of Aaliyah's arrival.

"I miss the food in Valshara," remarked Selena. "But this is not too bad."

The two women ate quietly, both of them glancing at the door each time the sound of footfalls drifted in from the hall.

"When do you think your kin will arrive?" asked Selena.

"It depends," she replied. "If this were a casual affair, I would say early. But as this is not, I would guess that we shall see them after midday."

Just then, a young servant girl arrived. She curtsied formally. "Your Highness. The elves from the harbor have arrived and are awaiting an audience."

Selena looked at Aaliyah. "It would seem either they think this a casual visit, or they are unwilling to wait."

Aaliyah thought for a moment and then stood. "After introductions, I would ask that you allow me to speak first, Your Highness."

"I think that would be best," Selena agreed. She turned back to the servant. "How many are there?"

"Three, Your Highness."

"Then have them brought to the king's library. I will receive them there."

The servant curtsied again and hurried away.

"I think it will be a better place than the throne room. A bit more ... personal."

Aaliyah nodded her approval.

The king's library was nearly as large as the council chambers, with every wall completely filled with shelf after shelf of leather-bound tomes. Rows of lamps were positioned in the middle of the room between two long mahogany tables, and there was a large desk to the far right.

"Lousis loves this room," mused Selena. "His passion for books rivals even that of my son."

They took their places behind the desk, with Aaliyah choosing to stand to the right of the queen. When the door opened, two guards escorted the three elves inside.

The middle elf was a tall female with long, sleek black hair similar to Aaliyah's. Her features were similar too, though a little less angular and delicate. Her eyes were azure and sparkled in the lamplight. She wore a flowing green dress tied at the waist by a white sash. Her two male companions, one with honey blond hair and ice-blue eyes, the other with auburn hair and eyes of deep violet, both wore white satin tunics with intricate, black threaded embroidery. Each carried a small dagger and a leather pouch on his belt.

Selena got to her feet as the trio approached. "You are most welcome to my city. I am Selena, Queen of Althetas. I regret that my husband, King Lousis, is not here to greet you as well. But sadly, he still fights in the east."

All three elves bowed in unison.

"I am Estrella, but this I am sure you already know." She gestured to the blond elf. "This is Bruhintu, brother of Nehrutu, and on my other side, Lhasari, who is a cousin of Mohanisi. I thought it appropriate that they should join us."

Selena bowed and smiled warmly. "You are indeed most welcome." She turned her attention to Lhasari. "I wish your cousin was here, but he is with my husband."

This drew a look of displeasure from the elf.

"And my brother?" asked Bruhintu.

"He is with Darshan," Aaliyah answered, quickly adding, "Or, as you know him—Shivis Mol."

"And where is Shivis Mol now?" asked Estrella, her eyes fixed firmly on Aaliyah.

"The answer to that will take much explanation," she replied coldly. "If you would sit, I will tell you everything that has transpired."

The three elves sat on the chairs offered.

"First of all, it would be best if you know the story from its very beginning," Aaliyah continued. "And that would be best told by Queen Selena."

Selena nodded and began the tale, first of all telling them everything she knew about the Dark Knight. For more than two hours, she explained all the events leading up to the war, including a background of the First Great War. Mention of this brought uncomfortable glances from the elves, but she ignored them and pressed on.

"And that is what has brought us to this present state of affairs," she finally concluded.

"Interesting," remarked Estrella impassively. "And what can you add to this story, Aaliyah?"

"Much," she replied. "But that will take at least as long to tell as did the queen's part. Perhaps you should take repast first."

"No," insisted Estrella. "I would hear what you have to say now."

Aaliyah bowed and folded her hands in front of her. "As you wish."

She spoke in detail of her time with Darshan, and of the part they had played in the war. When she mentioned her bonding with Nehrutu, both Estrella and Bruhintu's eyes widened.

"It seems you have been through much," Estrella said, once Aaliyah's tale had ended. She turned to Selena. "I would speak to Aaliyah alone."

A heavy frown formed on Selena's face. She leaned forward in a forceful posture. "I realize that you are Aaliyah's kin. But I was unaware you are not accustomed to displaying civility. You have docked in my harbor for days and we have not harassed you. You have been welcomed into my city and my home. And now you have been entrusted with knowledge reserved for only the trusted few among us. Yet you presume to order me about as if I were a simple servant." She rose to her feet, her eyes unblinking. "You will address me as Your Highness. I am the Queen of Althetas and deserve courtesy. Do you understand?"

Estrella bowed her head, though her expression remained unreadable. "I apologize if I have been discourteous. It was not my intent. But the events that have led us here, combined with hearing what you and Aaliyah have told us, have robbed me of all else but my purpose." She stood and bowed again. "Please, Your Highness. I would like to speak to my sister privately."

Selena's eyes shot to Aaliyah.

"Yes," she affirmed. "Estrella is my sister."

"I should have guessed," said Selena. "Very well. If you wish to talk alone, I could show Bruhintu and Lhasari around the manor. Your kin have taken much pleasure in the art my house boasts. Perhaps you will, too."

Both elves stood and bowed respectfully in acceptance of her offer. Once Selena had led them from the room, the two women sat, Aaliyah behind the desk and Estrella opposite.

"What have you done, sister?" scolded Estrella.

"Only what I knew to be right."

"You were sent here to bond with Shivis Mol. Not to get involved in the wars and politics of this savage world."

"I have already told you what has happened since we arrived," she retorted. "I was unable to bond with Darshan. He loved another. As did I."

Estrella's face darkened. "Yes. Nehrutu. I should have never allowed him to go with you. His feelings for you have clearly influenced your objectivity."

"You are wrong. My feelings for him had only been set aside out of a sense of duty. They were always as strong as his were for me. All we have done is complete a bond that should never have been ignored in the first place."

Estrella shook her head. "You have shamed yourself. And you have endangered our people."

Aaliyah sniffed. "Our people were already in danger. We were just unaware of it. I involved myself because there was a need. This world will not suffer isolation now that the barrier is down. We fight not only to save this land, but our own as well."

"Nonsense. What power could conquer us? Only the gods themselves possess such strength. You have allowed the fear that pervades the people here to infect you." Estrella clicked her tongue. "I pity you, dear sister."

Her smug, arrogant manner caused Aaliyah's anger to rise. "And you, *dear sister*, speak from ignorance."

"You see?" she chided. "Your rage comes out so easily now. Your passions govern your actions. No longer can you control yourself... and no longer can you be trusted it seems."

"That is not for you to say," she countered. "My loyalty has never been in question. And though you are my sister, do not presume to know my heart... or my motives."

"Are you not bonded to Nehrutu? Are you not engaged in a war that is not your own? Have you accomplished even a single task assigned you?" A hint of suppressed anger burned in Estrella's eyes. "And where are your ships?" She held out her hand before Aaliyah could reply. "Do not even bother to try and justify the death of so many of our kin. Or that you allowed those who survived to march off to certain death with the husband of this human queen. I am sorry, sister, but you are not worthy of the position you have been given."

She rose gracefully to her feet and turned her back before speaking again. "You may have wondered why I bothered to come here."

"I have," Aaliyah admitted. "Your work with the builders was only just beginning when I left. I am greatly surprised that you would abandon it."

"I came because I love you," she replied. Her tone was suddenly tender and kind. "You are my family. And now that mother is gone, my only family. When I was told of your encounter with Shivis Mol and the conflict ravaging this land, I knew I had to come to your aid."

"Then aid me," Aaliyah said. "Why berate and insult me?"

"I *am* aiding you." Her voice dropped to a mere whisper. "You are to board my ship immediately and return home."

Aaliyah sprang up from her chair. "I will not! You have no authority over me."

Estrella turned to face her sister again. There was both sadness and pity in her expression. "I am afraid that I do. I was sent by the elders to ascertain the situation and deal with it as I see fit. And given your current condition, I have no other choice. You will return home, and I will ensure that the bond between the elf Kaylia and Shivis Mol is broken."

Aaliyah let out a scornful laugh. "So that you may bond with him yourself?"

"If I can."

"Then you are a fool. You do not wield the power to sever their bond. And even if you did, Darshan would never join himself to you."

"Perhaps not," she said. "But I will try, nonetheless. And if that means the death of his current mate..." The idea of killing one of her own kind was clearly upsetting to her, and the final few words stuck in her throat for a moment. "Then so be it."

"None of this matters," Aaliyah told her. "You will never be able to get close to her. And I will not leave."

"I am truly sorry, but there will be no more debate. As we speak, a team of elves await my command to force your compliance, though I do hope you will come willingly. And, as far as the elf Kaylia is concerned, the human named Jacob gave us all the information we required. Believe me when I say that I did not enjoy playing on his trust, but it was necessary. And though the people here imagined we have been idle aboard our ships, we have not. I sent scouts out to gather the rest of what I needed to know. Long before you arrived, I knew that you had failed, and that another had bonded with Darshan." She reached out and touched Aaliyah's hand. "No matter. That has already been attended to. By now she is either dead—the bond broken—or both."

Aaliyah recoiled at her touch. "You have no idea what you have done. Darshan will..."

The door to the library suddenly burst open, causing the two women to spin around. Approaching them with long, confident strides was Kaylia, her eyes ablaze with unyielding intent.

"Darshan will not need to know of your stupidity," she said, her voice booming off the walls and startling Estrella. "And before you ask... yes, I am Kaylia, *unorem* of Darshan and mother to his child. And you are an arrogant fool who is lucky I am not the untempered youth I once was. Otherwise, I would burn you to ashes for what you tried to do."

Aaliyah's face lit up. "How did you know? How did you escape?"

Kaylia's furious gaze never left Estrella. "It was not *I* who needed to escape."

Estrella's look of surprise quickly faded, to be replaced by an imperious smirk. "So, you evaded my people, only to deliver yourself to me. And you think to call *me* a fool?"

"I did not evade your people," Kaylia corrected. "I allowed them to live. That they were my kin and thought they were doing right was the only thing that saved them." She took hold of Aaliyah's hand. "And what saves you now is that you are Aaliyah's sister. She is as a sister to me as well, so I will confine my wrath."

Kaylia looked deep into Aaliyah's eyes. "Are you all right?"

She smiled and nodded. "Though for a moment, I feared that you had been killed."

"Those she sent did not possess the power to harm me."

"But how did you know they were coming?" Aaliyah asked.

The corners of Kaylia's mouth turned up into a tiny smile. Pride washed over her entire aspect. "Jayden told me."

Aaliyah gasped, then laughed loudly for several seconds. After calming herself, she looked at her sister. "Forgive me, Estrella. But you really should do as Kaylia says."

Estrella closed her eyes, but they quickly shot open again, filled with frustration.

"You will not summon your people to come here," cautioned Kaylia. "I will not allow it. It would only result in needless deaths."

Estrella's face turned red with fury. "Just because you are able to block my connection to my kin, that does not mean you have the strength to prevent me from doing what I came here to do."

"I can do more than that," Kaylia warned. "I can trap your spirit, and the spirits of all your people, should you threaten me or those whom I love again."

Estrella snickered. "You lie. No elf possesses the power of the spirit."

"You think not? Aaliyah does. Nehrutu and Mohanisi as well. All of them have learned to use the *flow* of the spirit."

Estrella looked at Aaliyah. "Is this true? Have you achieved such power?"

Aaliyah nodded.

"How is this possible?"

Kaylia's face softened. "Through the same love that you would seek to destroy. You are so like Aaliyah was when she arrived on these shores. And had I not been so immature, I would have known what to do when we first met." Suddenly, the room lit up with a million tiny lights, and the tinkling of bells and laughter filled their hearts with unrestrained bliss.

"Behold—the spirit of this world," Kaylia continued. "It has been denied to you for far too long. Its beauty and majesty have been just out of reach. But no longer."

She paused to smile at Estrella. "You did not come here because you need the power of Darshan. Nor have you come to enlighten your kin. Though your powers are great and your spirit a match, you are really no different to the elves ... or even the humans ... of this land. And soon you will see that. And when you do, you will know the joy that both your sister and I feel when we imagine the future."

For a while, Estrella was unable to speak. She reached out to touch the lights with her fingertips, a tiny laugh escaping her lips each time. "How is this done?" she asked finally.

Kaylia took both of her hands. "Through love. Nothing else can bring you to this place. And you have it within you. We all do. It is the one thing all people, be they human or elf, have in common. But unlike humans, *we* are fortunate enough to be able to see it manifested."

Kaylia drew Estrella's spirit into her own. "Can you feel it now?"

"Yes," she whispered.

Kaylia let the *flow* slowly subside and helped Estrella into her chair. She and Aaliyah then sat close beside her.

After a few minutes, Estrella looked up at Kaylia, her face awash with regret. "Can you ever forgive my ignorance?"

"Of course," she replied. "Think no more about it. We are all guilty of ignorance at some point. And as I said. Aaliyah is as a sister to me. So I will think of you in the same way."

"And you, Aaliyah. Can you...?"

"There is nothing to forgive. I love you, and I know that you acted because of your love for me—and for our people."

"So what should I do now?" Estrella asked. "If the battle is already joined, we can be of no help to Darshan, or to King Lousis. What use can we serve?"

"War has ravaged this land," answered Kaylia. "Your people have skills that are desperately needed and would be most welcome."

"You shall have all that I can provide," Estrella assured her.

"The queen and Jacob will know where you are most needed," Aaliyah said.

"Then I will see to it at once."

"Not yet." Aaliyah gently squeezed her sister's arm. "We have some time, and I have missed you dearly. Will you sit with me and talk for a while?"

Estrella gave her a loving smile. "Yes. I would like that." She looked to Kaylia, who was about to rise. "And you should stay, too."

"You must forgive me," she said. "But I left my son in Valshara and am anxious to return to him."

Estrella nodded understandingly. "Of course."

After exchanging embraces with the two of them, Kaylia left the room.

"I did not want to ask her," said Estrella, once they were alone. "But are you certain that Darshan will prevail?"

Aaliyah smiled. "Certain? No. But I do have faith."

CHAPTER 16

King Lousis wiped away the blood dribbling down his face and steeled himself to face a fresh wave of attackers. Never before had he seen the armies of Angrääl moving with such alacrity and precision. The enemy's constantly repeated battle cry of "Never to Kratis" rolled across the field like ominous claps of thunder.

Their first battle had gone well. Mohanisi had been absolutely correct about the enemy's location, also their relatively few numbers. In less than a day, they'd had them on their heels and in full retreat. This new and unexpected engagement, however, was something completely different.

Whereas before they had easily outnumbered the enemy, this time it appeared as if the Reborn King had sent every soldier he had out to fight. Even so, with the elves easily able to navigate such obstacles, the rocky terrain should have given an advantage to Lousis's men. Only it wasn't working out that way. The positioning and adjustments of the enemy were uncanny.

"Fall back, Your Highness," shouted one of his guards. "They're coming again."

But Lousis knew there could be no retreat. He could hear the clashing of steel close behind him. Their right side had collapsed, and they had been flanked. To go back would only put him in greater danger.

"Then let them come!" he yelled.

It was almost with a feeling of relief when he saw that the soldiers bearing down on them were clad in the typical armor of Angrääl. The native barbarians, also fighting for the Reborn King, wore animal skins and carried giant axes or swords as long as a man. Their savagery had already gained them a fearsome reputation.

His guard took the brunt of the assault. The sound of steel clashing on steel, together with the crazed shouting of the combatants, combined to create a deafening demonic symphony. Hard as Lousis's guard fought, it wasn't long before two enemy soldiers slipped through the line and ran straight for the king.

He gripped his sword and broadened his stance. The first attacker to reach him swung his blade in a high arc, threatening to split him in twain. But it was a clumsy movement. Lousis had time to step aside and ram his shoulder into the man, sending him stumbling to the ground. Without hesitation, the king then crouched low and was just in time to thrust his sword straight into the second onrushing attacker's gullet.

He spun to finish off the first soldier, but one of his own men had already stepped back and plunged a knife into his neck. The king gave the guard a quick nod of thanks, but there was no time for him to return the gesture. Inch by inch, they were losing ground. Three more Angrääl soldiers forced their way through and came after Lousis.

Furiously, the king fought to keep them at bay. The flashing of blades and loud grunting of men straining every sinew to gain an advantage was growing ever more intense.

Again and again, the enemy pressed Lousis back, several times finding his flesh and opening shallow wounds.

Using his superior experience and sheer adrenaline to outmaneuver his foes, he did his best to ensure that only one soldier at a time could get through to him on the rock-strewn ground, and then only with the opportunity to attack directly from the front. This tactic was working for now, though he knew they would find a way of getting behind him soon enough. Either that, or more of them would break through and simply overwhelm him. Continuing like this was merely delaying the inevitable.

Well, I'll take at least some of them with me, he told himself.

Abandoning all further attempts at mere defense, Lousis lunged forward, slashing down hard. There was a moment of grim satisfaction when his blade cut deep into an enemy's thigh, but almost immediately after that, a loud hiss of pain escaped his mouth as cruel steel pierced his armor and cut into his ribs. This had been expected though. Fighting through the pain, he pushed himself farther forward. The soldier who had struck him was now too close to use his sword again and was scrambling back. In his haste, he stumbled on a small rock. This was all the invitation Lousis needed. His blade swiftly took the man's head.

In a flash, the third enemy moved in, stabbing hard at Lousis's chest. But fortune was with the king. He twisted sideways, and the point of the blade merely glanced off his breastplate. His armored elbow then shot out and smashed into his attacker's mouth, sending blood and teeth flying. Roaring with battle lust, he drew his dagger and sank it into the soldier's sword arm.

He glanced over his shoulder to see where the first man he had wounded was, only to find that he had now backed away, to be replaced by five more Angrääl troops racing into the attack.

Snarling, Lousis removed the head of the third soldier while he was still staggering about and clutching at his profusely bleeding sword arm. He then glared at the five new aggressors closing in on him. *So ends King Lousis*, he thought. He began to laugh. *I should have never made it this far, anyway.* Raising his sword high, he charged forward to meet his fate, the name of his queen springing forth loud and clear.

"Selena!"

He had taken only a few paces when searing heat suddenly hit Lousis dead in the face, bringing him to an abrupt halt. Just ahead, flames exploded from the earth, engulfing all five of the advancing Angrääl soldiers and yet more of the enemy behind them. Their screams of agony overcame even the desperate clamor of battle. Some victims began running wildly around in circles, while others were rolling on the ground in futile attempts to extinguish the flames.

Gasping from his exertions, Lousis scanned the area. It took him a moment, but eventually, he spotted Mohanisi walking toward him.

"Thank you," he said.

"Do not thank me yet," Mohanisi replied. "The enemy is still at our back. The left flank is holding, and the desert elves are reinforcing the right. But the day is far from over. Luckily, they have not yet unleashed their explosive bolts, but I suspect they do not want to risk killing too many of their own men. Once we re-establish the lines, that may change."

Lousis could see several deep gashes in the elf's armor, but thankfully no blood. "Suggestions?" he asked.

"First of all, I need to get you clear of the battle." He looked to where the king's guard was still fighting. Some had been killed, but the ball of fire had taken a deal of the spirit from the Angrääl soldiers. They were now giving ground.

"Help them," ordered the king. "They risk their lives to protect me."

Mohanisi thought to object, but could see that Lousis was determined. Holding out his hand, he caused a threatening wall of flames to hover immediately above the battling men. This terrified the enemy still more, driving them back at an even faster rate. In a flash, Mohanisi made the fire descend, so creating a barrier between the guard and the Dark Knight's soldiers.

"Protect your king!" he shouted.

The guard responded immediately and ran toward their monarch. Once they reached Lousis, Mohanisi led them to the rear. As they moved along, Lousis could see desert elves pouring in from the left and center.

"If they can clear out the enemy and reform the lines, we will last the day," Mohanisi remarked. "But we cannot sustain many more assaults."

The healing tents and the area surrounding them had not been breached. For this mercy, at least, the king was grateful. "They surprised us," he said. "But that will not happen again."

The only people within this relatively calm area were the wounded and the healers. All others were battling in the fray. Guilt gripped Lousis. He should be fighting with his people.

"You must stay alive," insisted Mohanisi, as if hearing his thoughts. "Your soldiers need you." He gave the king a sideways grin. "And I promised your wife that you would return safely."

Very little news came from the lines, but as dusk approached, the stream of wounded began to significantly lessen. Once Mohanisi was confident that the enemy would not again threaten the rear, he left to join the healers. He tried to persuade Lousis to go with him, but the king flat-out refused. "I am not so hurt that I need healing," he stated emphatically. "If I cannot fight, I will at least be here in open view so that my people know I am still with them."

The explosions Lousis was dreading to hear, never came. They had some of their own explosive bolts that had been captured in both the west and in Baltria, but the supply was fairly limited. It had been decided that they would only be used as a means to cover their retreat, should it come to that.

As the sun sank below the horizon, the sounds of battle faded away to virtually nothing. Only the cries of the injured and laments of those mourning the fallen could be heard above the howling of the stiff north wind.

Lousis was greatly relieved when he at first spotted Lord Chiron riding in from the front. But his relief quickly turned to concern on realizing that the elf had been badly hurt. His left leg was soaked with blood that still seeped from a heavy wound to his lower body. Also, his arm on the opposite side was hanging limply down.

"A hard day," called Chiron. His forced smile turned into a grimace when he pulled on the reins with one hand to halt his horse. "Perhaps tomorrow will be better."

"Go to the healers," commanded Lousis. "Or you may not see tomorrow."

Chiron looked down at his bloody trousers. "Oh, it's not as bad as it looks. A misstep on my part. I should look after my people."

Lousis's face hardened. "You will do as I say. If you don't, I will send for Lady Bellisia. I'm certain she will have a way of convincing you."

Chiron sighed. "As you wish, Your Highness." He pointed to Lousis's own injuries. "But you will accompany me. You have neglected yourself long enough."

"Very well."

Lousis grabbed the halter of Chiron's horse and led it toward the healers. On approaching, they saw Bellisia standing squarely in front of the biggest tent, one hand planted on her hip, the other wrapped firmly around her staff.

"It looks as though she's been waiting for us," remarked Chiron with a boyish smile. "I think I will tell her that you would not allow me to come earlier."

Lousis laughed. "So you would have me suffer her wrath alone? And I thought you were my friend."

"Even friendship has its limits."

Both men burst into laughter.

"And what is there to be so cheerful about?" Bellisia scolded. She motioned for two attendants to help Chiron down from his saddle.

"We live to fight again," Lousis replied, though with less humor. "For now, that is enough."

Ignoring his words, she quickly examined them both. "Take Lord Chiron inside. I can treat King Lousis here."

"I will join you when I can," said Chiron as the attendants led him away.

Knowing that she needed to conserve her strength as much as possible, Bellisia did not attempt to heal Lousis completely. However, she did do enough to close up his wounds and stop any further bleeding. Lousis thanked her and retired to his tent.

Once there, he stripped off his armor and put on a fresh shirt and pants. Shortly after that, just as he sat down at a small table, his commanders began to report in. The enemy had pulled back the moment the sun started to set. It was assumed they didn't want to engage elf fighters in the dark and lose their advantage. The right flank, once reinforced, had held fast and even gained ground, but the losses were terrible.

It was fully dark when Chiron returned from the healers. He looked remarkably restored, and had fully recovered the use of his right arm. As soon as he sat down, he produced a flask of brandy and pushed it across the table.

"A final drink for a doomed man?" joked Lousis.

"Maybe," he replied. "But then again, we might live one more day."

Lousis took a long drink. The sweet taste of the elf brandy soothed his parched throat and relaxed his tense muscles.

"If the only thing we learn from your people is how to make this, I would be happy." He handed the flask back. "And as you think we might live to see another day, I hope you have more of it."

Chiron took a drink and sighed. "Only enough for one more night, I'm afraid."

"Then survive we must."

After they had finished the brandy, Chiron could see that his friend was weary and in need of rest. He rose to excuse himself, but just as he was about to leave, a messenger entered and handed the king a folded parchment. As Lousis read, his face became dour.

"The enemy commander wishes to speak with me," he said.

"Where?" asked Chiron.

"Here. He asks if I will grant him safe conduct to and from our camp."

"He cannot be serious."

"It would appear that he is." He handed Chiron the note.

After reading it carefully, the elf elder tossed it onto the table. "It must be a ploy. More than likely, he will send an assassin in his stead."

Lousis's eyes narrowed. "I doubt it. He would know that I am well protected, and will take extra precautions. Besides, killing me under a flag of truce could possibly galvanize the soldiers and make the fight that much harder for him."

"Then why?"

"I think he just wants to see my face before he destroys me."

Chiron huffed a laugh. "You think it is so simple?"

"I do," he affirmed. "And that tells me much about who we fight."

"What does it tell you?"

"That our enemy is certain he will win tomorrow's battle."

"Arrogance!" spat Chiron.

Lousis shook his head. "No. Confidence."

He wrote a reply and then ordered a small pavilion to be erected at the front line. Quickly, he cleaned up and donned his armor and sword once more. His guards were waiting outside when he left to meet the enemy commander.

He didn't need to wait long. While sitting at a table under the pavilion, he spotted the silhouette of a lone horseman approaching across the moonlit field. The man rode tall and proud in the saddle with the skillful ease of a seasoned soldier.

"What can you see?" Lousis asked. Chiron was standing behind him, together with Bevaris and Lord Brasley Amnadon. His guard completely surrounded them.

"He definitely rides alone," Chiron responded. "And he looks to be unarmed."

Lousis rubbed his chin thoughtfully. "Brave," he muttered. "Very brave."

When the rider dismounted, Lousis could see that he wore a gold circlet on his brow that matched his flaxen hair. This, combined with resplendent black armor and his exceptionally broad shoulders, gave him a truly regal appearance. Though noticeably weaponless, the king's guard still stood in his path and motioned for him to raise his arms. The man politely complied while the guards searched him thoroughly.

"He is unarmed, Your Highness," announced the guard.

The man bowed low. "I am Prince Lanmore, heir to the throne of Angrääl and general of all the armies of the Reborn King."

Lousis bowed in return. "I am King Lousis of Althetas. Beside me is Lord Chiron, Lord Amnadon, who is Commander of the Western Armies, and Bevaris, Knight of Amon Dähl. I bid you welcome." He gestured to the chair that had been placed for their visitor. "Please sit."

Lanmore did as bidden and folded his hands on the table.

"So what is it you wish to discuss?" Lousis asked.

"Your surrender, of course," he replied, as though Lousis should have been well aware of this already.

Lousis laughed. "Then you have wasted your time coming here. I see no need for surrender. Just because you gained a temporary advantage through surprise does not mean you have won the war."

Lanmore heaved a sigh. "I implore you to reconsider. You are vastly outnumbered, far from home, and with no hope of reinforcements. Must more die for this foolish campaign? And even if you were to win the day, you could never take Kratis. Please stop this madness and go home."

"Did your king stop when he invaded my lands?" snapped Lousis. "Did he stop when he murdered my people and burned our cities?"

"That was an unfortunate misunderstanding," he replied. "And one for which the Reborn King would like to make amends."

Lousis could barely suppress his rage. "A misunderstanding, you say? Thousands of men, women, and children are dead, and you call it a misunderstanding?"

"Of course," Lanmore replied. His tone was *not* smug. Rather, it was sincere and self-assured. "Most war comes from misunderstanding. Surely a wise ruler such as yourself knows this. My king sought only to liberate the West from the tyranny of Darshan. Nothing more."

"Darshan is not our enemy," said Lousis. "Your master is. Darshan did not invade the kingdoms of the West. That was the work of the Reborn King. No one else!"

"And now he sees that he was mistaken and only wishes to make peace with you." Lanmore's face suddenly darkened. "But should you continue on your present path, peace will become impossible."

Lousis scrutinized the man for a long moment. He was confident... yes... but also somehow uncomfortable. Why? Why would a man of such stature and position seem so uneasy with himself? Then it came to him. A sly smile upturned the corners of the king's mouth. He leveled his gaze. "Let us not continue with empty conversation. The deceptive words of a noble are ill-suited to a man such as you. I do not know you personally, but I do know a real *prince* when I see one."

He leaned back and cocked his head. "You are no prince. A general and talented leader, I have no doubt. But you lack the nuance of true nobility." He could see that this was angering Lanmore. *Good.* He held up his hand. "Please do not misunderstand me. I congratulate you on your elevation. But if you would permit me to pass on some friendly advice?"

Lanmore regained his composure and nodded. "Of course. I am always in need of wisdom. Particularly from a king of your experience and ... reputation."

Lousis smiled. "Do not mince words and try to illicit anger from me. Such banter is not becoming of a fighting man. You came here to face your enemy before battle, and that is all. A brave act, granted. But it is the act of a warrior, not a prince." He allowed his words to sink in for a moment. "A noble would never put himself in direct peril unless there was no other choice. And if I were to accept your terms, you would allow us to withdraw to your borders, but no farther than that. Once there, you would move swiftly to crush us."

"You are very perceptive," Lanmore said. "And you are correct in saying that I *am* ill-suited to my station. I am not a noble... like you. But the Reborn King has seen fit to grant me status and power, and I will see that his confidence is well-placed." He chuckled softly. "And I did *not* expect you to accept surrender. As you said, I only wished to meet with you so that I would know the face of my enemy."

"And for that I am grateful," said Lousis.

The two men locked eyes for several seconds.

"Then I believe we have concluded our business," Lanmore said at last. He stood and bowed. Lousis did the same. "When the dawn comes, I will slaughter your army. But know that as I do so, I hold you in high regard. Truly,

I wish circumstances would allow your survival. The world will be diminished once you are gone."

"I thank you," said Lousis. "But I am not ready to depart this life just yet."

Without another word, Lanmore turned and mounted his horse. Lousis watched as he disappeared into the night.

"Should we have allowed him to leave?" asked Bevaris.

"I think there is nothing we could have done to stop him," Chiron remarked. "He possesses power that, as a human, you may not sense. But I can. The Reborn King has touched his spirit."

"It makes no difference," said Lousis. "I would not dishonor myself by breaking my word. And if the man wields the power that you say, then he probably could have killed me right then had he wanted to. But he didn't."

"So you think it really was just about facing his enemy?" asked Bevaris.

"I do. He is a man of valor. And that is what a man such as he does."

"So what happens now?" asked Amnadon.

Lousis continued to stare into the darkness. "Now? Nothing. But when the sun rises, Prince Lanmore will likely make good on his promise."

"Is there nothing to be done?" asked Bevaris.

Lousis turned to Chiron and gave a thin smile. "You told me that you have only one flask of brandy remaining. I think perhaps we should drink it now."

CHAPTER 17

When Gewey woke, he could see that a bowl of fruits and berries had been placed on the table, along with a clay pitcher and three cups. Nehrutu and Felsafell were both seated and talking in soft whispers.

"I was about to wake you," Nehrutu told him. "It's almost time."

After stretching and groaning the lingering effects of sleep away, Gewey took a seat beside the elf. His stomach immediately began to growl, but he knew it was not a good idea to eat. He'd likely be running for his life very soon, and that would be a lot more difficult to do with a full belly.

As they talked, the door opened and Cloya entered. For a moment, she just stood in the doorway, staring at Gewey. Then, with two massive strides, she was at the table just opposite of where he was seated.

"Will you really bring my people home?" she asked.

"I will," he assured her. "If I have to carry them here one by one, your people will see their home again."

After a long and thoughtful pause, she placed a vial on the table. "I don't know why, but I believe that you are who you claim to be. Even so, if your powers are diminished, you cannot hope to defeat the Ajagara alone. This might help."

Gewey picked up the vial to examine it. It was filled with a thick red liquid. "What is it?"

"If you are trapped, throw it as far as you can," she answered. "Be sure that it hits something hard enough for the glass to break. It will give you the time you need to escape."

Before Gewey could ask more, she had spun around and left the chamber.

He took a long look at the vial before tucking it into his belt.

"You see?" said Felsafell. "Fortune is in your favor."

A short time later, three *yetulu* arrived to escort Gewey from the room. As they wound their way through the halls, Gewey continued to marvel at their construction. Everything here appeared to be crafted from the earth, with absolutely no other materials used. *Did they simply will this place into being?* he wondered. The pulsing veins of blue light were everywhere. Had he not been cut off from the flow, he was sure that he would have felt it intensely in this place.

Occasionally they passed a room containing more *yetulu*. Mostly they were relaxing, just sitting, talking, and laughing. But some were busy crafting elaborately woven baskets or sewing colorful beads to leather bags and satchels. *Such a simple life,* he thought. It was becoming clear why they were afraid of discovery. And why Gerath had given them his protection. They could never adapt to the outside world. The fact that their kin who dwelled in Nehrutu's homeland had become feral was proof of that. These people were connected to this place, and to one another, in a fundamental way. It was deeper than anyone could fathom. They *belonged* here.

After walking for about three miles, they finally came to an ascending stairwell. His escort halted and gestured for him to continue up alone. After thanking them, he began to climb.

On emerging at ground level, the scent of flowers and jungle foliage was potent—almost intoxicating. He was in a small clearing carpeted by dense moss and surrounded by a half-circle of tall trees and thick vines that blotted out the bright morning sun. Within this shaded area, the air was cool and pleasant. Almost before realizing it, he found himself smiling.

Grunyal was standing at the far end. "Are you prepared?" he asked.

After checking his sword and feeling into his belt for the vial that Cloya had given him, Gewey nodded and confirmed that he was.

As he drew closer to Grunyal, the jungle behind the *yetulu* parted, revealing a walkway with dense undergrowth running along both sides. It was as wide as a city street, but unlike the rest of what he had seen, this was crafted from polished blue marble with onyx veins inlaid throughout.

Grunyal pointed down the path. "This will lead you to the hunting grounds of the Ajagara. Return from there alive, and you and your friends will be free to go. I wish you luck, Darshan."

Gewey gave a brief nod and moved forward. The moment his feet made contact with the marble surface, the jungle closed in behind him.

Glancing back, he gave a hollow laugh. "I guess there's only one way to go now."

The walkway stretched for more than two hundred yards. At the end stood a white stone archway with the symbol of Gerath carved into its apex. Beyond that, Gewey's vision was obscured by a heavy mist.

He took a moment to steady his nerves before stepping through the arch. Instantly, tiny beads of moisture began forming on his face and hair. In next to no time, his clothes felt as if they had been soaked in a rainstorm. The ground was now rocky and uneven, and the scent of the jungle had been replaced by the foul stench of rotting flesh and sulfur.

Ignoring his ever-increasing fear, he pressed on. After fifty yards, the mist thinned a little to reveal tall, thin rock formations and a few low bushes and brambles that had forced their way up through the craggy ground. His eyes darted left and right, but he was only able to see for a short distance. *If the Ajagara hunts in this*, he thought, *it probably sees* me *just fine*.

The regular escaping of his own breath sounded like gale-force winds against the dead quiet. Twice the clatter of a falling stone had his heart racing and his hand flying to his sword. But nothing came.

For half an hour, he stumbled on through the fog with no idea of where he was heading or what he was going to do. For all he knew, the Ajagara could be watching his every move. If the creature's young were any indication, his sword would be useless against it. Aside from the vial of liquid given to him by Cloya—which he was clueless as best how to use—he had no way of fighting. *I'm a bloody rabbit*, he thought, recalling his father's words after snaring one of these behind the barn. He had held up its lifeless body and said, "Be happy you're not rabbit. Everything eats rabbits." This sobering thought threatened to rob him of his courage and was quickly pushed aside.

After a few more minutes, Gewey found himself almost wishing for the beast to reveal itself. *Let this be over and done with*. As if in response, he heard a familiar hiss over to his right. This was followed by the scraping and clacking of talons on stone.

Drawing his sword, he prepared to flee. He strained his eyes in an attempt to catch a glimpse of the Ajagara, but it was useless. The creature was clearly an experienced hunter and knew exactly how far away it needed to be. The threatening sounds shifted from Gewey's right to his rear—then back to his right again. The dank air was muffling the noises a bit, but he knew that the rock formations and hard ground could deceive the ear. The beast was trying to confuse him.

He glanced to his left and spotted a pillar of rock less than twenty feet away. He cautiously took a step toward it. But the Ajagara had no intention of allowing him to reach it.

It charged at Gewey from slightly behind and to his right. In appearance, it was identical to the creatures he had encountered in the tunnel, but this adult was as big as a fully grown bull. And despite its size, it was moving with unbelievable velocity, its dagger-like talons churning up large chunks of rock and earth as it rushed forward.

Gewey ran with all the speed he could muster. Even without the *flow*, his naturally inherited power was considerable... and that was the only thing that saved him. He reached the pillar just in time. Even as he rounded it, he could feel the hot blast from the beast's foul-smelling breath. Faced with this obstruction between itself and its prey, the creature ground to a halt, at the same time letting out a high-pitched screech.

"You'll not get me that easily," Gewey shouted with a surge of defiance.

He spun around. The Ajagara was hissing and moving slowly around the rock, saliva dripping from its colossal maw. It was a keen reminder that one bite would be fatal.

Each time the Ajagara tried to advance around the pillar, Gewey backed away. The creature's yellow, reptilian eyes were unblinking, intent on its potential meal.

It swiped at him with a massive claw, and Gewey was only just far enough away to avoid being sliced to ribbons. But he knew he couldn't stay in this same spot forever, going around in circles. Sooner or later he had to do something. But what, he didn't know.

When the Ajagara struck out again, he brought his sword down hard on its foreleg. But it was as he had feared. The blade bounced off as if striking solid granite. And while the counter-attack hadn't injured the beast, it had certainly angered it considerably. Hissing with rage, it retreated a short distance and then charged at the pillar. Its massive shoulders crashed into the rock, sending pieces of loose stone raining down on Gewey's head.

Again the Ajagara charged, its impact this time causing large cracks to form in the pillar. One more assault like that, and Gewey knew it would collapse and his protection would be gone. He looked urgently around for alternative cover, but with the mist still shrouding his surroundings, there was nothing in sight.

As the beast backed away for a third assault, Gewey crouched low, his leg muscles tensed and ready to spring into action. Halfway through the Ajagara's charge, Gewey took off and raced past it in the opposite direction. It was to his left, so he veered right, hoping to give himself an extra second or two of advantage.

Unable to stop its forward momentum in time, the creature whipped its tail, attempting to take out Gewey's legs. But he'd already seen what damage the tail could do and was ready for this. He leaped high and clear of the lethal swipe, taking off again the moment his boots struck the earth. The crash of the crumbling pillar, together with the savage hissing of the Ajagara, followed his flight.

Within moments, he could hear the scrape of talons rapidly closing in. The Ajagara was faster than him, so outrunning it was not an option. His only hope was to outmaneuver the beast. Small boulders and bushes whizzed by, and his legs were already burning from the strain. His eyes searched desperately for another pillar, or at least a rock big enough to hide behind. But there was nothing.

He knew that in only a matter of seconds it would be all over... the beast would have him. Not daring to waste time by looking back, he tried to hear precisely where it was. The hissing was even louder now. And then came a gurgling sound.

It must be opening its mouth, ready to strike!

Gewey planted his left foot hard down, then swung his body as sharply to the right as he could, hoping that this would throw the Ajagara off-balance.

There was a loud snap of closing jaws. It had missed. But he only managed to run a few more paces before an outstretched claw caught his right heel, taking away his balance. While falling, in a final attempt to save himself, he twisted his body around in mid-air and stabbed upward with his sword. Tiny rocks ripped open his shirt and tore at the flesh of his back as he crashed onto the ground.

The first thing he saw after the jarring impact was wide-open jaws filled with jagged teeth directly above him. The tip of his sword had stabbed into the soft flesh at the roof of the Ajagara's mouth, with the forward momentum and sheer weight of the creature sinking the blade in even deeper. Gewey felt a flash of elation. But this was short-lived. The Ajagara thrashed its head wildly, jerking the sword clean out of his hand. He had missed the creature's brain, and was now completely unarmed.

He scrambled to his feet while the Ajagara was still clawing at the sword in an attempt to pull it free. Again, he spurred his burning legs into a fast run, praying that the creature would remain occupied with this for a while longer. But after less than twenty yards, he heard the clang of steel on stone as the weapon was thrown aside. Another piercing hiss of rage tore through the air.

Still looking urgently for anything he could use for shelter, Gewey ran on. But rather than finding another stone pillar looming before him from out of the mist, he saw a tall cliff face materialize. He was trapped.

For a wild moment, he cast his eyes around for a loose rock or a stick with which to defend himself, but quickly realized how ridiculous an idea that was. The Ajagara would be on him in moments. It was then that he remembered the vial. Caught up in all the stress of the situation, he had temporarily forgotten about it. Hastily, he fumbled at his belt to remove the small glass tube.

Looking up, he saw the Ajagara stampeding straight at him. Blood from the wound he had inflicted covered its lower jaw and was being splattered in all directions as it ran. Gewey threw the vial with all his strength. But the throw was too hard. The beast would be on him before it landed. He dove to his left, but found himself being slammed against the cliff face by a massive claw, the impact forcing every bit of air from his lungs. Pain shot through him as two of the talons dug spitefully into his chest.

He barely heard the tinkling of breaking glass over the feral hisses and snarls that were heralding his end. Unable to do anything more to protect himself, he held his breath and prepared to be torn apart. But incredibly, instead of that happening, the Ajagara suddenly ceased snarling and turned its head in the direction of the shattered vial. After licking the air with its long, forked tongue several times, it released its hold on Gewey. Gasping with relief, he slid heavily to the ground. Ignoring all else, the beast slowly turned away from him and walked off into the mist. Whatever was inside the vial, it was obviously far more important than its intended meal.

Gewey remained absolutely still for a moment, his heart pounding and adrenaline coursing like fire through his veins.

"Thank you, Cloya," he panted while getting to his feet. He promised himself that, should he make it out of this place alive, he would find some way to repay her.

He wanted to look for his sword, but not knowing how long the Ajagara would remain distracted, decided to leave it behind. He gazed up at the sheer wall of rock towering in front of him. It was far too high and smooth to climb. *So which way?* His thoughts raced. The sound of the Ajagara crying out in the mist forced him to choose quickly. *I'll go right,* he decided. *If not, I'm dead. So this has to be the way.*

He ran for a short distance, but the loss of blood that flowed from his wounds began to make him light-headed. Tearing off his shirt, he did his best to bind himself and continued at a walking pace. Another series of feral screams sent chills down his spine, though thankfully they did not sound as if they were getting any closer.

He pushed on for more than an hour, still not finding any way either over or around the cliff face. Grunyal had said that what he sought was beyond the Ajagara's hunting grounds. Not that this helped much right now. After fleeing from the creature through the impenetrable mist, he had completely lost his bearings.

Just as frustration was setting in, he noticed that the ground was beginning to change from rocks and hard earth to thin grass. Soon, this gave way to lush moss peppered with delicate white flowers. The foul odor of the hunting grounds was also gone, replaced by the smell of clean soil and damp turf.

He drew in a deep, cleansing breath. His wounds ached, but the bleeding had stopped. Even so, he was weak. Should anything else attack, it was unlikely he could put up much of a fight.

After another hour of walking, he came upon an opening in the cliff's rock face. It was just about tall and broad enough to allow him to enter. Its smooth sides and sharp corners made it obvious that this was not a natural cave.

"This has to be it," he whispered to himself.

As he stepped inside, the walls lit up with veins of blue light. With a rush of relief, he saw an iron door only ten yards farther down, etched with the symbol of Gerath.

He touched the thin blue veins with the tip of his finger. Almost instantly, he felt the injuries on his chest tingle and grow cold. It was the familiar sensation of a healer using the *flow*. Though he still could not sense the *flow* around him, it lifted his spirits to see evidence that it did, in fact, exist in this place.

He stood still until his wounds were completely closed. Satisfied, he walked to the door, pausing to run his hands over Gerath's symbol before turning the knob. It swung open easily, as if well-oiled and often used. Beyond was a twenty-foot square room with red granite floor tiles and marble walls veined with the same blue light.

At the far side of the room, his eyes fell upon what he had fought so hard to acquire. Two masterfully crafted golden pedestals had been placed on either side of a small round table. On top of the table was an unadorned silver box. But his heart sank as he looked more closely at the pedestals. Both of them were empty.

As he drew nearer, he could see piles of dust on the ground. *They have been destroyed!* He let out a frustrated cry and fell to his knees in defeat. Hope was lost. He knew he could not be a match for the Dark Knight without the power of the god stones.

He had no idea of how long he kneeled there. His mind was a storm of confusion and sorrow. Kaylia and Jayden would fall under the power of his enemy. His friends and allies would all be hunted. The elves would be slaughtered. And the world would burn.

"Why, father?" he shouted. "Why let me come so far, only to take away my one chance for victory?" Spitting out a curse, he got to his feet.

He turned his attention to the box on the table. It was far too small to contain the god stones. No—the dust on the floor was definitely what remained of them. He tried to raise the lid, but it was locked. He then attempted to pick the box up, but it would not budge.

Gewey frowned and rubbed his chin. He searched his belt for something to pick the lock, but had nothing that would work. Then he remembered something else... it was in his coin purse.

Suppressing a laugh, he reached inside and felt the tiny silver key that Felsafell had given to him at the Chamber of the Maker. He took it out and smiled.

"Let's see if you fit," he murmured.

The key slid in effortlessly. Gewey held his breath while turning it to the right.

Click! The lock opened, and he was able to raise the lid. Sitting inside was a crimson jewel about the size of a hen's egg. He stared down at it, uncertain what to do next. Finally, he shrugged and picked it up.

"I am so happy you are here, my son," came a voice from behind him.

Gewey spun around and gasped. There stood Gerath. Dressed in white robes, his entire body was surrounded by a silver aura. His face was just as Gewey remembered—dark hair and chiseled features. Handsome was not the word for him. Beautiful was more accurate. Beautiful in a way reserved only for the gods.

Gewey could feel the power emanating from his father and knew at once that, unlike the essence he had seen in the Black Oasis, this was not a shadow. He could feel a wave of strength and power that he'd only ever experienced once before—when battling Melek. *But how could this be? How is this possible?*

"You...?" he managed to say. "You're real."

Gerath gave his son a loving smile. "Yes. I am real. And I am here."

"But you're trapped in heaven? How can you be here?"

"I am here because I love you," he replied softly. "And I am here to help."

CHAPTER 18

At first, Gewey thought it must be some kind of trick or hallucination. Gerath—here the entire time. But there was no denying the power he felt. His confusion gradually turned into rage as a succession of realizations began to occur.

"How could you do this?" he demanded. "To me? To the people of this world? Why wait until now? Why allow so much death and suffering when you could have prevented it all?"

"I was powerless, my son," he replied. "As I am still powerless."

"That's not true," Gewey countered. "I can *feel* your power."

Gerath shook his head. "What you feel comes from within yourself, not from me. I am now a part of you." He sighed sadly. "There is so much I would like to show you. So much I would like to explain. But now it is far too late. Your time is at hand, and mine is done." He gestured to his right. Two chairs appeared from nowhere. "But I would at least like to sit and talk with you one time... as father to son."

Gewey stared at him with barely contained anger. But there was something in his father's expression that he was unable to resist. Eventually, he threw up his hands in exasperation and dropped heavily into the offered chair.

When Gerath was also seated, he gazed at his son with tear-filled eyes. "You have become everything I had hoped you would be. Strong, pure, and true. All the qualities my brothers and sisters feared you would lack. But I knew. I knew you were better than the rest of us from the moment I first saw you."

"That is *not* how you looked to me," Gewey snapped back. "Melek showed me my time in heaven when I was with him in Shagharath." He was well aware that his father had been trying to deceive the other gods through his mistreatment of him. But he was angry, and it was the only thing he could think of to say in order to lash out at him.

Gerath raised an eyebrow. "You met Melek? And in Shagharath, no less. You are even stronger than I imagined if you survived that encounter."

"I almost didn't," he explained. He began telling him about his time with Melek, and how he had eventually sent him back to Shagharath. But the moment he mentioned Jayden, Gerath seemed to hear nothing else.

"You have a son?" he whispered.

"Yes," Gewey replied. "It is for Jayden and Kaylia that I fight. And why I came here."

"Tell me about him," Gerath pleaded. He leaned back and closed his eyes. "Tell me about my grandson."

Gewey did as his father asked. He described Jayden's features and his smile. The color of his eyes and the tone of his skin. Every last detail. "He gives me courage beyond measure, father," he concluded.

Gerath was smiling when Gewey stopped talking. He remained motionless for more than a minute. Slowly, he opened his eyes and nodded. "Thank you."

Gewey nodded in return. "Perhaps when this is all over, you can see him for yourself."

A look of pain passed briefly across Gerath's face. "If only that were possible." He straightened his back. "Forgive my melancholy. Pleased continue with your story about Melek."

At the end of the telling, Gerath was smiling again. "It is good you have such friends. And fortunate. Melek would have never have guessed that a mortal could lay him so low."

Gewey grinned involuntarily. "I did enjoy seeing the look on his face when Weila sank the dart into his back."

Gerath let out a hearty chuckle. "A well-deserved fate. I pray he is never able to plague the world again."

"He won't," Gewey assured him. "Not if Maybell has anything to say about it."

The two gods both burst into cheerful laughter. For a brief spell, they were just a father and son sharing a pleasant moment together. But the moment soon passed and Gerath's countenance hardened.

"If Melek showed you your time in heaven, then you will have seen that I did not wish to abandon you, Darshan. You must know that I wanted to stay and watch over you."

"I know," he replied. "And I understand that the other gods would never have allowed it. I know all of this. Even so, I can't help but feel..."

"Betrayed?" he said, finishing off Gewey's thought.

"Yes. Betrayed." His anger began to rise again. "Why didn't the gods intervene? Why send me to earth? Why did I have to witness so much destruction and pain?"

"You have been in the moral realm for too long to understand one simple truth."

"And what truth is that?"

"That the gods are not wise. True, we are powerful. But without the Creator to guide us, we are like lost children. Humans and elves see us as beings with wisdom that surpasses their own. But that is simply not true. Strip away our power and we would not last a day in your world."

He took a deep breath. "Son, know that I did not send you here willingly. I was commanded to do so. When the Creator took me into *herself, she* passed *her* wishes on to me." His face grew dark and his tone sorrowful. "And for the very first time, I hated *her*. For the first time, I actually considered defying *her*. But I knew defiance would come at a terrible price."

"And so you obeyed and sent me here," said Gewey.

"Yes. I obeyed."

"And now what? The god stones are gone. You say you are powerless. Without help, I will not be able to defeat my enemy. Did you send me here to die?"

"I pray not," Gerath told him.

"Then what am I supposed to do?"

"You are supposed to do what you know you must," he answered. "You must face the Dark Knight and defeat him. You must put an end to his insanity."

"But who is he?" Gewey asked. "All this time, and I have learned almost nothing about him. Who he is? Where did he come from? And why is he doing this?"

Gerath sighed. "He is a mortal man. One with due cause for hatred and revenge, but still nothing more than a mortal. He feels betrayed by the gods, and by those he once held dear to him. Most of the details I do not know. I arrived here just before he seized the *Sword of Truth* and have only been able to discover a little. He was once a great knight who served Amon Dähl. However, he turned his back on them and sought the *sword* for himself."

"This much I have already heard," Gewey said.

"Then you know as much as I."

Gewey frowned, disappointed that he would not learn more about his enemy's past. "So why did you come here?" he asked. "Why choose this place?"

"It was the only place I knew where you were sure to eventually find me. When I told you that I had obeyed the

Creator, it was only partly true. I knew you would need my help." Gerath paused to give a small chuckle. "Here I am at the end of my life, and I lie to myself as would a dying mortal. The truth is, I knew I could not abandon you. At least, not entirely. Whatever the cost, I would not allow you to face your fate alone. So Ayliazarah and I came up with a plan. Though, had she fully understood the consequences, she would never have agreed to carry it out. But I understood all too well and hid them from her.

"We both knew that the others would not allow me to intervene. And if I remained in the mortal world, they would force me to return to heaven. So I came here, where they could not follow. I created this place to protect the *yetulu*. Here, my siblings' powers are useless. Even if they discovered where I was, they would never dare to go where they are powerless. They would be like fawns without the protection of their mother."

Gerath took a deep breath. "First, I tried to destroy the god stones, but was unable to find them all."

"Why did you do that?" Gewey asked. "I need their power."

"You could not have used them," he explained. "And if you had tried, it would have driven you mad. Only Melek might have been able to do so because he is not of our blood—we are of his. But you... I could not risk you trying."

"So how did the Dark Knight manage to do it? You said yourself that he is only a human."

"*Only* a human?" Gerath laughed. "My son, humans have far more power than you can imagine—though it may not be as obvious as it is with our kind, or even the elves. Their spirits have unlimited potential, and one day they will finally realize it. At least, that is my hope. The very fact that the Dark Knight *is* human and possesses the *Sword of Truth*—that is what has allowed him to steal the god stones' power and make himself stronger."

"Then how can I defeat him?"

"I will help you."

Gerath rose to his feet and turned his back. "Once you leave this room, my power will reside in you, just as my essence already does. But this time, everything I am and everything I was... it will all be yours."

Gewey could remember the same words being spoken to him through his father's essence. He looked at Gerath with suspicion. "And what will become of you after that?"

He bowed his head. "I think you know."

Gewey leaped from his chair. "No! I won't do it!"

Gerath turned to face his son again. "It is too late. I am already inside you, and my power is yours. Only my spirit remains. And once you leave, that will fade as well."

"Then I will not leave," he declared. Tears began to fall.

Gerath's face was awash with a father's love, but his voice was firm and unyielding. "Do you think I desire death? Do you think I would not know my son, or watch my grandson become a man? If I could, I would show you all the wonders of heaven and reveal the mysteries of the mortal world." He swallowed hard. "But that cannot be. I love you, Darshan. And I only do what I must. Would you not do the same for Jayden?"

By now, Gewey was weeping openly and unable to respond. Gerath stepped forward and placed his hands on his shoulders.

"Do not weep for me, my son," he said. "I will never leave you. Not really. You are all that is best in me, and that will continue long after my name is forgotten. I have lived long enough to see what you have become, and no father could wish for more. Or be filled with greater pride. I am sorry I was not there for you as a child. But I am truly thankful that Basanti kept her word and saw to it that you were loved and protected."

"I was," Gewey said, choking back his tears. "I was very well loved. My father... my human father... was a good and decent man. Everything I am, I owe to him."

Gerath nodded in approval. "Then my heart is less heavy by knowing this." He cleared his throat and wiped his eyes. "Now, it is time for you to go and fulfill your destiny."

The pair of them embraced. For a time, neither wished the moment to end. But then, reluctantly, Gerath pulled away.

"I will always remember you, father," Gewey told him. "And your name will never be forgotten." His tears were gone. It was time. The end of his long journey was nearly upon him.

"Thank you, Darshan," he replied.

After a final look at his father's face, Gewey turned and headed to the door.

"One last thing," Gerath called out. "Tell Ayliazarah, thank you... and that I love her."

Gewey nodded. "I will. I promise."

After passing through the door, Gewey suddenly became aware that he was still holding the jewel. But it was no longer red. It had now become clear and colorless.

He could feel the power of Gerath circulating inside him. At first, it was separate from his own, then, gradually it began to bind itself to him until they had become as one. All of a sudden, every bit of Gerath's knowledge and strength had penetrated his spirit, filling him completely.

It was done! Gerath was no more.

"Goodbye, Father," he whispered.

He left the passage and returned to the open air. The mist was still all around him, but now he could easily see through it. The *flow* in this place was tremendous and his ability to feel it had been fully restored. He could have used it to carry him through the air, but he wasn't ready to use the *flow* enhanced by his father's power just yet.

Without the mist hindering his perception, he could see that the landscape beyond the grassy area he was standing in was barren and colorless. But that was only on the surface. The power of the Creator was stronger here than anywhere he had been. He thought of the desert, and of the wonders that lay hidden beneath its sands. And now that he possessed Gerath's memories, he knew there were many more that even the elves had not yet discovered in all their long years of dwelling there.

After retrieving his sword, he sought out the wounded Ajagara. It was lying next to a large boulder, hissing and drooling blood. The moment it spotted him, it bared its teeth and charged. But Gewey was unconcerned. He held out his palm and sent waves of reassurance to the beast. At once, it slid to a halt and lowered its head.

He approached and placed his hands on its snout. "I'm sorry for hurting you, my friend. But I had no other choice. I couldn't very well have you eating me, now could I?"

Gewey closed his eyes. To heal the Ajagara, he would need to use the *flow*... and a part of that was his father's. He pictured Gerath's face. *It's all right, son,* came a distant voice. But Gewey knew it was just a shadow—a specter. He understood Gerath's mind and knew what he would say about the guilt his son was feeling.

Reassured, Gewey drew in the *flow* and quickly healed the Ajagara. Then, in a single motion, he leaped upon its back. With a thought, he urged it to carry him back to the *yetulu* and his friends.

Grunyal was waiting for him just beside the archway. His eyes shot wide on seeing Gewey atop the mighty beast. He lowered his head and bowed low.

"You are truly the son of Gerath," he said with humility. "Please forgive my doubts."

Gewey jumped down and rubbed the Ajagara's neck. "There is nothing to forgive. When I arrived, I was not as I am now. You had good reason to doubt. You have my gratitude for keeping the secrets of the god stones safe—my father's too. And I *will* keep my word. Your people will be returned to you."

Grunyal bowed again. "Then know that we are always at your service should the need arise."

Gewey smiled. "Thank you. I'll remember that."

"Come. Your friends will want to know you are safe."

Grunyal led him back to the room where Nehrutu and Felsafell were waiting. All the *yetulu* they passed by along the way gazed at Gewey in wonder. He guessed they were astonished to see him returning from the hunting grounds alive.

On his return, Nehrutu beamed a smile and leaped over the table. Felsafell simply nodded his approval.

"I was beginning to worry," Nehrutu said. "You have been gone a long time."

"I'm sorry," said Gewey. "It was ... a difficult trial."

"So you tamed the Ajagara?" the elf asked.

Gewey nodded. "I did. And I saw Gerath."

"So your father left more than one part of himself here," remarked Felsafell.

"No," he replied. He went on to recount all that had happened.

After he was done, there was a dead silence. A single tear fell down Felsafell's cheek. Only the opening of the door a short time later broke the solemn mood. Cloya came in and walked straight up to Gewey. She stared down at him for a moment before bowing low.

"Forgive me, Darshan." Her small, meek voice was ill-fitting to her massive frame.

Gewey laughed. "Forgive you? You saved my life. If not for the male Ajagara essence you gave me, I would have never made it through."

He could see the confusion on his friends' faces. Taking Cloya's hands, he led her to a seat.

"The vial Cloya gave me contained the essence of the male Ajagara," he explained. "You see, the young ones we encountered are all male. When the mother that lives in the hunting grounds reaches the end of her life, one of her children will automatically become female. The rest of them will then fight for the right to mate with her until only one is left alive. After the two remaining Ajagara mate, their young live within the mountain while the mother finds her way to the hunting grounds."

"And what becomes of the father?" asked Nehrutu.

"He dies."

"It is said that Gerath created the Ajagara to protect us," Cloya added.

"He didn't create them," Gewey said. "But he did alter their size and make them more aggressive so that they could prevent anyone from finding you."

He chuckled softly, seeing in his mind exactly how it was done. He had clear images of the quite small creatures Gerath had found wandering through the bowels of the mountain, and he could hear the words of his father saying, *"Yes. These will do nicely."*

"What will you do now?" asked Cloya.

"Nothing that you should be concerned about," he replied. His tone was kind and his expression yielding. "You and your people are safe. You can remain in this place for as long as you wish. No one will ever come here again."

"You will return, won't you?"

"I don't know," he said, trying to keep any hint of foreboding or melancholy from his voice. "Perhaps. In the meantime, I would ask that you give my friends some provisions and escort them back through the mountain after I leave. And don't worry; the Ajagara won't bother you. I've taken care of that."

Cloya stood and bowed. "I will see to it immediately."

Once she was gone, Nehrutu fixed his gaze on Gewey. "You are not coming with us?" he asked.

"No. I have things I need to do before I face the Dark Knight. And I must do them alone."

"Tell me," said Felsafell, a hint of suspicion in his tone, "Am I speaking to the same man who left this room? Or am I now speaking to Gerath?"

"I'm still me," Gewey replied. "I have gained my father's knowledge and experience, along with his power, but I'm not Gerath."

"Are you certain?" asked Nehrutu, suddenly suspicious as well.

"Yes," he quickly reassured the elf. "I am no more Gerath than I would be any man just because I knew everything about him." He paused for a moment. "Think of it like reading a book. If that book tells you every detail about someone's life, that doesn't mean you've actually become that person. What Gerath did with me is something like that. I know things. I can imagine his experiences—I even see them as clearly in my mind as I do my own memories. But what I do not experience is the flavor of the moment or the subtle nuances. I am unable to *feel* it in my heart."

Nehrutu nodded in understanding.

"When will you go?" Felsafell asked.

"Straight away. People are dying in the north. And as I said, I have something I must do before I fulfill my destiny."

"Then go with our love and prayers," said Felsafell. "And I hope this is not our final goodbye."

"Is there nothing we can do to help?" asked Nehrutu.

Gewey smiled warmly. "You have already done more than anyone has the right to expect. And no matter what happens next, I love you both." He rose calmly to his feet. "All I ask is for you to return to Aaliyah and Basanti ... and live well."

He embraced them both in an emotional farewell. Only with great effort were they all able to choke back their tears. After striding purposefully over to the door, Gewey hesitated for an instant longer to take a final look back at his two friends. Then he was gone.

The silence that followed was heavy with a sense of loss.

"Will we see him again?" Nehrutu asked.

Felsafell sighed and gazed thoughtfully at the empty space that Gewey had occupied only seconds ago. "I think we may have seen *Darshan* for the last time. In this life, anyway."

CHAPTER 19

Kaylia woke, unsure at first what had disturbed her. Instinctively, she looked at the crib where Jayden lay sleeping. And there beside it, silhouetted in the pale moonlight, was a familiar form.

"Gewey!" she cried out.

In a single motion, she was out of bed, and an instant later her arms were around him. Gewey held her close, bathing in the warmth of her body and the softness of her skin.

Eagerly, Kaylia tried to reach him through their bond, but found she was unable.

"Why are you keeping me from you?" she asked. "Surely the enemy knows you are here if you used the *flow* to travel."

He looked into her eyes and brushed the curls away from her face. "He knows."

"Then why?" Her tone had become nervous.

Gewey looked tenderly at his son and smiled. "He really does look more like you than me, don't you think?"

"Answer me, damn you!" she demanded. "Why have you not freed our bond?"

Gewey lowered his head and took a step back. "Because there is no bond to be freed. I have severed it completely."

For several seconds, Kaylia could only stare at him in utter disbelief. She reached out again, but there was still nothing. Her face contorted in fury.

"Why would you do this?"

It was breaking Gewey's heart to see her in such pain. "There is no other way," he told her. "When I am gone, the fate of the world will be decided. And the battle I am about to fight would destroy you if you were still bonded to me."

"None of this makes sense," she shot back. "I would have felt it. I would have known."

"I broke our bond in a way that would be painless to you," he explained. "I could not bear to see you suffer."

Her hand swung across in a blur to slap his cheek. The sound of the blow landing was like the crack of a whip. Jayden stirred, but to the relief of them both, he did not wake.

"You had no right to do this." Her voice was now an anguished whisper.

"I am so sorry, my love. I wish there was another way."

"Don't call me that," she hissed. "If you loved me, you would have never..." Her words faded away into soft sobs.

Reaching out, Gewey tried to wrap his arms around her. Kaylia struggled at first and began pounding her fists against his chest. But he refused to move back.

"I do love you," he insisted. "That is why I had to release you. And why I came here."

Kaylia gradually stopped fighting and allowed him to pull her close, her body shuddering as she continued to weep. Gewey kissed the top of her head repeatedly while the two of them simply held each other for a short while.

"Tell me what happened," she finally said. After wiping her eyes, she led Gewey to the edge of the bed.

"I can't," he replied. "There is no time. I was selfish to come here while so many others are dying. But I had to see you and Jayden once more before…"

"Before what? Before you die? Is that what you think is going to happen?" Her voice was hard and accusing.

"I have the strength to defeat the Dark Knight," he answered. "But doing so may still destroy me as well."

"It *may*?" she scoffed. "Then you aren't sure."

"No," he admitted. "I'm not sure. But even Melek feared him. And the knowledge I now possess tells me that he had good reason to."

"Then if you are not sure, I will not lose hope," she stated with stubborn resolve. "And even though we are no longer bonded, you are still my *unorem*. Do you understand me?"

Gewey smiled. "I understand. I really do."

He started to get up, but Kaylia pulled him back down.

She cupped his face in her hands. "You say that you have no time to tell me what happened. So be it. But you will not deny me my rights as your wife."

Even with her face racked with sorrow and anger, she was so beautiful to him. And though the end was looming near, she still made him burn with desire. His heart began to race as she touched his lips with the tips of her fingers.

"Please," he said. "King Lousis fights…"

"I don't care who lives and dies anymore," she declared sharply, yet somehow still not losing her seductive air. "I will have you with me before you go."

Gewey could no longer resist. He kissed her deep and long. Their love was absolute, and their passion so great that, even without the bond, he could feel her spirit within him. This was a love that the gods could never know or understand—one that only the Creator *herself* could fathom.

In that moment, he knew that this was the true strength of the mortal world.

Kaylia could hear the buzzing of hummingbirds coming from just outside her window. Jayden was cooing and fussing quietly in his crib. Even so, she knew that he would soon be in a more demanding mood if not fed.

Still, she did not want to open her eyes. Gewey was gone, and she was dreading the sight of the empty space beside her. He had been there only hours before, and though she desperately wanted to cling to hope, she could not escape the fear that last night had been a final goodbye.

Reluctantly, she opened her eyes. She wanted to weep, but her tears would not come. She wanted to cry out, but her voice was gone. All she could do was lay there and stare at the last place that she had been able to touch her *unorem*.

There was a soft knock at the door. Kaylia wanted to scream at whoever it was to go away, but wasn't able to.

"Kaylia?"

It was Aaliyah. Sensing that something was wrong, she immediately checked on Jayden, then sat down at the bedside. She only needed to glance at Kaylia's face to know what had happened. "How long ago did he leave?" she asked.

"Before dawn." Her voice was inaudible to all but elf ears.

Aaliyah continued to scrutinize her. "He will return. Whatever he may have told you, and whatever he might believe, I know he will return."

"I keep telling myself that same thing. And before he came to me, I had no doubts. But the look in his eyes and the sorrow in his voice..."

"It was nothing but his own fears," Aaliyah said, cutting her short. "He is not immune from fear any more than we are."

Kaylia grasped hold of Aaliyah's hands. "You don't understand. He has severed our bond. He told me I would not survive otherwise." She pulled herself up into a sitting position. "He said that his battle with the Dark Knight would kill me."

Aaliyah thought for a long moment. Slowly, from the corners of her mouth, a tiny smile began to appear. "Then he did the right thing. Bonds can always be reformed. Besides, your connection to Gewey is far deeper than any bond he could break. Your love for him—and his for you—that is your true bond. And when he is victorious, you will see him again." She glanced over at the crib. "But until then, there are more pressing matters needing attention."

Kaylia squeezed her eyes tightly shut in an effort to chase away her despair. Aaliyah was right. Gewey would return. She would not lose hope.

Her friend saw the change in her and gave a sharp nod. "That's better."

She stood and headed for the door. "Oh, by the way, I think there is something you should know." Her tiny smile grew until her entire face was shining with delight. "Just now, when I was holding your hand, I felt something. You are with child."

As Kaylia's eyes shot wide, Aaliyah burst into cheerful laughter and danced from the room.

Gewey gazed down at the vast expanse of the desert. With the power gifted to him by Gerath, he could look upon it with new understanding. He knew why the exiled elves were drawn here, and why they began to reject the *flow*. He knew so much more now. And yet, for all his strength, he was unable to alter the path set before him.

Gerath had spoken of his anger toward the Creator. *I feel it too, father.* He could see where he needed to go. And he knew that *he* was waiting for him. But first, he must repay the man who had saved him. What he must do now would break his heart. Only leaving Kaylia and Jayden would hurt him more.

It took just a few minutes to find the one he sought. He was wandering aimlessly a short distance from the Black Oasis. As Gewey reached out and touched the man's mind, his heart sank. He could feel nothing but rage and confusion. His will had been enslaved and his spirit broken. The gathering of the Vrykol was far away to the north, yet still, they controlled him—or at least, what was left of him.

He descended about fifty yards from where Lee Starfinder was standing. His friend's skin was pale and riddled with pulsating veins that were filled with corrupted blood. The clothes hanging off him were tattered and covered in dirt and grime. Though he wore no boots, the bare skin on his feet was unaffected by the scorching sands, and his black eyes were utterly devoid of life or intelligence.

The moment he spotted Gewey, he charged toward him, screaming maniacally. His speed was beyond belief, and he covered more than half the distance between them in a mere instant. But Gewey was not there to fight.

Using the *flow* of the earth, he enveloped his mentor in a pillar of sand all the way up to his neck. Lee struggled furiously, but the sand hardened into unyielding stone.

"I am so sorry," Gewey said. "But there is nothing I can do for you." He moved closer and touched his face. Lee grunted just once, then became unconscious. "You will join your wife in heaven soon, I promise you."

So many promises, he thought. How many of them will I be able to keep?

The bells and laughter of the *flow* of the spirit surrounded him. "Farewell, my good friend," Gewey said quietly. With that, he ripped Lee's spirit from his corrupted body.

The foulness of what the Vrykol had done to him wrapped around the light of his soul, strangling and biting into its purity. Before now, Gewey would have simply destroyed it and sent Lee into oblivion. But thanks to his freshly acquired knowledge, he knew a better way. With great care, he reached inside and pulled out the remains of his friend's soul. It was not enough to sustain a living body. But once heaven had been reopened and Lee was taken beyond its gates, he would be whole again.

"Until then, rest and be at peace."

Gewey willed Lee's spirit within the borders of the Black Oasis and asked the others waiting there to watch over him. That done, he rose skyward and looked out over the sands.

"I am coming," he roared. His voice shook the earth and echoed across the desert.

"I am waiting," came a soft reply.

CHAPTER 20

The First Temple of Valshara—53 years earlier

Aremiel tugged at the collar of his ill-fitting robes, almost dropping his books in the process. They had been made for a much older boy, and his mother had insisted that she hem them herself. Unfortunately, she was an appalling seamstress with no eye for aesthetic detail. Not that she was poorly dressed. But in her exalted position, she had others who attended to such mundane matters.

Since leaving his room that morning, he'd been constantly looking down at his feet, praying that the stitching would not come loose and send him tripping face-first onto the hard stone floor. He longed to ask for a new robe, but thought it might hurt his mother's feelings. She seemed to take great pride in the fact that she had attended to his needs herself. Besides, he was by far the smallest boy in Valshara... and the youngest. There probably wasn't anything that would fit him, anyway.

So far, his lessons had been easy enough, and his instructors were not as harsh as he'd feared. Even so, he had hoped to have made at least one friend by now. He'd been there a week, and still, no one had so much as looked at him.

He turned left down one of the hundreds of hallways, hoping it led to the next lesson. Valshara was so vast and complex that he spent most of his time feeling lost and confused.

Another reason to make a friend as soon as possible, he considered.

From the opposite direction, three boys were walking straight toward him. All of them were several years older and *much* bigger. They were talking and laughing—something about the ancient languages instructor smelling like rotten cheese.

On catching sight of Aremiel, their laughter stopped, and they all went quiet.

Now's your chance.

He did his best to make room for them, then put on his friendliest smile. "Hello. My name is..."

"We know your name," the boy closest to him said. He was taller than the other two, and obviously the leader of the group. "And we know why you're here."

"What do you mean?" he said. "I'm just here to learn... the same as you." He tried to remember the boy's name. *Come on. You're missing your chance.* Then it came to him. "You're Laraad, right?" He held out his hand.

Laraad sneered and folded his arms. "Look here, Aremiel, I had to earn my place in the temple, just like everyone else did. I spent two years in Baltria scrubbing floors and cleaning greasy pots for some stupid historian before they'd let me come. What did you do to get here?"

"I... I..." he stammered. "I'm sorry."

Laraad gave a mocking laugh and glanced at his friends. "You hear that? He's sorry." He took a quick step forward. The considerable size difference made it easy for him to loom over the younger boy. "What are you sorry for? Being the son of the High Lady? Is that it? I bet she wouldn't want to hear that. You're not ashamed of your mother, are you?"

This made him angry. But there was nothing he could do. If he fought, not only would he likely take a severe beating, but he would also have to face his mother afterward.

"Look boys," Laraad laughed. "I think the little piglet wants to hit me."

"Watch what you say," warned the boy to his right. "He might tell his mother you're calling him names."

"Yeah. I bet he would, too." He pressed his face into Aremiel's. "Look, you little runt. You may be the son of the High Lady, but that won't matter when it's time for combat training." He straightened his back, grinning viciously. "And I think today is the first day. Maybe I'll ask the instructor to match us up. Would you like that?"

"I think you'll be too busy with me, Laraad," came a voice from behind them.

"Stay out of this, Orias," he growled, turning and eying the newcomer.

"Why should I? So you can keep taunting a weaker boy? I don't remember *that* lesson when we were being taught about the knight's code of morality."

"What are you going to do? You going to tell his mom, too?"

"No," Orias replied, still grinning. "I'm going to wait until combat training this afternoon. Then I'm going to beat you until you can't move." He gestured to Aremiel. "Come on. I'll walk you to your lesson."

At first, Laraad refused to move aside. Orias shrugged. "Or I could say that you attacked me here in the hall, and that's why I sent you to the healing chamber with a broken nose. Like you said, his mother is the High Lady. I'm sure he will tell her exactly how it happened."

Laraad glared at Orias for a long moment, then sniffed. "Come on, let's go," he muttered, pushing roughly past Aremiel and stalking away, his friends following close behind.

"Thank you," Aremiel said once they were out of sight.

Orias nodded. His grin had vanished. "Listen to me. If you want to make it here, you need to be more than the son of the High Lady. You have to learn how to stand up for yourself."

"But I..." He hesitated and lowered his eyes. "I don't know how to fight."

"Hey! You see? This is what I'm talking about. You should be telling me to mind my own business and shut up." Orias tussled Aremiel's hair and lightened his tone. "Don't worry. You'll learn to fight soon enough, I promise. How old are you, anyway? I heard you were only five and some sort of child genius."

"I'm seven," he corrected. "And I'm not a genius. I'm a normal child, just like everyone else."

Orias threw his head back in laughter. "You keep telling yourself that if it helps. But I've heard the instructors talking. They say you're the brightest kid to come here since... well... since me, I suppose."

This time, it was Aremiel who laughed.

"Come on," Orias said. "I'll take you to your lesson. What do you have next?"

His face turned sour. "Healing Arts."

"Ah. Mistress Malicia. She's a mean one, all right. I used to call her Mistress Malice. Not to her face, of course. But if you're going to be a knight of Amon Dähl, then you'll need to know healing."

Aremiel didn't bother to tell him that he had no intention of being a knight. His mother wouldn't allow it.

The two boys wound their way through the halls until they reached the healing chamber. Aremiel was beaming the entire way. And to make things even better, he discovered that he had arrived before the other children in his group. Usually, by the time he'd figured out where he was going, the lesson had already begun.

He had heard Orias's name mentioned by the other children. He was said to be the most gifted boy ever to set foot in Valshara.

And he's my friend, he thought while taking his seat at the long table of herbs and strange liquids. If he hadn't been afraid of embarrassment, he would have jumped up and down with sheer happiness. Mistress Malicia gave him a displeased look and a funny kind of snort. *Mistress Malice*, he said with a grin... but not aloud, of course.

Despite Aremiel's raised spirits, as the day progressed, a sinking realization inevitably crept in. Today was to be his first day of combat training. He had never so much as threatened another child before, let alone fought one.

By the time he arrived at the door of the training room, his palms were sweating and his heart felt as if it would burst from his chest. The walls of the fifty-foot square room were lined with small, round shields and various wooden swords. Most of the other pupils were already there and gathered in groups of four. Aremiel's eyes searched desperately around for Orias, but he was nowhere to be seen. Laraad, however, was all too easy to spot. He was standing with the same two boys who'd been with him in the hall earlier.

He strolled over, a taunting sneer on his face. "Well, well, you actually showed up. What a shame your new friend Orias isn't here. But don't worry. You can partner up with us. We're one short in our group."

Aremiel just stood still in the doorway.

"Move it, boy," came a gruff voice from behind. "You're blocking the way in."

He felt a massive hand grip his shoulder and move him aside. Looking up, he saw a tall, broad-shouldered man with a shaved head and thick, powerful arms. His face was scarred and pitted, and his eyes burned bright blue. He looked back at Aremiel without expression for a moment, then strode to the center of the room.

"I am Master Kioshi," he bellowed. The room went instantly quiet. "I am a knight of Amon Dähl and your combat instructor. Should any of you so much as twitch without permission, you will face me in hand-to-hand combat. And let me assure you, you do not want that."

His eyes swept around the room. "Many of you have been in my class before." His gaze settled fleetingly on Aremiel. "Some of you have not. For those who are new here, listen, learn, and do what you are told. That way, we will get along fine. Test my patience and I will send you to the healing chamber without a moment's thought.

"I am hard. But I am fair. All will be treated equally. Some here want to become knights. Others will pursue different areas of expertise. But I don't care if you aspire to be a knight or a cook, you will still learn to protect yourself. My job is to see that you can... and I am very good at my job."

He began rearranging some of the groups. "Aremiel. Team up with Laraad. He needs a partner."

Aremiel's heart sank. He could see Laraad grinning from ear to ear.

"Now, boy!" shouted Kioshi.

Aremiel snapped to attention and hastily obeyed.

"I'm going to break your scrawny little neck," Laraad whispered.

Fear gripped him. He had heard that, from time to time, children were killed during combat training. Usually, it was an accident. *This won't be one of those times*, he thought.

"Today we will work on basic punches and blocks," Kioshi continued. "I know that you older students have been through this before. But you are to help the younger students learn. And I will be evaluating all of you. For the older children who want to join your friends at the end of the week in the advanced class, I had better see some fire. Those who want to stay here with the younger children..." He looked from group to group slowly. "That can also be arranged."

Kioshi reached into one of the groups and pulled a girl to the center of the room. Aremiel thought she looked to be about twelve years old. Her long, red hair was tied into a tight ponytail, and her gangly limbs made her look quite tall—though when standing next to Kioshi she appeared meek and fragile.

Kioshi allowed the girl to punch him several times. Aremiel was amazed at how fast and accurate she was. Though she couldn't hurt the instructor, had she been fighting another student, the impact would have been devastating. *I bet she'll be going to the advanced class,* he thought. Kioshi then showed everyone the blocks to counter these types of attacks.

"Now square off!" he shouted. "Older students block. Younger students punch."

Aremiel faced Laraad and held up his hands as he had seen the girl do. Laraad was still grinning.

"Go ahead," he said mockingly. "Punch me."

Without thinking, Aremiel's fist shot out and landed solidly on Laraad's chin. The boy stumbled back, his eyes wide with surprise.

"That's good, Aremiel," Kioshi called from the other side of the room. "And, Laraad. If you plan to move on from this class, you had better show me something."

Laraad's face turned red and his jaw clenched tight. "Try that again, runt."

It took all of Aremiel's control to keep from trembling. *What did I do? He's going to kill me for sure now.*

They faced each other again. Aremiel shifted right and crouched low before throwing another punch. His fist made contact for a second time, on this occasion hard into Laraad's ribcage. The boy let out a grunt and doubled over.

"Laraad!" yelled Kioshi. "What the hell is wrong with you? Let that happen again and you *will* stay here with the younger students."

The humiliated boy could see the other children snickering and whispering to each other about him. Aremiel groaned inwardly. *This just keeps getting worse and worse.* He could think of only one way to help ease the situation.

They faced up yet again. But this time Aremiel made sure Laraad could see what he was intending well in advance. In a clumsy and exaggerated motion, he stepped left and threw a punch at the boy's right cheek. Laraad raised his arm and easily deflected the blow. After giving a snort of satisfaction, his cocky grin suddenly returned.

Three more times, Aremiel threw awkward punches, allowing Laraad to block each one. He spotted Kioshi looking on with interest.

"Now switch," said the instructor. "But do not use full force."

This brought a sinister look to Laraad's face. "Now you're going to taste blood," he warned. It was clear he had no intention of obeying Kioshi's order.

Aremiel readied himself. Laraad threw a straight right aimed for the bridge of his nose. But he tilted his head and raised his arm quickly to deflect the blow past his right ear. Though it was a miss, the contact with his forearm was hard and pain shot all the way up to his shoulder. Gritting his teeth, he did his best to ignore the injury.

Almost before he was ready, Laraad struck again—this time at his abdomen. Aremiel dropped his elbows just in time to successfully block once again, though the force was still hard enough to promise painful bruises later.

Laraad's frustration and anger were growing; his fists were clenched so tightly that his knuckles had turned white. He threw a wild punch at Aremiel's jaw, but he ducked and spun away. The enraged youth snorted—he still wasn't done.

Letting out a wild growl, and in complete defiance of the rules, he unleashed a whole barrage of punches. Amazingly, Aremiel found that he was able to block most of these, but a few glancing blows did manage to make it through his defense.

"Laraad, enough!" roared Kioshi.

Laraad instantly stood at attention, his chest heaving and his face bright red.

"What did you think you were doing?" the instructor demanded.

Aremiel cut in quickly. "Sir, it's my fault. I asked him to do that. I wanted to see if I could block more than one blow at a time."

Kioshi looked from Laraad to Aremiel, and then back again. "Is this true?"

"Y-Yes, Master Kioshi. He asked me to do it. I wasn't *really* trying to hurt him."

Kioshi scrutinized the two boys for an uncomfortably long time. "Aremiel. What you did was dangerous. And you Laraad—you should know better."

"Yes, sir," the two boys said in unison.

"Both of you are done here for today," he said. "And you had better pray to the gods that I don't decide to report this to the High Lady. Now get out of my sight."

The boys bowed and hurried from the room. They walked down the hall together in silence until stopping at a point where the passage split left and right. Here, Laraad grabbed Aremiel by the collar and thrust his face in close.

"This isn't over, runt," he snarled. After shoving Aremiel to one side, he set off down the hallway leading left.

Why did I even come here? Aremiel asked himself. But he already knew the answer. It was his mother. She wanted him close. And in truth, he had wanted it, too.

The rest of the day passed uneventfully. Laraad was nowhere to be seen, and no one else tried to bother him. However, he did notice that he was receiving more stares than usual from the other children. It was obvious that word of what had happened in the training room had spread. This only made him feel even more alienated and alone. He wished that he would see Orias. But there was still no sign of his new friend.

For the first time since arriving in Valshara, he was glad he was staying in his mother's chambers, and not in the boys' barracks. Laraad would be there. And even if he wasn't, the other children would only talk and whisper behind his back.

After completing his final lesson of the day, he decided to skip supper and go for a walk in the gardens. They were usually empty at this time, and he found the solitude enjoyable.

It was spring, and the roses were in bloom, filling the air with their distinctly sweet scent. He walked along the winding slate paths, scarcely noticing the exquisite beauty surrounding him. On reaching the far side of the grounds, he found a bench and sat down. For a time, he went over the day's events in his mind, wondering if there was anything he could have done to make a better outcome.

His mother's words echoed in his head. *"Be kind and considerate."* That's what she had told him just before they'd walked through the gates here together for the first time. *"If you do that, people will do the same to you."* How wrong she was!

Just then, he heard the sounds of approaching footfalls. "I thought I saw you come this way." It was Laraad. He was standing just a few yards down the path. His usual two friends were with him.

"What do you want?" Aremiel asked. But he already knew the answer to that.

"I told you it wasn't over." The other two boys began cracking their knuckles. "I bet you thought that was funny—humiliating me in class. Didn't you?"

"I wasn't trying to humiliate you, I swear."

"Save your breath, runt. Let's see how tough you are without Master Kioshi to save you."

"Please. Don't do this. I didn't mean to embarrass you. I'm sorry."

Laraad laughed. "Not yet, you aren't."

Aremiel glanced to his right. The path ended just beyond the bench. He was trapped; there was nowhere to run. Just as this thought was forming, the three boys charged in.

He leaped to his feet and tried to duck beneath them. But they were too many, and they were too strong. Laraad's friends each grabbed one of his arms, hauling him up straight. With a sneer on his face, Laraad stepped forward, his hand balled into a tight fist. Instinctively, Aremiel flicked up his foot, planting it hard into Laraad's groin. The boy let out a sharp yelp of pain and then dropped to his knees.

Aremiel began to thrash about wildly in an effort to make the other two boys lose their grip on him. But his hopes were dashed. They held on tight until Laraad had recovered. He moved in close again. Thick knots of veins were now protruding from his brow, and his eyes were ablaze with hatred.

"You'll pay for that," he growled.

"Don't hit him in the face," one of his friends advised. "His mother will know."

Aremiel gasped for air as Laraad struck him hard in the stomach. But that was only the beginning. Again and again, the same vicious punches sank into his body. He began seriously fearing that he might die from being unable to breathe. His ribs were on fire, and he felt as if he would vomit at any second.

"I think he's had enough," he heard the boy holding his right arm say.

Laraad spat on the ground. "I'll say when he's had enough." He grabbed Aremiel's chin and pushed up his head. "Ready for more, runt?"

"Are you?" responded another voice.

It was Orias. He was standing right behind Laraad, a dangerous-looking smile on his face.

Laraad barely had time to turn before Orias's fist crashed into his nose. Blood flew from his nostrils, splattering streaks of red all around his mouth. The other two bullies immediately released Aremiel and moved in, but Orias was prepared. The heel of his boot sank into the stomach of the first boy. The second managed to throw a punch, but Orias spun sideways to avoid it and then struck him on the temple with the tip of his elbow. After going down, neither boy attempted to get up again.

Laraad, on the other hand, was still standing, even though blood was still gushing from his broken nose and by now soaking almost the entire front of his shirt. All semblance of sanity appeared to have temporarily deserted him.

"I'll kill you!" he screamed, throwing a cluster of wild, uncoordinated punches at his tormentor.

But Orias merely stepped to one side and rammed his knee up into Laraad's midsection. One final punch to the jaw then sent the enraged youth into deep unconsciousness.

Orias hurried over to Aremiel, who had collapsed to the ground immediately after being released. "Can you walk?" he asked.

Aremiel merely nodded, for the moment still unable to speak.

Bending down, Orias wrapped an arm around his shoulders and pulled him up. "We need to go before anyone sees you here," he said.

After a few yards, Aremiel insisted that he was able to move along under his own power, albeit while bent forward and gingerly clutching at his ribs. Luckily, it was getting dark and most of the temple was at supper. The few people they did encounter were preoccupied and took no notice of them.

Orias guided him to a door near the west guard tower and up a narrow stairwell leading to the ramparts. On reaching the top, they walked north until well behind most of the temple's structures.

"No one can see us here unless they come up," Orias told him.

By now Aremiel could just about speak, though his body was still aching terribly. "But we're not allowed to be up here," he croaked.

"Don't worry," Orias said confidently. "I bring the night sentinels wine from time to time. They won't say anything."

Aremiel was about to protest, but the look of assurance and kindness on the other boy's face calmed his fears and reservations.

"Thank you," he said. "If you hadn't helped me..."

Orias held up a hand to silence him. "Forget it. Friends don't need to thank one another. You would have done the same for me, I'm sure."

Friends. The very sound of the word brought Aremiel a sense of peace and belonging that he had not felt since arriving. "Why would you want *me* as a friend?" he asked.

Orias laughed and slapped him on the back. "Because one day we'll both be knights. That alone makes us friends."

"You really think I can be a knight?"

"If what I heard about your first day of combat training is true, I'm sure of it." He leaned his elbows on the edge of the wall and gazed out toward the distant forest. "You do want to be a knight, don't you?"

Aremiel shrugged. "My mother wants me to be a historian. She says that I'm smart enough, and that they lead a good life."

"A historian? Really? Well, I suppose they have their place." He locked eyes with Aremiel. "But what do *you* want?"

"I don't want to disappoint my mother. But I don't want to just watch people and write things down either. I... I want to be a knight."

"Then you will be," Orias said. "Then people can watch us and write about our deeds."

Aremiel was grinning from ear to ear. "Why do you want to be a knight?"

"My father," he replied, his head held high. "The first time I saw him fight, I knew what I wanted."

"So... your father is a knight of Amon Dähl?"

"My father is the greatest knight alive," he boasted. "Ask anyone about Morzahn. They'll tell you. Of course, my mother wants me to be an agent like her. She's afraid that I'll end up getting killed."

"Your mother is an agent and your father a knight." Aremiel was greatly impressed. "No wonder you're so good."

Orias raised an eyebrow. "Me? You're the one who trounced a boy twice your size on your first day of combat training. They'll be talking about that for weeks."

This dampened Aremiel's mood. "I wish they wouldn't. And I wish my mother wasn't the High Lady. Everybody hates me. They think I'm only here because of her. They say I didn't earn my place like they did."

Orias laughed contemptuously. "Who says that? Laraad and his bunch of morons? Who cares what those toads think? People said the same thing about me. I was the youngest student ever to be accepted here." He gave Aremiel a playful punch on the shoulder. "That was until you arrived. And don't worry about Laraad. I don't think he'll be bothering you again."

Though Aremiel was indeed relieved that Laraad would be leaving him alone from now on, he couldn't help but wish there had been another way of resolving the problem.

"Aremiel! Orias!" a deep, stern voice called to them from their left. It was Master Kioshi.

The two boys snapped to attention.

"The High Lady orders you to come to her chambers at once."

Without a word, they started off.

Kioshi caught Orias by the arm as he passed by. "And we'll talk later about you walking the ramparts."

While they made their way to the High Lady's chambers, Aremiel felt himself dreading what was about to come. Someone must have told her what had happened in the garden.

"Just let me do the talking," Orias told him. "This isn't the first time I've been in trouble. I know the best things to say."

Aremiel could only nod.

Normally, he would simply enter his mother's chambers. But this time, he knocked.

"Enter." There was steel in her voice.

The two boys stepped inside. The High Lady was standing just beyond the door, her eyes narrowed and her face red with anger.

"By the gods!" she shouted. "Just what were you thinking of? Laraad is in the healing chamber with a broken jaw and nose. And the other two aren't in much better shape."

"But High Lady..." Orias began, but a fierce glare silenced him.

"When I want to hear from you, Orias, I'll speak to you directly."

"But, Mother," Aremiel cut in. "Orias didn't do anything wrong. Those other three boys were beating me. If he hadn't come to... well..."

Each word he spoke seemed to incite an even angrier look from her. He steadied his failing courage and stiffened his back. "He saved me. That is the truth."

"He saved you, did he?" she scoffed. "From what I have seen, it was Laraad who needed to be saved?" Her eyes shifted to Orias. "Well? What do you have to say for yourself?"

His expression did not change. Aremiel dearly wished he were as fearless as his new friend.

Orias's tone was steady and calm. "It was all my fault, High Lady. I saw Laraad and his friends follow Aremiel into the garden and suspected they were going to attack him. So I followed them in."

"And what should you have done?"

"I should have reported it at once to the nearest sentinels and allowed *them* to handle the matter."

She folded her arms. "And why didn't you?"

"I wanted to teach Laraad a lesson."

"You wanted to teach him a lesson," she chided. "And are you an instructor?"

"No, High Lady?"

"So what qualifies you to teach Laraad a lesson?"

"Nothing, High Lady."

She scrutinized him for a time before speaking further. "This is not the first time you have been brought before me, is it?"

"No, High Lady."

"And what did I tell you would happen if you broke the rules again?"

Aremiel saw Orias's mouth twitch.

"You told me I would be expelled, High Lady," he replied.

"No!" cried Aremiel. "You can't!"

"Silence," she snapped.

Orias placed a hand on Aremiel's shoulder and shook his head as a warning to say no more. "I'll pack at once, High Lady. If you would be so kind as to inform my father that I'll be leaving for Baltria to join my mother."

Her eyes darted from Aremiel to Orias several times. "I will do no such thing. You will leave only when I order you to do so, and not a moment before. Do you understand me?"

"Yes, High Lady," Orias answered. This time, he could not disguise the emotion in his voice.

Aremiel was positively beaming at his friend's unexpected reprieve.

"I don't know what you're smiling about," his mother said sternly. "The two of you will be working in the kitchens for the next month. And after tonight, you will bunk in the boys' barracks." She looked back at Orias. "And since you have set yourself up as my son's guardian, you can move your things from the older boy's quarters and bunk *with* him." She waved her hand dismissively. "Now get out of my sight before I come to my senses."

Orias bowed. "Thank you, High Lady." While hurrying from the room, he flashed Aremiel a wide grin.

In spite of pardoning Orias, the High Lady's features remained firm and unforgiving as she regarded her son.

He gave her a formal bow. "Thank you, Mother."

Slowly, her expression softened. She shook her head and sighed. "I only spared him from expulsion because I understand why he acted the way he did. Orias may be a bit of a troublemaker, but he has a kind heart. And If I discovered that someone had hurt you... well, let's just say that a beating from Orias would be the least of their worries."

Aremiel embraced her tightly. "Thank you, Mother. I'm so happy that you brought me here."

She kissed the top of his head. "How could I not bring you? I love you."

"I love you, too. And don't worry. I'll make you proud of me."

She squeezed him even tighter. "I'm already proud, son."

CHAPTER 21

The First Temple of Valshara—49 years earlier

Aremiel circled left, his sword gripped tightly in his right hand. Each step he made was well practiced and measured. The light armor he wore was the only thing hindering him. Just like his first robe when arriving at Valshara, it was ill-fitting and awkward. But it would have to do.

Orias stood before him. *His* sword was a far superior weapon, and his armor had been made to fit his dimensions exactly. The tiny smile on his face told of his confidence as he matched Aremiel's movements.

"What are you waiting for?" he taunted. "Let's get this over with. I'm feeling hungry."

This time, Aremiel refused to be goaded. He feigned right and then left, trying to lure Orias off-balance. But he was far too good to fall for such simple tricks. *Better to wait and hope he makes a mistake,* he thought.

He didn't have to wait long. With a grunt of irritation, Orias lunged in, his sword thrusting low. Aremiel twisted away, at the same time bringing the hilt of his sword up toward Orias's jaw. But his friend had anticipated such a move and leaned back. Aremiel felt a fist strike his temple and was sent stumbling back.

"Is that what Kioshi taught you?" Orias scoffed. "No wonder the elves killed him."

The mention of Master Kioshi's recent death sent torrents of rage coursing through him, and the grin on Orias's face fueled the flame even more. He charged in, his blade swinging in a tight, controlled arc. Orias deflected the blow and countered with a series of his own.

Aremiel's anger was giving him extra strength, but not nearly enough to overcome his older and stronger opponent. Soon, he found himself being forced to yield ground. Other than Master Kioshi, Orias was by far the best swordsman he had ever faced. There were even rumors that he had actually once disarmed Kioshi during a sparring lesson—though Aremiel couldn't really believe such a story.

After another flurry, Orias stepped back and scowled. "Are you going to fight me or not?"

Aremiel spat on the ground and spun left, and attacked. Small sparks flew from their clashing steel blades. He couldn't match Orias in strength—that much was certain—but he was not without his own strategies. He ducked and rolled forward, rapidly regaining his feet and drawing his dagger the moment he was behind him.

Orias stepped back and left, then grabbed Aremiel's wrist. "Not bad," he smiled.

Aremiel released the dagger before Orias could twist his wrist. Jerking his trapped arm free, he swung his sword wildly with the other to prevent his opponent from taking advantage of their close proximity. He was only just able to get away in time to reset his feet.

"I think your mother is right," mocked Orias. "You *should* be a historian."

Aremiel renewed his attack. After three more futile attempts at penetrating Orias's defense, he was sure that he had at last spotted an opening. Orias was leaning his weight much too far back. Ducking low, he thrust high. But even while in the middle of delivering the strike, he realized his mistake... it was a trap. He would miss, and as a result, was now badly overextended. Orias simply turned and brought his sword down onto Aremiel's exposed neck.

The cold steel of the blade resting on his exposed flesh was a stark reminder that, had this been a real fight, he would now be dead.

"Damn it!" Aremiel shouted in disgust. "I almost had you this time."

Orias laughed while sheathing his sword. "Actually, you did. If you had drawn your dagger before you rolled, you would have won."

Aremiel sheathed his own weapon and glared at his friend. "How could you say that about Master Kioshi?"

"Because of what the master taught me," he replied flatly. "Elicit anger in your opponent, if you can. It makes them careless. And never fight with rage as your ally. Passion gives you power and focus. Rage only blinds you."

Aremiel nodded. He remembered the same lesson well. But since hearing news of the master's killing by a band of elves near Tarvansia, he had been unable to focus on his combat training. Kioshi had become a mentor to him over the past four years. Aside from his mother, only Orias held a more treasured place in his heart.

"Why do the elves still hate us so much?" he asked. "The Great War has been over for hundreds of years."

Orias began to remove his armor. "They're savages. Soulless savages. We should have wiped them out when we had the chance."

The part of Aremiel that was still mourning Kioshi agreed, but there was also something in his heart telling him that such thoughts were wrong.

"But what do we really know about them? Maybe if we tried to—"

"Tried to what?" Orias barked with a sudden flash of anger. "Reason with them? Make peace? We made peace, and yet still they plague us. Their hatred of the gods has turned them into nothing but brutish vermin." He met his friend's eyes. "Trust me. There can be no peace between human and elf."

Aremiel gazed back at Orias, and for the first time could see the pain behind his eyes. When the message had come about Kioshi's death, he had seemed unaffected, continuing with his studies as if nothing had happened. In fact, when a new combat instructor arrived two days later, he seemed quite happy. He even remarked that he was learning more than he ever had from Master Kioshi. But Aremiel could now see the truth in his friend's expression. The master's death had wounded him deeply.

Orias forced a smile, as if he knew that Aremiel could see through him. "Come on. They're serving roasted pork today. And I hear the cook has made apple pie."

"I can't," said Aremiel. "I promised Mother I'd have lunch with her."

Orias laughed as he hung his armor and sword on a peg fixed to the wall. "Very well then. But I can't promise I'll save you some pie."

Aremiel knew this to be a lie. He placed his equipment on the next peg and shrugged. "That's fine. Then I can't promise I'll bring you some sweets from Mother's chambers." This, naturally, was another lie.

Orias slapped him on the back and hurried off to the dining hall. Aremiel hated it that his mother would never allow his friend to join them. But there was no convincing her otherwise. Each passing year as his studies progressed, there were more demands put on his time. This meant less time with her. He could tell she was bothered by this, though she would never actually say so openly.

When he arrived at her room, the door was already ajar. A young girl was placing their meal on a small table at the far side of the room, just beneath the window. His mother was seated and sipping a cup of honeyed wine. Her face lit up when she saw him.

"I was beginning to think you weren't coming," she said.

Aremiel smiled in return and took his seat. "I would never defy High Lady Velinia." Something about using his mother's given name always made him feel awkward.

She looked at him with sad eyes. "You have matured so much since you arrived here. My little boy is nearly a man."

This was an exaggeration, of course. He still had many years to go before his studies and training were complete.

"Are you still insisting on this *knight* nonsense?" she asked, her disapproval clear.

"It's not nonsense," he shot back. "The knights are what is best about Amon Dähl. They protect the people and ensure that we can continue to do the work the gods have set before us."

His mother shook her head and frowned. "You know, Mistress Frasia says you are a quick learner. She thinks you would make a fine historian one day."

"I don't want to be a historian," he contended. "I want to be a part of history, not an observer of it."

"Those are Orias's words, not yours," she said. "I don't like how much sway he has over you. He's a good student and will make a fine knight, but some of his ideas are dangerous."

His mother had always been distant from Orias. She'd never objected to their friendship, but clearly believed that his wish to become a knight was a result of Orias's influence. And he had to admit that there was some truth in this.

He often daydreamed of himself and his friend setting off together on an important mission and fighting side by side.

"He's not dangerous," he said with a grin. "Just stubborn."

His mother blew out an exasperated breath. "Not as stubborn as you, it seems. And I did not say that *he* was dangerous, only some of his ideas. In some matters, the boy is ... obsessed. He thinks he must be the knight his father is. And I'm afraid that one day he'll attempt something stupid to prove himself. And if he does..."

"If he does," Aremiel said, cutting her off. "I will be fighting by his side—where a true friend should be."

Velinia glared at her son. "You will be the death of me. You know that?"

His mother's stare could always make him feel guilty. "I didn't mean to upset you. I'm sorry."

She sighed and took her son's hand. "I just don't want you getting yourself into trouble over Orias's foolishness. I know that he's your friend and you think you understand him. But I see something within that boy. A single-mindedness of purpose that disturbs me."

"He just wants to be the best knight he can be," Aremiel said. "That's all. And I won't let him get me in *too* much trouble."

"I hope you are right."

The two ate their meal quietly. Afterward, Aremiel told her about his studies and the day-to-day goings on of his life. He knew how important it was to her to know these things. If a week went by without an update, it was well known throughout the temple that she would be in a foul mood. This prompted members of the Order to often remind him that, if he had not been to see his mother in the last few days, then to do so very soon.

Aremiel was just about to leave when there was a soft knock at the door. A courier handed the High Lady a sealed parchment and then hurried away. As she read it, her expression grew dire.

"Go find Orias," she commanded. "Tell him that I need to see him at once."

"What's wrong, Mother?" he asked.

"I said go!" The sudden increase in the volume of her voice startled him.

He raced out and ran at full speed to the dining hall. Orias was sitting at a table, talking with some of the older boys. He smiled when he saw Aremiel approaching.

"I see you didn't bring me the sweets," he said lightheartedly. "Well, it just goes to prove that I'm the better friend." He gestured to a slice of pie sitting on the vacant chair beside him.

Aremiel did not waste time returning the banter. "The High Lady wishes to see you right away," he said, breathing quite hard from his run.

The urgency in his voice dispelled his friend's smile. "Did she say why?"

Aremiel shook his head.

"What did you do this time, Orias?" teased one of the boys.

But Orias didn't answer. He and Aremiel set off immediately toward the High Lady's chambers. When they arrived, two knights and another man—who, from the plain clothes he wore, was likely an agent—were waiting.

"Your lessons are canceled for today, son," the High Lady said. "Go now. I must speak to Orias alone."

Aremiel reluctantly obeyed. Whatever had happened, he knew Orias would need him. He went to the courtyard and waited near the door that led up to the ramparts. If Orias was upset, that's where he would go.

Several hours passed without a sign. Then, just as the sun was going down, he saw his friend leaving the main temple door. The two knights were with him. They walked for a few yards before stopping and talking quietly for a while. Aremiel wished that he could hear them. He had learned to read a person's lips, but the knights had their backs turned and Orias was saying nothing to them in reply. Finally, both knights touched him on the shoulder and left. Once left alone, he stood there absolutely still for more than a minute.

Aremiel was just about to join him when his friend looked across and walked over.

"What happened?" Aremiel asked.

"It's my father," he replied. His expression was unreadable.

"Is he... is he...?" Aremiel could not bring himself to say the word *dead*.

"No. He is accused of murder and treason."

Aremiel had met Orias's father only once. Morzahn was widely considered to be the finest knight in the order. Perhaps the best in its history. Tales of his deeds had already reached mythical proportions. "That can't be true," he said.

"It is," Orias replied, still without a hint of what he was feeling. "Your mother says there is undeniable proof."

"I don't believe it. There has to be some mistake."

"There's no mistake. He killed four knights and was caught *interrogating* a fifth."

"Interrogating? Why?"

"He was looking for the *sword*."

Now his friend's tone did reveal a trace of emotion—it was hate. But hate for who?

"You don't believe that, do you?" Aremiel asked.

"Like I said. The proof is undeniable. And he has already admitted his guilt."

"Where is he now?"

Orias looked up. His eyes had become hot coals of fury. "The knights who captured him are arriving tomorrow. They are bringing him here for execution."

Aremiel wanted to give words of comfort, but could think of nothing suitable to say. Instead, he simply asked, "What will you do?"

"I will speak to him myself." The stone conviction in Orias's voice had taken on an alarming quality. "And if he is guilty, then I will smile as he dangles from the gallows."

"Is there anything I can do?"

"Other than be my friend... no."

Aremiel reached up and grasped Orias firmly on the shoulder. "I'll always be your friend. You know that."

The two boys climbed up to the ramparts and stayed there until well past the time they should have been in bed. Orias barely spoke throughout. Instead, he spent his time staring bleakly in the direction from which he knew his father would be coming. But unlike Morzahn's previous visit, this time he would be a prisoner in chains.

Aremiel's heart ached for his friend. To look upon your own father and know him to be a traitor and a murderer must be simply unbearable.

When Orias was finally ready to go back down, it was nearly midnight. On arriving at the barracks, Aremiel found that a note had been placed on his bunk. It was from his mother.

"She wants to see me before I go to bed," he explained.

"Then you should go," Orias told him. "I'm sure she wants to know my condition. You can tell her I'm fine."

Aremiel set off straight away to his mother's chambers and knocked on the door. It was opened by a tall man wearing typical villagers' clothing. He looked at Aremiel for a moment, then departed down the hallway.

His mother was sitting at her desk, a grave expression on her face. She gestured for him to take a seat and rubbed the bridge of her nose.

"Orias said that he is fine," Aremiel blurted out before she could speak.

"I'm sure that's what he said. But I doubt the poor boy is. How could he be?"

"Is it true?"

His mother took a moment before nodding. "I'm afraid there is little doubt regarding his father's guilt. He was captured while torturing another knight. The bodies of those he had killed were still lying close by."

"Orias said that he was looking for the *sword*."

"Yes," she confirmed. "But what we don't know is *why* he was looking for it." The High Lady studied her son for a moment. "I have not always approved of how close you and Orias have become. You know that I think him to be unpredictable."

"He's my friend, Mother," he protested. "He's always been there for me. And I trust him."

"Do you trust me?"

He cocked his head. "Why would you ask me that? Of course, I do."

"Then trust that what I am about to ask of you is for Orias's benefit. I need you to stay close to him."

"Stay close? Of course, I will. He's my best friend. And right now, he needs me. Why would I leave him?"

There was a long pause. "When Morzahn arrives, Orias will wish to speak to him. And when he does, I need you to be there."

The full meaning of his mother's intentions suddenly became clear. "You want me to spy on him?" he asked, appalled.

"I want you to observe and listen," she corrected. "I will not allow Orias to be alone with his father. He may well be vulnerable to his influence. The boy has far too much potential for me to allow him to be corrupted."

"Then why let him speak to his father at all?" Then it occurred to him. "You want to know if Morzahn has actually discovered where the *sword* is kept."

"Yes."

"You really think he'd say anything with me there?"

"I doubt it," she replied. "But Master Karlio tells me that you would make a gifted agent if you chose to pursue it. I spoke to him, and he says you may be able to read the meaning of Morzahn's words."

Aremiel frowned. "You should just ask Orias. He'd tell you. And he's much better at agent craft than I am."

"I simply can't risk it," she replied. "If Morzahn has found a way to reach the *sword*, he may have left clues for others to follow. I need to know. *Everything* depends on it." She leaned in. Aremiel could see the wearied circles under her eyes. "Will you help me, son?"

Aremiel stared at his mother. As much as he hated it, he knew she was right. If Morzahn had indeed discovered the *sword's* location, the Order *must* know.

"I'll help you," he said. His voice was small and quiet.

His mother smiled weakly. "Thank you. Now get some sleep. Tomorrow will be a trying day."

Aremiel stood up and kissed her goodnight. When arriving back at the barracks, he found Orias still awake, a candle burning low on the little wooden nightstand beside his bed.

"Did she ask you to spy on me?" he asked.

Aremiel opened his mouth, but no words came out.

"It's all right," his friend said. "I would have asked you to do the same. If my father was searching for the *Sword of Truth*, then she needs to know how much he has discovered. And torturing a man like Morzahn would do no good at all. He'd *never* talk, so they're hoping he'll say something to me."

He smiled at Aremiel. "Don't feel you're betraying me for agreeing to do it. You're not. You're my best friend. But you are a member of Amon Dähl first. The well-being of the order is the most important thing of all."

"I'm sorry." It was all Aremiel could think to say.

"Like I said. It's all right." He sat up and blew out the candle. "Now get some rest."

The next morning, the temple was abuzz with activity. News of Morzahn's betrayal had already spread, and as the two friends made their way to the main dining hall, countless whispers followed them. Words such as *murder* and *treason* could be heard echoing off the stone walls. Everyone avoided looking at Orias, but if this bothered him, he didn't show it.

As they ate, the quiet of the normally noisy hall was painfully obvious. Morzahn would be arriving soon, and the tension was building.

Laraad slid into a seat beside Orias. "Well now. Can it be true? The mighty Morzahn—a traitor?" He clicked his tongue and shook his head. "How horrible that must be for you."

"Don't you have a door to fix?" Aremiel snapped.

Laraad had failed to make it into the advanced combat classes, completely dashing any hopes he held of becoming a knight. Instead, he'd been made a builder's apprentice. It wasn't a bad way to spend one's time. The builders of Amon Dähl were highly respected and their skills greatly prized. But nothing carried with it the same prestige as becoming a knight.

"Thanks to Orias's father, all work and classes are suspended," he replied with a sneer. "So tell me... how does it feel to be the son of a traitor?"

Orias didn't reply or even look up.

"Leave him alone," Aremiel said. He slowly rose from his chair. "Otherwise I'll..."

Laraad burst into wicked laughter. "You'll what? You'll give me a beating? Right here in front of everyone?"

Aremiel sat back down. "No. A *knight* learns to show restraint when dealing with fools. But I wonder if Master Builder Drekol knows that you've been stealing wine from his quarters."

This shook Laraad for a moment. "You can't prove that," he blustered. Then his smirk returned. "Anyway, last I heard, you weren't a *knight*. So quit pretending you are."

"He may not be a knight yet," Orias chimed in, his head still lowered. "But he *is* the youngest student ever to make it to advanced combat training. The very same class you failed, as I recall. And to answer your question, being the son of a traitor makes me feel angry. Very angry. And though I would never lay a hand on someone who tried to hurt me with cruel words, there are many forms of revenge. You would know this if you paid attention in agent training—assuming that you haven't been kicked out of that as well. I have never actually considered becoming an agent, but it's still amazing what you can learn there. There are several ways of causing severe harm to someone that leaves no trace."

He finally looked up and locked eyes with Laraad. "And I know them all."

The blood drained from Laraad's face. "Well... I..."

"If I were you," said Aremiel. "I'd leave now."

Laraad growled angrily. "One day you'll get what's coming. Both of you." Springing up from his seat, he stalked away.

"I'm sure he's right," Orias muttered. "But I think we all get what's coming to us in the end."

At that moment, the blare of a trumpet rang out. Morzahn had arrived. Everyone in the dining hall instantly jumped up and hurried to the nearest door. With just three narrow exits, it took several minutes for the crowded room to empty.

Only the two friends remained in their places. When the last person had finally departed, Orias let out a deep sigh. "I suppose it's time," he said.

They entered the main courtyard just as the gates were swinging open. Orias pushed through the crowd and made his way to the front. Aremiel followed him. Then a hush fell over the temple as a line of horses carrying the knights filed in. Aremiel held his breath until he spotted Morzahn.

Even when stripped of weapons and armor, and bound in chains, he was still an intimidating sight to behold. Tall, and possessing the mighty shoulders of a blacksmith, his medium-length, black, curly hair and beard were unkempt and wild from the miles of travel. His skin had the texture of tough leather, while his face, together with heavily muscled limbs, bore a multitude of scars from past battles. But for all this, it was the man's penetrating green eyes that captured the most attention, issuing the clearest warning imaginable of the awesome power that could be unleashed whenever necessary. Aremiel shuddered at the thought of fighting him. How could anyone ever defeat such a warrior?

He rode with head held proudly high, looking straight ahead and only glancing briefly down as he passed his son. Orias glared back with seething hatred. But if this affected Morzahn, he gave no outward indication of it.

The accompanying knights dismounted, then set about pulling Morzahn roughly down from his horse. It was obvious they would have liked nothing more than to kill the traitor there and then. But their code demanded justice... not vengeance.

They led him through the temple's main entrance, and then down to the cells in the basement. Aremiel had been there once when he was younger. It was a morbid place, with dank air and mold-covered stone walls. He had heard stories of elves being kept imprisoned there for decades, being fed nothing but stale bread and fetid water until they eventually wasted away and died.

Orias waited until the courtyard was cleared before entering the temple. Just inside the door, a knight was waiting.

He bowed to the two boys. "I am Dresher. The High Lady asked me to stay with you until Morzahn has been locked away. When they are ready, you will be sent for." He led them to a small parlor in the west wing and offered them seats near the unlit hearth.

"The High Lady tells me that both of you want to be knights," he said.

The boys nodded.

"Good. We can use more strong men. And I hear that both of you are exceptional fighters. Kioshi mentioned your names to me a few weeks before he died." He looked at Orias. "You in particular. He said that your skill with a sword was uncanny for one so young."

"I am grateful that he thought so," Orias responded.

"And as for you," the knight continued, turning to Aremiel. "He said that you were second only to Orias. And that you even surpass him in some areas."

"I can't think of anything in which I can surpass Orias," he responded truthfully.

Dresher scrutinized the two boys for a moment. "You have been friends for some time, yes?"

"We have," affirmed Aremiel. "Orias was the first friend I made here."

"Then you will be pleased to know that friends are kept together once they become knights, if it is possible."

"Assuming they will still allow me to become one," said Orias. His tone wasn't angry. He spoke as if simply weighing the balance of possibilities.

"Why wouldn't they?" asked Dresher.

"With all due respect. My father..."

"He is not you," the knight interrupted. "And though I cannot say how others in the temple may treat you after this, be assured that the knights judge a person on their merit, not their heritage. My father was a thief and a pirate. He was hanged from the Baltrian city walls when I was only four years old. Yet here I am. A knight of Amon Dähl. Your father's crimes are only yours if you make them so. Never forget that."

Orias bowed his head in gratitude. "Thank you. I won't."

Soon the door opened and a young man in plain clothes gestured for the boys to follow.

Just as they were leaving, Dresher called out, "Be careful. Morzahn is a murderer, but not a fool. And his reputation was well earned."

His words struck home. Aremiel had been wondering how Orias would handle speaking to his father. Seeing him in chains would do nothing to lessen the impact of his presence. His legend alone would make even the bravest of men think twice before confronting the mighty Morzahn.

As they descended into the basement, the air quickly became thick and putrid. Only a few dim torches lit the small room at the foot of the stairs. Here, a middle-aged man with a bald head, olive skin, and narrow features was waiting for them, along with an older, silver-haired woman.

Agents, thought Aremiel.

"Your father is through there," said the woman, opening a door leading to the cells. "Take as long as you need, but do not approach the bars for any reason."

Orias led the way. The room beyond was at least fifty feet long and twenty feet wide. To the right was a series of iron-barred cells, and at the far end, another door that it was rumored had once been a torture chamber—though it was now empty.

Morzahn was in the third cell along, still dressed in a simple shirt and trousers... and still shackled. He was sitting on a stool, back straight against the wall and eyes closed.

"So they send my own son to question me, do they?" he muttered. His voice was as deep and powerful as his frame would suggest.

"They didn't send me," said Orias. "I came of my own will."

"Did you?" He chuckled. "Did you really?"

Orias stood in front of the cell, with Aremiel just behind and to his left.

Morzahn opened his eyes. "You've grown. You'll be as big as me one day, I'd wager."

His gaze fell on Aremiel. "And this must be your friend Aremiel, son of the High Lady of Valshara, leader of the Order of Amon Dähl." His words were filled with contempt. "Does my son know that you're here to spy on him?" He paused, then nodded. "Of course he does. He's no fool. And unless I've been told wrong, you're too good a friend to have kept such information from him."

"I asked Aremiel to be here," Orias said. "And yes, I know his mother asked him to report back to her. But that won't be needed. I plan to do so myself, anyway."

"I'm sure that you do." Morzahn rested his huge forearms on his knees. "You'll need to prove yourself many times over now that I've been branded a traitor. No one will ever look at you the same way again. And for that, I am truly sorry."

"Is it true?" he asked. "Did you do what they say?"

"I think you know the answer to that."

Anger flashed across Orias's face. "Tell me!"

Morzahn sighed heavily. "Yes, it's true. I killed those men. And yes. I *was* looking for the *sword*."

Tears welled in Orias's eyes. "Why?" His voice cracked.

"Because I had to. Because things are not always as they seem. One day you'll see that."

"And did you find it?" He forced his words out through stifled sobs.

"That's what they really want to know, isn't it?" Morzahn sneered. "They want to know if I discovered a clue that would lead to the *sword*. Well, they can all go to hell. I'm not saying anything else about it."

"But why did you want it?" Orias was doing his best to govern his emotions in the way he'd been taught, but each word his father spoke was bringing forth more rage and anguish.

"Because the madness must end." This time, his father's voice was soft and kind. "You must not ask me more."

"Why not? Surely I have the right to know why you have betrayed everything we were taught to believe in."

"You have the right to know only what I decide you should know," Morzahn countered calmly. "And son of mine or no, seeing as you are still a part of the temple, you cannot be entrusted with my reasons."

Orias glared furiously at his father for a full minute before speaking. "Then if you have nothing more to tell me, I will go."

"There is one thing," said Morzahn. "Tell your mother that I am sorry we never got to walk the beaches of Skalhalis again. And that I love her."

"Is that all?" he asked. Though tears were streaming down his cheeks, his voice was steady.

"Yes." Morzahn lowered his head. "That is all."

"Then we are done." Orias gave a sharp nod and walked smartly to the door. Just before opening it, he paused to glance back. "I'll smile when you hang. I wanted you to know that."

Morzahn said nothing, nor did he look up.

The two agents looked highly displeased when the two boys returned.

"That didn't take long," said the man. "You should have pressed him harder. I knew it was a bad idea to send a child in with him."

"You would have done no better," the woman scolded. "So stop being an ass." She turned to Aremiel. "Did you glean anything from his words?"

"He may not have," Orias cut in quickly. "But I did." He started toward the stairs.

"And where do you think you're going?" said the man.

"To see the High Lady," he replied.

Orias sped from the room and up the stairs so rapidly that Aremiel found himself struggling to keep up. But instead of taking the left hall leading to his mother's chambers, he took a right and then motioned for Aremiel to follow him into a rarely used storage closet.

"I wanted to speak to you alone before we see your mother," he whispered. He looked outside to check that they weren't being followed. When satisfied, he closed the door. "My father mentioned Skalhalis. He said to tell my mother he wished they could walk again on its beaches."

"Yes. So?"

"*So* they have never been there together," he explained. "He's trying to send her a message."

Aremiel thought for a moment. "Are you going to tell this to my mother?"

"No. But the agents were certainly listening in. If they picked up on what he said and thought it worth noting, they would go straight to the High Lady. I don't want my father involving my mother if I can prevent it."

Aremiel didn't want to say what he was thinking, but knew that he must. "How do you know she's *not* involved?"

"I don't," he admitted. "But she will certainly come here after word of all this reaches Baltria. *I* will speak to her first."

"And if she *is* involved?"

His face tightened. "Then I will lose two parents." He grabbed his friend's shoulders. "I need you to keep quiet about this until I can speak with her. Will you do that?"

Aremiel nodded slowly. Even though he felt this was something that his mother should know, he could understand why Orias would want to wait.

"Thank you," Orias said. He cracked open the door. "Come on. Let's go see the High Lady."

When they arrived, she was talking with Dresher at her desk.

She motioned for them both to sit. "So, have you said all that you needed to say?"

"Yes, High Lady," replied Orias. "And he doesn't know where the *sword* is. He wants you to think that he might... but he doesn't."

"Are you sure?"

"Yes, High Lady. I'm sure."

She studied him for a moment. "As your father has confessed and there is no doubt of his guilt, his execution will not be delayed. If you would like, I can send you away with Dresher until it's over."

"If my father is a traitor, I would see him hanged. There is no reason to send me away."

The High Lady frowned. "Naturally, it is your right to be here. But I urge you to reconsider. This is not something you want to see."

"Begging your pardon, but it is."

She sighed and rose to her feet. "Very well. You have two days to change your mind. In the meantime, stay with Dresher. I'm sure there is much you can learn from him."

Both Orias and Aremiel stood as well.

"Stay here, son," she said.

Orias gave his friend a nod and then left with the knight.

His mother sat back down. "There is more. Isn't there?"

Aremiel plopped heavily back into his seat and remained silent for a long moment. His mother could always see through him. He desperately wanted to tell her what Orias had said. But the thought of betraying his best friend repulsed him.

"You can tell me, son," she assured. "Orias is confused right now. He may not show it, but seeing his father has wounded him. He cannot possibly know what the right thing to do is." Her smile was tender and compassionate. "I know you don't want to betray his trust. But this is important. If he withholds information, it could end his chances of becoming a knight. So if you truly want to help him, you must tell me what you know."

"If I tell you," he said. "You must swear to keep it to yourself."

His mother shook her head. "I'm sorry, but I can't make that promise. If there is a danger to the temple, I must act."

"There is no danger," he promised. "You have to trust me on that."

"I do trust your intentions, son," she said. "But you are still too young to understand certain things."

Steadying his resolve, he sat up straight. "Either you swear, or I won't tell you."

The two locked eyes. Finally, it was the High Lady who relented. With an exasperated sigh, she lowered her head.

"Very well," she said. "I swear."

Satisfied, Aremiel conveyed what Orias had told him.

"Then I see no harm done," she remarked, speaking as much to herself as to her son. "Word has already been sent to his mother this morning. And as it will take a few weeks for her to arrive here, I suppose there is nothing to do but wait."

There was a knock at the door. A moment later, the old woman from the cellar entered.

"I beg your pardon, High Lady," she said. "But there are matters we should go over."

The High Lady nodded. "Of course."

Aremiel got up and embraced his mother firmly. "Thank you."

She kissed his cheek and watched him leave.

Being that the execution was scheduled in two days, the builders began erecting the gallows at once. Laraad, who was helping in their construction, made a special point of smiling broadly at Orias every time they saw each one another.

Orias, however, appeared unconcerned by his taunting. Most of his and Aremiel's time was spent with Dresher. The knight had ridden with Morzahn on many assignments and knew him well. At first, Aremiel thought it rude when he spoke of the man so casually in front of Orias.

"Morzahn was not always as he is now," Dresher explained. "His crimes will cost him his life. But he did many great deeds before his fall. There are hundreds, if not thousands, of people who owe their lives to the courage of Morzahn. And I would have his only son know of that."

As it turned out, Orias seemed glad to hear Dresher's stories, and even asked questions about certain details.

When the day arrived, Aremiel expected to see Orias's demeanor change. But instead, he was as cheerful as he had ever been. They ate their morning meal and afterward made their way to the courtyard. By the time they got there, it was filled nearly to capacity.

The High Lady was standing beside Dresher atop the gallows, with six knights guarding the pathway leading from the main building. Each one wore a black cloak with the hood pulled over his head.

Aremiel scanned the crowd. Laraad and a few others were perched atop the ramparts, laughing and talking as if they were at a fair rather than an execution. He had never hated the boy more than at that moment.

They pushed their way through the throngs of people until arriving directly in front of the gallows. Murmurs and whispers could be heard as eyes fell on Orias. But he ignored them all and simply stood there, stone-faced and silent.

When the temple doors swung open, a hush fell over the crowd. Out walked Morzahn, closely escorted by a knight on either side. They slowly led him to the foot of the gallows and up the steps. Dresher looked him in the eye for a second, then turned away to position himself beside the trapdoor release lever.

"I'm glad it's you, old friend," Morzahn told him.

Dresher simply nodded.

The High Lady stepped forward. "You have been brought here to answer for the crimes of murder and treason. Through your own admission, you have been found guilty. And as you have offered up no cause for leniency, you are hereby sentenced to death. Do you have any final words you wish to say?"

Morzahn looked out at the crowd until he spotted Orias. His voice carried clearly. "I should have told you this when we spoke before... I love you, son. No matter what I've done, always remember that."

Aremiel expected tears, but instead, Orias reacted by quickly climbing atop the gallows and placing his hand just above Dresher's on the release lever.

Gasps of both wonder and revulsion reverberated through the crowd. The High Lady simply looked on in amazement.

Morzahn nodded and huffed a quiet laugh. "I should have expected this. But it doesn't matter. My heart is still with you, son... even if yours has abandoned me." He looked at the High Lady. "Let's get on with it."

Tearing her eyes away from Orias, she stepped in front of the condemned man and secured the noose tightly around his neck. "Are you prepared to answer for your crimes?" she asked.

"Prepared?" He let out a disdainful laugh. "I'm eager."

She turned to the crowd. "Then let justice be done." After a brief sideways glance at Orias, she descended the stairs.

Time stood still as everyone waited. There was total silence. Orias then looked up at Dresher and nodded.

In unison, they pulled the lever.

Two weeks had passed since the execution of Morzahn. Though Aremiel was concerned about his friend, he seemed to be carrying on with his business as if nothing had happened. He'd tried talking to him about it on a few occasions, but Orias just laughed and slapped him on the back.

"I'm fine, you old mother hen," he would say. "Worry about your sword practice instead."

It was just after their evening meal when Orias was called to the High Lady's office. When he returned to their sleeping quarters later, Aremiel could see that all the color had drained from his face and his eyes were distant, as if in a trance.

"What's wrong?" he asked.

For a moment, Orias said nothing. Then he pulled a parchment from his pocket and handed it over.

Aremiel opened it apprehensively, dreading to see what was inside. After reading, he placed the parchment on the nightstand and touched Orias's shoulder.

"I'm so sorry," he said.

"The High Lady said that they found her lying in her bed," Orias whispered. "Her throat had been cut and her house ransacked. A robbery, they said." He looked up at Aremiel, tears flowing freely. "A bloody robbery."

A terrible thought occurred to Aremiel. Could his mother have ordered this done? He quickly dismissed the idea. She would never do such a thing. That much he knew for a fact.

"Now I'm truly alone," Orias sobbed.

"You'll never be alone," said Aremiel. "Not as long as I live. I swear it."

Orias reached out and embraced his best friend, desperate for comfort.

As they stood there locked together, Aremiel once again swore his oath to always be there for Orias... though this time it was just as much a prayer as a promise.

CHAPTER 22

The road from the Northern Steppes—40 years earlier

After reining in their horses to a slow trot, Aremiel looked over his shoulder. His face was twisted in anger.

Orias laughed boisterously. "Stop worrying. We lost them."

"We would never have needed to lose them if you would just obey orders," Aremiel snapped.

"Your mother warned you not to make me your lieutenant," he replied, still laughing. "She said I would be nothing but trouble."

He glared at Orias. "And she was right."

"Anyway, I don't know why they're so upset," Orias said, feigning innocence. "It was only a pair of horses."

"We were there to negotiate with the men of the steppes in order to *buy* horses. We were not there to *steal* them."

"I was intending to leave some gold."

Aremiel snorted. "That's not the point, and you know it."

"Well, anyway... it's a good thing they aren't as smart as their mounts." He gave his friend a devilish grin. "Otherwise they'd have caught us, and I might have to save your skin again."

Just then, both men caught the sound of distant hoofbeats. They halted their horses and continued listening, but the sound slowly faded away.

Orias burst into another round of laughter. In spite of himself, Aremiel could not help but join in with him.

"Next time, at least try to tell me *before* you do something stupid," he said, shaking his head, though unable to wipe away a broad grin.

"I'll try," Orias replied. "But sadly, I rarely know that it's stupid until after the deed is done."

They rode on until reaching a small village on the borders of the steppes. It was little more than a trading post, but Amon Dähl had agents there. And that meant decent food and a warm bed.

They both felt a tingling in their medallions telling them that a member of the order was nearby, though identifying who that was might prove to be difficult. If it was a knight, it would have been easy. Even without the charm, they would be able to recognize him simply by the way he moved. But agents were another matter. They were trained to blend in and pass unnoticed.

Orias spotted the village's solitary inn and spurred his horse toward it. "At least we can have a drink while we wait. The gods only know how long we'll have to sit there. Bloody agents."

Aremiel shared Orias's dislike of agents. "I should have found out who was assigned here before we left. At least we would know who we're looking for."

"Hey! Did I just hear Captain Aremiel admit that he did something wrong?"

Aremiel smirked. "Of course not. Just like I didn't hear *Lieutenant* Orias making fun of his commander."

In truth, it should have been the other way around. Both of them knew that it was only Orias's propensity for making trouble that had prevented him from being made Aremiel's superior officer. His high spirits had got him into more than his fair share of scrapes. Even so, there was no denying that he was the finest swordsman in the Order. He also had a keen intellect and an uncanny sense of when danger was near. Several knights owed their lives to him... and Aremiel was one of them.

But of all Orias's virtues, his kindness was by far his greatest. And the one that held him back the most. Knights of Amon Dähl were not expected to involve themselves in local disputes or politics. But if his friend saw an injustice, he was compelled to act. Though Aremiel admired him for this trait, it frequently caused their superiors to question Orias's ability to lead.

When Aremiel was promoted to captain, he'd insisted on having Orias as his lieutenant. No one was pleased by this decision, least of all his mother. She feared Orias's recklessness would eventually get him killed, and that their close friendship would have her only son lying dead beside him.

He had often pleaded with Orias to behave less impulsively, but he would only smile and say it was the will of the gods that drove him to act in such a way. At first, Aremiel thought this was just a joke. But over time, he realized it wasn't. Orias truly believed he could feel their will, and that they had a special purpose for him.

After tying up their horses, they stepped inside the inn. The place was typical for a town such as this. Just a few tables surrounding an iron stove in the center of the common room, and a small bar to the right.

"Order us a bottle of wine," Orias said. "I'm going to check out the area."

Before Aremiel could object, Orias was gone. *Check out the area,* he thought. *You're going to find another shrine.* It was the same in every town they visited. Orias would very soon locate a local shrine or temple to pray at, though he tried hard to hide this fact. His cavalier attitude and lighthearted ways were a surprising contrast to his deeply held faith. He was by no means a monk or priest, but he was equally as dedicated.

Aremiel thought to join him from time to time, but knew it would likely embarrass his friend. In any case, though he loved the gods as much as anyone, he never could really see the point of prayer. Such beings were probably far more concerned with larger issues. The life of a single knight couldn't possibly matter much to them.

The inn door opened to reveal a swarthy man in dingy clothes. He came over and sat down.

"I'm Vurin," he said. "I've been expecting you. When you're ready, my house is nearby."

"I'm Aremiel," he replied, nodding politely. "My friend Orias will return very soon."

"I saw him in the street," Vurin told him. "He's already there."

There was a note of urgency in the man's voice that disturbed him. They left the inn immediately and went to a small hovel at the end of the main avenue.

The interior was far more accommodating than the dilapidated exterior suggested. Four comfortable beds were at the rear, and a hearth was burning brightly to the left. The floor was covered by a plain yet well-made rug, and the walls were lined with bookshelves filled to capacity with dozens of leather-bound volumes.

Orias was sitting at a wooden dining table near the stove, a bottle of wine gripped firmly in one hand, and a piece of parchment in the other.

"I see you couldn't wait for us to return," scolded Vurin.

Orias ignored the agent. Grinning boyishly, he tossed the parchment to Aremiel.

"Can you believe it?" he said. "We've made the list of prospects."

Aremiel read the message carefully. Both men then simultaneously burst into laughter.

"Why are they bothering us with this nonsense?" Aremiel said. He sat down and handed the parchment to Vurin.

Orias took a drink. "I really don't know. It's not like she would choose either one of us to guard the *sword*."

"This is not a matter to be taken lightly," scolded Vurin. "It is a great honor, and you should treat it as such."

Aremiel took the bottle from Orias and turned it up. After wiping his mouth with his sleeve, he gestured for the agent to join them. "I know it is. I truly do. But I am the son of The High Lady of Valshara. My mother would cut off her arm before she would send me to a place where she could never see me again."

"And I am the son of Morzahn," said Orias. This caused Vurin's eyes to widen. "Can you imagine the turmoil choosing me would cause? No, my friend. This is just a ploy to get Aremiel to come home for a while. His mother misses him."

"That, and the fact she's afraid if I stay away too long, you'll get me killed," he added.

"That too," agreed Orias.

"Whatever the case," said Vurin. "You should leave in the morning."

Orias sighed and leaned back in his chair. "Then I hope you have plenty of wine for us to drink tonight."

The next day, though they were up early, Vurin was already gone.

"Off spying on people, I suppose," Orias said.

"So long as it's not us, I don't care."

Valshara was only a week away, and the journey passed uneventfully. The two of them spent most of it talking about past exploits, both their own and those of other knights. Aremiel loved the fraternity between the Knights of Amon

Dähl. He often thought back to the days when his mother was still insisting he become a historian. It always made him laugh. He could never have been happy with such a boring life.

When they finally arrived at the gates of Valshara, ten men stood upon the ramparts and announced their arrival with a call of golden trumpets.

"Well, that's new," remarked Orias. "If I didn't know better, I would begin to think they are happy to see us."

"I wouldn't get too used to it," Aremiel said. "When the new guardian is chosen, they'll go back to ignoring us again."

The courtyard was packed with cheering people. Aremiel could feel his face flushing with embarrassment, but Orias was clearly reveling in the attention. He waved and smiled as they rode in, making sure to give each young woman he saw a playful wink. When they reached the base of the stairs leading up to the main temple building, two grooms took their horses and gear.

Aremiel's mother stepped out through the doors. On her left was Jylias, chief of the agents and a difficult woman at best. But the person standing to her right gave both men pause. It was Laraad. His head was held high, and he was smirking with thinly veiled contempt.

The High Lady's face was expressionless. Aremiel knew at once that something was wrong. He could think of no circumstances that would prevent her customary smile every time he returned to Valshara.

"I see her look too," whispered Orias, sensing his friend's concern.

"Welcome, brave knights," she said when they reached the top of the steps. "Your presence has been eagerly anticipated. Only two candidates have yet to arrive. Your rooms have been prepared and your meals will be brought to you once you've cleaned and changed."

Even her speech was odd. She was never this formal with him.

Both Orias and Aremiel bowed low.

"Thank you, High Lady," Aremiel said, mirroring her reserve. "But Orias and I would prefer to stay in the barracks."

"That would be inappropriate under the circumstances," Laraad told them.

Aremiel raised an eyebrow. "I was unaware of your elevation. Or do you make a habit of speaking out of turn?"

"Laraad is representing the *builders*," the High Lady said. "His master is ill and chose him to come in his place."

Aremiel bowed. "Then I congratulate you, *Master* Laraad."

"And I, you," he replied, unable to hide his scorn. "Both of you. This *is* quite an honor. One well-earned if the tales I've heard of your exploits are true."

"I'm afraid they may have been exaggerated," said Aremiel. "We are simply servants of the Order."

"Indeed," Jylias interjected. "And yet you have been set apart by your fellow knights as the best they have to offer. Such respect coming from the bravest among us *must* be warranted."

"Where are the representatives from the other vocations?" asked Orias.

"They are in council," Laraad replied. "We were given the honor of greeting you. But now we must return."

This confused Aremiel. *In council?* Rarely did the different branches of the Order all meet at once. There was no need. Healers had little business with historians or builders with agents. *So why would they need to be in council now?*

His mother's eyes told him that the answer was not going to be to his liking. They were then shown to their rooms and provided with bath water and fresh clothing.

Once changed, Aremiel went immediately to his mother's chambers. She was awaiting him at her desk. Her expression was grave and her eyes bore the lines of age and fatigue.

"What's going on, Mother?" he demanded. "Why are they in council?"

"They are discussing who is to be the next guardian," she replied.

Aremiel nearly leaped from his chair. "What? How can this be? That choice belongs to you."

"I'm afraid that as my son is a candidate, I was forced to defer to their judgment," she explained.

Aremiel felt ill. He had been certain that his inclusion was incidental. Now, there was a real possibility that he might be spending the rest of his days alone.

"Don't worry, son." She was doing her best to force the anxiety from her voice. "There are twelve candidates. And all of them have been a knight far longer than you. Most outrank you as well. It's likely one of these will be chosen."

"I need to tell this to Orias."

"Orias can wait," she said. "I haven't seen you in almost a year. You *will* spend time with your mother. I've already sent for our meal." She got up and stepped around the desk. "For now, push everything else from your mind. There is nothing to be done."

Aremiel smiled at her. "Of course. You're absolutely right. I'm sorry."

They spent the next few hours together, talking quietly. He then excused himself, promising to return early the next day.

Later that evening, he told Orias what he had learned. But his friend only shrugged and dismissed any possibility that either of them would be chosen.

"The fact remains that you are the son of High Lady Velinia, and I am the son of Morzahn. I, for one, would most certainly not want to face your mother if they chose you."

Aremiel tried using this logic to calm his nerves. But he couldn't shake the feeling that something was very wrong.

It only took two days for the final candidates to arrive, but by then, rumors were circulating that the new guardian had already been chosen. Even so, a feast was held to honor all who had been considered. Orias and Aremiel stayed at this only as long as courtesy required, after which they spent the rest of the evening in the training room. Sword practice always took Aremiel's mind off things, and he was eager for the distraction.

The night before the announcement was to be made, he was unable to sleep. He wandered the halls for a time, then made his way to the ramparts. Orias was already there, waiting for him.

"At least we don't have to bribe the wall sentinels any-more," he joked.

Aremiel thought about the first time they had been up here together.

"You were so scared," Orias said, reading his thoughts.

Aremiel chuckled. "So were you. I just didn't know it."

"I still am."

There was a long silence.

"If I am chosen, I don't think I can go through with it," Aremiel eventually said. "I can't imagine my life without you at my side."

Orias placed a hand on his shoulder and gave it a fond squeeze. "If you *are* chosen, you will take a piece of my heart with you, my friend. But you *can* do it. And as much as I hate the thought of you leaving, I can think of no one better to guard the *sword* than you."

"I can," he replied.

The two men stared out into the night in quiet contemplation. They had been together for most of their lives. That Orias was older and had become a knight first was the only reason they had been separated at all. For both of them, it had been a long three years. And as soon as Aremiel took the oath, he insisted that he be partnered with Orias. Now, it could all end.

The next morning, Valshara was a beehive of activity and excitement. The High Lady would be given the council's choice, and she would then read it aloud in the courtyard at midday. Every member of the Order who could attend would be there.

Orias and Aremiel spent their time in the training room instructing the students. For them, it was an honor to have two candidates there. But for the two knights, it was a thrill to see the new talent that would one day be riding into honor and glory.

When the time finally came, they were escorted to the courtyard. A platform had been erected, on which all the candidates were lined up at the rear.

Trumpets sounded as the High Lady exited the temple and then ascended the platform. In her hand was a sealed parchment that contained the name of the chosen one.

She raised her hand to quiet the crowd. "For thousands of years, the Order of Amon Dähl has been charged with protecting the greatest power in the mortal world. And for thousands of years, we have never failed in our duty. It is the reason the Order was founded, and our most important purpose of all. For that reason, only the very best amongst us is picked to reside in the *Sword of Truth's* resting place. There he lives, and there he eventually dies. This sacrifice is made to ensure the safety of all people, and is an honor not given lightly.

"Behind me are the bravest and most honorable knights our Order has to offer. Their character and deeds have earned them all a special place in our hearts, and I feel that any one of them would be a worthy guardian of the *sword*. I know that I am not alone when I say that we are so very grateful for their loyal service."

She closed her eyes for a moment before opening the parchment. "But only one can be chosen." She opened her eyes and looked at the name. For several seconds, she did not speak. The crowd began to stir with impatience. "The one chosen is..."

Her voice cracked, and she was forced to clear her throat. "Aremiel."

The crowd erupted and immediately began chanting his name.

Aremiel was unable to move. The sound of his own name did not seem real. His mother reading it aloud was like remembering a dream of years past, though it had happened only a moment or two ago.

He felt someone take hold of his hand and pull him forward. It was his mother. He had not seen her, even though she'd been standing right in front of him. Tears were streaming down her face as she lifted his arm aloft. The sound of the cheers increased until the excitement reached a fever pitch.

He was still unable to move on his own when his mother embraced him.

"It will be all right, son," she whispered into his ear.

He wanted to say something, but had been robbed of his voice. After a time, the crowd became calmer. Eventually, after managing to shake off the initial shock, he stepped down from the platform. Orias was close behind him.

Ignoring the calls of congratulations from those he passed, he made directly for his mother's chambers and waited there until she arrived. Orias sat beside him and said nothing. As soon as his mother entered, he leaped up from his chair.

"I won't do it," he shouted. "I won't spend the rest of my life in seclusion."

The sadness in her eyes was immeasurable. "You must. And you will not really be alone. The gods will be with you."

"Bah! Tell that to Orias. He's the one dedicated to the gods." He looked down at his still-seated friend and immediately felt guilty. "Forgive my hasty words. I meant no insult."

Orias smiled warmly. "I know you didn't. But your mother is right. The gods will be with you. You will hear their voices, and it will fill your heart with joy."

Aremiel dropped hard back down into his chair and put his face in his hands. "Why did they choose me?"

"Because you are the best of us all," Orias replied. "Everyone knows it."

"I know you don't want to leave your life behind," added the High Lady. "Or your friend. But it will be many years before the current guardian dies. Until then, you are free to do as you wish."

Aremiel looked up. "Then I will continue with my duties as a knight and hope the current guardian is blessed with immortality."

"I think both Orias and I wish that as well," she said.

Orias got up and slapped his friend on the back. "Who knows? With me around, you might not even live long enough to take the position."

Normally this would have brought an angry remark from his mother, but on this occasion, she instead cracked a tiny smile. This quickly grew wider and wider until turning into outright laughter. Soon, all three of them were laughing loudly together... though no one really knew why. It was like an island of joy amidst an ocean of despair.

"I think I will stay here for a few months," Aremiel said after calming himself down. "I'd like to help instruct the new students."

"Sounds like fun," agreed Orias. "I can show them why *I* am the superior swordsman."

"We'll see about that," he shot back, grinning.

Orias winked. "We will indeed."

CHAPTER 23

Baltria—32 years earlier

"I hate this city," complained Aremiel. "Too many agents."

"You hate every city," said Orias. "All for the same reason."

"I just don't like them. They're far too devious."

The two men rode past the city gates, pausing only to ask the guard for directions. Not that they really needed them. But it was always better to appear as if you were new to a place. It helped to keep people from wondering why you were in areas that you shouldn't be. And though this trip was not dangerous or covert, it was an old habit.

"At least the food here is good," said Orias. He spotted an attractive woman in a short skirt and thin blouse. "And the Baltrian women are much easier on the eye than those in the dirty little trading posts you prefer."

Aremiel shook his head in mock disapproval. "Then I take it I won't be seeing you tonight."

"Not unless you come with me," he replied. "You could keep me out of trouble."

"I doubt even I could do that."

"Agreed. But it's an excuse to do something other than sit in your room and read."

In truth, Aremiel would have very much liked to go with him. But the time was fast approaching when he would have to take his place as guardian of the *sword*. There was still much he needed to know before that happened, and being that he had chosen to spend most of his time away from Valshara, he had to learn what was required during their travels.

"I'll think about it," he lied.

Orias scowled. "As you wish, Commander. But you really need to get some enjoyment from life before you take up your position as guardian."

Aremiel didn't like it when Orias spoke of their impending separation. "According to you, my heart will burst with joy when that time arrives. So why worry about what I miss out on today?"

"There is no talking to you, is there?" his friend grumbled.

They wound their way through the streets to the inn where they would be staying. Their assignment was simple: remain at the inn until the agent contacted them, then escort her to a location in the Eastlands. As usual, there was no way of telling how long they might be required to wait. On their last assignment, they had been held up in Helenia for more than a week.

Naturally, during their time there, Orias soon found a way of getting himself involved with a group of merchants who were extorting the temples. He had at first intended to simply frighten them off, but ended up beating two of them nearly to death. At the end of it all, in spite of Aremiel's reprimand and outward anger, it was hard to deny that his intervention had greatly improved the situation. What's more, he'd managed to do it without anyone knowing that Amon Dähl was involved.

On arriving at the inn, they ate a quick meal and retired to their rooms until the evening. The agent would know who to ask for whenever she showed up, so Aremiel took the time to relax. The place wasn't upscale, but the beds were soft and the rooms clean. After weeks of sleeping in the open, it was a welcome respite. Unfortunately, his pleasure was not destined to last for long.

Just as he was dozing off, there came an urgent tapping on his door. Experience had him grabbing his dagger before he even realized he was doing it. But before he could fully raise himself from the bed, the door opened, and a woman entered. She looked to be in her sixties, though not frail. Her tanned skin hid many of her wrinkles, and only thin wisps of gray hair peeked out from beneath her bonnet. She carried a cloth-covered bundle in her arms.

"You are Aremiel?" she asked.

"I am. And you are?"

"It doesn't matter who I am," she replied.

Aremiel could hear the anxiety in her voice. "Has something happened?"

"Many things have happened," she answered. "But what you should be concerned with is in here." She laid the bundle on the nearby table.

"What is it?" he asked, suddenly suspicious. He felt uneasy around agents. Particularly agents who kept dangerous secrets. And this seemed dangerous already.

"There isn't time to explain," she said. "But there are things you must know before you take over as guardian of the *sword.*"

His uneasiness rose. "Who are you?" he demanded.

She moved close to the door before replying. "I was a friend of Orias's mother. And to my eternal shame, *I* was the one who murdered her."

Before a stunned Aremiel could say a word, she hurried from the room. He gave pursuit, but she was out of the inn and lost in the densely crowded street before he was able to stop her.

His head spinning with questions, he returned to his room and carefully opened the bundle. Inside was a thick, leather-bound book and a folded parchment. Picking up the parchment, he began reading.

Aremiel,

I come to you because my heart will no longer allow me to remain silent. I hope that you are the man people claim you to be. If so, you will find a way to use what I have given you for the good of Amon Dähl.

First of all, you should know that the death of Orias's mother was not a robbery. I killed her under orders from my superiors. Please know that I was told a lie and acted with the understanding that I was doing my duty. They said that she had found the location of the Sword of Truth and was planning to pass this information on to her husband. I now know this to be untrue. If Morzahn ever did discover the sword's location, she was not the one who divulged it to him.

The book I am giving you was written by Orias's mother and details the reasons Morzahn was driven to betray the Order. The corruption and greed described are beyond anything you can imagine. How deep it goes and exactly who is involved, I cannot say. But as you are the son of the High Lady, I can think of no one better to bring this to. Should I attempt to take it to her myself, I would be discovered and likely never make it to Valshara. I think they already suspect that I am aware of them, and if they knew I possessed this book, I would quickly find myself in a shallow grave.

I am sorry to involve you in this, but I have nowhere else to turn. I pray that you can undo the evil that has been done in the name of the gods. Tell Orias that I hope he can forgive me for taking his mother from him, even though I can never forgive myself.

I will now try to go east to the borderlands, and then into the deep desert. There are rumors of nomadic tribes there. Perhaps my enemies will not think to look for me in such a desolate place. Please do not seek me out.

Good Luck,
-S-

Aremiel re-read the letter several times, unwilling to believe what he was being told. His eyes then shifted to the book and lingered there for several minutes. He tried to reach out and pick it up, but was unable to. It was as if he had lost command of his muscles. Only a loud pounding at the door jerked him out of his stupor.

Orias poked his head in. "Are you coming or not?"

"I... um... no." He wanted to tell his friend what had happened, but something inside said that he should wait. "You go ahead."

Orias shrugged before shutting the door again. "At least I tried."

With movement now restored, Aremiel picked up the book. His hands trembled as he placed it on the table in front of him and turned to the first page.

For the next few hours, he pored over the text in absolute horror. It contained explicit details of the most heinous crimes imaginable, nearly all of them being committed by actual members of the Order. It seemed that they had been manipulating just about everyone for decades—the temples, kings, lords, merchants, and even the common people—all to advance their own hidden agenda. Orias's mother believed that their ultimate aim was to maneuver and corrupt the nations of the world until they were literally unable to function. Then, when all was on the brink of disaster, a small core group of conspirators would be able to seize power and rule all humankind.

The temples were their chief means of exercising influence, and they had corrupted members within every single one of these, from the Abyss to the desert.

He continued to read until hearing Orias returning from his night out. Though still only halfway through the text, he had already uncovered hundreds of atrocities—murders, thefts, and treacheries of every conceivable kind.

His door opened and Orias stumbled in, smiling broadly and clearly a little worse for drink. "You look terrible," he grinned. "I said that you should have come with me."

Aremiel gestured for him to sit down. "There is something you need to know."

Orias rubbed his eyes. "I think I've had a bit *too* much fun tonight. Can't it wait until morning?" But the expression on Aremiel's face quickly conveyed the urgency of the matter.

It took Orias a moment or so to focus after Aremiel handed him the letter. But the second he came to the part about his mother, his eyes shot wide and the effects of the wine vanished. Just as Aremiel had done, he read it again several times. Then, as if it were made of thin glass, he placed the parchment delicately on the table.

"And you believe this?" he whispered.

"I do."

Orias's breathing was becoming rapid and shallow. "Let me see the book."

Aremiel handed it over. Orias studied the first few pages, then closed it again.

"It is my mother's handwriting," he confirmed. He looked at Aremiel with hollow eyes. "Have you read it all?"

"Much of it," he replied. "Your father was right. All this time we believed him a traitor... and yet he was right."

"How can you say that?" Orias demanded. "Even if this is all true and the men he killed were a part of the conspiracy, he still was seeking the *sword*. That alone makes him guilty."

"Then what do you think he should have done?" Aremiel shot back.

"The same thing that you are about to do. Go to the High Lady and report what you know."

"And if *she* is involved?" The words stung, even as he spoke them. He didn't want to believe it. But he knew he couldn't deny the possibility.

"Your mother is a good and honest woman," Orias countered. "Do not allow this to poison your heart. She is *not* involved."

"You can't know this," Aremiel said. "But you are right. I must speak with her."

"I'll go with you."

"No. You stay here and complete our assignment. If this runs as deep as I think, we must act as if there is nothing amiss. I am the chosen *guardian*. If I return to Valshara alone, no one would think it out of place." He lowered his head. "But before I go, there is something more I must tell you."

"Speak," Orias urged. He could see the conflict on his friend's face. "Whatever it is, I'll understand."

The next sentence caught in his throat. "If the High Lady is involved, then I am partly responsible for your mother's death."

Orias furrowed his brow. "What is this nonsense? Of course, you're not."

"I told her what your father said to you," he explained. Guilt racked his spirit. "I told her about his message to your mother."

Orias gave him an understanding smile. "I thought you might, even then. You never could keep secrets from her.

But that was a long time ago. And like I said, I know she is not involved."

"But what if she is?!" He hadn't wept in years, but now tears were starting to fall quite freely. "What if I'm responsible for..."

Orias's hand came up, silencing him. "You are *not* responsible for my mother's death. And if I am wrong, I still do not blame you. You were only a child then, and you did what you thought was right at the time."

Aremiel could only nod.

"Whatever happens, trust that the gods will guide you," he continued. "Listen to what they say and all will be well."

Mention of the gods only brought forth anger in Aremiel's heart. They had allowed their own temples to become corrupt and vile. Where were the gods when an innocent child was murdered just so someone else could inherit power and wealth from its father? Where were the gods when villages were burned to the ground because they would not sell their land to local lords? Where were the gods when husbands were slain in order to marry the wife into a more influential family? These and countless other crimes had been committed by the temples—and all of them covertly orchestrated by members of Amon Dähl. Yet still, the gods remained silent. But Aremiel dare not say any of this aloud. Orias would never accept it. He was a man of absolute faith. To him, even the evil that had infected the temples and the Order was being allowed by the gods for some greater purpose. Aremiel could see that in his expression.

"I trust in *you*, my friend," he said. "That has to be enough."

His ride to Valshara was plagued with rain. It was as if the storm was following his every mile. On the morning he departed, Orias had suggested he join him in prayer at the temple of Gerath. He had refused.

So the gods care nothing of evil, he thought bitterly. But when I refuse to pray, they send a deluge to torment me.

When the walls of the Valshara came into view, he stopped and stared at them for more than an hour. All his life he had believed in the principles taught there. Over the years, he'd watched good men die fighting in the name of Amon Dähl. Now he was discovering that it was all a lie.

With a violent crackle, a streak of lightning split the sky. It was time. He would now discover if his worst fears were to be realized. As he spurred his horse to a slow walk, deep rumbles of thunder heralded his approach.

The greeting and bows from the sentinels went unnoticed, as did the voices of the people expressing their delight in having the guardian return to Valshara. Nor did he thank the groom who took his horse and gear. His eyes remained fixed resolutely on the door leading into the main temple complex.

"I will see the High Lady at once," he told the servant who met him inside.

"Would you not prefer to dry off first?" the man asked.

Aremiel shot him a furious glance. "I said at once."

The servant lowered his eyes. "I will let her know that you're here."

"There's no need for that." He brushed his way past and stalked down the hall.

With every step he took, his feet felt heavier. He had gone over in his mind what he would say a hundred times. And each time, the scene ended differently, leaving him more confused than before. If she knew and *was* involved, what would he do? He still had no answer to that. And even if she wasn't, did that really change anything?

On reaching her door, he knocked and quickly entered before his mother could respond. She was sitting at her desk in her casual robes, reading a book and sipping on a cup of hot tea.

"Aremiel!" She sprang up and rounded the desk, but stopped just short of him. "You're soaked. Why didn't you change first? You may be a knight, but you can still get ill."

Aremiel wanted to speak, but even after pondering for so long over what to say, he still didn't have any idea how to begin.

His mother's expression quickly changed from joy to concern. "What is it? What's happened?"

"Sit down, Mother," he said. "We must talk."

The despondency in his tone startled her. "At least let me get you something to dry off with."

She retrieved a towel from her closet. Aremiel hesitated before accepting it, then quickly dried his face and arms.

Velinia sat back down. "Now tell me what is wrong."

Without a word, Aremiel reached inside his shirt and pulled out the bundle of cloth containing the book and letter. He tossed them both on the desk in front of her.

She opened the book and began reading. After only a few pages, she looked up, her face pale and her eyes filled with tears.

"Did you know?" he asked, desperation seeping into his tone.

"Yes."

Her voice was less than a whisper, yet the single word echoed in Aremiel's ears like a hammer striking an anvil. His head began to swim and his vision blur. His worst nightmare had just come true.

"How can you be a part of this?"

She shook her head, tears dripping onto the desk. "I'm not a part of it, son. But there is nothing I can do to stop it."

"What do you mean?" His focus was slowly returning... along with his fury. "You are the High Lady, are you not?"

"This has been going on long before I ascended to the position," she explained. "And when I first found out, you were but an infant. I was afraid..."

"You were afraid of what?" he demanded.

"I was afraid they would do to you what they did to your father," she replied meekly.

"You're telling me that they killed my father?" His hands began to tremble. His father was an Amon Dahl builder. He had been told all his life that he had died from a fall while constructing a temple in Helenia.

She lowered her head. "Yes. And I was given a choice. Stay silent, or see you suffer the same fate."

Part of him understood. She had acted out of a mother's love. But another part of him could not forgive her lack of courage.

"When I was a child, you may have had reason to fear," he contended. "But I have not been a helpless boy for a long time. You could have told me. I could have done something about it."

"There is nothing you could have done. They are everywhere. No matter how strong you have become, they would have found a way to silence you."

"Like they silenced Orias's parents?" He leaned in. "Did you have anything to do with that?"

"Not the death of his mother," she replied. "I swear it. But I suspected Morzahn had unearthed the truth, and that it was this knowledge that had sent him into insanity." She straightened her back and leveled her gaze. "Morzahn sought the *sword*. No one should ever possess such power. He knew this better than anyone. Yet he did it anyway."

"He didn't deserve to die!" Aremiel shouted.

"He committed the one crime that is unforgivable by the Order," she countered.

He sneered. "Yes. It seems that any other crime is simply a part of the routine, with no one there to punish them or challenge their authority. Well, all that is about to end."

"Son... please." She knew her child well and could see the conviction building behind each word he spoke. "There is nothing you can do about this. They'll kill you."

"Will they?" He laughed. "Perhaps."

Rising from his chair, he reached inside his shirt and grasped the medallion of the Order. For an instant, he paused. Then, in a single determined motion, he ripped it from his neck and tossed it contemptuously onto his mother's desk.

She stared at it, pain and panic striving for supremacy in her eyes. "No! I'm begging you. Take your place as guardian. The old guardian will be gone soon. Once there, you won't need to worry about anything ever again. The gods ..."

"Never speak to me of the gods again," he hissed. "They have done nothing to prevent this. And yet we give them praise and worship. For what?" He turned his back and strode to the door. "Morzahn was right. The madness must end."

He paused for just a moment to look over his shoulder. "Tell Orias that I am sorry. I must follow my own path from now on."

"Son, wait!"

But it was too late. Aremiel was gone.

CHAPTER 24

Althetas—19 years earlier

The streets below were quiet as Aremiel watched carefully for his prey to emerge from the tavern. The small shop he had chosen for his perch was closed, though unfortunately for the shopkeeper, he did not close early enough. He now lay bound and gagged in a broom closet.

Aremiel's breathing was controlled and his hands steady. In spite of the fact that what he was about to do would almost certainly lead him to the prize he had sought for so long, his training and experience allowed him to keep his focus.

It was regrettable that another knight would have to die. It troubled him each time, even after the scores he had slain. He could never completely rid his heart of the fraternity and kinship he'd once felt when he was one of them. But that was long ago, and he was a different man now.

The Order of Amon Dähl had stricken his true name from the record, and even his own mother had been forced to denounce him. In fact, it was an offense to merely speak the name of Aremiel. But they had given him a new one anyway—one that suited him much better. He had heard it cried out in terror more times than he could easily count by the men and women he was about to kill. It was also spoken with dread in hushed whispers within every temple from the desert to the sea.

The Dark Knight. It was more than a name. It was what he had become.

He shifted his weight and took a deep breath. The Master Builder should be coming out any time now; the man wasn't much for drinking and was a terrible gambler. As the Dark Knight, Aremiel had often studied his prey for months before striking. It was a lesson learned from matching wits with agents. Patience was their greatest strength. Twice they had cornered him, and only his prowess with a blade had saved his life—though be bore three deep scars to remind him of his carelessness.

But he had learned the agents' weakness. Arrogance. They had lived in the shadows for so long, they had begun to believe they were truly invisible. And to most people, they were. But not to him. Sometimes he had to watch a town for weeks before picking them out. Usually the arrival of a knight gave them away, and once they realized this, they abandoned all contact with the Order except via messenger bird.

He smiled every time he thought about the panic it had caused. He had picked off more than a dozen agents before they became aware of what was happening. They tried everything to stop him. He was a fugitive within every kingdom in the land; his description had been given to every magistrate and constable in every city and town. But their feeble attempts to apprehend him were useless. He had made his home in the one place they all feared to go.

Soon he would return there and consolidate his power. Then the earth would tremble. And at long last, the reign of the wicked, and the tyranny of the gods, would come to an end.

The tavern door opened and the Master Builder stepped outside. His knight escort was close to his side, his eyes constantly alert and his hand poised ready to draw his sword.

A young one, Aremiel thought. A pity. How foolish to send a newly ordained knight to guard the Master Builder.

He watched as they rounded the corner, then jumped down from the roof. The impact jarred his knees, causing him to wince briefly. Age was catching up with him. But soon, age would no longer be a matter of concern.

He followed the duo, running in silence from shadow to shadow. Though the knight was young, he had been well trained. He took a seemingly random route through the city, stopping from time to time to check that they were not followed. But the Dark Knight was far too skilled to be caught by such basic tactics.

When they finally reached the Master Builder's small house, his escort ushered the man inside and then took a walk around the building as a security measure. But none of this would do him any good.

When the knight returned and followed his charge through the front door of the house, Aremiel prepared to move. Watching from an alley twenty yards away, he waited for a few pedestrians to pass before bolting across the street. Creeping along the side of the house, he made his way to the back. The sound of the knight talking came to him quite clearly.

Experience told him to stay put until he knew precisely where everyone was. From the sound of the footsteps and the creaks in the floor, he was able to get a reasonable idea of the interior layout. The Master Builder was clearly not in a mood for conversation, and was saying nothing while the obviously now relaxed knight prattled on.

He would prefer for both men to be in the same room when he made his move, so he decided to enter straight through the back door. If he was fast enough, he should be able to take the knight by surprise and end the fight before he could even arm himself.

He drew his dagger and stepped forward. The knight would be in the room just to his left. He took a breath and smashed the rear door in with his the heel of his boot.

Without hesitation, he stormed to the door of the next room. It was slightly ajar, so he ran into it shoulder first and burst through. He was expecting to see a solitary knight caught unawares by the suddenness of the attack. Instead, there stood three knights, each one well prepared and carrying a long dagger.

The younger man was in the center, and flanked on each side by an older veteran. The man on his left the Dark Knight recognized, the other he did not.

Aremiel grinned viciously. "I see I wasn't as careful as I thought."

"It ends here, demon," the young knight said. "You have drawn your last drop of blood."

"And you think you will be the one who kills me?" he scoffed. "For your bravery, I will spare your life if I can."

"You will pay for the lives you have already taken," he spat in return.

The older knight on the left spoke. "Take care. I have seen him fight. He was the only knight in the Order who could challenge Orias."

"That is why I called for you," the youthful knight shot back. "I am young, but I'm no fool."

Hearing his old friend's name sent a tinge of pain shooting into Aremiel's heart. But in an instant, the pain had turned to anger. He could hear the Master Builder's rapid breathing in the next room. He needed to end this and complete his task. Still, he felt a liking for the young knight. He was reminded of himself as a youth. So full of confidence and resolve.

"I suggest that you prove you are no fool," he said. "Leave now." But the young knight said nothing. Aremiel's eyes narrowed. "Such a waste."

As his opponents rushed forward in a narrow semi-circle, he grabbed a small throwing knife from his side. The steel was painted black, making it virtually invisible against his black armor. It sank into the thigh of the man to his right, who instantly let out a cry of both shock and pain before collapsing sideways directly in the path of the young knight. Aremiel could see the fierce determination in the young man's eyes as he fought to prevent himself from stumbling over his fallen comrade. Somehow, he managed to avoid entangling his feet, and, with balance restored, charged on.

The Dark Knight's blade flashed as it struck out at his oncoming foe's heart. The young man twisted away, his training guiding his movements. He countered by attempting to open Aremiel's throat with his knife, but the blade found only air.

In his eagerness to strike, he had stepped beyond his reach. In an amazing display of skill, Aremiel kicked the young knight in the groin while simultaneously plunging his dagger into the injured man's chest.

The young knight doubled over, his face creased with pain and turning purple. Yet still, he was able to thrust his blade upward. It caught the Dark Knight's breastplate, but he did not have sufficient leverage to penetrate the armor.

The man now at his rear, enraged by the sight of his companion's death, roared with fury and stabbed hard at the Dark Knight's back. But like his younger comrade, his blade also found nothing but empty air.

Aremiel spun around and trapped his attacker's extended arm beneath his own. In a single movement, he then brought his own blade across the knight's neck. The man let out a ghastly gurgling sound as blood spewed from the terrible wound. He then sank to his knees and toppled over onto his back.

By now, the young knight had recovered sufficiently to regain his stance. Aremiel could see the rage in his eyes and knew that more blood would need to be spilled.

"Come then," he said. "Join your friends if you must."

The young knight charged in with speed that was remarkable for a man of such large proportions. Aremiel jumped to one side and was only just able to avoid having steel sink into his chest. Instinctively, he caught the man's wrist and countered. But the young knight was ready for this, and pressed hard to one side, causing the dagger to pass behind him. The sheer force of his movement was immense. Both men slammed into the wall, grunting loudly as they did so. The old timbers, unable to withstand such a battering, shattered asunder. With an ear-splitting crack of wood and glass, the pair tumbled completely through and landed in the small area of ground behind the house.

For a second, panic seized Aremiel. His opponent was larger and heavier... and on top of him. But his hand holding the dagger was still free, and at the other man's back. He turned the tip down and struck. The young knight yelped and rolled to one side.

This was all the Dark Knight needed. Going with the sideways momentum, he exerted even more force until able to roll over completely and reverse their positions. Now on top, he still had an iron grip on the young man's knife hand. After pinning this to the ground, he pressed his own blade to the flesh of his opponent's throat.

"It is over," he growled. "Drop your weapon."

The young knight glared furiously. But his situation was undeniable. He had lost... and now he would die. He loosened his hold on the knife and allowed it to roll off the tips of his fingers.

"Some men close their eyes when they know the end has come," said the Dark Knight. "But not you. No. You have courage. And as I told you—I would spare you if I could."

"Don't bother," he hissed. "I have no fear of my own end."

"This I can see," he replied approvingly. "And before you meet that end, I will know your name."

There was a long pause. "Bevaris," he finally said.

"It was an honor to meet you, Bevaris. May you live long enough to find a good death. For today, it has eluded you." With a heavy grunt, Aremiel sent his fist smashing into the young knight's jaw, dispatching him into unconsciousness.

He rose to his feet and went back into the house through the ruined wall. The Master Builder was still in the next room, sitting in a rickety chair against the far wall.

The Dark Knight chuckled as he entered. "It would seem you ended up finding your true calling after all, didn't you, Laraad?"

"I have always contended that one's true nature will surface in the end, Aremiel," he replied.

He raised an eyebrow. "I thought speaking my name was a crime."

Laraad sniffed. "As this is to be my end, I don't think I need worry about the consequences."

"Your end? Why should that be so?"

"Don't play games with me," he said. "We are no longer children, and I have not the patience. Just do what you came here to do."

"You've gained some courage over the years." Aremiel took a chair from the other side of the room and placed it in front of Laraad. "I would have never imagined that to be possible."

"And you have become even more arrogant," he shot back. "I would have never imagined *that* to be possible."

Aremiel laughed softly. "Perhaps you're right. Perhaps I am arrogant. But that does not explain why you chose me as the guardian of the *sword*."

Laraad sneered. "You think I would choose *you*? I voted for Orias, but was overridden. He was always a man of faith. More so than any of the others... especially you. Whatever you may think of me, I am devoted to the Order. I would not allow my personal feelings about you or Orias to influence the most important decision of my life. He was always the better man."

"And from what I have heard, you now have your wish. Is he not the guardian?"

"You know that he is," Laraad replied with disgust. "You know it because you tortured members of the Order for the information. How many innocent men and women have fallen to your wrath? A hundred? A thousand? Or do you even know?"

"I have only done what needed to be done," Aremiel replied calmly. "You can serve the gods if you choose. But I will no longer be blinded by their lies. The time is at hand for humankind to be rid of them ... forever."

"And will it end there?" he countered. "Once you have defeated the gods, will you simply lay down the *sword* and live your life in peace?"

"Peace? When has there ever been peace? Have the gods brought peace, or do they simply watch the never-ending slaughter from heaven?"

"So that is what you think you will do, is it? Bring peace? How can you be so blind?" He shook his head. "You swim across an ocean of blood and think peace will await you on the other side? I was wrong about you. You are not arrogant. You're insane."

Aremiel locked eyes with him. When they were young, Laraad would have quickly looked away. But this was not the same cruel boy he had known in Valshara.

"Give me what I came for," he commanded sternly.

"This will only end in your doom." Laraad removed a gold ring from his index finger and held it up. It was set with an oval jade bearing the engraved symbol of Amon Dähl. "And I fear that many others will share your fate."

Aremiel snatched it from his grasp. "I will create my own fate. And when it is over, you shall see that I am right. The world will be free."

Laraad laughed with woeful eyes. "Men like me will not survive to see what you have done to the world."

Rising to his feet, Aremiel placed the ring on a nearby table and drew his dagger. With a grunt, he smashed the pommel end of the weapon into the green stone. The jade shattered, revealing a tightly folded piece of parchment. With the utmost care, he opened it and read. A tiny smile crept up from the corners of his mouth.

"Do you have what you came for?" Laraad asked solemnly.

"Yes," he replied. "I do indeed."

The High Lady of Valshara inched her way along the passage toward her door, the young cleric on her arm a constant reminder of her increasing age and infirmity. No longer could she walk the halls of the temple whenever she felt restless. Most of her time was now spent in her chambers. In fact, the vast majority of Amon Dahl's business was now conducted from there.

On reaching the door, she patted the young girl on the hand and dismissed her. She was not so feeble that she couldn't dress for bed unaided—though that time must fast be approaching.

The first thing she did after entering the room was to glance at her desk. She let out a sigh of relief. No letters. Every day, she feared receiving word of more deaths at the hands of her son. Her dear boy. Where had she gone wrong?

The day she denounced him was long ago, yet it was still fresh in her memory. *The one thing that is not failing me is the one thing that causes me the most pain*, she thought. Slowly, she rounded her desk and eased herself into the chair.

"Hello, Mother." The voice seemed to come from the dark corner across the room.

She froze, at first thinking she had imagined it. Then, from the shadow, her son stepped out.

"Aremiel." Her voice was barely audible. "How...?"

"Don't worry," he said. "I killed no one in coming here. But you will want to have someone check the ramparts after I leave so they can untie the sentinels."

"Why are you here?" she asked. Her eyes were already welling with tears.

"I am here to tell you that it is over," he replied. "I know where the *sword* is. And when I leave here, I will have it."

Anguish instantly clouded her face. "I will only say this once, though I know you will not listen. The *Sword of Truth* was never meant to be wielded by mortal hands. If you take it, it will destroy you. Please, son. Has there not been enough death? You have made war on the Order, the temples ... and me ... until your heart has completely turned away from the light. Come back to me. I'm begging you."

"There is nothing to come back to," he said. "Amon Dähl is nothing to me now."

"Am I?" she asked. "Am I nothing?"

He gazed at his mother, trying to see her as he once had. But the woman he knew then was long gone. He understood this now. And in that moment, he knew that coming to see her had been a mistake. It would only serve to cause her more pain. And in spite of his anger, he did not want that.

"You are my mother," he replied. "And regardless of what you might think, I do love you."

"I know you do, son. And no matter what you have done, or will do, I love you, too."

Aremiel moved closer to kiss her on the cheek. She took his hand, squeezing it desperately. For a brief moment, he was the child she had brought to the temple so many years ago. But then he pulled away, and without looking back, left the room.

For more than an hour, she sat there in silence, tears soaking her face. Finally, she reached into her drawer and removed a small, silver-handled dagger.

"It has been long enough," she whispered.

The pain was insignificant. She knew how and where to place the blade. Soon her eyelids grew heavy as more blood spilled onto the floor. And as she faded, a vision of her precious boy entered her mind. His smile was bright and warm, and his love unquestioning and complete.

She smiled back and her spirit reached out to him.

Still together, they passed into memory.

As he neared the location of the *sword*, his thoughts turned to Orias. Would he be there? Of course he would be. He was the *guardian*. Yet still there was a part of him that longed for his old friend to have abandoned his duty, so making the inevitable confrontation unnecessary. But this was a futile hope. Orias was still blinded by his faith and a slave to the will of the gods. And now fate was upon them both. A final death to cause... and his ultimate sin to commit. He pressed on.

It was all the Dark Knight could do to keep his teeth from chattering. The chill mountain air was thick with a dense fog that soaked into his skin, making every movement of the wind feel like torture. The only sounds were the crunch and clatter of his horse's hooves and his own labored breathing.

He could feel that he was drawing near to his destination, yet could see nothing but dull gray fog and the gnarled, vicious shadows of long-dead trees...

CHAPTER 25

Gewey rose from the slithas and landed gently on the sandstone terrace that surrounded the vortex. He stared into its depths for a moment, marveling at the sight. As the rushing sand flowed down, it changed from the light beige color typical of the desert into a luminescent blue, then vanished completely into a well of nothingness. The *flow* was so strong here that it took his breath away. It was several seconds before he was able to adjust and focus his vision.

The surrounding area was broad and smooth. Shadows danced and flickered from multiple directions, yet the only light here was emanating from the vortex itself. His memory, or rather, the memory of Gerath, told him that this was where all life had first spawned. At least, that was what the gods believed. He was still shocked at how, in spite of their vast knowledge, there were still numerous mysteries that remained elusive to them. In many ways they were no different from humans or elves. All were limited in their wisdom, and all continuously sought the meaning in their existence.

But this was not the time for such contemplations. He took a deep, cleansing breath and stretched out with his spirit. In an instant, he knew that his foe was near. Gewey smiled and centered his mind on what his human eyes were unable to see.

Then he saw him. The Dark Knight. He was sitting on a large earthen chair he had created with the *flow*. His form was that of a man. He was broad in the shoulder—nearly as broad as Gewey himself—and even through the gleaming black armor, the sinews of his powerful arms and legs were obvious. His dark curls fell down his neck, pulled away from his face by a thin golden crown resting upon his brow.

But it was his face that was startling. His penetrating brown eyes, square jaw and handsome nose would have made most women swoon. But his flesh... if that's what it could be called, had all the appearance of polished marble. Pitch-black, and veined with thin crimson lines, it was like looking at a superbly crafted statue of an ancient warrior. Only the fact that his eyes blinked occasionally indicated that he was indeed alive and not made of stone.

"Does my appearance bother you?" he asked. His voice boomed and echoed with unrelenting power. A mortal man would have fallen to his knees in terror, but Gewey easily dismissed the display. "I'm afraid that the sword's power has had some unanticipated effects." He held out his hand, and the *Sword of Truth* immediately appeared there. The ghostly light of its blade spilled down and drenched the floor with its energy.

Gewey used the *flow* to create another chair facing his enemy. His eyes never left him as he sat down. Then he noticed the body of a woman on the ground behind the Dark Knight.

"Was the death you've already caused not enough for you, Aremiel?" he asked.

The Dark Knight smiled, his white teeth giving his already unworldly appearance an even more startling quality. "You know my name?"

"Of course I do. The power you used to erase it from memory no longer affects me."

"Good," he said approvingly. "It is pleasing to hear it spoken aloud after all this time. But I did not kill the wife of Lee Starfinder. She was as you see her when I arrived here."

Lee's wife! Gewey reached out and felt her spirit still residing within her body. Yet her physical life was completely gone.

"Release her if you wish," offered Aremiel. "I will not stop you. Her usefulness to me has come to an end."

Gewey took hold of Penelope Starfinder's spirit and pulled it from her body. He could feel her confusion and frustration. *Be calm*, he told her. *You will be with Lee very soon.* He then released her and guided her from the chamber.

"Now we can concentrate on the matters at hand," Aremiel said.

"Yes," agreed Gewey. "But there is something I would know. Why did you wage this war at all? Why not simply fight a war against the gods? Why did so many others need to suffer?"

"That you care so much for the suffering of mortals separates you from the rest of your kind," he replied. "But I am afraid there is no easy answer as to why I have done this. My ambitions were small before I took the *sword*. I simply wanted to free the mortal world from the cycle of lies that corrupted our hearts and ruined our spirits.

"For thousands of years, the gods have demanded worship. And for thousands of years, they have interfered with the lives of humans. But to what end? The very temples erected in their names have become dens of vermin and disease. And what did they do to stop it? Nothing. When it amuses them, they enforce their will and move us like pieces on a board.

Then they watch as cities crumble and people are slaughtered. When they are needed most... they disappear. They leave others to put back together the pieces of the world that they themselves have helped to tear apart."

He paused for a moment. "But after I took the *sword*, my eyes were opened. The malady of the world was far beyond any remedy mortal man could provide. For he has become infected as well. The gods have held sway for too long. I quickly discovered that the very people I had hoped to save were now as much a part of the disease as were the gods. It was then that I realized what must be done. The world needed to be wiped clean so that life could begin anew. And only I had the power and the will to do it."

Gewey could hear the conviction in his voice... and the madness. "You were once a believer in redemption. Do you have no hope that the mortal world can be healed?"

"I was once a believer in many things," he countered. "And just as you were once a naïve farm boy, I grew up. Even one such as you must admit that humans and elves are beyond redemption. The Great War settled nothing. To this day, they continue to squabble and bicker. How long before this festering boil of hate explodes into another war?"

"That may be," said Gewey. "But you have no right to interfere. You are becoming like the very beings you despise. But instead of merely misguiding the mortal world into disaster the way they do, you seek to destroy it completely."

Aremiel laughed. "No. Not completely. There is still virtue in the world. There is still strength. Once all else is cleansed, I will create a new world and a new people. And with my hand to guide them, they will finally know true harmony and happiness."

"So you intend to become the Creator? Is that your ultimate plan?"

"The Creator?" he mocked. "Is there even such a being? I see no evidence of it. And if there is, then it is as much responsible for the insanity of the world as the gods are. Moreso, in fact."

"There *is* a Creator," Gewey stated emphatically. "And to aspire to rise so high will only result in your greater fall."

"And are you not here to ensure that I do fall? Are you not here to stop me? It seems to me that I have more to fear from *you* than from some mythical Creator."

"If it is *her* will, then I *will* stop you. Perhaps that will be the only proof you will accept."

"And if stopping me means your own death?"

"Then so be it," Gewey replied. The resounding boom that issued from his lips caused the Dark Knight to flinch. His enemy could feel the power raging within him. Equally, he could feel the strength of his enemy. They were evenly matched. And they both knew it.

"There is another way," he offered. "Leave this world to me. Take your wife and child and return to heaven where you belong. I can use the power of the *sword* to let you pass through. Leave here and be contented."

Gewey scowled. "That you think I would abandon the world and its people to the fate you describe tells me you know nothing of who I am. The world you seek to mold would be as loathsome as the one you now revile. More so, as it would be devoid of kindness and pity. You speak of strength and virtue, but you never once mention love and compassion. You seek a throne that will make you the one and only god of this world. But a god has no use for thrones. So what does that make you?" He sneered and waved his hand dismissively. "Just a mortal man with grand ambitions and egotistical dreams of glory."

He let out a short, ironic laugh. "I once feared this day. I envisioned you as some colossal fiend that I would have to conquer. But I was wrong. You are just a man. Small-minded and unable to wield power with wisdom." He could see the rage building in his enemy's eyes.

"You might destroy me, Aremiel," he continued, "But I no longer fear you. Whatever happens now, I know that you were never a god. In fact, you are barely a man. And I pity you."

The Dark Knight rose to his feet, and the chair turned to dust behind him. "Then let us finish this now, Darshan, son of Gerath."

Gewey stood, and his chair disintegrated as well. "May you find forgiveness in the next world."

Aremiel snorted. "I need no forgiveness. Only your blood."

Gewey did not waste time with more words. Instead, he drew his blade and readied himself. When he'd fought Melek, the battle had been waged between their spirits. But his adversary this time was not a god, and he was unsure of how he would be attacked.

"I have always wondered what it would be like to fight one of your kind in the flesh," the Dark Knight said softly, almost as a gentle muse.

In a blur of motion, he rushed in. The curtain of light radiating from his sword sharpened, making it appear as if he were wielding a thunderbolt rather than cold steel.

As they came together and their swords met, the ringing of steel on steel was far louder than Gewey had ever known before. More than that, each time their blades clashed, angry flames shot out in every direction. For a while he was forced steadily back, and twice his feet nearly slid from beneath him.

The Dark Knight pushed forward relentlessly, then suddenly switched his method of attack from high sweeps to a series of low thrusts and tightly controlled strikes. Gewey fended these off rather more easily. With his balance now restored, he countered furiously. But the Dark Knight parried and avoided his attempts to draw blood with no more effort than if fighting a young boy.

It suddenly became clear to Gewey that his enemy was toying with him, and that he was no match for the man's skill. In that case, he decided, he must rely on brute strength. There was just one thing worrying him. Though he could easily heal from a wound made by a normal sword, he had no idea what an injury from the *Sword of Truth* might do to him. For all he knew, one small cut might mean instant death.

Putting this from his mind, he stepped right, and using all of his strength, swept his sword violently across at the Dark Knight's hip. The blow was easily deflected, but the sheer force sent his enemy stumbling back several paces.

"For a moment, I thought this would be too simple," he said with a half-smile. "Your physical strength is truly impressive. But your skill with a sword…"

He rushed in again, this time sending a hail of strikes raining down. Gewey did his best to counter, but even with his godlike speed, the Dark Knight's skill was quickly overcoming his defenses. Finally, steel found the flesh of his left arm. His eyes went wide. But with a flash of relief, he realized that the *sword* had done no more harm to him than any other weapon might have.

As droplets of his blood spilled onto the floor, the Dark Knight grinned. "That is what I wanted to see. The blood of a god drawn by my own blade." He took several steps back and gripped the hilt with both hands. "And now we shall see how powerful you *really* are."

The ground began to shake violently. Gewey could feel the *flow* radiating from his enemy like heat from the desert sun. Even Melek had not felt so powerful as this. Rocks fell from the high ceiling of the chamber, shattering on the stone floor all around him.

He'll bring the whole place down around us.

From the corner of his eye, he saw that the vortex was growing and consuming the terrace surrounding it. The Dark Knight rose ten feet into the air, both hands still gripping the *Sword of Truth*. His eyes were burning with fierce rage; his mouth was twisted into a vicious snarl.

Panic briefly threatened to take hold of Gewey, but then he heard a small voice in the back of his mind whisper, *Use your strength. Use your knowledge.* He smiled and nearly laughed out loud. Gerath was still with him.

He rose up, matching the Dark Knight's elevation. When level, he met the gaze of his enemy and raised both his arms. The vast mass of splintering earth above them instantly exploded upward, sending millions of tons of rock and debris flying out in every direction. Light from the noonday sun streamed over them like water released from a broken levy.

Gewey shot skyward through the opening; the Dark Knight immediately did the same. Below, Gewey could see that the vortex was still continuing to expand. The massive crater he had just created would be consumed within minutes.

"Impressive," said Aremiel. "You have learned to use your gifts. And you are far more powerful than I anticipated. So much the better. I will make your strength my own."

He lowered the *Sword of Truth* and pointed it directly at Gewey. Before he could move away, a ray of pure white light shot out and struck him in the center of his chest. At once, Gewey felt the *flow* within him beginning to drain away. He drew in more, but it left him just as quickly as it came. After only a few seconds, he realized that the *sword* was not simply draining away the *flow* he was channeling, it was stealing the power within his spirit... all of it.

He began falling toward the swirling mass below. He tried to resist, but the harder he fought, the weaker he was becoming.

He is not a god. It was the voice of Gerath once again. *Remember that.*

Spurred by the voice, Gewey clenched his fists tightly together and released a primal roar. All the remaining force and power he possessed shot forth, instantly engulfing the Dark Knight.

Aremiel screamed in agony. "No!" he bellowed, the volume of his voice louder than a thousand trumpets. The light from the *sword* was already receding.

Gewey halted his descent, but his head was reeling. He could barely see his enemy, and the *flow* within him was still drastically weakened.

He thought to ascend higher. That might give him the time he needed to recover. But before he could do this, the sky above turned red and a blast of heat seared into his exposed skin. His eyes cleared just in time to see a massive ball of fire streaking toward him. Instinctively, he used the *flow* of the air to part the flames. Even so, his hands and face began to blister as the inferno rushed past. He gritted his teeth and pushed the pain away.

His strength was returning, but not fast enough to save him from a second ball of fire, twice as large as the first. Again he tried to part the flames, but this time the power of the Dark Knight was too great.

He screamed in agony as the fire began to roast him alive. He tried desperately to push it away, but he was trapped within a burning hell.

The Dark Knight began to laugh maniacally. "Yes! Now do you understand? Do you see it? This was always going to happen. The other gods knew it... and they sent you to the slaughter, anyway. Beg for mercy and swear to serve me and I will release you from your torment."

Gewey's will was breaking. No human could have endured so much. The stench of burning flesh filled his nostrils, and he could feel pieces of himself dropping off.

It is only flesh, echoed the voice of Gerath. *Nothing more.*

"But the pain!" he wailed. "I can't bear it."

No! I must not yield, he told himself, making a last effort at resistance. But he knew he was at the very limit of what he could endure. In desperation, he began healing his own ruined skin. The pain lessened a little.

The Dark Knight sensed what he was doing and quickly increased the flame's intensity to the limit of his own strength. Gewey's clothing had long since burned away, and now his sword was beginning to melt.

He redoubled his efforts to heal, and in moments found that he could outpace the damage being done. *It is only flesh.* The words repeated in his mind again and again. He could see it now. How uncomplicated the flesh was... yet how miraculous. He marveled at its creation, nearly forgetting that a nightmare was raging all around him.

He looked down at his naked form and laughed. "This won't do." He used the earth below to create a suit of armor. Just as it was complete, the flames vanished. He looked up at his enemy and released a blast of air that sent him tumbling from the sky. His descent halted only a few feet above the vortex.

The Dark Knight glared. "You think you are winning? This fight has only just begun."

With these words, the ground immediately beyond the vortex erupted, sending hundreds of rock hard little balls of earth shooting toward Gewey. He responded by raising a shield of swirling wind that dispersed all but a few of the missiles. The ones that did make it through crashed into his chest and legs, but his armor absorbed most of the impact.

Though the air was almost completely dry, he was still able to extract enough moisture to form a wave of tiny, razor-sharp ice crystals. He hurled these at the Dark Knight, but a blast of flames melted them when only a few feet away from their target.

Before the Dark Knight could counter, Gewey followed this with a blast of air that struck his foe's breastplate with unbelievable velocity. His body was sent flying for nearly a mile before hitting the earth. Sand flew everywhere as he continued to slide across the ground for fifty yards before stopping, leaving a deep trench in his wake.

He scrambled to raise himself off the ground, but a gesture from Gewey had sandy tentacles reaching up and gripping his ankles. He swiped at them with his sword, but they reformed as fast as he could sever them. Relentlessly, they pulled him down into the earth until he was completely buried. Gewey hurried to solidify the sands and turn them to rock. He then sent waves of heat to roast his enemy in an oven of stone.

For a brief few seconds, he thought that he had won, and a feeling of elation lifted his heart. But then the earth began to shake with terrible violence. Gewey called on everything he had to keep the ground intact, but the Dark Knight overpowered him. A colossal explosion sent them both, together with huge chunks of semi-molten rock, hurtling a hundred feet or more into the air.

Free again, Aremiel glared at him with hate-filled eyes. Gewey could see his burned flesh already rapidly healing. There was a large dent in his breastplate, and black smoke was rising from the smoldering cloth beneath his armor.

With a feral cry, Aremiel raised the *sword* aloft. A cyclone of sand rose up from the earth and began to expand. Gewey readied himself for another barrage of missiles, but they did not come. Instead, the Dark Knight stepped into the tempest. Gewey tried to send a spear of fire into its heart, and growled with frustration when the flames vanished as soon as they touched the storm's outer surface. As he moved closer, a bolt of lightning shot forth. His earthen armor absorbed most of its energy, though its light momentarily blinded him.

His vision quickly returned, but the Dark Knight was already upon him. Gewey ducked just a fraction of a second before the *Sword of Truth* would have taken his head. A gauntleted fist then smashed into his jaw. He tumbled across the sky until he was once again hovering above the ever-expanding vortex.

He regained his bearings just in time to see Aremiel streaking toward him. Gewey glanced at his warped sword and tossed it aside. Just as he did so, the familiar sound of bells and laughter filled his ears as the *flow* of the spirit wrapped itself around him. When the Dark Knight was only a few feet away, both of their spirits suddenly sprang forth and ascended even higher.

At last, the two faced one another in their true forms. Gewey looked down. He could see their earthly bodies, frozen in time and space above the vortex, which had increased to more than a mile across.

The Dark Knight was now in gleaming silver armor, sword in hand and a jewel-laden crown atop his brow. His face was no longer of stone, rather, it glowed brightly with his spiritual power. And yet, for all his beauty, there was a dark force emanating from deep within his heart. It surrounded him with a vile aura that tarnished the purity that was once Aremiel, Knight of Amon Dähl.

Gewey was dressed in the simple garb of a farmer. His form and his sword glowed with a cool blue light. He looked at his enemy and shook his head sadly.

"Look at what you have become," he said. "Your strength and majesty have putrefied and become diseased. Your spirit is corrupted."

The Dark Knight sniffed. "And look at you. You are nothing more than a lowly peasant. That is what you have always been. How I could have considered you a threat is beyond reason. Such weakness cannot defeat me. Now I will cleanse the world. And I will begin by ridding it of you."

As their swords clashed, the entire earth rumbled with such mighty force that both men were thrown back several yards. But the Dark Knight quickly renewed his attack.

Though Gewey was no match for his opponent in human form, here they were equals. Each combatant struck and parried, their weapons taking turns ruining spiritual flesh.

It soon became clear that the Dark Knight was growing frustrated. He had not faced an opponent able to withstand him in many years.

Eventually, he stepped back for a moment, a sinister grin on his face. "You should know that once you are gone, I will take great pleasure in flaying your wife and child alive. Their screams will fill my heart with joy."

Gewey felt the rage within him building. *But this is what he wants*, he thought. *He wants me to fight with blind fury.*

"Or perhaps I'll spare them," the Dark Knight continued. "I will make a slave of the boy and your wife into my concubine." He grinned viciously. "I very much look forward to meeting them."

"The only thing that you will be meeting is your Creator," Gewey told him. His voice was calm and purposeful.

He stepped in, bringing his sword down in a sweeping arc that the Dark Knight was able to block without too much trouble. Undeterred, Gewey spun and struck out hard with his fist. This was more successful, and connected solidly with his opponent's jaw. The Dark Knight staggered back, but many years of experience controlled his movements. After shifting right, he thrust at Gewey's throat, forcing him to turn and step away.

With his enemy slightly off-balance, the Dark Knight pressed his advantage. In a series of calculated strikes, he maneuvered his way to Gewey's right. A dagger appeared in his left hand just before he dived forward and rolled behind him.

Gewey's eyes shot wide as the weapon plunged into his back. Pain racked his spiritual body. He spun around and tried to back away, but a fist smashed into his temple. This was quickly followed by a knee to his abdomen. In desperation, he swung his sword at the Dark Knight's legs. Though this made him step back for a moment, Gewey knew he was still losing the fight.

The pain was increasing from the deep wound, and this time he was not able to heal himself as he had done before. He somehow managed to defend against the next series of blows, but his strength was depleting... and the Dark Knight was clearly aware of this.

"It's over," he said triumphantly. "You are done."

Gewey gritted his teeth as another wave of pain shot through him. "That's not for you to say," he roared defiantly.

The Dark Knight laughed with contempt before moving in for the finish. It was in that moment that Gewey saw it. His opponent's overconfidence had left an opening. He could see it clearly. But if he exploited this opportunity, it would also mean his own end. He would be leaving himself wide open, and they would die together. Was he prepared to make that sacrifice?

Thoughts of Kaylia and Jayden only weakened his courage, and the possibility of surrender flashed through his mind for the first time. He remembered the vision that Ayliazarah's essence had shown him. He had surrendered then, and it had cost him everything. He had sworn that it would never come to pass. Even so...

Have courage, came a voice.

At first he thought it was Gerath again, then realized that there were two voices speaking in unison. He looked across and saw that the spiritual aspect of the Dark Knight was completely frozen, just like their physical bodies below.

Have faith, said the voices.

"Father?" cried Gewey. "Where are you?"

We are here, they replied. Both of us.

Two figures appeared between him and the Dark Knight. At first, Gewey refused to believe what he was seeing. It was the familiar smile of Harman Stedding. Gerath was at his side, his hand resting on Harman's shoulder.

"Have faith, my son," Harman said. "Be strong."

"Father," Gewey cried out again, now utterly convinced of their presence. He desperately wanted to embrace them both, but like the Dark Knight, he was unable to move. "Please forgive me. I have failed you. I tried to be brave, but my end has come and I am so afraid."

Harman shook his head and sighed. "You have failed no one. Least of all me. Now, though, you must face your true destiny. I know you are afraid. But be assured that we will be there with you all the way."

"We will see you through this trial," added Gerath. "We love you, my son. And now it is time to come home."

As the two fathers faded, Gewey could feel their love penetrating his spirit.

"Yes," he whispered. "It's time."

The Dark Knight's form burst back into life. Gewey stepped forward. The opening was still there, and he no longer hesitated. Both men gasped as their swords plunged into each other's chest.

Instantly, their spirits evaporated, and they were back in their physical bodies. Gewey could see the *Sword of Truth* protruding from his chest. At the same time, his sword hand had punched right through the Dark Knight's armor and pushed the man's heart out on the other side. Blood dripped from both of their mouths, spilling down into the vortex directly below.

Gewey looked into the Dark Knight's eyes and could see the vacant stare of death gazing back at him. As their bodies plummeted, darkness took him. Only the whistle of the wind in his ears told him that some life still remained. But it was to be fleeting, and he knew it.

When their bodies reached earth and plunged into the gaping depths, the world shook from its core one final time. The vortex gradually slowed its spinning and then began receding. When it was only a few yards across, the sands burst up in a mammoth explosion. It took many minutes for the earth to settle again.

The vortex was gone... and with it, both Darshan and Aremiel.

CHAPTER 26

As the dawn rose, King Lousis said a silent prayer. The vast army of the Reborn King would soon be upon them. And though his men would fight with valor and honor, he knew that this would be his final battle.

His thoughts turned to Selena. He could still see her smile when lying with him on their wedding night. Their love had made them both young again. For the briefest of moments, there was no war, no death, and no sorrow. There was only their love... and that was enough.

And if that is all I shall ever have, he told himself, it was still far more than I deserved.

Mohanisi and Lord Chiron rode up to join him. To Lousis, they looked like warriors of legend. Tall and proud, with unwavering courage. To think that this would be the day that claimed the lives of such of such magnificent elves brought a monumental sadness to his heart.

"They come soon," said Mohanisi.

Lousis gave him a thin smile. "Then let us ensure that this is a day they will never forget."

As if in response to his remark, the ground began to tremble with the pounding of thousands upon thousands of boots. Lousis surveyed his army with immeasurable pride. Not one man was so much as stirring in the face of their oncoming doom.

Drawing his sword, Chiron spurred his horse toward the vanguard. "For freedom!" he shouted. "For freedom and King Lousis!"

The army of men and elves erupted in thunderous cheers. Lousis felt a lump in his throat as he heard his name called out repeatedly.

"And for Selena," he whispered.

Mohanisi closed his eyes and said a prayer.

The long ridge on the horizon was soon filled with the banners of Angrääl. Armor-clad warriors and their swords glittered in the sunlight like a vast galaxy of stars. Wave after wave of them descended, ready for battle. Lousis shook his head and drew a nervous breath. There were so many of them.

He steeled his nerves and drew his weapon. "I will not wait to be trampled over," he grumbled. He looked at Mohanisi. "Are you with me?"

The elf simply smiled and drew his own blade.

"Sound the advance," Lousis shouted.

Trumpets blared out the order. Within seconds, his men were screaming the bloody cries of war. As they charged forward, Lousis could see that this aggressive tactic had taken the enemy by surprise. Angrääl had halted and was hurrying to form tight battle lines.

He knew that this would be only a momentary advantage. Prince Lanmore would quickly adjust. Lousis could only hope that his men engaged the enemy before they had time to unleash their terrible weapon.

But these hopes were quickly dashed as hundreds of white balls came streaking across the sky. The elves desperately tried to deflect them with the *flow*, but many still got through. One bolt landed directly in front of Lousis, but thankfully the speed of his horse carried him beyond it a moment before it exploded. Even then, the force of the blast sucked the air from his lungs and very nearly threw him from the saddle. The sounds of the repeated explosions were soon joined by a macabre symphony of screams from the wounded and dying.

Two more volleys were loosed before the armies came together. However, in anticipation of facing such blasts, Lousis's commanders had spread their advancing ranks well apart, so greatly reducing the casualties. This tactic had weakened their lines, though, and almost from the onset of battle, Angrääl was pushing them back.

Mohanisi maneuvered his horse in front of Lousis and began shouting for the guards to surround the king. Lousis roared with anger.

"Fight!" he cried. "Forget about me and fight!"

He looked up as yet another salvo of explosive bolts was launched. After passing over his head, it appeared as if they would land exactly where his reinforcements were waiting at the rear. But just as the deadly missiles were reaching the apex of their trajectory, the ground began to shake ferociously. Lousis's horse reared in terror, throwing him from the saddle and dumping him hard onto his back. The bolts overhead exploded in mid-air, sending tiny balls of fire raining down all over the battlefield.

The violent earth tremors continued for more than twenty minutes, keeping both armies too occupied with their own survival to bother fighting. A wide fissure suddenly opened just beside Lousis, and he was only just able to scramble away in time to avoid plunging down into the bowels of the earth. The desperate cries of terrified men told him that not all had been so fortunate.

When the quake finally subsided, an eerie hush settled over the field. Stunned men and elves cautiously regained their feet, and the two armies simply stared blankly at one another.

King Lousis surveyed the scene. Neither side knew what to do next. He grabbed one of his guards by the collar and shook him until snapping the man out of his stupor.

"Tell the commanders to pull back," he ordered. There was no other choice. They were in disarray and needed to regroup. He could only hope that Angrääl would do the same.

A minute later, the trumpets blared and the lines slowly backed away. The enemy did nothing to stop them. When they were far enough out of bow range, Lousis ordered them to halt. By then, most had recovered their wits, but still, the mystery of what had happened remained.

One by one, Mohanisi, Chiron, Bellisia, and the other commanders joined Lousis.

Finally, Mohanisi said what the others dared not to hope. "The war may be over. I believe Darshan has won."

"I pray you are right," said Lousis. "But until we know more, we should reform ranks and prepare to charge."

Chiron and the commanders departed to carry out his orders. Only Mohanisi and Bellisia remained.

Gradually, the lines came together and the soldiers readied themselves for more battle. But across the devastated field, things looked very different. The Angrääl troops still appeared to be in total disarray. They had yet to make any attempt at regrouping; in fact, most of them were wandering back and forth with no obvious purpose in mind. Confused shouts and desperate calls were the only sounds that could be heard coming from their direction.

Though Lousis was still unconvinced that it was all over, Mohanisi was not. He sat atop his horse with a wide smile on his face.

"Could it really be true?" said Bellisia. A single tear fell down her cheek.

Lousis called for a messenger. "Send word to our commanders that if the enemy begins to regroup, we charge. Otherwise, we will hold our positions."

Two hours passed, and the king was still staring intently across the field. But his optimism was growing, albeit cautiously. *Please let Mohanisi be right,* he prayed. *Let this be the end.*

A few minutes later, a group of three men on horseback emerged from the scattered Angrääl army. They were carrying a flag of truce.

The sight of this caused Lousis's heart to nearly rupture from the elation he felt surging in his breast. He spurred his horse to a run, leaving his guard struggling to catch up and place themselves between the enemy envoy and their king. They halted at the edge of bowshot range and waited. Mohanisi and Chiron rode up just as the enemy soldiers arrived.

"Are you King Lousis?" asked the man in the center. He was clearly the eldest of the three. His face was scarred and weathered—his eyes full of fatigue.

"I am," Lousis replied. "And who are you?"

"I am Dwylin, Your Highness. I come seeking your terms."

Lousis struggled to keep his hands from shaking. "In whose name do you speak?"

"My own," he replied. "Our commander, Prince Lanmore, is dead, and our officers have lost their wits. I have been chosen to represent Angrääl in their stead."

"And what is your rank, soldier?" asked Lousis.

"I am a sergeant, Your Highness."

Lousis shot a quick glance at the elves, then turned back to Dwylin. "And what of your king?"

"I don't know," he replied. "But as near as we can tell, we believe that he is also dead. That is what our officers keep mumbling to themselves, though none of us are really sure." He reached into his saddle and drew an elegantly decorated sword.

The guards immediately closed in, but Dwylin merely held it up by the blade and lowered his head. "This is the sword of Prince Lanmore. I offer it to you as a prize for your victory."

One of the guards took it from him and passed it to the king. For a long moment, all Lousis could do was stare at the weapon in disbelief. He then handed it to Chiron.

"We can no longer fight," said Dwylin. "Our army is scattered and leaderless, and we have no desire to continue."

Lousis thought for a moment. "And if I allow you to leave the field, what will you do?"

Dwylin shook his head. "I... I don't know."

"Then tell your men they are to lay down their arms and return to their homes. Those who do so will be allowed to pass. Those who remain on the field when the next dawn breaks will die. These are my terms, and they are not subject to debate. Do you understand, sergeant?"

"I understand, Your Highness." Dwylin bowed his head and rode away.

The king sat motionless in the saddle for a full minute before also riding back. Once within his lines, he told the commanders what had transpired and had them form a path down the middle of the ranks through which the defeated enemy could pass.

This done, he slid wearily from his saddle and started toward his tent. But after taking only a few steps, he fell to his knees. Mohanisi was at his side in an instant.

"Are you ill?" he asked.

"No, my friend. Not at all." Tears soaked the king's face. His voice dropped to a barely audible whisper. "Thank you, Darshan. Thank you."

Mohanisi helped him to his feet. Cheers and praises followed their every step. Chiron was already waiting just outside the tent, his face beaming.

"I lied, Your Highness," he called. He pulled a flask from his belt. "I saved us one more."

The old king burst into laughter. "You are absolutely forgiven."

They entered the tent and shared the brandy while listening to the joyous celebrations building outside.

Bellisia came in soon after and placed herself directly in front of Chiron. Her face was grim, one hand gripping her staff, the other planted firmly on her hip. Chiron frowned with confusion at her demeanor.

"Give me your sword," she commanded.

Without hesitation, he obeyed.

She looked at the weapon with disgust before tossing it into the corner. "If you are to be mine, you shall never wear that again. Do you understand me?"

Chiron could only look at her with his mouth agape.

"That is, unless you object to a union with me," she added.

Lousis and Mohanisi both shifted in their seats, trying to contain their laughter.

"I didn't know that you held such feelings for me?" Chiron said. "I had always thought your heart belonged to Lord Theopolou."

Her features softened. "He was indeed dear to me. And yes, I loved him. But love takes many different forms."

Chiron rose to his feet. He met her gaze with a tender smile. "And what form has it taken for me?"

There was a brief silence.

"As when a fool has love for an even greater fool," she then replied, feigning irritation.

"Then there is little doubt that we are well-matched," he replied, taking hold of her hand. "And I will try to be less of a fool in the future." He leaned down and kissed her gently.

"This is truly a day of miracles," Lousis remarked. "We emerge from the jaws of death and fall into loving arms.

Though sadly, my love is far from here, so I must wait a while longer to hold her."

They continued to sip the brandy together. Once it was all finished, Bellisia left and returned soon after with a bottle of wine.

"The enemy is already leaving," she said. "Across the field, there is an enormous pile of weapons that they have abandoned."

The king nodded and took a long drink.

"What happens now?" asked Chiron.

Lousis leaned back in his chair and gave everyone a contented smile.

"Now... now we can go home."

CHAPTER 27

Basanti sat in the cramped shack she had built for herself, deep in thought. The sound of the ocean and seagulls were constant companions. In truth, they were her only companions. The tiny island where she now dwelled was not suited for any sort of life other than the occasional sea turtle and the ever-present birds.

On first arriving here, she had wept continuously for weeks. And when she could shed no more tears, terrible nightmares replaced her sobs with screams. The darkness that now lived inside her would not permit rest. She couldn't imagine how Yanti had lived this way for so long.

This is what must have driven him mad, she thought. She recalled his final thoughts... or rather, emotions. The overwhelming feelings of relief, joy, and gratitude. Would anyone come to pay her the same kindness? Or would she remain here and slowly slip into insanity?

The pull to Angrääl had left her some time ago, which meant that the war was over and Darshan had won. This was the single point of light able to penetrate her grief. The people were now free, and the gods were released from heaven. But even the tiny smile that this thought created was quickly wiped away.

Felsafell. He would have discovered by now what she had done—and why. How hurt he must be. How angry. The broken promise of a life together once the danger had passed clawed at her heart, perhaps even more painfully than her grief over the damage her violence had caused.

When she first became aware that the Dark Knight was gone, the temptation to leave the island was almost too much to resist. But resist, she must. If not, she knew that she would become the next plague on the world, just as Yanti had been when he became King Rätsterfel.

But the world would be safe if she stayed here. Not even Felsafell knew of this island, and its tiny size meant that it held no interest for humans and elves. There was very little food apart from a dozen or so coconut trees, and no fresh water. Not that she needed either to survive. But she did enjoy eating and drinking anyway, and this was another pleasure that her choice had stripped her of. Even so, she was not regretful. Jayden and Kaylia lived. And because of this, the future held hope.

She got up and walked outside. The gentle waves were lapping rhythmically upon the white sands. The orange sky of the setting sun—a scene she had so often felt to be the Creator's greatest beauty—now seemed grotesque and miserable. It was a harsh reminder that yet another day had passed by, and that another must soon be endured.

She walked the length of the island several times. The coming night always made her restless. When she was still the oracle, she would often sneak away and wander the forest north of the city for several hours. Those who knew her best constantly scolded her for going off by herself.

"You have no business being alone." The words of Allie, her very first personal attendant, came to mind. "There are brigands and bandits and

bears out there. The gods help me, but if something happened to you... well... I just don't know what."

She had watched Allie grow from a young girl to a woman, and then pass into old age. In the end, it was Basanti who attended her as life drained away from her frail and withered body.

But Allie was only the first of many. She had seen scores of mortal lives turn to dust; the exact number she had long ago lost count of. Yet through it all, she had remained unchanged. *How fitting*, she thought. *Now I will be forever changed.*

She took a final look at the sun disappearing beneath the horizon and returned to her shack. After lighting a candle, she sat down on a straw mat in the corner. She didn't really need the candle to see, but staring at its flickering light was mildly soothing.

Some nights, she would choose to drift off to sleep quite early. Even the nightmares could be preferable to the solitude of her waking life. But tonight, the nightmares would have to wait for a while longer to torment her again.

A stiff breeze blew in through the cloth flap that covered the entrance, extinguishing the candle. Muttering with annoyance, she relit it. But another gust of wind quickly blew it out again. Sighing with irritation, Basanti threw herself down on her mat.

"My beautiful child."

The voice was like sweet music. Basanti recognized it at once and sat up. Sitting beside her, dressed in shimmering silver robes, was Pósix. Her flawless features and loving expression instantly brought tears to Basanti's eyes.

"Why are you crying?" she asked.

Basanti wiped her cheeks. She tried to answer, but speech had temporarily abandoned her. Instead, she threw her arms around the goddess in a desperate embrace. Her body radiated an intense heat that would have burned any mortal, but to Basanti, it was like a warm blanket she could lose herself within.

"There, there," whispered Pósix. She stroked Basanti's hair and rocked her gently.

"I've been so alone," she wept.

"I know. And you did right by coming here." She eased Basanti back so she could look into her eyes. "Had you not, you would have certainly fallen into darkness. But all that is over now. The enemy is dead and can no longer do you harm."

"I know," she said. "But I am still a danger to the world."

Pósix nodded. "Indeed, you are. And one that cannot be allowed to roam freely."

Basanti closed her eyes. "So you've come to kill me?"

Pósix laughed and pulled her close again. "Of course not. After all you have done for the world, what kind of reward would that be?"

"Then what is to become of me?"

Pósix stood up and offered Basanti her hand. "Come. Let us walk together."

Basanti allowed herself to be pulled to her feet. The strength in the goddess's grasp was shocking, yet tempered. She felt as if she were a small girl being helped up by her mother.

They left the shack and began walking along the shore. Pósix's movements were fluid and graceful beyond words, and her bare feet left no impression in the sand. Her godly flesh gave off a slight aura that melded with the light from the full moon to illuminate the way forward.

"Am I to be healed?" Basanti asked, unable to hide the desperation in her tone.

"I am sorry," she replied. "There is no way for me to heal you. And I do not believe it would be right to do so, even if I could. The sacrifice you made must stand."

"Then what becomes of me? I cannot leave this island as I am. And if you will not end my suffering..." Her tears returned.

"My dear," Pósix replied tenderly. "I did not say that you would continue to suffer. And I will not leave you as you are. But when you killed, you changed the very nature of what you are. When all those years ago you asked me to heal your brother, I told you that I was not permitted to do so. And though I did not lie, I did not fully understand the reasons."

Basanti halted. Vivid memories of pleading for Yanti's spirit to be healed raced through her head. It was the only time she had ever shown anger toward the goddess, and the only time she had seriously considered abandoning her duties.

"Gerath instructed me that I was to leave Yanti as he was," Pósix explained. "He said that I did not possess the power to heal him. I had thought he meant that it would take a combination of our powers to accomplish it, but I was wrong. Once Yanti's spirit was altered, death was his only release. Gerath declared that Yanti still had a role to play, and therefore was not to be harmed." She took Basanti's hands. "I now see that his wisdom came not from his own mind, but from the Creator *herself*."

She gave Basanti's hand a gentle squeeze. "I'm sorry that you had to see what your brother became. I know you loved him dearly. But take comfort in the knowledge that now the door to heaven has been re-opened, his spirit resides with us... and he is happy."

Basanti lowered her head and smiled. "Thank you."

They continued to walk.

"So what happens now?"

"Thanks to Darshan's courage and self-sacrifice, the world is free and the gods are no longer needed—though often I wonder if we ever were. The elves and the humans will now make a new life as one people."

Basanti's mouth twisted into a doubtful expression.

Pósix laughed softly and nodded. "I know. They are two stubborn races who are resistant to change. And the change will be fraught with obstacles. But in the end, I trust that they will find their way. Whatever happens, they will no longer need to fear our interference. We will become what we were always meant to be... shepherds of the spirits. The mortal world is no longer ours to wander."

"And what about Darshan?" she asked. "Is he dead?"

"Darshan was born to serve a single purpose." Pósix's voice was distant and reflective. "And now that purpose is complete. In the end, he knew what must happen and faced his destiny with the valor befitting of a god." She gave Basanti a sideways grin. "But you should not concern yourself with Darshan. He lives on within the memories and legends of all the people he saved. His name will be in songs as long as mortals roam the earth."

Pósix stopped walking and placed her hands on Basanti's shoulders. "And now it is time for you to receive your reward. You have served me and the people of this world for countless centuries, never asking anything for yourself. You have forsaken your heart's desire so that the hope of all mortals would be saved. For these reasons, and for many more, you have my eternal gratitude. But now your work has ended and it is time for you to live again." Pósix glanced over to her right, a playful grin on her face.

Basanti's eyes followed her gaze. She caught her breath sharply. There, to her delighted amazement, standing ankle-deep in the water, was the tall, muscular form of Felsafell. With the moonlight reflecting off his smooth ebony skin and silver hair, never before had he looked more beautiful to her. She wanted to run to him, but Pósix held her fast.

"When you touch his hand," the goddess explained. "You will once again be mortal."

Basanti felt a flash of fear at her words. "Mortal? You mean..."

"I mean, you will be as you once were ... human. Frail, but free." Pósix stroked her cheek with the back of her hand. "But you will not be alone. Felsafell has also earned his reward. The moment you touch him, the two of you will be irrevocably joined." She could see that Basanti was confused. "He will become mortal as well. It was the only reward he asked for... and I was happy to give it."

"But I thought the *first born* could never become mortal."

"Never before has a *first born's* spirit been bonded to that of a human," she replied. "He will share your mortality. And when the time comes to leave this world, you will both find your peace in heaven."

Basanti was speechless.

Pósix kissed her tear-soaked cheek. "Now go to him. You have waited long enough."

Basanti looked again at Felsafell. No longer was he the tall, imposing figure of a *first born*. He was now the young flaxen-haired human she had first met in the forest thousands of years ago; the one who had taken her by the hand and led her to safety. His bright smile conveyed all the love he held in his heart for her. She turned back to Pósix, but the goddess had vanished.

"Thank you," she whispered.

Basanti broke into a dead run. Felsafell did likewise. He swept her into his arms, spinning her around and kissing her with complete abandon. As soon as their flesh touched, they both felt their spirits meld as one. They were no longer alone within themselves.

"I can feel you," she said, laughing joyfully.

"And I, you," he replied. He kissed her yet again, then looked down at his new form and frowned. "It would seem that I am to be human in body, as well as spirit."

Basanti cupped his face and smiled. "You will always look the same to me—beautiful."

Felsafell laughed. "And at least we won't draw attention to ourselves. We can go wherever we will, unnoticed."

"And where shall we go first?" she asked.

Felsafell pointed down the shore to a small boat. "First, we should leave this wretched island. Then... well... I have never been across the Abyss. We could start there."

"Sounds exciting," she replied.

Hand in hand, they walked to the boat. Basanti remembered how she had envied the bond the elves shared. Now she knew it was all she had imagined ... and so much more. She could feel Felsafell's love and commitment; it went deeper than she could ever have fathomed. Together, they pushed the craft into the sea and Felsafell raised the small sail. She sat beside him and rested her head on his shoulder while he steered the boat north toward the mainland.

"A thought just occurred to me," she said. "As we have become mortal, we will need to provide for ourselves. I don't know about you, but I have no gold or silver. And now that I am no longer the oracle... not even my tent to sleep in."

Felsafell burst into laughter. "Yes. Many things will be different. But you needn't worry. The same thought occurred to me after I spoke to Pósix." He pointed to a box sitting beside the mast.

Basanti reached over and opened it. Inside were hundreds of gold coins.

"Where did you get these?" she asked.

"I may be human now," he said, a roguish grin appearing. "But I have lived long enough to know where the ancient treasures of the world are buried."

Basanti nearly rolled over with over laughing. "Then I hope you bought some food. For the first time in thousands of years ... I'm famished."

CHAPTER 28

A year and a half had passed by since King Lousis returned triumphantly to Althetas. The people had greeted him with a festival, the like of which had never been seen before. For nearly a week, the city had been in a state of continuous celebration.

Now once again, Althetas had cause for joy. Today would see the departure of the old king and the coronation of his heir. But this was no ordinary event—if a coronation could ever be considered ordinary. No longer would the lands of the west be divided. For today would see the coronation of the first High King of the Western States.

"Are you all right?"

The sound of Selena's voice snapped Lousis from his trance. He was staring out of the window over the city, smiling as he recalled the memories of his youth. He rubbed his hands together. He could feel the scars of war on every inch of his flesh. *Old and battered*, he thought.

"I'm fine," he replied, placing an arm around his wife and kissing the top of her head.

"Good. Because after today, I plan for us to take a very long holiday. And it wouldn't do if you are ill. Particularly once we're at sea."

"Are you sure you want to take such a long journey?" he asked. "There are plenty of places to visit that are much closer."

"And decline Mohanisi's invitation? I wouldn't think of it. Besides, I want to go while I still have the energy to make such a trip."

Lousis chuckled. "Then I am at your command, my queen. We go where your heart desires."

There was a knock at the door and Jacob entered.

"Shouldn't you be preparing for the coronation?" asked Lousis.

"I've done all I can do," he replied. "And I'm tired of servants fussing over me. Father would have..."

He stopped in mid-sentence as he saw the pain in his grandmother's eyes at the mention of her son. "I'm sorry," he said. "I wasn't thinking."

Selena forced a smile. "There is no reason to apologize. Your father would be so very proud of you. And yes. He would be having no end of fun at your expense right now. He was not a man who enjoyed being pampered and fussed over either. It's good to remember him at times like this. It's just that I..." She swallowed hard and stifled her tears. "I never had the chance to say goodbye. Not really. When he left Valshara, it didn't occur to me that he might not return. That was foolish of me."

"With the door to heaven now open," said Lousis. "He is in the arms of the gods. And I believe he hears your words and knows how much you love him."

Selena saw a glimmer of pain on Jacob's face. "Now I am the one who needs forgiveness," she said. "You lost both mother and father to the evil of Angrääl."

"Yes," he replied. "But it is as King Lousis said. Thanks to Darshan, they are both safe and at peace. And I know that one day we will all be together again."

Selena nodded, then kissed his cheek. "But enough sad talk. Today is a day for happiness."

"Indeed," agreed Lousis.

"There are a few hours left before I need to get dressed," said Jacob. "Grandmother tells me that you have a secret supply of elf brandy hidden away somewhere, courtesy of Lord Chiron."

Lousis cast an accusing, yet lighthearted glance at Selena. "Your grandmother was not supposed to know about that." He sighed and nodded. "But she's right. I do. Though I'm not sure how wise it is for you to be drinking just before your coronation."

Jacob gave a wry grin. "I don't see how I can get through it otherwise," he countered.

Lousis chuckled. "It was the same with me. I was so nervous, I very nearly emptied my stomach when they placed the crown on my head. Come. A few small sips should set you to rights."

He retrieved the brandy and poured each of them a glass. With the sweet scent filling the room, Lousis found his mind wandering again.

"Has there been word from the north?" Jacob asked him.

Selena had to nudge her husband before he responded. "No. At least, nothing to be concerned over. With the Reborn King dead, his armies have completely disbanded and the soldiers returned to their homes."

"I heard that the elves have sent a delegation to Kratis to learn the secret of their explosive bolts," Jacob said.

"If you ask me," Selena interjected, "they should leave that particular horror a mystery."

Lousis took her hand and nodded in agreement. "Yes. This world has seen enough destruction. But such matters are no longer my concern." He looked at Jacob. "It is for you and the new leaders of this world to decide what is best. My time is done."

"I do wish Darshan was still among us," Jacob remarked. "He would be such a great help."

"He gave his last full measure of life in the desert," said Selena. "But his memory and deeds will continue to guide us, I think."

"As will all those who fought and died," added Lousis.

There was a long pause. Jacob then raised his glass. "May their spirits guide us forever."

Soon, it was time for him to get ready. After he had gone, Lousis and Selena spent their time discussing all the things they intended to see once they were across the Abyss. Mohanisi had spent hours telling them of the wonders and beauty of his land. They felt like children leaving home for the first time.

Normally, a coronation would take place in the royal manor or at one of the temples. A few times in the past, when the new monarch had been particularly popular and the crowd too large, it had been held in the open air. Today, however, such was the size of the occasion, that they were being forced to hold it completely outside of the city walls.

Jacob was already well loved in Althetas due to his many good deeds to improve the citizens' lives while Lousis was away. After the war was over, he continued to earn their love during the reconstruction with his tireless efforts and selfless generosity. And being that he was to rule over all twelve of the western kingdoms, people from far and wide had been flocking to the city. It had been agreed that the current rulers would remain in place and govern locally, but they be oath-bound to enforce the will of the High King.

It was King Victis who had first proposed this, and Lousis who had added the elves to the council. There would now be one nation, under one flag, with one king... all peoples united.

As Lousis stood upon the immense platform, he stared out over the crowd. Lord Chiron and Lady Bellisia were in front, standing beside Aaliyah, Nehrutu and Mohanisi. King Victis and the other rulers were atop a small dais to his left that had been specially erected so they could have a clear view of the ceremony. Alongside him on the platform and to his right was Ertik, High Lord of Valshara, while Queen Selena was positioned just off to his left beside the pedestal that held the royal crown. He had offered Linis and Dina a similar place close to his side, or at least a seat on the dais, but they had chosen to remain in the crowd and were standing near to a large group of other elves.

He continued looking out upon the sea of happy smiles. Occasionally, he thought he recognized someone from memory, but found that it was nearly impossible to focus on a single face for very long among the throngs of people.

A short time later, a trumpet blared, announcing that the royal procession had passed through the city gates and was now slowly making its way to the platform. As the throngs of cheering people made room for the new king to pass, Lousis could see Jacob sitting atop a white steed—the guard of honor surrounding him made up of both humans and elves. The banner they bore did not bear the sigil of Althetas, but rather the new symbol that had been adopted. Woven upon a red background was a white eagle with a ribbon clutched in its talons. Across the ribbon, written in the ancient language, was the motto: "Once broken, now restored."

When they reached the platform, Jacob dismounted and ascended the stairs.

"Are you sure I have to go through with this?" he whispered, smirking.

"There's no backing out now," Lousis told him. "Not unless you intend starting a riot."

Jacob solemnly kneeled on a satin cushion placed in the center of the stage. Once again, the trumpet rang out, prompting Lousis to step forward and address the crowd. The volume of cheers was almost overwhelming, and it took more than five minutes before he was able to be heard.

"Today is a day deserving of great joy and celebration. After thousands of years of separation and hardship, we have at long last been united as one people, with one purpose, and now ... under one king.

"I say this because Jacob Starfinder will not be king of the humans in the west. Nor shall he be a ruler of a separate nation in which elves are merely tolerated—as has been the case under my rule. We have spilled too much blood together for that. And the old ways are gone forever.

"King Jacob will be a king for all peoples. A hand of justice for elf and human alike. A voice of compassion to reach all ears. And I gladly step aside to usher in this new age and new way of thinking.

"It has been my deepest honor to serve Althetas and her people. I want you all to know that, though I may no longer be your king, my heart remains with each and every one of you. Through war and sorrow, you have taught me the true meaning of strength and courage. Without your undying support, I could have never endured."

He turned and stepped over to the pedestal upon which Selena handed him the crown. After bowing, Lousis approached Jacob.

"Do you swear to honor and protect your people, both meek and strong, to use your authority for the betterment of the kingdom and its citizens, to be fair and just in all things, and to rule with kindness and understanding?"

Jacob closed his eyes and bowed. "I so swear."

"Then it is my pleasure and great privilege to place this symbol upon your brow. For it is only a symbol. A thing of metal and stone. The true source of its power comes from within you. May your reign be long and filled with happiness." After placing the crown atop Jacob's head, he took a step back.

Ertik then stepped forward and touched the new king's shoulders. "May the gods bless you and keep you safe. And may the Creator grant you wisdom and long life."

Jacob rose slowly to his feet and bowed low. He then turned to face the crowd.

"I give you King Jacob Starfinder," Lousis called out. "High King of the Western Nations."

At this declaration, the crowd went into a frenzy of cheering that lasted for fully ten minutes. Jacob could only wave and smile until the noise had subsided.

"I am truly humbled to be here today," he began. "I have much to live up to. I now sit upon the throne once occupied by a great man. For there could be no greater monarch than King Lousis. All the free people of the world owe him a debt of gratitude that can never be repaid. Without his courage, everything that you see around you would now be just ashes upon the ground. He marched into the jaws of certain death to save the lives of his people. He was willing to sacrifice all for the sake of our freedom. For that, and for countless other reasons, I say, long live King Lousis the Great!"

The crowd cheered again, repeating his salutation to the former king.

"I shall use his example as I move us forward into the future. But I think now is also the time to remember the men and women—both elf and human—who sacrificed their lives so that I can stand before you today with hope and optimism in my heart. Because of them, we live in a land free from tyranny and oppression. May their spirits reside in heaven for eternity."

Jacob bowed his head. The people did the same. The whispered names of countless loved ones carried on the air like spring pollen. From behind, he heard his grandmother offering her own private tribute. "Lee Starfinder."

"Penelope Starfinder," he added quietly to this, then looked up to continue his speech.

"Finally, let us remember the one man to whom not only do we owe our lives, but the lives of all future generations. Through his sacrifice, he saved both heaven and earth from annihilation. And though I call him a man, we know that he was much, much more. A god bound in spirit to this world who chose to die for the sake of all living things. Only *he* could have stood against the power that sat upon the throne of Angrääl. And only *he* could have cast down the Reborn King. Even now, the eastern desert bears the scars of his sacrifice. And though he is no longer among us. His name will live on in our hearts forever. Darshan..."

Barely had the name escaped his lips when the crowd began repeating it in steady unison. But it was not the uninhibited chanting that Darshan's name had engendered in so many previous gatherings. This was a solemn and reverent murmuring. Many people wept, while some fell to their knees and covered their eyes.

"But let us now lift up our hearts," Jacob called out with a joyous tenor that shattered the somber atmosphere. "Let this be the first day of a new age. A golden age. Together we can make it so. Now come. All of you. Let us rejoice and revel in the freedom so dearly bought. And may *love* be the word that defines this day... and in all the days to come."

"Long live King Jacob," came a voice from the crowd.

A host of others quickly took up the same call. Soon, the people were shouting and cheering as never before. Jacob felt his grandmother's hands on his shoulders.

She whispered in his ear. "You did well. And you will make a fine king."

"Thank you," he replied, smiling. "But I wonder. Is Darshan *really* gone?"

"No one knows for sure," she replied. "His body was swallowed by the sands along with that of the Reborn King. But I'd like to think he is still with us... even if only in spirit."

The celebration lasted for three days. And when it was over, Lousis and Selena met Mohanisi at the harbor to set off on their new adventure. They said their goodbyes, and Jacob watched as they sailed into the horizon. It felt ... permanent. As if a book had been closed, never to be re-opened. Yet, as he rode back to the king's manor, he understood that a new tale was now beginning. A new story for the ages. He smiled and looked up to the heavens.

He was sure that the loving eyes of his parents would be there, watching as it unfolded.

CHAPTER 29

Kaylia sat in the old wooden rocking chair that had once belonged to Gewey's mother. As she stared into the hearth and watched the flames dance and crackle, she was reminded of the days before her father died. He had built a small house just like this one, deep in the forest. It was a place that only a few close friends and relatives knew how to find.

Each spring, he would take her there for at least a month. He would tell her that it was his time for meditation and reflection, but mostly they just played and hunted wild game.

Normally, these memories would produce a smile and a warm feeling in her heart. But this was not a normal night. And she felt no warmth... only sorrow.

Jayden's voice broke the daydream.

"Mommy! Do you have to go?"

She could see Gewey's eyes looking back at her as she lifted him onto her lap. "Of course I do. You know that."

"But I don't like it when Miss Melli watches us," he said. His pleading expression would usually get him what he wanted, and he knew it. "She makes us go to bed too early."

"Well, she just doesn't understand that you're half elf," Kaylia explained. "Melli is human, and human children go to bed early."

"But I'm five already!" he protested. "And I'm never tired when she tells us it's time to sleep."

Kaylia tried her best not to laugh at his pouting little face. "I don't hear your sisters complaining."

"Yeah. But they're girls," he replied. "They never complain. They just lay in the bed and whisper to each other all night. They think I can't hear what they're saying... but I can."

"That's not true," two tiny voices called out in unison.

With auburn hair and bronze skin, the twins were the spitting image of their mother. But their eyes, like Jayden's, unmistakably came from Gewey.

They flashed him an angry look. "We don't stay up *all* night. You're a liar."

"Maybell and Penelope Stedding," scolded Kaylia. "You will apologize to your brother at once."

"But mommy..." Maybell began.

"But nothing," she snapped back. "You don't call him a liar. Especially when Melli has told me exactly the same thing about what you get up to."

Both girls did their best to meet their mother's gaze, but within seconds, they were looking at the floor and shifting their feet. "We're sorry, Jayden."

Kaylia could not help but notice how unusually close Maybell and Penelope had become over the past four years. The women of the village had told her that this was common for twins. But the fact was, they were *not* common in any way. It was almost as if they shared the same spiritual bond that adult elf mates had. Jayden often felt excluded by this, but there was still no doubt that he loved his sisters very much. In spite of their occasional spats, they generally got along wonderfully well. When they played together in the hayfields, he would watch over them as if he was their parent rather than an older brother.

A knock at the door brought squeals of delight from the girls, and a sour frown from Jayden.

"You are to be on your best behavior," warned Kaylia softly before calling out, "Come in."

Linis and Dina entered, followed by Miss Melli. Melli was the wife of a local horse trader and a leading member of the Village Mothers. When Kaylia arrived in Sharpstone, she had been the first villager to welcome her, and was constantly inviting her to join the Mothers at their monthly meetings. It was an invitation that Kaylia invariably declined.

The girls ran headlong across the room and into Linis's waiting arms. He lifted them off the floor and spun them around.

"Have you missed me?" he asked.

"Yes, yes," they replied, giggling as Linis put them down and playfully tickled their tummies. "Did you bring us something? Did you?"

He stood up straight and placed his hands on his hips. "Bring you something? When do I ever bring you anything?"

"Stop teasing," said Maybell. "I know you did."

Linis paused, still attempting to look as if he had no idea what they were talking about. Then, slowly, he smiled and reached into his pocket to pull out a small bag. Penelope snatched it from his hand and opened it as fast as her little fingers could manage.

"Elf candy," the girls cried out with glee. They each pulled out a small green ball and popped it into their mouths. "Thank you, Uncle Linis."

"And what about me?" asked Dina, pretending to be hurt by their lack of attention. "No hugs for your auntie?"

The twins laughed and embraced her while she showered the tops of their heads with kisses.

Jayden did not seem as excited. Still, he forced a smile and hugged them both.

"What's wrong, Jayden?" asked Linis.

The boy shifted and kicked the floor with the toe of his shoe. "It's nothing."

"I think I know," said Dina. She produced a small piece of cloth and handed this to Jayden.

His eyes lit up when he unfolded it and saw that it contained a bar of chocolate.

"He doesn't like elf candy," Dina told Linis, as if he should have known this all along.

"What?" he cried. "What's not to like?"

"It's just too sour, that's all," said Jayden.

Dina kneeled down and whispered into his ear. "Don't worry. I don't like it either."

This brought a smile to his face. He hugged her again, this time with more enthusiasm.

"Now all of you need to get ready for bed," announced Melli.

Her words brought moans of discontent from all three children.

"You heard her," said Kaylia.

They lowered their heads and filed from the room with angry little faces and dragging steps.

"You should let them stay up just a short while longer," Kaylia said quietly, after they'd gone. "Elf children have a bit more energy than a human child."

Melli smiled. "Of course. I sometimes forget that they are half elf. It's the ears that throw me. They're not pointed and..."

Her eyes widened and she covered her mouth. "Oh my. I'm sorry. I hope I didn't... I mean, your ears are lovely... What I meant to say..."

"It's fine," Kaylia told her. "I know you meant no offense. Just let them stay up a wee bit longer tonight. But not too late, of course. After all, they are half human, too."

Melli's face was still red with embarrassment. "I'll read them some stories before bed. That should tire them out."

Kaylia smiled in approval, then went into the children's rooms to kiss them goodbye.

Linis had a wagon waiting outside, drawn by a pair of sturdy work horses. "A far cry from the steeds we once rode," he said. "But they serve my needs."

They climbed aboard the front and Linis cracked the reins. The sun was just below the horizon, painting the sky in hues of red and purple. Linis took a deep breath and wrapped his arm around Dina.

"It's still hard to imagine you as a farmer," remarked Kaylia.

Linis shrugged. "I enjoy it well enough. My uncle was a farmer. He taught me some of the skills when I was a boy. Well ... before I was sent to train as a *seeker*."

"I love him as a farmer," Dina chipped in. "He stays at home."

"That was our bargain," said Linis. "Dina would retire from the order, and I would settle into a life befitting a family man."

"Do you miss it?" asked Kaylia. "Being a *seeker*? Adventuring?"

"The travel, yes," he admitted. "But I have seen all the danger I care to see."

"And when do you intend to start this *family* of yours?" Kaylia teased. "How long must I wait for good news?"

Dina's face twisted into a scowl. "Unfortunately, becoming a farmer did not relieve him of his caution. He insists that we wait until after our fourth harvest."

"I will not make beggars of my offspring," Linis countered. "If we live alongside the humans, then we must adapt to some of their ways. And a hunter and tracker makes very little gold."

Kaylia threw her head back in laughter. Linis had refused to accept any kind of reward from King Jacob for his service, while Dina had donated the retirement grant she was allotted as a former High Lady of Valshara to the victims of the war. Of course, this made them essentially penniless.

"I have paid back the loan I took to buy our farm last year," Linis continued, his tone defensive. "And this year I'll make enough for us to provide the things befitting a son or daughter of mine."

Dina kissed his cheek. "Always the proud elf *seeker*." She turned to Kaylia. "You know, Melli made me promise to ask…"

Kaylia's hard stare cut her off. "I'm not going to be a bloody village mother," she snapped. "It's bad enough that they are constantly at my door pestering me to tell them elf stories and teach them elf cooking. I'm not going to willingly put myself among them."

"Not enjoying living among humans?" asked Linis.

"I like it just fine," she replied. "But I have never liked gossipy women. I don't care to hear about what store clerk's husband was found passed out drunk in the streets, or whose wife was flirting with the Baltrian trader who came to town last week."

"They do more than that," Dina protested. She had become a village mother the year before, though was less deeply involved than Melli. "Well… they try to do more." Kaylia's eyes never blinked. Dina sighed. "Okay, they *are* a bunch of gossips. But you could at least come with me once in a while. I could use the company."

"I will consider it."

They talked of simple matters for the rest of the ride. Finally, they arrived at Starfinder Manor. Millet was already standing outside the front to greet them, a welcoming smile on his face.

Torches lit the drive all the way up to the entrance, and the aroma of mint lamb wafted on the breeze through the open door.

Kaylia immediately jumped down from the wagon and threw her arms around Millet. "It is always wonderful to see you."

"And you, my dear," he replied. "Though I do wish it was more often. This house gets lonely, and I am in dire need of sophisticated company."

"I hear that the mayor visits you quite often," joked Linis. He gave Millet's shoulders a fond squeeze.

Millet huffed. "If only Barty would run for office. Then I wouldn't mind the ... *honor* ... of a mayoral visit."

"He's too busy these days," said Dina. "And that's your fault, really. If you hadn't suggested to King Jacob that he bestow the Nal'Thain fortune to Randson, he would most likely be staying in Sharpstone a lot more."

"Don't remind me," said Millet sourly. "Now we are stuck with that fool Melton Fathing. If ever there was a more annoying man born, I haven't heard of him." He grinned at Linis. "Perhaps it is time we had an elf mayor."

Linis laughed boisterously. "The people here may be accommodating. But I doubt they are ready for that."

"Perhaps one day," Millet responded. He gave an elaborate wink. "Perhaps even one day soon. You'd be amazed at how convincing a man of wealth and influence can be in a small town."

"And you certainly have wealth," teased Kaylia. "I heard that you brought back ten wagonloads of gold from Baltria."

"Gossip is unbecoming an elf," scolded Millet. "You know good and well that it was only two wagonloads."

This produced a round of laughter from everyone.

Millet led them inside to where wine and fine cheese was already waiting. They each took a seat. Kaylia glared at the empty place beside her.

"What is it, my dear?" asked Millet.

Kaylia shot him an accusing stare. "I think you know. Where is he?"

Millet held up his hands. "I'm sure I have no idea what you mean."

"Is that right?" She slid her chair back and looked at the open door at the far end of the dining hall. "You had better come out before I drag you out."

Millet sighed and glanced in the same direction. "Do as she says, Gewey. I don't want her breaking my things over your thick skull." He turned back to Kaylia. "I was going to tell you of his return, I promise. But he made me swear to wait so that he could surprise you."

Gewey appeared, smiling boyishly. His hair was still damp from a recent shower, and his fresh white shirt and brown pants were neatly pressed.

He strode over to the table and kissed her on the cheek. "You have no sense of humor, my love," he told her.

At first she pretended to resist, but soon her arms were wrapped around his neck. He then embraced both Dina and Linis before sitting down.

"I thought you might miss it this year," said Dina.

"I thought so, too," he replied. "But I managed to settle things in Gath in time. They'll be purchasing all of their hay from me next year."

"That's no excuse for being late," chided Kaylia. "You had plenty of time to get home. The children miss you."

In reality, she knew very well why he had chosen to come directly to Millet's. As much as Melli was after her to join the Village Mothers, she was twice as adamant that Gewey should take his place on the council. But his hatred for politics was immeasurable. The constant bickering and shouting was far more than he cared to deal with.

"I know," he said, using his most humble tone. "I'm sorry."

Kaylia sniffed and gave him a playful pinch on the arm. Just then, the sound of horses arriving at the front of the house reached them.

The group looked at one another in surprise—all but Gewey, who smiled knowingly.

Moments later, the door opened to reveal Aaliyah and Nehrutu. Kaylia flew from her seat and wrapped her arms around them both, nearly weeping with joy.

"Did you not know we were coming?" asked Aaliyah. "I sent a message to Gewey several months ago to say that we could attend this year.

"Another surprise," he smiled.

Kaylia kissed him lightly. "For this one, you are certainly forgiven."

After greeting the others, the new arrivals took their places at the table. Soon, the wine was flowing and the time apart melted away.

"So, what news from across the sea?" asked Linis.

"Strange things, actually," Nehrutu replied. "The Morzhash have vanished. There is not a trace of them to be found. It is as if something has plucked them from the face of the earth."

"Interesting," remarked Millet. "As I understand it, they had been raiding your villages for many years."

"Indeed," he affirmed. "No one is lamenting their departure. But it is odd, nonetheless. However, it *has* opened up new space for those coming from this land to settle."

"Has there been a lot of them?" asked Dina.

"A fair number," he replied. "Too many for some of my folk's taste. But they will grow accustomed to new people in time."

Aaliyah turned to Kaylia. "We were hoping that you and Gewey would return west with us when we depart." She looked to Dina. "The two of you as well. I am certain your mother would be pleased to see you."

"My mother visits us quite often actually," she said. "And it's bad enough hearing Kaylia go on about Linis and I having a child. When *she's* here and they join forces..." She shook her head.

"I would love to go," said Linis. He kissed Dina's hand. "But there is much to do here, and I simply can't spare the time."

"Also, I think Gewey and I returning west might not be the best idea," said Kaylia.

"No one there even remembers you," Aaliyah countered. "Which, by the way, still amazes me. You would be safe from notice."

Gewey shook his head. "When I erased all connections between Darshan and Gewey Stedding, it took every bit of my power to accomplish it. I would not risk someone remembering who I really am. To the world, Darshan is dead and Gewey Stedding spent the war hiding in Hazrah. Neither are connected in any way."

"Well, at least we still remember you," said Dina.

"That actually surprised me," he admitted. "I didn't intentionally exclude anyone." He saw the sour expression flash across her face and held up his hand. "Not that I would have wanted any of you to forget me, but I honestly didn't know how to be that specific. I used the same power that the Dark Knight had used to erase all memories of him. But I knew he'd only partially succeeded. I needed more. Which is why I went to the Chamber of the Maker. It increased my power and hopefully my influence on people's memory."

Linis shifted in his seat. Gewey could tell he wanted to say something.

"What is it?" he asked.

"Well," he began hesitantly. "In all the time we have been living here in Sharpstone, you have never once spoken of what happened in the desert. This is the fourth annual gathering we've had, and still you avoid any talk of it when asked."

Gewey sighed. "I suppose it was too soon... still too fresh in my mind. And there was so much of it that I didn't really understand."

"This is the first gathering Aaliyah and I have attended," said Nehrutu. "So, if you are able, I would ask you only one thing. When you met the Creator, what was it like?"

Gewey's eyes grew distant for a moment. Then Kaylia touched his shoulder and he smiled faintly.

Nehrutu spoke again. "If you cannot answer, I understand."

"No," said Gewey. "For a time it was difficult. But not because of the Creator. There were memories I was trying to push from my mind. It has taken me a few years to make peace with what happened. Those who were lost... those that I failed to save."

Though unspoken, everyone knew he was thinking about Lee.

"No one alive today has caused more death than I have," he continued. "How do you live in a world with such a burden on your heart?"

"But we were at war," Linis told him. "You did not kill simply for the joy of it."

Gewey nodded. "I know this. But knowing something in your mind and understanding it in your heart are often very different."

"And how do you feel now?" asked Dina.

"With Kaylia's help, I have learned to accept the past," he replied. He took hold of her hand. "I try to remember that I am truly blessed. And that my family needs me. They get me through the dark times when the guilt I carry becomes too much to bear." He sat up straight and banished his melancholy. "But as to your question..."

The room went silent.

"When the Dark Knight and I sank into the vortex, I truly thought that was the end. There was no sense at all of my spirit living outside of my body. Only blackness. And even the blackness was fading. I knew I was facing oblivion, and I was terrified. I tried to cry out for help, but I didn't have a voice. No matter what I did, I knew the end was coming.

"It was in this moment of utter despair that I finally realized there *was* nothing to be done. This was the sacrifice I had agreed to make. My life for the lives of everyone else. So I accepted it and thanked the Creator for giving me the courage to go through with my task."

He looked up and shook his head. "I can honestly say that, had I known in advance about the sheer terror of oblivion, I couldn't have done it."

Dina cocked her head. "But oblivion is just ... nothing. How could you have felt fear?"

"We live in this world secure in the knowledge that there is a life beyond this one," he explained. "The only reason we fear death is because the spirit world and heaven are mysteries to us. There is always that little bit of doubt. Will I go there when I die, or will something *else* happen? Is this world everything there is for me, or is there more to come? No matter what we think we know, we can't help but wonder. But this was different. I knew for certain that the complete end was coming. It would be as if I had never existed. My love for Kaylia and our children, my friends, everyone ... all gone. More than that, I wouldn't care about it because I wouldn't exist."

He could see that no one aside from Kaylia understood.

"It doesn't matter. Just know that in that moment, I was more terrified than I ever thought possible. And then there was nothing."

Now the group truly looked confused.

"Nothing?" said Millet. "You mean you *did* die?"

"No," he replied. "I mean, I ceased to exist. I have no memory of what happened. I was no longer of this, or any other world."

"Then how is it you are here now?" asked Aaliyah.

"I'm not," he replied. There was a long, uncomfortable pause. Then Gewey burst out laughing. "I'm sorry. That was a bad joke. But I really was gone. And for how long, I can't say.

"My first memory was of standing in the middle of the desert, naked as the day I was born, trying to figure out what had happened. It was then that I saw her." He shook his head. "No. *Saw* is not the right word. I did see a blinding light, but it was more like I felt *her*."

"And how was that feeling?" asked Dina in a half whisper.

"How much do you love Linis?" he asked in return.

"With all of my heart."

"Try to imagine that love. Then multiply it by the number of drops in the ocean. That is what I felt... and it hurt."

"It hurt?" repeated Millet incredulously. "How can love hurt?"

"Any strong emotion can cause pain," he replied. "Love most of all."

Millet's eyes grew suddenly distant, as if recalling a memory of long ago. "That is true. But you're describing this as if it was a physical pain. Not a broken heart."

"It was," he replied. "No one, not even a god, is capable of bearing the full force of the Creator's love. It's beyond anything we can fathom. I fell to my knees, screaming for it to stop. But it didn't. It got worse and worse until I was yearning for death. And still, the pain continued increasing."

Gewey leaned back in his chair, a strange little smile on his lips. "And then something remarkable happened. I returned it. I couldn't tell you why—or how—but in that moment of the most excruciating pain of my life, I loved *her* back. And then, all at once, the pain went away."

"So, the Creator only wants our love?" asked Aaliyah. "Is that what you are saying?"

Gewey chuckled. "No. And yes. What I began to understand was that I hadn't really given *her* anything. I had given my love to *her* creation. And the more I began to understand this, the angrier I became. Not at the Creator, but at myself for being so stupid and blind. It was all so very simple."

"What was?" asked Dina.

"That all I ever needed to do was surrender myself," he replied. "If I had, *her* true power would have been mine, and I would have become invincible. The Dark Knight could have never stood against me. And as I returned the love I was given, I suddenly knew *her* will."

"And what was that?" asked Linis.

"For me, it was to return home and raise my family," he replied.

Dina obviously expected more. "Yes. But what about me? And Linis? And Aaliyah? Everyone?"

"For you, who knows? But if you listen, you will be able to feel it. It's simple for each one of us as individuals, but unclear for the world as a whole. It's one message, while at the same time being many. There *may* be a single message for everyone... I just don't know. But I doubt it. I think *she* has something different in mind for each of us. Otherwise, we would all be the same person."

"So what happens if we don't listen?" asked Millet.

"Look around you," Gewey said. "There is still hatred and mistrust in the world. People still seek vengeance and retribution. *That* is what happens when we don't listen. The Creator only wants us to be happy... and that's all. Nothing more. It's really that simple. And *she* doesn't need us to earn *her* love. We already have it."

"What about evil?" asked Nehrutu. "Surely *she* doesn't love evil."

"And why not?" asked Gewey. "Could you stop loving your child for any reason? Even if it did bad things? That's what we are to *her*. Children. And naughty children at that. But *she* still loves us. All of us."

Dina furrowed her brow. "Are you saying that the Dark Knight...?"

"*She* loves him too," he said, cutting her short. He smirked and rubbed the spot on his chest where the *Sword of Truth* had pierced his flesh. "All the same, I have to admit I'm glad *she* didn't expect me to feel the same way about him."

"What else did she tell you?" asked Aaliyah.

"*Tell* me?" He spread his hands. "Nothing in words that I could repeat. But *she* let me know that I had done well, and that *she* was proud of me. And when *she* did, I wept like I have never wept before. I was overjoyed to know that the Creator... my mother... was proud of me. And that *she* loved me so much that she would bring me back from the depths of oblivion. I felt so much joy that I thought my heart would burst."

"So, did you say anything to *her?*" asked Millet.

"No," he replied. He could see the disappointment on their faces. "I couldn't. Being in *her* presence was almost more than I was able to stand. I wanted to say thank you... I love you... anything at all. I just couldn't form the words. And then *she* was gone. Well, not *gone* exactly, but the force of *her* presence had disappeared.

"From there, I just came home. Kaylia was already here waiting for me. And you know the rest." He folded his hands on the table and watched with a smile on his face as the group absorbed all that he had said.

The reflective silence was broken by the clamor of dishes and footsteps as two young girls entered carrying platters of thinly sliced mint lamb, fresh bread, and spiced carrots.

The mood lightened as they ate and talked of their past adventures. Gewey told of his first meeting with Kaylia in the forest, and how it had nearly cost him his life. And Kaylia told about the time she drugged him with jawas tea for asking too many questions.

After the table was cleared, they retired to a small intimate parlor and sat around the hearth. The stories continued until midnight, on the exact hour of which, Millet poured everyone a glass of plum brandy.

He raised his glass. "I want to thank you all for coming. It's wonderful to see everyone together again. I only wish it could last forever. I want you to know that I love each and every one of you." He closed his eyes. "Here's to friends. Especially those who are no longer with us."

Everyone bowed their heads.

"Theopolou," said Kaylia.

"Maybell," said Dina.

"Lee," said Linis.

"My fathers Harman and Gerath," said Gewey.

"My kinsfolk, who fought and died bravely so very far from home," said Aaliyah.

Nehrutu wrapped his arms around her shoulders and kissed her brow.

"And to all the other people who sacrificed their lives so that we can be here on this night and share these simple pleasures as friends," concluded Millet.

They turned up their glasses and finished every last drop. For another hour, they talked and laughed, remembering the people they had lost and missed so dearly. Gewey was telling of when he nearly killed Linis using the *flow* for the first time.

"I had no idea how to channel it, and when I let it go, the ground exploded right underneath him," he said. "It must have thrown him twenty feet in the air. I was so scared that I'd killed him, I nearly broke down crying."

"Do you miss it?" asked Linis

"Miss what?" said Gewey, feigning ignorance.

"You know what. All that power you once had. Now you are just like the rest of us."

Gewey shrugged. "I still have my strength. And I can still feel the *flow*. I just can't use it."

"Did it affect your bond?" asked Dina.

Gewey shook his head. "Not at all. In fact, after I returned and we reconnected our spirits, it was stronger than ever."

"Come on," said Dina with a playful grin. "Are you saying you don't miss being able to fly off anywhere you want whenever you feel like it?"

"There's nowhere I'd rather be than here with my family," he replied. "So no. I really don't miss it. Losing my power was the price I paid to remain in the mortal realm, and I'd do it again in an instant. Actually, in some ways, I'm happier without it. Powers such as I possessed can be as much a burden as a gift. Aaliyah knows what I mean."

"Yes," she agreed. "My powers are but a mere fraction of what yours were, and I too have found it to be so. The responsibility that goes with them is great, and the desire to misuse them is sometimes overwhelming."

Dina smiled and sighed. "Yes... but to go anywhere you wanted..."

"And where would you go, my *wife*?" asked Linis in an accusing tone. "Would you leave me to tend the farm while you go adventuring?"

Dina ignored his apparent irritation and laid her head on his shoulder. "Of course not. I'd take you with me. And I wouldn't go adventuring. I'd go to the hot springs west of the fire hills. The water there is so warm and pure..." She moaned with pleasure at the thought. "I could bathe in it for weeks." She looked up at Linis and gave him a tender kiss. "I meant to say, *we* could."

He smiled and pulled her close.

A few minutes later, Gewey and Kaylia stood up.

"We should be going," Kaylia said. "I promised the children that we would be home before they wake up."

"Linis and I are staying the night," Dina told her. "But you can take our wagon if you want."

"That's not necessary," said Gewey. "It's nice out. I think we'd rather walk."

They said another heartfelt goodbye, then left the manor. Hand in hand while walking along, they talked of how much they had missed their friends, and how long it would seem before they would see them again once they had departed.

When the farmhouse came into sight, Kaylia stopped and closed her eyes for a moment. "They're asleep," she said. "And it's still several hours until dawn."

"What are you suggesting?" asked Gewey, but with a knowing smile.

"I am saying that the hot springs Dina mentioned sounded wonderful."

Gewey wrapped his thick, powerful arms around her waist and held her tight. "Very well. But this time, let's get home *before* they wake up."

Kaylia kissed him long and deep. "I'll try to keep my mind on it."

The wind rose and swirled around them. In an instant, they shot skyward, hurtling west like a blazing comet. Though no one could ever know the truth, whenever they basked in the warm waters of the springs, sat upon the highest peak of the Razor Edge Mountains, or even strolled the beaches of some remote island, they were not simply Gewey and Kaylia.

They were Darshan, God of the Wind and Sky, and Kaylia, savior of his soul.

Their love, like their spirits, would live on ... forever.

BOOK CLUB QUESTIONS

1. Who is your favorite character? Why? And what about them make them enjoyable to read about? Has your favorite character changed since the last book?

2. How well does the author follow the formula of the hero's journey while making the story unique in its own right? Has the journey held true from book to book?

3. How well developed do you feel the character arcs are? And how do you think they develop throughout the book and series?

4. Do you feel Gewey will be the savior he is prophesied to be or will he succumb to the temptations of power? Have your feelings on this changed since the last book?

ABOUT THE AUTHORS

Brian D. Anderson was born in 1971 and grew up in the small town of Spanish Fort, AL. He attended Fairhope High, then later Springhill College, where his love for fantasy grew into a lifelong obsession. His hobbies include chess, history, and spending time with his son.

Jonathan Anderson was born in March 2003. His creative spirit became evident by the age of three when he told his first original story. In 2010, he came up with the concept for The Godling Chronicles. It grew into an exciting collaboration between father and son. Jonathan enjoys sports, chess, music, games, and, of course, telling stories.

Don't miss out!

Click the button below and you can sign up to receive emails whenever Brian D. Anderson publishes a new book. There's no charge and no obligation.

https://books2read.com/r/B-A-UEAF-JRKW

Connecting independent readers to independent writers.

Did you love *The Godling Chronicles,* books 4-6? Then you should read *The Godling Chronicles Bundle 1-3* by Brian D. Anderson!

The world is under siege and the door to heaven is sealed. The Reborn King and his armies are preparing to ravage the land, leaving only death in their wake.

But there is hope. Gewey Stedding. He alone possesses the strength to save both human and elf. But only if he can harness his power.

Discover more at
4HorsemenPublications.com

10% off using HORSEMEN10